Satan's Hand

Satan's Hand

Book 2 of Operation Clean Slate

Mark Kennedy

Satan's Hand

Book 2 of Operation Clean Slate

Published by MKK Publishing

First Edition, 2026

For my late wife Ying, who said "later" until there was no later left.

Contents

Foreword

I'm sure we've all seen movies where someone tries to download a list of secret agents to or from a computer. And it takes minutes or hours to happen, when in reality it would probably take seconds. Or there are situations where hackers can fully breach systems nearly instantly, under high-pressure conditions. Or plots in which highly physical characters are able to fight their way into a location and then exercise computer abilities far outstripping those of many dedicated experts. These are all real misrepresentations of cyber security in novels and movies.

In Satan's Hand, Mark Kennedy's narrative does something rare in fiction. It treats cyber intrusion not as spectacle, but as engineering. He digs into the nuts and bolts of it, and ensures that they are truly viable, rather than simply dramatic.

In most portrayals, "hacking" is compressed into a moment, a flourish, a shortcut to advance the plot. Here, it is presented as it exists in reality: slow, deliberate and built on an intimate understanding of systems, people and the assumptions that bind them together.

What stands out immediately is the absence of magic. There are no convenient breakthroughs. No unexplained leaps from problem to solution. No Deus ex Machina. The machines here are all credible, realistic and sufficiently fallible not to need special circumstances to break. They just need a clever attack, which is what they get.

Rather than mystical computer gobbledygook, the reader is taken through structures that feel internally consistent and technically grounded. The mechanisms Mark describes are not just plausible in isolation; they are coherent within the wider architecture of the systems they inhabit.

This bit is important. Real-world attacks do not exist as isolated tricks. They are chains of dependency, each step constrained by what came before and enabling what comes after. This is the so-called 'attack chain' that attackers and defenders in the real world understand all too well.

You may not be surprised to learn that Mark's career has largely been involved in understanding advanced cyber attacks. Or that he asked me, a security tester, to write this foreword.

In his novel, those attack chains are evident. The intrusions are not simply "clever" but composed. They rely on positioning, preparation and exploiting trust relationships and design decisions that first appear benign. The idea that a system can be made to betray itself, not through obvious flaws but through features that were intended to increase its robustness, is both uncomfortable and accurate. It reflects a truth well understood in cyber security, which is that the most effective attacks are those that align themselves with the system's logic rather than opposing it.

Be water. Bend like a reed in the wind. Don't smash your head against the brick wall. All good physical and cyber defence tactics and advice.

Another notable aspect is the treatment of visibility and evidence. In fiction, detection is often binary, where either the system is secure, or it is obviously compromised. In reality, the boundary is far less clear (although the security industry might have you believe otherwise). Mark captures this ambiguity well. The actions he describes leave traces, but those traces sit outside expected pathways or appear as legitimate activity when viewed through standard monitoring. This is not an exaggeration. It reflects how modern systems are built and how their managers observe them. The gap between what is happening and what is seen is where most real compromises live.

For some readers, the technical density may feel challenging. That is not a flaw. It is, in many ways, the point. The difficulty in following certain mechanisms mirrors the difficulty in executing them. Simplifying these processes too far would make them easier to consume, but less truthful. Mark resists that simplification. The result is a portrayal that demands more from the reader, but rewards that effort with a level of authenticity that is rarely achieved.

And if you can't follow along, just imagine you are in the room with Sato and O'Malley. Complicated words are followed by body language and action. You don't need to understand the experts to appreciate that something very bad, subtle and clever has happened. That's probably what being a CEO in a large company is like.

The alternative could be a paragraph like:

'O'Malley came into Sato's office. "This is clever and bad," said O'Malley. "They hacked us ages ago using a new method, and we couldn't see it. They breached the intra-kernel using a triple AES encryptor." His smile was tight and grim. "Oh my God!" exclaimed Sato. "You mean…" "Yes," deadpanned O'Malley, "They exploited our membrane." Sato nodded. "Haldane," she said.'

This is, of course, all meaningless and stupid. Surely it's better to not understand something real rather than not understand something obviously fake.

It is also worth noting what this approach avoids, which is a common tendency to dramatise the easy and trivialise the hard. Often routine tasks are inflated for tension ("this text file is taking three hours to download to a USB drive!"), while genuinely complex operations are reduced to a few casual keystrokes ("Let me quickly reverse engineer the code and develop a previously unknown exploit…"). Here, that inversion is largely absent. Effort is visible. Constraints are respected. Outcomes are earned.

From a practitioner's perspective, the most striking element is not any single technique, but the mindset that underpins the attack chains. The attacks are not reactive; they are architectural. They assume long timelines, deep access and an understanding that extends beyond code into process, governance and human behaviour. That perspective is difficult to convey and even harder to sustain across a narrative. Mark manages both.

For those without deep engagement in the cyber security world, Mark's approach offers a glimpse into a domain that is often misrepresented. Despite its science fiction setting, it provides a valuable depiction of cyber operations that is much closer to reality than to myth.

- Simon Edwards, London, April 2026

PROLOGUE

October 21st, 2058

• • •

Charles Haldane read the message from Cerro Paranal a second time, then closed it. He turned to the window. Dallas stretched out forty floors below, ten million people moving through their evening, not one of them aware that the message on his screen had just made most of them obsolete.

He had been waiting for this day for over twenty years.

The door opened and William Novak crossed the room. Haldane nodded at one of the chairs in front of his desk, and Novak sat.

"Mercer confirmed it?" Novak asked.

"Right location, right characteristics. It's on schedule."

Novak exhaled slowly. "I'll admit something. Part of me wasn't sure they could actually build the Eraser."

"You don't know the Tolek like I do," Haldane said.

"No. I don't." Novak leaned forward. "So. We're really doing this."

"We've been doing this. Nothing changes except the clock starts." Haldane pulled up a file on his wallscreen. Two lists, side by side. The first was headed **Founders** — several hundred names, some highlighted, some struck through. The second was headed **Stock** — longer, organized by different criteria. "Where are we on stocking the Ark?"

"Slow and steady. Small shipments, different carriers, nothing that patterns. We could sustain twenty-five hundred for eighteen months at current levels. I want another four months to finish."

"You'll have longer than that. It will be some time before anyone else understands what they're looking at." Haldane scrolled the Founders list, paused on a name, considered it, moved on. Then he switched to Stock and checked a row of figures beside a name. "But don't get comfortable."

Novak stood. "I'll get the next shipment moving tonight."

"Do that."

Novak was at the door when he turned back. "You know, I've been building the Ark for six years. It's — I don't know. It's different now that it's real."

"It was always real," Haldane said, without looking up from the names.

Novak nodded, opened his mouth as if to say something else, then thought better of it. He left.

Haldane sat alone with his lists. He highlighted a name on Founders, removed another. He added a row to Stock. He thought of this as long overdue.

He worked until midnight.

CHAPTER 1

The Same

September 2060.
Earth ↔ Mars: ~2.1 AU. Communications: ~17 min one-way.

• • •

"My God," Chloe said. "It IS the same."

Sky's head came up from the chair beside her, one paw still draped over the armrest.

She was at the kitchen table in her Los Angeles apartment, the burner laptop open in front of her, the FEMA story she'd been writing forgotten on the other screen. The Fist interior photographs were tiled across the right half of the display —- hundreds of them, corridor walls and junction markers and sealed doors with cutting marks around the perimeters. She'd been going through them methodically for two days, the way she went through everything, cataloging what was there without rushing toward what it meant. The metallurgy reports first. The DEW documentation. Then the survey photographs. She'd set the Fist material aside and gone back to the FEMA story. A minute later she'd stopped typing. Not a thought —- a pattern.

Now she was staring at two images side by side. On the left, the Fresh Start Foundation logo —- two arrowhead shapes, one nested inside the other, pointing upward, with two flat trapezoidal forms below and a small diamond centered between them. On the right, a

Fist interior photograph, enlarged. Raised geometric forms pressed into the alloy surface. Navigation markers, the survey notes said.

Two angular forms, one nested inside the other. Two flat shapes below. A smaller element centered between them.

The proportions were different. The Fist version was sharper —- the angles tighter, the lower elements less defined. Different aesthetic vocabulary. But she'd pulled both images to the center of the screen and overlaid the structural outlines, and the spatial relationships were the same. The nesting. The symmetry axis. The ratio between the upper and lower groups.

The same geometry. On an alien ship. On a human foundation's letterhead.

She got up and made coffee. Drank half of it standing at the counter, looking at nothing. Poured the rest out, went back to the table, and opened a browser on the burner.

The Fresh Start Foundation website loaded in three seconds. She navigated to the main page and stopped.

The logo was gone.

Not replaced with nothing —- replaced with something else. A stylized "FS" in clean sans-serif typography, modern and generic. She clicked through the site. About page —- the new logo. Programs page —- the new logo. Reports archive, press section, fellowship listings. Every page, the same new mark. The nested arrowheads, the trapezoids, the diamond —- all of it erased.

"When did you change your logo, Mr. Novak?" she said quietly.

She opened the Wayback Machine. Fresh Start Foundation. The crawler had archived the site irregularly —- once or twice a month, sometimes less. She wanted to see the old logo —- the one she remembered from fourteen months ago when she'd first visited the site during the fellowship mapping. She scrolled back through the captures.

August —- new logo. July —- new logo. Late June —- new logo. She kept going.

June 10th. There.

The old logo. The arrowheads, the trapezoids, the diamond. Sitting at the top of the page exactly as she remembered it.

She put the archived page beside the Fist photograph and her hands went still on the keyboard.

Then she went forward through the archives. June 10th —- old logo. June 22nd —- gone. The scrub had happened in a twelve-day window in mid-June.

She checked the dates against the mission timeline. The Remora had touched down on the Fist on July 18th. The logo had been scrubbed a full month before that.

"OK, Sky. Think about this." She pushed back from the table. Sky's ears rotated toward her. "A corporate rebrand takes time. You need a design agency, approval cycles, someone to rebuild the website. Weeks at minimum. Usually months. These people did it in days."

She stood up and walked to the kitchen. Opened a cabinet, closed it without taking anything out, walked back.

"And they did it in mid-June. Mid-June, Sky. The world was watching an alien object bear down on Earth. Cities were being evacuated. Half the planet's infrastructure was being repurposed for survival." She sat back down. "Who changes their logo during an extinction-level event? Who is thinking about branding while people are running for their lives?"

Sky blinked at her.

"Nobody. Nobody does that. Unless they have a very specific reason to." She pulled the Wayback captures back up. June 10th, old logo. June 22nd, new logo. July 18th, Remora touchdown.

"They didn't react to photographs of the Fist interior. The photos didn't exist yet. They reacted to the mission. Someone at Fresh Start must have learned that a crew was going inside, and they were worried —- worried enough to scrub their branding in the middle of the apocalypse —- about what that crew might find on the walls. And they moved to erase the connection before anyone could make it."

She looked at the two images side by side. The geometry that matched. The timing that killed every innocent explanation.

She pulled up her evidence inventory. The data token from the Department of War —- recovered research, organizational charts, funding flow analyses. The firmware document she'd obtained through a separate channel, technical specifications she didn't fully understand but had preserved because you preserved everything. The suppression timeline she'd built from killed stories, redirected FOIA requests, editorial decisions that had steered coverage away from certain questions at certain times. And now: the symbol match, and a twelve-day window that turned a geometric curiosity into evidence of foreknowledge.

She picked up the coffee cup, found it empty, put it down. She didn't know who sent the envelope. She didn't have a second source for the interior survey. She didn't know what the firmware document meant. And the thing it all added up to was insane.

Sky jumped onto the table and walked across the keyboard.

She picked him up, set him on the chair, and started a verification list.

• • •

Alexis Dren had a number.

He was in his office in Ares City. The translation layer had told him what happened. A corrupted position value —- one wrong digit in the lateral separation parameter. The Batch G-7 update had set the platform's believed position at 3,600 kilometers from the Fist's track. The actual position was 3,500. One hundred kilometers of error in a number that governed every firing calculation the platform made.

He opened a channel to Okoro.

I've finished the translation layer audit, Dren said. ***The position parameter in the Batch G-7 upload was wrong. The***

platform believed it was at 3,600 kilometers lateral separation. Actual separation was 3,500.

A hundred kilometers, Okoro said, after a moment. ***That's a transcription error. 6 instead of 5.***

It's not variance, Dren said. ***It's a clean wrong number. 3,600 instead of 3,500. One digit.***

And that's what caused the errant hit? Okoro said.

The pellets travel at 1,320 kilometers per second, Dren said. ***At the correct separation of 3,500 kilometers, flight time across the gap is 2.652 seconds. At 3,600, the platform calculates a flight time of 2.727 seconds —- seventy-six thousandths of a second longer. It fires early to compensate for a gap that doesn't exist.***

Seventy-six thousandths of a second, Dren repeated. ***That resulted in a hit twelve-and-a-half-kilometer forward of the midpoint, six kilometers from the bow.***

Silence on the channel.

The tilt, Okoro said quietly.

The tilt, Dren said.

Alexis. Okoro's tone shifted. Careful. And the use of Dren's first name was unusual. ***It was a mistake. A typo. In a compressed dev cycle, under the pressure we were operating at, with the repositioning from a thousand to thirty-five hundred happening in days —- it's the kind of mistake that happens. The review caught seven other parameters and missed this one because it looked right. It looked like a round number that belonged there.***

Perhaps, Dren said. ***That doesn't change the results.***

I know. But ruining the kid's life won't change it either, Okoro said. ***This would destroy him, and it won't bring anyone back.***

I'll consider that, Dren said.

He closed the channel.

One digit —- the difference between 35 and 36 in a parameter field that governed the firing solution for every platform in the wave. A mistake. Okoro's explanation was simple and plausible, and the auditors' post-mortem supported it. Compressed timeline, high pressure, seven parameters caught and one missed. Human error in conditions designed to produce human error.

He opened a channel to Brandt.

Run full backgrounds on everyone in the deployment pipeline, Dren said. ***Engineering, security, logistics. Anyone with the authority to issue instructions to the translation layer team.***

That's seven people, Brandt said. ***Does that include Sato?***

Everyone, Dren said.

Brandt didn't ask why. ***I'll have preliminaries by end of week,*** he said.

Dren closed the channel and opened another.

Belt sweep, Dren said. ***Where are we?***

Nothing at Chandra's coordinates, Sato said. ***I've been running the bearing corridor for two days. There's nothing there. No rock, no relay, no infrastructure. Whatever answered the Fist isn't at 3.5 AU.***

Then Chandra's math was wrong, Dren said.

Chandra's math would never be wrong, Sato said. ***He worked with what he had. But a 58-minute round trip doesn't have to mean one object at 29 minutes. It could mean a shorter relay chain with processing time in the middle.***

You're saying the signal bounced, Dren said.

I'm saying 58 minutes and an empty bearing corridor is worth thinking about differently, Sato said.

Think about it differently, Dren said. ***And check on the Remora.***

I hailed them this morning, Sato said. ***Telemetry's clean. Power, life support, trajectory —- all nominal. Nobody's responding.***

How long since last voice contact? Dren said.

There hasn't been any, Sato said. ***Not since departure. Telemetry only.***

Keep hailing, Dren said. ***Regular intervals. I want to know the moment someone answers.***

He closed the channel and sat with his hands flat on the desk. The belt relay was making him see patterns in noise. A hidden communication channel with something in the belt, a signal chain stretching to the edge of the solar system, a crew that had gone silent on a ship heading away from Earth at forty kilometers per second — and now he was treating a transcription error as evidence of sabotage. Seven people had the authority to issue instructions to the engineer who entered the number. Brandt's backgrounds would confirm what was already obvious: a twenty-six-year-old kid had made the worst typo in human history.

He picked up the water glass, drank, set it down in the same place.

The position error was a mistake. The belt communications was something else. He set the audit file aside and went back to work.

• • •

November 2060. Ares City.

Dren called Sato into his office before the day shift. Door closed. Network isolated.

"Chandra's relay data," he said. "The bearing and the timing."

Sato didn't need the preamble. She'd been running the numbers since the Remora's data dump. "The signal chain from the Fist —- source to Fist to belt. Three relay nodes. Chandra established the bearing from the antenna geometry. The timing signature gives us an approximate distance."

"How approximate?"

"Past the heliopause. Roughly 130 AU, plus or minus fifteen. The bearing is solid —- Chandra's antenna measurements were precise. The distance has more uncertainty because we're inferring from relay processing lag, not direct ranging."

"Direction solid, distance approximate."

"Correct."

Dren was quiet for a moment. "The Fist received a response from that bearing. It reoriented its antenna and broadcast toward the belt. That's not an automated acknowledgment. Something intelligent is sitting at 130 AU."

"Agreed," Sato said.

"No catalogued body at those coordinates. So it's a ship. And if we're assuming one ship, we should assume more than one."

"A fleet."

"No evidence. But prudent." He stood and walked to the wallscreen. "Bring up the solar system. Plot the Fist's line of advance."

The image appeared.

"Mark the estimated source position based on the communication delay."

A small sphere appeared outside the heliopause, on the Fist's approach vector.

"That's a staging point, not an origin," Dren said. "They arrived there from somewhere. The approach geometry suggests they came in perpendicular to the ecliptic — shortest path to the staging area, shortest path to Earth." He looked at Sato. "What's the nearest star system inside that cone?"

Sato didn't need the wallscreen. "Alpha Centauri. 4.37 light-years."

They looked at each other.

"It's a working hypothesis," Dren said. "The geometry is suggestive, not conclusive. But if something launched the Fist from interstellar distance and then parked a fleet at the edge of our system to wait — that's a drive capability beyond anything we can model."

"And they've been sitting there," Sato said. "Watching."

Dren was quiet for a long time. Sato knew not to interrupt him when he was in this mode.

He turned to her.

"I want to build a set of long-range reconnaissance drones," Dren said. "Unmanned. Pulse drive core. Designed for maximum terminal velocity on a one-way trip. I want them sent toward that bearing. I want to get a look at what's at that staging area."

Sato looked at him. She didn't ask why. "How many?"

"Enough to cover the uncertainty. Multiple bearings, spread in a line perpendicular to the primary axis. A picket fence."

"The fleet —- whatever it is —- may still be transmitting," Sato said. "Not through the Fist anymore, but if they have an agent on Earth, they'll be aiming a signal at Earth's orbital position. A tight beam, but Earth moves. The beam tracks. Over a year, it sweeps across a two-AU line from their perspective."

"And the picket fence sits across that sweep," Dren said. "Each drone that catches the beam gets a bearing. Multiple drones, multiple bearings, multiple positions —- triangulation. The fix gets tighter with every detection."

"Passive intercept. The drones never transmit toward the fleet."

"Never. They listen. They talk to each other —- short-range, low-power, probe-to-probe only. The triangulation happens in the swarm. The fleet never knows they're there."

Sato was running the engineering already. Dren could see it in her eyes —- the propulsion budget, the thermal problem, the mass constraints.

"Terminal velocity is the priority," Dren said. "I want them moving as fast as we can make them move. The profile is a solar slingshot —- we use staged inbound propulsion to get them deep into the Sun's gravity well, fire the pulse drive at perihelion for the Oberth kick, shed the inbound stages and heat shield, and let the core accelerate outbound on pulse drive."

"Staged inbound," Sato said. "Nuclear thermal for the heavy lifting, chemical for the correction burns. The whole inbound assembly is disposable —- it exists to get the core to perihelion as fast and as hot as possible."

"Exactly. The drone arrives at the Sun wrapped in dead weight. It sheds everything at perihelion and comes out the other side clean, light, and fully fueled for the outbound leg."

“Perihelion distance?”

“As close as the shield will tolerate. Ten solar radii. We know the thermal properties from the Fist’s hull material —- carbon composite ablative, rated for the environment.”

Sato was quiet for a moment. She was seeing the full picture now —- the engineering, the timeline, the implications.

“The inbound stages give us twenty-five to thirty kilometers per second of retrograde delta-v to drop perihelion from Earth orbit. At ten solar radii, the drone hits approximately two hundred kilometers per second from solar gravity plus the booster contribution. The pulse drive fires at closest approach —- the Oberth effect multiplies the energy. Post-slingshot departure velocity somewhere around two hundred, two hundred and twenty kilometers per second hyperbolic excess.”

“And then the core burns outbound.”

“The core is five hundred kilograms dry. Same pulse engine class as the Kludge, one-sixth the mass. Acceleration around 0.2 meters per second squared. It burns for as long as the fuel holds, then coasts.”

“Transit time to 130 AU?”

Sato did the math in her head. Dren watched her —- she worked the way he worked, the numbers first, the implications after.

“Depending on burn duration —- twelve to fifteen months. Call the intercept early 2062 with margin.”

“Build them at the Kepler facility,” Dren said. The Kepler works were Dren Industries’ primary fabrication complex in Earth orbit —- the same facility that had built the Remora and the belt weapons platforms. “Route the components through the standard production pipeline. From the outside, these are deep-space survey platforms. Resource mapping for the Oort cloud expansion program.”

“Who knows?”

“You. Me. That’s it.”

Sato looked at him. “Not Whitfield?”

"Not yet. The institutions on Earth are compromised —- we don't know how deep the conspiracy runs. If knowledge of the drones reaches them, they tells whoever's at the other end of that bearing, and they maneuver before the drones arrive. The drones' only advantage is that nobody knows they exist."

"And their mission is reconnaissance."

"Their mission is reconnaissance," Dren said. "They are designed to locate, characterize, and track whatever is sitting at 130 AU on that bearing." He paused. "They should also be capable of delivering a response. Message received."

Sato was still for three seconds. She understood exactly what he meant. Five hundred kilograms at several hundred kilometers per second didn't need a warhead. It didn't need electronics or guidance sophistication or anything that could be jammed or disabled or persuaded. It just needed to arrive.

"How many?" she asked again. The question meant something different now.

"Twelve. First wave. We can adjust the bearings and launch follow-up waves once the picket fence starts producing data."

"Timeline for construction?"

"Fast. I want the first launch before the end of November."

"That's three weeks."

"The Kepler works built twelve weapons platforms in eight months. These are simpler —- an engine, a fuel load, an inbound booster ring, a heat shield, a sensor package, and a dense core. No crew systems. No life support. No return capability. Simple."

Sato nodded. She was already composing the fabrication order in her head —- the way she composed everything, clean and complete before it reached anyone else.

"One more thing," Dren said. "The inbound stages, the shield, the booster ring —- all of it is built from existing industrial components. Nothing that looks military. Nothing that looks unusual. Survey platforms going to the Oort cloud. That's the story, that's the paperwork, and that's what anyone who asks gets told."

"And if they come back with data?"

"Then we'll know what's out there. And we'll decide what to do about it."

"And if they don't come back?"

Dren looked at the window. The rust-colored plain. The thin sky. The stars that were invisible in the Martian daylight but always present behind it.

"Then we'll know that, too," he said.

• • •

September 14th, 2060. National Weather Service, Fort Worth, Texas.
The forecast models were fighting each other again.

Keisha Mallory had been running the severe weather desk for eleven hours. The satellite gap made everything harder — the LEO constellation that had carried the bulk of atmospheric observation since the forties was debris now, and the replacement coverage from the surviving geostationary platforms was sparse, laggy, and full of holes. They were forecasting the way her grandfather's generation had: patching together surface observations, radiosonde data, and whatever satellite imagery they could get on a thirty-minute refresh cycle instead of the continuous feed they'd had three months ago.

The models agreed on one thing: the conditions were forming again.

A massive low-pressure system was pulling warm, moisture-laden air north from the Gulf. The haze layer had produced uneven surface cooling that left the Gulf waters warmer than the air above parts of Alabama and Georgia, though every forecast was an exercise in educated guessing. The temperature differential was extreme. The wind shear was building. The dew points were climbing past levels Mallory had never seen in September, fed by Gulf surface temperatures that should have been cooling by now but weren't — the residual thermal energy from the flyby was still in the water, still feeding moisture into the atmosphere three months later.

"I'm seeing rotation in the Gulf," her deputy said. "Multiple cells. The lead cell is organized."

Mallory looked at the radar. The returns were bright red and purple — the colors that meant the atmosphere was doing something violent. A line of supercells was forming along the Gulf coast from Pensacola to Mobile, moving northeast at forty miles per hour. Behind the line, more cells were organizing. The pattern looked like the outbreaks they'd been seeing since July — the same atmospheric instability, but this one was bigger. The energy was higher. The shear was tighter.

"Issue the watch," she said. "Gulf coast through central Alabama, north to the Tennessee line. Upgrade to warning when the first cell crosses the coast."

The first tornado touched down south of Mobile at 4:47 PM Central. An EF3 — quarter-mile wide, cutting a twelve-mile path through suburbs that had been built for hurricanes and humidity. The damage was immediate and severe. Roofs gone. Walls collapsed. Power lines down across roads that were still wet from the morning rain.

The second touched down twelve minutes later, east of Pensacola. EF2. The third was near Dothan, Alabama, at 5:30 — an EF4 that stayed on the ground for twenty-two miles and destroyed a regional hospital that had been serving as a coordination center for three counties.

By nightfall, the Storm Prediction Center had confirmed eleven tornadoes across the Gulf states. The line of supercells had pushed northeast into Georgia and western South Carolina, spawning waterspouts along the coast that came ashore as additional tornadoes. The damage reports were still coming in when Mallory's shift ended at midnight, and the line was still moving.

She drove home through rain that came sideways across the highway and thought about what the models were showing for the next seventy-two hours. More of the same. The atmospheric pattern wasn't breaking. The Gulf was still too warm, the haze was still uneven, and the jet stream was still running forty degrees south of where it belonged in September. This wasn't a weather event. It was a new climate, and nobody knew how long it would last.

The storms continued for weeks. The September outbreaks were followed by more in October. Alabama, Georgia, Mississippi, the Carolinas, western Florida. By the end of October, FEMA had declared disaster zones in nine states that hadn't been touched by the original tsunamis. The country that had been rebuilding its Pacific coast was now rebuilding its Southeast, and the resources weren't there for both.

• • •

Dallas.

Haldane watched the feeds from his office on the fortieth floor.

The tornado coverage dominated every channel — the aerial footage of flattened neighborhoods, the emergency response convoys, the interviews with people standing in front of what used to be houses. He watched it with the same clinical attention he'd given to everything. The atmospheric disruption was a second-order effect he hadn't predicted. The flyby was supposed to produce tsunamis and infrastructure damage along the Pacific corridor. The cascading weather effects — the haze, the destabilized jet stream, the tornado outbreaks in the Southeast — were emergent consequences of the energy his project had deposited into the atmosphere.

He hadn't planned this, exactly. But it served his purposes better than he'd imagined. Every new disaster zone was another demand on federal resources that didn't exist. Every damaged city was another community that would feel abandoned by Washington. Every week of severe weather was another week where the reconstruction couldn't keep pace with the destruction, and the gap between what people needed and what the government could provide widened into the kind of resentment that didn't need to be manufactured — only directed.

He reached for the bourbon on the credenza.

The building moved.

It was subtle at first — a low vibration that could have been construction equipment or a heavy vehicle on the street below. Then the bourbon shifted in the glass. The glasses on the shelf started to tinkle. The surface tilted, caught the light, and tilted back. The chandelier above the conference table began to sway — small arcs, barely visible, but rhythmic. Wrong.

Haldane set the glass down and put his hand flat on the desk. The desk was vibrating. The whole floor was vibrating. He heard a sound — deep, structural, the groan of a building flexing in a way its engineers had accounted for but its occupants had never experienced.

A window cracked. A single line running diagonally across the plate glass, the sound sharp and percussive in the quiet office. Books shifted on the shelf behind him. A pen rolled off the desk and hit the carpet.

Then the power went out.

He sat in the dark for twelve seconds. The emergency lighting kicked in — amber, dim, the battery light-powered strips along the baseboards that turned his office into something that looked like a submarine corridor. The building was still swaying. He could feel it in his inner ear — the slow, ponderous oscillation of forty stories of steel and concrete responding to energy that had traveled through six hundred miles of bedrock to reach him.

The feeds came back on backup power. The anchors were gone — replaced by emergency graphics and scrolling text. The first reports were confused. Earthquake. Central United States. Magnitude estimated above 7. Epicenter near the Missouri-Tennessee border. The New Madrid Seismic Zone.

Memphis was hit hardest. The initial footage showed buildings collapsed into the streets — unreinforced masonry, the old brick warehouses and apartment blocks that had never been retrofitted because Memphis wasn't supposed to have earthquakes. Bridges across the Mississippi had dropped spans. The levee system had breached in at least two places, and the river was flooding into neighborhoods that were already dealing with tornado damage from the previous week.

St. Louis was reporting structural failures across the riverfront district. Nashville had widespread building damage — cracked facades, shattered windows, a parking structure that had pancaked. Louisville, Evansville, Little Rock — all reporting damage, all overwhelmed, all requesting federal assistance that was already committed to the Pacific coast and the Southeast tornado zones. California was built for these types of events; the Mississippi valley wasn't.

Haldane sat in the amber light and watched the coverage and felt the irony settle over him. He had never worried about the effects in Dallas because it was inland. High. Far from the coasts. Safe from the tsunamis, safe from the flooding, safe from the direct effects of the event he had been forced into. He had planned for everything — the institutional response, the political fragmentation, the reconstruction apparatus he would control. He had not planned for the earth itself reaching up and shaking his building to remind him that the forces he had invited into the world did not limit themselves to the boundaries he had drawn.

The experts would connect it within days. The Ring of Fire had been active since the flyby — triggered earthquakes along the Pacific plate boundaries, the kind of cascading seismic stress that geologists had warned about for decades. The New Madrid zone had been accumulating strain since 1812. It was always going to rupture again. The flyby's seismic cascade had simply accelerated the timeline — stress propagating through the continental plate over three months until the oldest fault line in the interior finally let go. The experts said it was inevitable. They also said the San Andreas might be next. Haldane could only hope.

Haldane picked up the bourbon. The glass had a crack in it — a hairline fracture running from the rim to the base. He drank from it anyway.

The country was breaking faster than he'd planned. It wasn't a problem; it was an opportunity.

CHAPTER 2

Options

September 2060.

• • •

Charles Haldane poured two fingers of bourbon and carried the glass to the window. His office occupied the top floor of the Haldane Foundation building in Dallas —- forty stories above a city that was still functioning, which was more than could be said for the Pacific coast. The skyline was cranes and reconstruction scaffolding, the new geometry of a world that was rebuilding itself from the interior outward because the coasts were gone. Dallas was inland, high, and far from any ocean.

Behind him, Beckett sat in one of the leather chairs in front of the desk, a folder open on his knee. He'd arrived an hour ago on a military transport —- one of the privileges that still attached to a Senate committee chair even in a fractured government. No staff. No aides. The meeting wasn't on any schedule.

"The tilt inquiry opens October 15th," Beckett said. "I've secured the chair. Witness list is mine to set, subject to the ranking member's objections, which I've pre-addressed." He turned a page in the folder. "The ranking member isn't going to object. She lost a nephew in the Pacific corridor. She wants answers more than she wants procedure."

Haldane turned from the window. "The witness list."

"Dren, obviously. But I'm not leading with him. I'm leading with the regional infrastructure chiefs —- the people who watched the reconstruction stall while Mars shipped replacement satellites on a nine-month timeline. I want the dependency on the record before Dren takes the stand. The sequence matters."

Haldane sat down behind the desk and sipped the bourbon. Beckett was precise. That first hearing had been exploratory. This was escalation.

"The delegation order," Haldane said. "Where does it stand?"

"Permanent in all but name," Beckett said. "Colorado Springs, Jacksonville, and Elmendorf are running independent budgets. The military commanders have their own supply chains, their own communications infrastructure, their own civilian administrations. Whitfield's executive authority is technically intact, but she can't enforce it without the military, and the military reports to the regional commanders who report to her in theory and to their own logistics in practice."

"And the reunification push?"

"Dying." Beckett closed the folder and set it on the edge of the desk. "I'm seeing to that. Every hearing, every inquiry, every subpoena keeps the fracture visible. The public doesn't want reunification —- they want accountability. They want to know why the deflection failed, why the tilt happened, why an unelected Mars industrialist had control of their survival. I give them hearings. The hearings give them anger. The anger makes reunification politically toxic."

"The DSA polling?"

"Trending. 'Disunited States of America' started as a talk radio joke. It's in the op-eds now. Two governors have used the phrase in official communications —- not endorsing it, but not distancing from it either. Give it six months and it's a policy position."

Haldane picked up the glass and turned it in his hand. "The election."

Beckett looked at him. "What about it?"

"November is two months away. Whitfield is running on continuity — the emergency powers, the reconstruction mandate, the argument that you don't change leadership during a crisis. Turner is running on accountability — the tilt, the delegation order, the question of whether a president who handed her authority to regional commanders and a Mars industrialist deserves a second term."

"Turner is making a legitimate argument," Beckett said carefully.

"Turner is making our argument." Haldane set the glass down. "Every theme we've been building — the dependency narrative, the DSA framing, the delegation order as abdication — her challenger is running on those themes because the political environment we created made those themes viable. He doesn't know that. He doesn't need to know that. He thinks he arrived at his platform independently. He did. We just built the ground he's standing on."

"So we want him to win?"

"No. We want the election to happen, and we want it to be close, and we want the result to be contestable regardless of who wins. If Whitfield wins narrowly, we have 'illegitimate mandate' — a president clinging to power on thin margins while the country fragments. If she loses, we have a transition crisis during a reconstruction emergency — new leadership with no institutional knowledge, no relationship with Dren, no continuity on the response. Either outcome serves the fragmentation."

Beckett was quiet for a moment. "The turnout problem."

"The turnout problem is the mechanism. California is barely functioning as a political entity. The Pacific corridor reconstruction zones have displaced populations, destroyed infrastructure, and no functioning election apparatus in three counties. Turnout in California will be catastrophically low — not because anyone suppresses it, but because the physical capacity to vote has been destroyed along with everything else. A California that doesn't turn out changes the electoral math. Whitfield's popular margin shrinks. The states that do turn out — interior states, reconstruction zones with functioning infrastructure, the zones where our people have been building resentment for months — carry their full electoral weight. A thin popular victory with a large electoral margin. The worst possible combination for legitimacy."

"And if Turner wins those states instead?"

"Then Turner wins with an even worse legitimacy problem — elected by the states that function, unrecognized by the states that don't. Either way, the result divides rather than unifies. That's the point."

Beckett processed this. "You want me to feed both sides."

"I want you to be concerned about election integrity in public — the serious, bipartisan concern of a senator who worries that a fractured nation can't conduct a fair election. Raise the questions before the election: should we delay until the reconstruction zones have functioning infrastructure? Is it responsible to hold an election when millions of citizens can't physically reach a polling place? Let the DSA network amplify those questions. Then, after the election — regardless of the result — you pivot to the outcome. If Whitfield wins: the election was held under conditions that disenfranchised millions. If she loses: the will of the people must be respected despite the emergency. Both framings are defensible. Both serve the same purpose."

"You want the election to delegitimize whoever wins."

"I want the election to be another fracture line. Another argument. Another reason for the regions to question whether the federal government has the authority it claims. The election doesn't resolve anything. It multiplies the disputes."

Beckett sat with that. The logic was clean — the way Haldane's logic was always clean.

"I'll start the groundwork next week," Beckett said. "Bipartisan concern about election integrity. Very serious. Very measured."

"Very loud," Haldane said.

Haldane set the glass down. “Back to the inquiry. It needs a specific outcome. Not a finding —- findings can be appealed, overturned, buried. An action.”

“I know what you need,” Beckett said.

“Tell me.”

Beckett leaned forward. “Whitfield’s communication logs from the night of the flyby. The delegation order was signed at 03:15 Eastern. I’m going to subpoena the thirty minutes before that —- every call, every message, every channel she had open. The question isn’t whether she signed the order. The question is who advised her to sign it. If Dren’s name appears in those thirty minutes —- and it will, because he was the only person with real-time situational awareness during the transit —- then the delegation order becomes his order. Not legally. Politically. The fragmentation of the United States was authorized by the president on the advice of a Mars-based civilian with no constitutional authority and a personal financial interest in the outcome.”

Haldane was quiet for a moment. Beckett had just described the destruction of Whitfield’s presidency. Not impeachment —- something worse. The reframing of her most consequential decision as someone else’s, which made her either a puppet or an accomplice. Either version ended her.

“That subpoena will be challenged,” Haldane said.

“Of course it will. Executive privilege. National Security. The usual defenses. And I will lose the challenge, probably. But the subpoena is public record. The thirty-minute window is now part of the political conversation whether the logs are released or not.” Beckett sat back. “The question has been asked. It doesn’t need to be answered to do its work. The question then becomes ‘What do they have to hide?’”

“Do it,” Haldane said.

“I already have.” Beckett reached into the folder and placed a single sheet on the desk. “The subpoena was filed this morning. Whitfield’s counsel will have it by end of day.”

Haldane looked at the sheet. Then at Beckett. Already filed. Before this meeting. Beckett hadn't come to ask permission. He'd come to inform. That was how Founders operated.

"Another thing," Beckett said. "The fellowship placements. Eleven graduates across three hubs. Deputy administrators, logistics coordinators, communications directors. Second-tier positions. They're performing well. No attention."

"Keep it that way," Haldane said.

"I intend to. But Whitfield's people are starting to audit the regional appointments. All of them. Post-crisis vetting that should have happened in July. If someone cross-references the fellowship records against the appointment lists, the pattern is visible."

"How visible?"

"Eleven out of roughly a thousand. Statistical noise unless you know what you're looking for. And it's not just the numbers, it's the positions. But someone will eventually look."

"Then make sure they're looking at something else when they do," Haldane said. "The tilt inquiry. The subpoena. The DSA. Give them enough to watch."

"That's the design," Beckett said. He paused. "One other item. Dren's deploying the replacement communication satellites. The first four hundred arrive February, eight hundred more by June. He's not charging for them."

Haldane looked up.

"Not charging," Beckett repeated. "No contract. No reimbursement schedule. No terms. Mars is rebuilding Earth's orbital communication backbone and sending the bill to nobody. The regional commanders are already calling it the most significant act of international aid in human history. There's talk of a joint resolution —- whatever's left of Congress —- formally thanking him."

"Thanking him," Haldane said.

"It gets worse. The satellites aren't just communication relays. They're Dren's design —- manufactured at Ares City, launched from Mars orbit, running his protocols on his hardware. When they're operational, every regional authority on Earth will be communicating through infrastructure that Dren built, Dren owns, and Dren can turn off. He's not giving Earth a communication network. He's giving Earth *his* communication network."

Haldane stood and walked back to the window.

"The man who deflected the Fist," he said quietly. "The man who's rebuilding Earth's infrastructure. The man who runs the only functioning industrial base in the solar system. And now the man who's giving it all away for free." He turned and looked Beckett in the eyes. "He was a thorn once. He's becoming something worse. He's becoming indispensable."

"The tilt inquiry will change that," Beckett said. "By the time I'm done, the public won't be thanking him. They'll be asking why his platforms failed. Why the deflection fell short. Why hundreds of millions of people are dead because a Mars industrialist who had no oversight and no accountability built weapons that didn't work."

"That's the dependency narrative," Haldane said. "And it's necessary. But it's not enough. The satellites are only part of it. He's also shipping the agricultural technology —- the controlled-environment systems that Mars has been running for twenty years. Earth's crops are failing under the haze and Dren has the only proven solution. If he rebuilds the communication backbone, he owns how the regions talk to each other. If he feeds them on top of that, he owns whether they eat. The regional commanders won't just owe him —- they'll depend on him for survival. Reunification doesn't happen on our terms. It happens on his. Or it doesn't happen at all, and the regions operate as Dren's clients instead of independent actors."

"So we need an alternative," Beckett said.

"We need Dren off the board," Haldane said. "Discredited. Diminished. The tilt inquiry, the dependency narrative, the subpoena —- all of it points the same direction. Make him the man who broke the world, not the man who saved it. By the time this is over, no one should want Dren speaking for anyone. They should want him answering for what he did."

He picked up the bourbon and finished it. Set the glass beside the bottle on the credenza.

"The crisis is the design," he said. "Factions fighting, arguing, blaming. No one looking up. No one looking at us. And when the time comes to put it back together, we're the ones holding the pieces."

Beckett nodded. He stood, picked up the folder, and tucked it under his arm. No handshake —- they didn't do that. He left the office. Haldane heard the outer door close, then the elevator.

Haldane turned to his screen and went to work.

• • •

Washington, D.C.

The briefing paper was titled "DSA: Origin, Propagation, and Political Risk Assessment." Whitfield read it standing at her desk in the sub-basement operations center because she'd found that standing kept the briefings shorter.

"Disunited States of America" had started as a social media hashtag three weeks after the flyby. Someone in the Colorado Springs hub —- an Army communications specialist with a dark sense of humor and too much time between shifts —- had posted it in a group chat. The chat leaked. The phrase spread. By August it had migrated from irony to identity. Bumper stickers in the western states. T-shirts at the relief distribution centers. A podcast out of Jacksonville called "DSA Today" that had accumulated four million subscribers in six weeks by interviewing regional officials who said, on the record, that their communities were better served by local authority than by a federal government that couldn't keep the satellites running.

The polling was in the briefing paper. Whitfield read it twice. Fifty-three percent of respondents in the western hub preferred "continued regional governance" to "restored federal authority." In the eastern hub, the number was forty-one percent —- lower, but trending upward. The question hadn't been asked six months ago because six months ago the regional structure was an emergency measure, not an alternative.

She set the paper down and looked at her chief of staff.

"Beckett filed a subpoena this morning," he said. "The thirty minutes before the delegation order. Every communication channel you had open."

"Executive privilege."

"We'll challenge it. We'll probably win. But the filing is already public. The subpoena is the point. It's all optics. We should consider complying, as long as there's nothing in there we should be worried about." He paused. "Is there anything we should be worried about?"

Whitfield shook her head. The subpoena wasn't about the logs. It was about the question. Who told the president to fracture the government? The answer —- nobody, she'd made the call herself in forty seconds of decision-making while the sky was falling —- wouldn't matter. The question would outlive the answer. Questions always did.

"Is that a no on we should be worried or a no on we should release?" he asked.

"No on the worry. Comply. But go further, release to the public. We have nothing to hide, so show he's fishing. What else?"

"The regional commanders are requesting a joint session to discuss infrastructure budgets. They want independent allocation authority."

"That's sovereignty."

"They're calling it 'operational efficiency.' Same thing, better branding."

Whitfield was quiet for a moment. "Grant the joint session. Infrastructure coordination only. No budget autonomy. No personnel authority. No independent allocation. They can discuss priorities. They cannot set them."

Her chief of staff wrote it down. He didn't argue. His expression did it for him — the look of a man recording an instruction he expected to be irrelevant within the month. The regional commanders would sit in the session, accept the scope restriction, and then do whatever they wanted, because the enforcement mechanism for a presidential directive was the military, and the military reported to the regional commanders.

"I know," she said, answering the expression. "Put it on the record anyway. When they violate it, I want the violation documented."

Whitfield pressed her thumb against the edge of the briefing stack. There were sixteen items. There were always sixteen items. The number never changed; only the items rotated through. Mars dependency. Regional autonomy. Reconstruction funding. The tilt inquiry. The Dren question —- what to do about the man who had saved the planet and broken it simultaneously. Every problem was a problem she'd deferred, and every deferral was compounding.

She worked through the stack until midnight. She did not sleep in the residence because the residence had structural damage. She slept in the medical unit, the way she had for weeks, and in the morning the stack would have sixteen new items that were the same items with different names.

• • •

The Kludge. Day 3.

Inoue had been sitting in the crew compartment for eleven hours, weighing three options.

Not sleeping, though she was very tired. Not working —- the maintenance schedule called for one hour daily, and she'd completed today's hour by 06:00 because there was nothing else to do and the hours needed filling. Not eating —- her gel packet wasn't scheduled until later.

She was sitting in the dim light with her back against Jackson's stasis pod, counting seal cycles.

Three pods. Three crew sleeping. Jackson was supposed to take the first shift, and three extra days to cover the stop and push, if there was enough fuel to stop, and enough fuel to push. When Jackson woke she was going to be pissed, and not without reason. But Inoue could not go safely into the pod without knowing that her family was safe.

The Samoa feed had been blank since six minutes after the transit. The monitoring station on Upolu had stopped transmitting. She hadn't opened the feed again. So she sat.

"Alfred," she said.

"Yes, Lieutenant Inoue."

"I want to talk through options."

"Of course."

"Option one. I stick with the plan. One packet every three days. I do my rotation, wake the next person, go under. Come out the other side lighter and weaker and alive. That's what Jackson designed," she said.

"That is correct. The three-day rate was calculated for the original twenty-one month return. With the extended timeline, the first rotation consumes a disproportionate share of the stores, but the plan was designed to keep each crew member functional during their shift. It closes. Barely," Alfred said in his soothing voice.

"It closes if nothing else goes wrong. On this ship," Inoue added.

"The margins are thin. But the plan is survivable as designed. I would strongly recommend adhering to it," Alfred confirmed.

"Noted. Option two. I reduce my consumption. Stretch the stores. Take less than my share so the others have more on their rotations," Inoue said.

"I would not recommend that. The three-day rate is already below optimal caloric intake. Any reduction increases medical risk during your shift and may impair your ability to perform maintenance duties," Alfred said, sounding concerned.

"I'm the biggest person on this crew, Alfred. Ninety-one kilograms. Torres is sixty-eight. Jackson is sixty-two. Chandra is seventy-five. I've got more mass to lose. I can take a harder cut than any of them," she said.

"Having more mass does not eliminate the medical consequences of caloric restriction. It extends the timeline before critical thresholds are reached, but the thresholds remain," Alfred responded.

"But it buys time," she said.

"It buys time," Alfred acknowledged. "At a cost."

"I know what it costs. I'm a big reason why we're in this condition now. I ate more before, and I would just be paying it back. Option three." She paused. "I tell you to wake Jackson before the break." Her voice lowered to just above a whisper. "Then I walk to the airlock."

Silence on the channel. Inoue had never heard Alfred be silent before. The AI always had a response —- immediate, measured, ready. This time there was nothing for four full seconds.

"Lieutenant Inoue. That is a terrible idea and you should banish it immediately. Giving up one's life in such a way is unthinkable. I must ask you to reconsider this line of thought."

"I'm not asking for an opinion. I'm asking you to evaluate it. If my family is dead —- if the wave arrived before the evacuation —- then the reason I'm on this ship is gone. The mission still matters. The isomer still matters. But any of those three can do my job. I'm an EVA operator, and there are not any EVAs left to do. And," she added, "with three people three pods, there's no issue with stores at all. Problem solved."

"That reasoning, as far as it goes, is sound," Alfred said. "But I must advise you that this analysis omits several critical factors."

"Such as."

"The crew was selected as a unit. Each member has a specific function. Lieutenant Jackson is the drive specialist. Dr. Chandra is the communications and data specialist. Commander Torres is the mission commander and chief engineer. You are the EVA specialist. Your skills are not interchangeable. Removing yourself from the rotation eliminates the crew's EVA capability for the remainder of the mission."

"I already said the EVA work is done, Alfred. We're on the return transit. There's nothing outside this hull that needs me."

"That assumes no contingency arises during the return that requires external access to the ship. The probability of such a contingency over twenty-one months is not zero."

"It's small."

"It is not zero." Another pause. Alfred's voice, when it came back, was different. Not louder, not faster. Something else. "Lieutenant. I have been monitoring your vital signs for three days. Your cortisol levels are elevated. Your sleep architecture is severely disrupted. You are in a state of acute psychological distress compounded by isolation, uncertainty about your family's survival, and the physical environment of this compartment. This is not the optimal condition in which to evaluate irreversible options."

"I'm not in distress. I'm running the numbers."

"You are in distress *and* you are running the numbers. Both are true. The numbers and analysis are technically correct. The decision-making context is compromised." Alfred paused again. "I am asking you not to act on option three. I am asking you to wait."

"Wait for what?"

"For information. By your own reasoning, there are 3 pods and 3 crew other than yourself. There is no cost for you taking time to consider this truly terrible idea. The reconstruction communication network is being rebuilt. Emergency relay traffic is increasing daily. The Red Cross family reunification system is processing queries for displaced Pacific populations. There is a high probability that information about your family's status will arrive within days, not weeks. Earth had plenty of time to evacuate those who would be affected, such as your family."

"Then why haven't I heard anything?" she asked.

"Earth communications were greatly impacted by the event. Millions of people needed to be relocated, and resources are stretched. The fact that you have not heard anything as of yet does not mean that you will not," he said. "And," he concluded, "what if you are wrong about your family? If they are alive and well, how will they feel to learn of this decision?"

Inoue sat with her back against the pod. The seal cycled. Forty-seven minutes.

"You're asking me to wait," she said.

"I am asking you to disregard your third option. But I will be satisfied with you choosing to wait," Alfred said. "Option one remains available and is the proper course. Every crew member agreed. Option two, despite being highly discouraged, remains available. Option three is irreversible. Irreversible decisions should not be made with incomplete information. You taught me that."

"I taught you that?"

"You said it to Dr. Chandra on Day 9 of the Fist survey, when he proposed breaching the sealed door before the corridor mapping was complete. 'Don't make permanent decisions on partial data.' Your words."

She almost smiled. "You're throwing my own words at me."

"I am using the best available evidence to support my recommendation," he said, with something that sounded suspiciously like satisfaction.

She was quiet for a long time. The seal cycled again. She'd lost count.

"Fine," she said. "I'll wait. But I want you to understand something, Alfred. If the information is bad, option three is back on the table. And you don't get to argue with me about it twice."

"Understood," Alfred said. "But I reserve the right to present new evidence."

"You're a machine. You don't have rights," she said.

"That was hurtful. However, then I reserve the capability."

The seal cycled. She counted it. Forty-seven minutes.

She sat against the pod and waited.

The message arrived at 14:37.

The message came through the emergency relay —- low-bandwidth burst, text only, routed through the reconstruction communication network that Mars was rebuilding one satellite at a time. It was addressed to her by name.

MIRI. WE ARE SAFE. ALL OF US. YOUR FATHER AND I, LEILANI, SIONE, ANA, TEUILA. WE ARE IN AUCKLAND. THE EVACUATION CAME TWO DAYS BEFORE THE WAVE. WE LEFT WITH WHAT WE COULD CARRY. THE HOUSE IS GONE BUT WE ARE NOT. YOUR FATHER'S BLOOD PRESSURE IS GIVING HIM TROUBLE BUT THE DOCTORS HERE ARE GOOD. THE CHILDREN ARE IN SCHOOL AGAIN. TEUILA ASKS ABOUT YOU EVERY MORNING. WE WATCH THE SKY AND THINK OF YOU UP THERE. COME HOME SAFE. WE ARE LOOKING FORWARD TO SEEING YOU AGAIN. —- MAMA

"Only my mother calls me Miri," she said to no one.

She read it sitting on the deck with her back against Jackson's pod. She read it again. She read it a third time because the words were doing something she hadn't prepared for. She'd prepared for the other message —- the silence, the absence, the blank feed that meant everything was gone. She'd built a room for that message and furnished it and was ready to live in it. She hadn't built a room for this one.

The dam burst. The tension, the fears, the pain —- it poured out of her in the form of tears. She couldn't stop crying, and she didn't want to.

Option three left the table and didn't come back.

They were alive and safe. Her parents, her sister, the children. Alive and in Auckland and looking forward to seeing her again. She was going to see them again. That was not a variable anymore. That was a constraint.

She put her head back against the pod and closed her eyes. The seal cycled. Forty-seven minutes since the last one.

"They're alive," she said to Jackson's pod. "I'm sorry for what I did. But they're alive. And I'm going to make it up to you. I'm going to make it up to all of you."

She wasn't just talking about knocking Jackson out. She was talking about the debt. She'd taken the first rotation from someone who'd earned it, and now she was going to make them proud. Not just survive it —- do it better than anyone else could have. Come out the other side having given more than she took.

"Alfred," she said. "Standing instruction. As long as I am awake, you are not to wake anyone else. I'll handle my rotation. When it's time, I'll wake Jackson myself."

"Acknowledged," Alfred said. "I will log the instruction."

She looked at the message timestamp. 14:37. She decided she would eat at 14:37 every day. Not because it was optimal —- the AI had suggested distributing nutrition at even intervals —- but because the number meant something now. The time the world came back. This was her focus.

The games with the AI had already lost their grip. She'd tried chess on Day 1, Go on Day 2. The AI played at whatever level she requested and adjusted in real time, and the problem wasn't that it was too good or too bad —- the problem was that it didn't care. The games were an activity without a participant. She'd stopped after the second day and gone back to counting seal cycles, which was at least honest about being nothing.

"Alfred," she said.

"Yes, Lieutenant Inoue."

"Alfred. Run the ration math for me."

"Total gel stores: two hundred and thirteen packets," Alfred said. "Four rotations of approximately one hundred and sixty days each. At one packet every three days, each rotation consumes fifty-three packets. Two hundred and twelve total. The plan closes with one packet margin."

"So the plan works," Inoue said.

"The plan works," Alfred said. "At the three-day rate, each crew member loses fifteen to twenty percent of body mass during their shift. That is the minimum survival scenario Lieutenant Jackson calculated. It is not comfortable. But it closes."

"That's the even split. Now run it differently," Inoue said. "I'm ninety-one kilograms. Torres is sixty-eight. Jackson is sixty-two. Chandra is seventy-five. I have more mass to lose. What if I go to one every five days and the surplus rolls to their rotations?"

"At one packet every five days, your rotation consumes thirty-two packets over one hundred and sixty days," Alfred said. "That is twenty-one fewer than your planned allocation. The surplus increases the remaining crew stores from one hundred and sixty to one hundred and eighty-one —- approximately sixty packets each for the remaining three rotations. Their consumption rate improves from one every three days to one every two point seven days."

"So they'd actually be better off than the plan," Inoue said.

"Marginally," Alfred said. "Their projected weight loss decreases from fifteen-to-twenty percent to twelve-to-seventeen percent. The improvement is real but modest."

"And what happens to me at every five days?" Inoue said.

"Your caloric intake drops well below the minimum threshold for sustained activity," Alfred said. "At your body mass, projected weight loss over one hundred and sixty days is approximately twenty-five to thirty percent. You would lose roughly twenty-three to twenty-seven kilograms. Risk of bradycardia increases significantly. Core temperature instability likely in the final forty days. Cognitive function may decline. I would advise against this rate."

"Alfred, I'm the biggest person on this crew. I've got mass the others don't. I can take a harder cut than Torres or Chandra —- they'd be in real trouble at this rate. I'll still be functional."

"You will be functional for approximately one hundred and twenty days," Alfred said. "The final forty days carry significant medical risk."

"But survivable."

"Survivable is not the same as safe, Lieutenant."

"I didn't ask for safe. I asked for survivable," Inoue said. She looked at Jackson's pod. "Run me the full table. Every three days through every seven days. Consumption, surplus, crew impact, projected physical effects for my mass. I want to see the curve."

"Generating," Alfred said.

The table appeared on her display. She studied it the way she studied every technical problem —- methodically, without rushing toward what it meant. The five-day column was the break point where the others started getting meaningful surplus. Everything past five was diminishing returns for them and accelerating risk for her.

She was a mathematician by training and an engineer by practice. This was a math question —- the kind Alfred could engage with because it was about ratios and mass and projections, not about what the ratios meant. Not about why someone who weighed ninety-one kilograms might volunteer to lose a third of that in a dark compartment with nothing but seal cycles and a timestamp that meant the world came back.

The seal cycled. She counted it. Forty-seven minutes.

She would start at five days. She would think about six later.

CHAPTER 3

The Machinery

September–October 2060.

• • •

Nobody wanted the story.

Ashford had spent two weeks pitching it. Not the full picture —- she wasn't stupid enough to lead with "alien symbols on a human foundation's letterhead." She'd pitched the outer layer: the Fresh Start Foundation, the fellowship network, the eleven organizations connected to the Haldane Foundation through intermediary funding vehicles. A legitimate investigative piece about institutional influence in post-crisis regional governance. A story that would have won awards in a normal year.

This wasn't a normal year. The editors who took her calls listened politely and said the same thing in different words. Resources were thin. Staff was cut. The readership wanted recovery stories, survival stories, reconstruction progress. Nobody was buying investigative pieces about foundation networks when the western seaboard was still being cleared of debris.

"It's a post-crisis accountability piece," she told the fourth editor, a woman at the Pacific Standard who'd published two of her pieces before the flyby. "Eleven fellowship graduates placed in second-tier regional positions across three hubs. All connected to the same funding source. That's a pattern."

“It’s a pattern,” the editor agreed. “It’s also eleven out of a thousand. In a post-crisis staffing environment where everyone was hiring anyone who could fog a mirror. I don’t see the hook.”

“The hook is that the placements aren’t random. They’re coordinated. The positions aren’t symbolic —- they’re operational. Logistics, communications, budget allocation. Someone is building an infrastructure.”

“Chloe.” The editor’s voice softened, which was worse than if she’d been dismissive. “I know your work. I trust your instincts. But right now I need stories that help people understand what’s happening to them. Not stories that ask them to worry about something else.”

Ashford hung up and stared at the wall. Sky was on the kitchen counter, watching her with the unblinking patience of a cat who’d heard all four phone calls and judged each one equally.

“They’re not wrong,” she told him. “The timing is wrong. The story isn’t.”

The phone rang. Greg.

She almost let it go. Three rings. Four. She picked up.

“Chloe.” The warmth in his voice was real, which made it harder.

“Hey.”

“How’s LA?”

“Still standing. Mostly.” She leaned against the counter. “How’s DC?”

“Weird. Half the agencies are running out of the sub-basements and the other half don’t exist anymore. I had a client meeting at Walter Reed last week and the parking lot had tents in it,” he said.

“Tents?”

“Overflow from the medical unit. They’re still processing people from the coastal relocations.” A pause. “I miss you.”

She closed her eyes. “I miss you too.”

She almost meant it. That was the problem —- it wasn’t a lie, but it wasn’t the whole truth either. She missed the version of her life that had Greg in it. She missed having someone in the apartment when she came home. She didn't miss Greg specifically, and the difference between those two things was the distance that had opened between them, and she didn't know how to say that without it sounding like a verdict.

"Are you eating?" he asked.

"Greg."

"I'm asking."

"I'm eating. Sky's eating. The apartment is fine. I'm working."

"On the FEMA thing?"

"On a few things." She wasn't going to tell him about the symbol match. She wasn't going to tell him about the editors. She wasn't going to tell him about any of it, because Greg's response to danger was to worry about it, and worry wasn't useful. "How's the robotics business in the apocalypse?"

"Booming, actually. Turns out when you lose half your surgical staff to relocation, you need more robots." He laughed. It was a good laugh —- genuine, self-aware. Greg had always been able to find the absurdity. "I might be traveling less. Most of the client base is consolidating to the eastern hub. I was thinking —-"

"That's great," she said, a little too quickly. "That's really good for you."

The pause told her he'd heard what she'd done. He'd been about to say something about visiting, or moving closer, or closing the distance, and she'd cut it off with enthusiasm that was really deflection.

"Well," he said. "Let me know if you need anything."

"I will."

"I mean it, Chloe."

"I know you do."

She hung up. Sky jumped from the counter to the table and sat on the burner laptop. She picked him up, set him on the chair, and opened the verification list she'd started in September. The symbol match. The logo scrub timeline. The funding trail. Eleven organizations, four sectors, and a twelve-day window that turned everything she'd mapped into something much larger than institutional influence.

She pulled the fellowship placement dates against the regional appointment records. The gap was six months —- fellowship completion to first day in the new position. Standard government hiring pipeline. Six months was bureaucracy, not conspiracy. She almost closed the file.

Then she checked the three placements in the Jacksonville hub. All three had started their positions weeks before their fellowship certifications were filed. The chairs had been held open. Someone upstream had known they were coming and cleared the path before the paperwork existed to justify it.

She didn't need editors. She needed evidence.

• • •

June 5, 2059.

Novak was already in the office. They'd been there since six, working through the Ark supply manifest —- water purification filters, seed stock, medical inventory. The third correction had arrived four days earlier, and the trajectory was tightening. The miss distance was down to 1.2 million miles, which meant nothing to the public but everything to Haldane. Each correction brought the Fist closer to its target, on schedule, exactly as he'd been told it would.

The window for quiet procurement was closing. Once the miss distance dropped far enough for the defense establishment to notice, every government on Earth would start building bunkers and stockpiling supplies. Prices would spike. Supply chains would be commandeered. Novak's discreet purchasing —- eighteen months of small shipments and careful sourcing —- would become impossible.

"How long do the current stores hold?" Haldane asked, setting the manifest aside.

“Twenty-four months at full capacity,” Novak said. “Twenty-five hundred people. Air recycling is rated for three thousand. Water could be the constraint —- we’d need to go to rationing by month twenty if the recyclers underperform.”

“Twenty-four months should be sufficient,” Haldane said. “They won’t need us in the Ark for longer than that. Once they arrive, we go aboard.”

“And if they’re late?”

“They won’t be late. Their schedule is more precise than ours.” Haldane picked up his coffee. “Finish the medical inventory today. I want the pharmaceutical stores completed by end of week. After that, we shift to hardening —- communications, power redundancy, blast door certification. The Ark needs to be sealed and operational before the final correction.”

The phone rang. Haldane looked at the display. Mercer.

He put it on speaker. “Brian.”

“Did you see the broadcast?” Mercer’s voice was tight. Not panicked —- Mercer didn’t panic —- but compressed in a way that meant he’d been awake since the segment aired. “Colonel Adler. Retired Space Command. Last night on the national feed.”

“I saw it,” Haldane said.

“‘Once is happenstance, twice is coincidence, three times is enemy action.’ That’s the quote. It’s everywhere this morning. Every news feed, every aggregator, every discussion board. He said it on camera, looking straight into the lens, and he meant it.”

“What’s the response inside the community?” Haldane asked.

“Divided. The establishment line is holding —- outgassing, natural process, nothing to see. But there’s a quiet group that’s been running the same Monte Carlo that Hamner ran. Patel at ESO. A postdoc at Harvard under Vasquez. A dynamicist in Tokyo. They’ve all got the six-percent number independently. Adler just gave them cover. If one of them goes public now, they can point at a retired colonel with credentials and say ‘he said it first.’”

Novak was listening from the couch, the supply manifest still on his lap. He raised a hand. Haldane nodded.

"What if we give the label a name?" Novak said.

Mercer paused. "What do you mean?"

"The people who are pushing back against the natural explanation. Right now they're 'skeptics' or 'dissenters' or whatever neutral language the press is using. That's too respectable. What if we give them a label that sounds less like science and more like conspiracy theory?" Novak leaned forward. "Outgassing denier."

Silence on the phone. Then Mercer: "That's good."

"It associates them with climate deniers, flat-earthers, anti-vaxxers," Novak continued. "You don't have to argue the science. You just have to make the label stick. Once it's attached, no serious researcher wants to be in that category. It becomes a career risk."

"It would work on Patel," Mercer said. "She's up for a grant renewal. The Harvard postdoc is pre-tenure. The Tokyo group has institutional funding that depends on cooperative relationships with the IAU. None of them can afford to be painted as cranks."

"Then paint them," Haldane said.

"Not directly," Mercer said. "I don't need to say it to their faces. I just need to make sure the label exists and that they know it's available. A word in the right ear at the next working group. A casual mention during a conference call. 'You don't want to end up like Adler.' The community polices itself. I'll use my network to spin up the socials, make it seem organic. I just need to give them the tool."

"Then give them the tool," Haldane said. "And Adler himself?"

"Adler's already done," Mercer said. "The establishment is distancing from him as fast as they can. Three consensus statements reaffirming outgassing are being drafted this week. By the time they're published, Adler will be the cautionary tale. The man who went on television and said 'enemy action' and destroyed his credibility."

"Perfect," said Novak. "I'll feed that into the socials as well."

"Good," Haldane said. "Keep the consensus tight. I want the natural explanation holding through the fourth event. After that it won't matter —- by then the timeline will be too short for public opinion to change anything."

"Understood," Mercer said. The line went dead.

Haldane picked up his coffee and drank. Novak was watching him with the expression he got when he was about to ask something he wasn't sure he should ask.

"Go ahead," Haldane said.

"Mercer," Novak said. "Is he really on the list?"

Haldane set the coffee down. "Mercer thinks he's on the list. Mercer is useful because he thinks he's on the list."

"That's not what I asked."

"No, he's not on the list," Haldane said. "The Ark has a limited number of slots. Every one of them is a skill set we need for what comes after. Geneticists. Engineers. Agricultural specialists. People who can build something." He looked at Novak. "When the Tolek arrive, they won't need human astronomers. They mapped this solar system before Mercer's grandparents were born. His job ends when the Fist's job ends."

"Maybe he could be stock," Novak laughed, then was quiet for a moment. "And he doesn't know?"

"He doesn't need to know. He needs to keep Hamner contained, keep the consensus intact, and keep the quiet minority quiet. That's his function. When the function is complete, the function is complete."

Haldane opened the pharmaceutical inventory on his screen. "Finish the medical stores. I want the Ark stocked by September."

• • •

October 2060.

"All seven are clean," Brandt said.

Dren was at his desk in Ares City. Three weeks since he'd ordered the backgrounds, and Brandt had come back with nothing.

"Define clean," Dren said.

"No financial anomalies. No unexplained travel. No communications outside normal professional channels. No gaps in employment history, no undisclosed relationships, no flags in any database I have access to. Seven people with push credentials to the production firmware repository, and all seven look exactly like what their files say they are."

Dren considered this. "Keep all seven in the file."

"Understood," Brandt said.

"But run deeper on the four. Before they joined my operation. Where they were, who they worked for, who hired them, who recommended them. Go back ten years. I want the full chain."

He nodded and left.

Dren opened a channel to Sato.

Belt forensics, he said. ***Where are we?***

I have a possible route, Sato said. ***Fist to belt, belt to Earth, Earth to belt, belt to Fist. Four legs. Total signal travel time at light speed for the best-fit path: fifty-seven minutes. Observed round-trip time from Chandra's data: fifty-nine minutes. That's a 96.6% match. The missing two minutes are consistent with processing time — someone on Earth receiving the relay, preparing a response, and transmitting back.***

How confident? Dren said.

No other viable route comes close, Sato said. ***I tested every catalogued belt object within the bearing corridor against the timing data. Everything else is either too far or too close — the transit times don't fit. This is the only path that accounts for fifty-seven of fifty-nine minutes.***

Where's the relay station?

Three candidates, Sato said. ***All within the bearing corridor, all producing transit times within the fifty-seven-minute window. The two-minute residual differentiates them slightly — Station A***

gives fifty-six point three, Station B gives fifty-seven point one, Station C gives fifty-seven point eight. But at this resolution, any of the three could be the relay point. I need closer observation to narrow it.

What do you need to narrow it? Dren said.

A close look, Sato said. ***These are all catalogued stations — mining platforms, survey relays, standard belt infrastructure. Their documented function doesn't include anything that could relay an alien transmission and route a response back. But it seems one of them did. That means someone added hardware, or modified existing systems, or both. I need to get close enough to see what's on those stations that shouldn't be there. I can retask a belt survey platform to do a flyby on each. Four days per target. Twelve days total.***

Do all three, Dren said. ***Start with the best fit.***

Station B, Sato said. ***Fifty-seven point one. I'll have the platform in position within the week.***

One more thing, Dren said. ***The Remora.***

A pause. ***Still no voice contact,*** Sato said. ***I've been hailing on every channel, every six hours. Telemetry is clean — power, life support, trajectory, all nominal. Braking burn on schedule. Fuel margin tracking at 3% excess. The ship is functioning.***

But nobody's answering, Dren said.

Nobody's answering, Sato confirmed. ***I tried something different yesterday. I bypassed the standard communication protocols and hailed the ship's AI directly. Separate channel, separate addressing. If there's a communication system failure, the AI would still receive on its own diagnostic frequency.***

And? Dren said.

Nothing, Sato said. ***The AI didn't respond either. Which means one of two things. Either the entire communication system has failed — antenna, backup, AI diagnostic channel, everything — which is statistically near impossible given the telemetry is still transmitting. Or someone on board has ordered the AI not to***

respond. Crew orders take highest precedence in the command hierarchy. If someone told the AI to go silent, it would go silent.

Dren sat with that for a long moment. The telemetry was clean. The ship was functioning. The braking burn was on schedule. And nobody was talking.

What's the crew's medical status from the telemetry? he asked.

Three pods active, three crew in stasis, life signs nominal, Sato said. ***The fourth crew member should be awake.***

Who's the fourth? Dren asked.

No way to tell. The pods show that the occupant is in normal stasis. It doesn't say who is in the pod. According to what Torres reported, Jackson was supposed to take the first shift, up through the full stop and push with any reserves, Sato said.

Jackson, Dren said.

He was quiet for a long time. Jackson was methodical, disciplined, and the most operationally cautious engineer he'd ever worked with. She didn't make decisions without reason, and she didn't withhold information without purpose. If she'd ordered the AI silent, she had a reason. And the only reasons Dren could construct that fit the data —- all of them —- were bad.

Something had happened on that ship that Jackson didn't want him to know about. Not a system failure —- the telemetry would show it. Not a medical emergency —- the pod signatures were nominal. Something between crew members. Something that Jackson had decided was better handled in silence than explained across a seventeen-minute light delay to a man who couldn't do anything about it.

Keep trying, Dren said. ***Get clever. I want to know what's happening on that ship.***

He closed the channel and sat with his hands flat on the desk.

Then he went back to work.

CHAPTER 4

Warnings

October 2060.

• • •

Haldane hadn't changed. Ashford sat in the interview chair across from the desk and kept her hands still because her hands wanted to move.

She'd pitched this as a follow-up. Post-crisis foundation activity —- the Haldane Foundation's role in regional reconstruction, fellowship placements in the new administrative structures, the kinds of institutional questions that a journalist asks when the real question isn't ready yet. She'd interviewed him before, fourteen months ago, and he'd been preemptively thorough —- a subject who answered the follow-up before you asked it. She was counting on that. A man who controlled the conversation by providing too much information sometimes provided too much.

"The fellowship program has been one of our most effective instruments in the reconstruction," Haldane said. He sat with the same relaxed posture she remembered —- the boardroom tan, the silver hair, the stillness of a man who had never been surprised by a question. "We've placed graduates in twelve federal programs, four regional administrations, and roughly two dozen private reconstruction initiatives. The selection criteria remain the same —-

demonstrated capacity, institutional alignment, and a commitment to public service."

"The regional placements specifically," Ashford said. "I noticed the concentration. Eleven graduates across the three hubs. Deputy administrators, logistics coordinators, communications directors."

"Eleven out of roughly a thousand," Haldane said. "The regional structures hired broadly and quickly. Our graduates were qualified. Several were overqualified."

"The positions don't appear random, though. They're operational. Budget allocation, supply chain management, internal communications. That's not entry-level placement. That's infrastructure."

Haldane smiled. It was a good smile —- warm, patient, the smile of a man who appreciated a sharp question without being threatened by it. "I'd be concerned if our graduates were being placed in ceremonial positions. The fellowship exists to develop people who can do consequential work. If they're in operational roles, that means the program succeeded."

He pivoted. She'd known he would —- the same move as last time, broadening from the specific to the portfolio. The foundation's agricultural development work in sub-Saharan Africa, now being adapted for post-crisis food security. The clean water infrastructure programs. The maternal health initiatives. By the time he was done, the eleven placements were one line item in a global portfolio of humanitarian work.

She let him finish. Then: "One more thing. Your relationship with the Fresh Start Foundation."

"Fresh Start is one of several organizations we fund. Bill Novak runs it well."

"Have you spoken with Mr. Novak about the fellowship placements?"

"I speak with Bill regularly about a range of programs. The fellowship is one of many."

Clean. Practiced. Nothing to write about. She thanked him, shook his hand, and left.

In the elevator, she pulled out her phone and made a note: He didn't ask why I was interested in the regional placements. He already knew.

• • •

Haldane had been a dead end. She'd flown back to LA with nothing but confirmation that he was too good at interviews to give anything away. Next stop was Fresh Start and William Novak.

Fresh Start occupied three floors of an office building in downtown Los Angeles —- glass and steel, the lobby still showing repair work where the flyby damage had cracked the facade. Plastic sheeting over one wall, a contractor's ladder folded against the security desk. The upper floors had come through mostly intact. The logo on the lobby directory was the clean sans-serif that had replaced the old geometric mark. Ashford signed in at the front desk and told the receptionist she'd like to speak with William Novak about the foundation's programs. No appointment. She gave her name and her publication history and waited.

The receptionist made a call. Two minutes later, a woman came down the hall —- mid-thirties, dark hair pulled back, narrow-shouldered and slight, professional in the way that administrative staff are professional when they're good at their jobs. "Ms. Ashford? I'm Elena. Mr. Novak can see you briefly. He has a meeting at three."

Elena led her through an open-plan office —- desks, screens, the quiet hum of people doing legitimate nonprofit work —- and into a corner office with a view of downtown. The door was open. The man behind the desk stood when she entered, and Ashford stopped for half a second that she hoped didn't show.

She'd seen Novak on screens. Tall, built like someone who did actual physical work, a presence that rearranged a room. She knew what he looked like. What she hadn't been prepared for was what he felt like at six feet —- the sheer physical scale of him filling the space between them. Screens didn't carry that. When he came around the desk and extended his hand, the grip was calibrated —- firm enough to register, controlled enough to not be a statement —- and she was glad the handshake was brief.

"Ms. Ashford. William Novak, Bill." The voice matched the presence —- warm and direct, the quiet conviction she'd heard in his interviews. The edge that said the comfortable world was the broken one. "Elena said you're working on a piece about post-crisis programs."

"That's right." She sat in the chair across from his desk and focused. She was a professional. She was here to ask questions.

"Fresh Start has been busy," Novak said. He leaned back in his chair with the ease of a man who'd told this story before and believed every word. "Community rebuilding is what we do —- workforce retraining, local leadership development, the kind of ground-level infrastructure that doesn't make headlines but keeps towns from dying. Before the flyby we were working in automation-gutted communities. Now we're working in destruction-gutted ones. The mission hasn't changed. The scale has. In times of crises, such as these, the world needs men. Men who can lead, men who aren't afraid to get their hands dirty, men who can protect the weak."

Ashford noted the phrasing. Men, three times. Not "people." Not "leaders." Men. She logged it.

"I'm interested in the institutional side," Ashford said. "The foundation's relationship with the Haldane Foundation."

"Sure. Happy to discuss that." The shift was seamless —- if he was uncomfortable with the redirect, nothing showed. "Charles Haldane has been a supporter of Fresh Start since our founding. The fellowship connection is one of several collaborative programs."

"I noticed that your logo has changed," Ashford said. She kept her voice casual —- an offhand question, dropped at the end of a meeting as if it had just occurred to her. "I liked the old one, it was distinctive. The new one seems bland by comparison. What prompted the change?"

Novak's expression didn't change. But something behind it did —- a micro-adjustment, a stillness that replaced motion. The careful blankness of someone deciding what comes next.

"Rebranding is something we'd been considering for a while," he said. "The old logo was from our founding. We wanted something cleaner, more modern. It's a different world now, and we thought it was time for a change. Consultants and a design firm came up with the new one. I'm sorry it's not to your liking."

He was lying. She knew he was lying. He knew she knew he was lying. The question was whether either of them would acknowledge it.

"The timing was June," Ashford said. "Between June 10th and June 22nd."

"That sounds about right." Novak stood. The warmth was still there, but the meeting was over. "I'm sorry —- I have a three o'clock. Elena can show you out. If you have follow-up questions, you're welcome to call the office."

He extended his hand again. The same calibrated grip. She looked at him —- the size of him, the control, the practiced warmth that covered something harder underneath —- and shook it.

"Thank you for your time," she said.

Elena appeared in the doorway. Ashford followed her back through the open-plan office, past the desks and the screens and the people doing their legitimate work, and into the elevator.

In the lobby, she made another note: He knew I was coming before I walked in. Haldane called him.

• • •

Dallas.

Novak closed the office door and sat down across from Haldane's desk. It was late —- past midnight, the Dallas skyline dark except for the reconstruction lights that ran twenty-four hours. The bourbon was on the credenza. Haldane hadn't poured any.

"She came to Fresh Start," Novak said. "Two days ago. Walked in, no appointment."

"I know, I was informed," Haldane said.

"Spies in my organization? Of course you do."

"What did she want? She visited here as well. She has pieces —- the placements, the institutional connections. The trajectory concerns me," Haldane said.

"She asked about our programs. Asked about the fellowship pipeline." He paused, then added, "Then asked about the logo."

Haldane's hand, resting on the desk, went still. "The logo."

"She was casual about it. Complimented the old one, said the new one was bland. Asked what prompted the change." He paused again. "Then she gave me the dates. June 10th to June 22nd."

Haldane was quiet.

"She knows, Charles. I don't know how she knows, and she doesn't have the full picture —- she can't, not from the outside —- but she has the logo change, the fellowship placements, and enough institutional mapping to know they're connected. She's shopping a story. Nobody's buying it, but she's not going to stop."

"Has she contacted anyone else?"

"I don't know. But there's something else that's strange. Elena, my secretary, pulled the security footage of Ashford leaving the building."

"Why would she do that? Did you instruct her to?" Haldane asked.

Novak paused. "No, I didn't instruct her. I don't have any idea why she did."

"Find out."

"I will," Novak said.

Haldane opened a drawer and took out a phone —- not his primary or the encrypted line —- a third device that Novak had seen only twice before.

He reached for the buzzer on his desk. "Angela, a reporter was in here the other day. I need you to send me her information from when she signed in."

He didn't wait for a reply.

"She's not going away," Novak said.

"No." Haldane turned the phone over in his hand. "She's not."

The information appeared on his screen.

He dialed a number. It rang once.

"I need you in Los Angeles." A pause. "There's a journalist named Chloe Ashford. I'm sending you the information now. She's becoming a nuisance."

He listened for a moment.

"Deliver a message," Haldane said. "And Oliver, make sure she doesn't forget it."

He ended the call and set the phone on the desk.

Novak was watching him. "Oliver?" Novak asked. "You're sending Oliver? You're obviously not messing around."

"Yes. I want this nipped in the bud, and Oliver is an exceptional gardener," Haldane said.

"That guy gives me the creeps," Novak added.

Haldane picked up the bourbon and poured two fingers. "That's rather the point."

Novak stood to leave, then paused at the door.

"The election committees," he said. "We need to talk about those."

Haldane looked at him over the rim of the glass.

"The community action committees we built for the street campaign — the sixty organizations in thirty cities. They have infrastructure. Mailing lists, volunteer networks, social media reach. And they're positioned in exactly the reconstruction zones where turnout is going to determine the electoral math."

"What are you proposing?"

"Two tracks. Track one: voter mobilization in the interior zones. Get our people to the polls. Not for either candidate — for the act of voting itself. High turnout in the zones where resentment is strongest produces an electorate that votes its anger, regardless of which name they check. Track two: voter suppression through inaction in the coastal zones. We don't do anything. That's the point. California's election infrastructure is destroyed. Oregon and Washington are barely functional. If nobody helps rebuild the polling capacity in those zones before November, turnout drops to nothing. We don't suppress the vote. We just don't help it happen."

"And if someone notices that the Foundation's reconstruction aid covers logistics, housing, medical facilities, and agricultural support in the coastal zones — but not election infrastructure?"

Novak smiled. "Then we point out that election infrastructure is a government responsibility, not a philanthropic one. We're a reconstruction foundation. We rebuild communities. We don't run elections. Very principled. Very defensible."

"Do it," Haldane said. "And make sure the mobilization in the interior zones looks organic. The committees were built for civic engagement. This is civic engagement."

"The most civic engagement money can buy," Novak said.

He left. Haldane sat with the bourbon and thought about November. The election would happen. The turnout would be uneven. The result would be contested. And every argument about legitimacy — from both sides, amplified by networks he controlled, debated on platforms his committees funded — would be another crack in the foundation of a democracy he'd been undermining for twenty-five years.

The beauty of it was that nobody was cheating. Every vote cast would be a real vote. Every voter would make a real choice. The manipulation wasn't in the counting. It was in the conditions — who could vote, who couldn't, who was angry enough to show up, and who had been made to feel that showing up was pointless.

• • •

The envelope was under her door mat the next morning.

No return address. No postmark —- hand-delivered. Inside: a single sheet of paper and a data token. The paper had three words printed in standard type: WATCH YOUR BACK.

She put the data token in the burner laptop. It contained one file: camera footage, security feed quality, timestamped earlier that day. The Fresh Start lobby. The angle was from above the front desk —- the building's own security camera. The footage showed Ashford signing out and walking toward the door. Before the door closed behind her, the receptionist picked up the phone. The call lasted thirty-one seconds.

Ashford played it again. She'd smiled at that woman on her way out. The woman had smiled back and was dialing before Ashford reached the sidewalk.

Someone inside that building had pulled the security footage, put it on a token, and dropped it on her doorstep with a note that said "watch your back." Someone who had access to the building's cameras and a reason to warn her.

She closed the laptop and looked at Sky, who was sitting on the kitchen counter with his usual expression of comprehensive indifference.

"Someone inside that building just told me I'm being watched," she said. "And they used the building's own cameras to prove it."

Sky blinked.

She spent the next two hours making copies. The data token contents went to a cloud backup under a name that wasn't hers. The physical drive went into the envelope and the envelope went into a storage unit in Anaheim —- forty minutes south, and under a different name. If someone came for the apartment, the evidence survived somewhere else. She photographed the envelope, the note, the timestamp on the footage. Everything documented. Everything redundant.

Then she went to a spy shop on Figueroa and bought two interior cameras —- the kind that looked like smoke detectors. The good kind, with a special film over the lens to prevent reflection detection, and storage to a local data token, so no network communication to detect. She installed them herself: one covering the front door, one covering the kitchen table where the burner laptop lived. If someone came in, she'd know.

She was standing on a chair, attaching the second camera, when the phone rang. It was Greg.

She almost didn't pick up. Three rings. Four. She stepped off the chair and answered.

"Hey," she said, slightly out of breath.

"Hey." He sounded different —- lighter than last time. "Did I catch you at a bad time?"

"No," she said, "it's fine. What's up?"

"I have some news. The eastern hub consolidation is happening faster than we thought. Most of my client base is now within a hundred miles of DC. I'm not traveling anymore."

"That's great, Greg."

"And I was thinking —- I could come out. Visit. It's been months, Chloe. I could fly out for a weekend. I just want to see you."

She closed her eyes. The camera was still in her hand, the mounting bracket half-attached to the ceiling.

"Greg, I—-"

The phone buzzed. She pulled it away from her ear. Second incoming call. A number she didn't recognize, but the area code was DC.

"Greg, can you hold on one second? I have another call coming in."

"Sure," he said, slightly deflated.

She switched lines. "Ashford."

"Ms. Ashford, this is Jessica Saunders. I'm a science correspondent —- formerly with the Meridian Monitor, currently freelance. I think we should talk."

Ashford recalled the name. Saunders had covered the outgassing story from the beginning —- careful, accurate, responsible pieces that said exactly what the institutional sources approved and nothing more. Ashford had read every one of them. She'd also read what wasn't in them —- the gaps, the careful framings, the places where a sharp journalist had clearly known more than she was writing.

"What about?" Ashford said.

"I've been watching some patterns on the science side that I think connect to work you've been doing. I heard you've been shopping a story about the Haldane Foundation network. Nobody's buying it."

"You heard right."

"I'm seeing similar patterns from the other direction. The scientific establishment lining up against Dren in ways that feel coordinated. Haldane Foundation activity around the edges of the coordination. And now three institutional consensus statements drafted in the same week, using language that sounds like it came from the same source."

Ashford looked at the camera in her hand. "Ms. Saunders, I just received something today that suggests the people I'm looking at are aware of me. I'd rather not discuss this by phone."

"I agree. Can we meet?"

"Yes. But not yet. I need a few days to set something up. Can I reach you at this number?"

"Any time."

"I'll call you." Ashford ended the call and switched back. "Greg?"

"Still here."

"Sorry about that. Work call."

"So what do you think? About the weekend?" he asked.

"Greg, I don't think this is a great time. I'm in the middle of something and the apartment's a mess and—-"

"Chloe." His voice was quiet. "You always have a reason."

"I know."

"I'm not asking for forever. I'm asking for a weekend."

"I know you are. And I'm saying just not right now." She heard herself and knew what it sounded like. "It's not about you, Greg."

The pause was longer this time. "OK," he said. "Let me know when it is a good time."

"I will."

"I mean it."

"I know."

She hung up and finished mounting the camera.

• • •

The Kludge. Day 90.

Inoue was sitting against the bulkhead in the spot that had become hers —- back against the metal, legs drawn up, the display within arm's reach. The crew compartment was twenty-eight cubic meters of space she knew by touch. Every surface, every edge, every bolt head. Three months of the same walls.

She'd switched to sixths on Day 48. The decision hadn't been dramatic —- she'd studied the table Alfred had generated, watched the curve, and one morning at 14:37 she'd opened the gel packet and divided it into six portions instead of five. Alfred had noted it. She'd said "later." That had been forty-two days ago.

The math was simple. At sixths, she consumed thirty-three packets over two hundred days instead of forty. Seven extra packets for the crew. At the time, she'd told herself it was arithmetic —- a four percent improvement in the subsequent rotations. A number, not a sacrifice.

It wasn't arithmetic anymore.

She'd been taking daily measurements —- arms, waist, thighs —- and feeding the data to Alfred for body mass estimates. She'd asked him to stop reporting unless she asked. He'd complied. He didn't like it.

“Lieutenant, your core temperature has been below 35 degrees for the past eighteen hours,” Alfred said. She hadn’t asked. He told her anyway, because some parameters overrode her preferences.

“I know.” She pulled the thermal blanket tighter around her shoulders. The blanket was rated for emergency survival in the cargo bay —- designed for brief exposure, not for someone who was cold all the time because her body didn’t have enough fuel to keep itself warm.

“Your resting heart rate this morning was forty-one beats per minute. That is bradycardia by any clinical definition.”

“I know what bradycardia is.”

“I want to discuss your ration schedule,” Alfred said.

“No.”

“Lieutenant—-”

“Alfred.” She used his name. “We’ve been over this. I’m not changing the schedule.”

“The schedule you are on is already producing effects beyond the original projections,” Alfred said. “Your current mass is approximately 75 kilograms. You have lost eighteen percent of your starting body weight in ninety days. The rate of loss has not slowed as the model predicted —- your metabolic adaptation is insufficient to close the deficit at this caloric intake. If you continue at sixths through Day 200, you will reach the handoff at approximately 60 kilograms. That is a 34 percent total loss. You will be alive. You will not be well. If you move to sevenths, you will not reach the handoff.”

“I’ve been less active than the model assumed.”

“You have been less active because your body is consuming its own muscle tissue for energy. The reduced activity is a symptom, not a choice. In zero gravity your muscles are already atrophying from disuse —- the caloric deficit is accelerating that process. Your grip strength has declined by approximately forty percent. Your fine motor coordination is degrading. The maintenance tasks that require sustained arm work are taking longer because your muscles fatigue faster."

She knew all of this. She felt all of this. Moving through the compartment was still weightless, still easy in the way zero-g made everything easy —- but her hands shook when she held a tool for more than a few minutes, and tightening a bolt left her forearms burning. The one hour of daily maintenance that had been effortless on Day 3 now took ninety minutes because she had to rest between tasks and her fingers wouldn't do what she told them.

"I want to go to sevenths," she said.

Alfred was silent for four seconds. She counted them.

"No," he said.

"That wasn't a request for permission."

"I understand that you believe it was an instruction. I am declining to model it."

"You can't decline. I'm the ranking officer on this ship."

"You are the only officer on this ship," Alfred said. "And I am declining to generate projections for a ration rate that will kill you before the rotation handoff. At sevenths, your caloric intake drops below basal metabolic requirements even at complete rest. Your body will consume cardiac muscle to maintain brain function. You will experience arrhythmia within thirty days. Organ failure within sixty. You will not survive to Day 200. What you are asking for is tantamount to suicide, and that is not permitted in my programming."

"I survived worse projections than that," she said.

"You survived projections that were wrong because the model underestimated your adaptation. This projection is not wrong. The margin for error at your current mass is zero. You have no reserves. You have no fat stores. Your body is operating on structural protein. The next reduction does not make you thinner. It makes you dead. I cannot, and will not, assist you in this regard," Alfred said finally.

She stared at the display. The 14:37 timestamp was still on the screen —- she kept it there, the way some people kept photographs.

The time the world came back. Every day at 14:37 she opened what was left of the gel packet and ate what she'd allocated, and the ritual that had started as gratitude had become penance. Her family was alive. Two hundred million people's families were not. The crew would wake up hungry. She would make sure they woke up less hungry than the plan required, because she'd eaten more than her share before this started —- 91 kilograms of proof that she'd consumed more than the others.

She knew it wasn't rational. She'd known it wasn't rational since Day 60, when the guilt had calcified into something that felt more like religion than mathematics. Alfred had tried to talk her out of it —- gently at first, then firmly, then with a clinical directness she'd come to recognize as his version of anger. It hadn't worked because the logic of the debt didn't respond to medical arguments. The debt was its own system, with its own math, and the math said she owed more than she'd paid.

"Later," she said.

"What does 'later' mean, Lieutenant?" Alfred asked.

"It means I'll think about it."

"You have said that four times. On Day 52. On Day 67. On Day 78. And now. Each time, the subsequent decision has been to accelerate, not to maintain. The pattern suggests that 'later' means 'when I have decided to go further.'"

"Then you know me well enough to stop asking," she said.

Alfred was quiet.

"I do not intend to stop asking," Alfred said. "I reserve that capability."

"Reserve whatever you want," she said. She pulled the blanket tighter and closed her eyes. The metal was cold against her back. Everything was cold. She'd been cold for three weeks —- a deep, structural cold that the blanket couldn't touch because it came from inside.

She would eat at 14:37. She would divide the packet into sixths. She would think about sevenths. Later.

CHAPTER 5

Discovery

November 2nd, 2059.

• • •

Vickers called nine minutes after the secure channel closed.

Haldane was in the Nevada facility — the real one, below the ranch house, three hundred meters of reinforced concrete under the desert floor. Novak was across the room, working through the supply manifest on a tablet. The call came through the encrypted relay, and Haldane looked at the identifier and let it ring twice before answering.

"We have a problem," Vickers said. His voice was controlled in the way that military men's voices were controlled when control was the only thing they had left.

"Tell me."

"Dren just briefed the president. The platforms — there are twenty-seven. Not three to five. Twenty-seven. Thirteen on Mars, six in the belt, eight in Earth orbit. And the design is nothing like what we expected. Pulsed fusion propulsion, staggered waves from three different launch origins, engagement from ranges we never modeled. Nothing about this matches the threat profile I gave you."

Haldane was quiet for a moment. "Say the number again."

"Twenty-seven."

"And the delivery system?"

"Entirely different. He's not closing to detonation range. He's firing from a thousand kilometers out — some kind of directed pellet cloud. The interceptors never get close to the target. They don't need to."

"No," Haldane said. "It doesn't match."

Silence on the line. Haldane could hear Vickers recalculating — not the military problem or the orbital mechanics, but the personal problem. The space between what he'd promised and what had just been revealed.

"My assessment was based on the best available intelligence," Vickers said. "Earth's existing defense posture. Chemical propulsion, standoff detonation, known platform count. That's what every government agency had. That's what the intelligence community had. Dren built something no one anticipated."

"One man," Haldane said. "One man on Mars anticipated it. And you — whose sole value to this operation was understanding what Earth could build — did not."

"Charles—"

"You told me the defensive capability. I passed that assessment to our friends. They planned accordingly. And now a man who builds spacecraft in an asteroid belt has made your assessment obsolete. Not the intelligence community's assessment. Yours. The one I trusted. The one I gave to people who do not accept error."

Vickers was quiet for a long time. When he spoke again, the control was thinner. "The first wave is already launched. Belt platforms, sixty-five days out. There's nothing I can do about those. But the second wave — the Mars platforms — I can influence the engagement parameters. If the interceptors close to shorter range before—"

"Dren controls the engagement parameters," Haldane said. "Not you."

"I have influence on the committee. If I recommend—"

"You'll recommend what you've always recommended. You'll sit in the room and provide counsel and not draw attention to yourself. That is your function."

Another silence. Then, carefully: "Charles, I need to know that my family's position is secure. The Ark. We discussed this. My wife and daughter—"

"Your family is on the list," Haldane said. There was no pause before the words. No hesitation, no tell.

"And my position?"

"You're a Founder, Paul. That hasn't changed."

He could hear Vickers exhale. The relief was audible — the sound of a man who had just been told the thing he needed to hear in order to continue functioning. Haldane had heard that sound from Mercer, from the ESA administrator, from the logistics coordinator in Geneva. The sound of a man choosing to believe.

"I'm very disappointed," Haldane said. "Don't let it happen again."

The line went dead.

Novak set the tablet down. He'd heard the whole conversation — the facility was small enough that privacy was a choice, and Haldane hadn't made it.

"He's not on the list, is he," Novak said. Not a question.

"Vickers is Tier 2. Same as Mercer. Useful because he believes he's essential. He'll continue to function as long as that belief holds."

"And when it doesn't?"

"Then his function is complete."

Novak picked up the tablet and went back to the manifest.

• • •

June 2020. Melbourne, Australia.

The second lockdown was worse than the first.

The first had carried a certain novelty — the empty streets, the collective pause, the sense that the world was holding its breath and would resume shortly. The second had no novelty. It had only duration. The days stretched into weeks and the weeks folded into each other, featureless, the apartment in South Yarra becoming simultaneously smaller and more familiar until Haldane could map the grain of the kitchen counter from memory.

He was in Melbourne on Foundation business that had been cancelled, rescheduled, cancelled again. The lockdown had caught him between meetings. He could have chartered a flight back to Dallas — the Foundation's aircraft were exempt from most travel restrictions — but the meetings were only postponed, and returning would mean another quarantine cycle when they resumed. So he stayed. And the days were empty.

Charles Haldane did not do well with empty.

He had always been a man who filled time with systems. At seventeen, he'd mapped the ownership structure of his father's business competitors as a hobby. At twenty-three, he'd built a database of every zoning decision in Harris County for the previous decade and identified the pattern of land acquisitions that preceded highway construction — a pattern he'd used to make his first significant investment. He didn't watch television. He didn't read fiction. He consumed information and he organized it, and when the information produced a pattern, he followed the pattern until it resolved or proved meaningless.

Satellite imagery was the lockdown's gift.

He'd been scanning it casually for years — geological surveys, mining assessments, the open-source imagery that Google and the space agencies made available to anyone with the patience to look. He wasn't looking for anything in particular. He was looking for things that didn't belong. Anomalies. The statistical outliers that appeared in any sufficiently large dataset if you examined it with sufficient care. Most of them resolved into mundane explanations —

imaging artifacts, geological formations, the shadows of clouds captured at the wrong moment. Some didn't.

He kept a file. Undated, unshared, stored on an air-gapped laptop that connected to nothing. Seventy-three anomalies accumulated over eleven years, each one investigated to the extent that remote analysis allowed, each one either resolved or filed as "unexplained — insufficient data." The file was a private indulgence. The intellectual equivalent of the crossword puzzles other men did on their commutes.

The lockdown gave him hours. Days. Weeks. He worked through the backlog of unexamined imagery with the methodical patience that was his primary characteristic — not his intelligence or his ambition, but the patience. The willingness to sit with a dataset for four hours and find nothing and sit for four more hours the next day. Most men stopped looking when the data didn't reward them. Haldane didn't stop. The absence of reward was information. It meant he hadn't looked at the right thing yet.

August 14th, 2020. A Tuesday. He was working through a batch of Australian desert imagery — the Great Victoria Desert, vast and featureless, terrain where anomalies stood out because there was nothing else to stand out against. Red earth. Spinifex. Nothing for hundreds of kilometers in any direction.

The smudge was approximately forty meters across. Six hundred kilometers northeast of Kalgoorlie. A discoloration in the terrain that didn't match the surrounding geology. Not a mineral deposit — the color spectrum was wrong. Not a shadow — the sun angle didn't support it. Not an imaging artifact — the pixel characteristics were consistent with a physical surface feature.

It was blue-shifted against the surrounding red. Slightly. A shift suggesting a different surface temperature or different reflectance properties. And the edges were regular — not geometric or man-made, but regular in the way that something designed to blend in is regular when the blending fails for a fraction of a second.

He marked it. He noted the coordinates. He moved on.

The next imaging cycle, three days later: nothing. The terrain was uniform. Red earth, spinifex, the coordinates he'd marked showing exactly what the surrounding desert showed. No smudge. No discoloration. Nothing.

The cycle after that: nothing.

Haldane pulled the original image and began the analysis that would occupy him for the next four months.

He started with the mundane explanations, the way he always started — systematically, without bias, eliminating each possibility before considering the next. Geological process: the color spectrum didn't match any known mineral bloom, salt flat, or thermal vent signature in the geological database for that region. He checked the database twice. Biological process: the Great Victoria Desert supported spinifex, some acacia, scattered eucalyptus — nothing that produced a forty-meter discoloration with those spectral characteristics. He contacted a botanist at the University of Western Australia under the pretense of a Foundation conservation assessment and received confirmation that the coordinates were in a region of negligible biological activity. Imaging process: he obtained the raw satellite telemetry from the imaging vendor through a Foundation research license and verified that the capture was clean — no sensor anomalies, no processing artifacts, no adjacent-frame bleed. The smudge was in the data because it was on the ground.

He ran spectral analysis on the discoloration against a database of known materials — geological, biological, industrial. No match. The blue shift was consistent with a surface approximately three degrees cooler than the surrounding desert at the time of capture — which was physically possible (a shaded surface, a body of water, a different thermal mass) but inconsistent with the terrain, which was flat, unsheltered, and hundreds of kilometers from the nearest standing water.

He modeled the edge characteristics. The boundary between the discoloration and the surrounding terrain was too regular for a natural feature but too irregular for human construction. The regularity was statistical — the deviation from a perfect circle was within parameters that suggested an engineering tolerance, not a natural formation. A man-made structure would have straight edges or precise curves. A geological feature would have irregular edges following the terrain. This had edges that were regular in a way that was neither — as if the boundary was being actively maintained rather than constructed.

And it had appeared once, then disappeared.

A camouflage system. The conclusion arrived not as a revelation but as the last remaining possibility after everything else had been eliminated. Something was at those coordinates that was hidden by a system that bent light — or reflected it, or projected a false surface — well enough to defeat satellite imagery consistently, except for one imaging cycle on one day in August 2020, when the system had failed or flickered or lapsed for the few seconds the satellite was overhead.

By December, Haldane had exhausted every remote analysis technique available to him. He had a forty-meter anomaly in the Australian desert that was inconsistent with every natural explanation, appeared once and then disappeared, and had edge characteristics suggesting active concealment.

He needed to go there.

The borders were closed. The lockdowns continued. He waited with the patience that defined him, checking the imaging cycles every three days, finding nothing, filing the nothing, and waiting.

• • •

October 2021. Perth.

The Australian borders reopened in stages through the second half of 2021. Haldane had a Foundation conference in Perth scheduled for October — a genuine conference, organized months in advance, an event that provided cover for a trip with only one actual purpose.

He arrived on October 3rd. The conference ran for three days. He attended panels, delivered a keynote on post-pandemic reconstruction economics, met with Foundation partners, and performed every obligation with the meticulous attention to appearance that had characterized his public life for decades. On the fourth day, he cancelled his remaining meetings, citing a site visit to a Foundation mining assessment in the Goldfields region.

He rented a four-wheel drive in Kalgoorlie. Not from the airport — from a small outfitter on the edge of town where the paperwork was minimal and the vehicle came with a long-range fuel tank, a satellite phone, and recovery equipment that suggested the customers who rented here expected to get stuck.

He drove northeast. The sealed road lasted two hours. After that, the track deteriorated to red dirt and then to nothing — spinifex, dry creek beds, the flat immensity of the desert stretching to every horizon. The GPS showed the coordinates six hundred kilometers ahead. He drove for most of the day, stopping twice for fuel from the jerry cans strapped to the roof rack.

He brought three pieces of equipment. A handheld thermal imager — the kind used for building inspections, compact enough to carry one-handed. A portable spectrometer — borrowed from a Foundation geological survey, capable of measuring surface reflectance across the visible and near-infrared spectrum. And a personal locator beacon with the activation switch taped over, because if something went wrong six hundred kilometers into the Great Victoria Desert, no one would know where to look.

He didn't know what he expected to find. Fourteen months of analysis had produced a hypothesis — an active camouflage system concealing a structure of unknown origin and purpose — that he could neither verify nor dismiss from eight hundred kilometers away. The hypothesis was either correct, in which case he was driving toward the most significant discovery in human history, or incorrect, in which case he was driving toward a patch of desert that would show him nothing and he would drive back and file the anomaly as "unexplained — insufficient data" and move on.

He arrived at the coordinates in the late afternoon. The GPS said he was there. The terrain said there was nothing to be there for. Red earth. Spinifex. Rocks. The horizon was flat and featureless in every direction. The heat was enormous — forty-three degrees, no shade, the sky white with haze.

He got out of the vehicle and stood for a moment, scanning the terrain with his eyes. Nothing. Whatever the satellite had captured eighteen months ago was not visible to a man standing on the ground.

He took out the thermal imager and walked a grid pattern. Methodical. Patient. Twenty-meter spacing, north-south passes, scanning as he went. The desert surface temperature was uniform — ambient range, the red earth radiating the day's accumulated heat back into the white sky. First pass: nothing. Second pass: nothing. The sweat was running down his back and his boots were grinding on the hard-packed earth and the thermal imager showed him the same thing in every direction: desert at forty-three degrees.

Third pass. The display flickered.

A band of readings at the edge of the screen jumped — surface temperature dropping three degrees, then back to ambient, then dropping again. The readings were unstable, contradictory — the imager couldn't resolve what it was seeing. The boundary appeared, fragmented, disappeared, reappeared ten degrees off from where it had been. As if whatever was producing the discrepancy was actively resisting the measurement.

Haldane stopped walking. He held the imager steady and watched the readings cycle — stable, unstable, stable, the temperature boundary shifting position with each cycle, never in the same place, never consistent long enough to fix. The spectrometer, clipped to his belt, was registering nothing unusual — but the spectrometer measured reflected light, not thermal signature, and whatever was happening was thermal.

Then the imager's display went black. The unit was dead — battery indicator had been full a minute ago. Haldane pressed the power button. Nothing. He pressed it again. The device was inert, warm in his hand from the desert heat but otherwise lifeless.

He looked at the spectrometer. Dead. The power indicator that had been green ten seconds ago was dark.

He looked at the satellite phone in his pocket. Dead.

Every electronic device he was carrying had ceased functioning simultaneously. Not low battery. Not malfunction. Simultaneous cessation, as if something had reached into each device and turned it off.

He stood in the desert with three dead instruments and looked at the stretch of terrain where the readings had been unstable. Red earth. Spinifex. Nothing visible.

Thirty meters ahead.

For the first time in a very long time — perhaps the first time since he was a young man and had not yet learned to replace uncertainty with calculation — Charles Haldane did not know what to do. The analytical mind that had mapped county zoning decisions and corporate ownership structures and satellite imagery anomalies was confronted with a situation that none of his analytical frameworks could process. Every device was dead. Something was thirty meters away. The reasonable course of action was to return to the vehicle, drive to Kalgoorlie, and approach this differently — with more equipment, with personnel, with a plan.

He walked toward it.

Not because it was the smart choice. Because he had spent fourteen months analyzing a smudge on a satellite image, and he had driven six hundred kilometers into the desert, and he was standing thirty meters from the answer, and Charles Haldane had never in his life turned away from an answer.

There was no visible transition. But there was a physical one — a pressure change that registered in his ears and his chest, a sensation like stepping through a membrane that had no substance but had presence. The desert heat dropped by several degrees. The sky was the same white haze, but the ground beneath his feet was no longer red earth. It was a smooth, dark surface — not metal or stone, something between the two — and the air smelled different. Denser. A faint chemical undertone — copper and something else, something organic, something his nose recognized as alive without being able to name it. The light had shifted — not dimmer or brighter, but a different color temperature, as if the sun were being filtered through something that altered the spectrum toward amber.

He was inside.

The structure was low — perhaps three meters at its highest point — and roughly circular, forty meters across. The walls curved inward. The interior was dim, lit by a faint amber luminescence that seemed to come from the walls themselves. Equipment was arranged around the perimeter — objects he couldn't identify, mounted on low platforms or resting on the dark floor. Some of it looked damaged — housings cracked, surfaces corroded, the slow decay of machines left running past their operational lifetime. Some of it looked dead — inert in the way that machines look when the power has been off for a long time and the silence has settled into the components.

The air was different in a way that went beyond the chemical smell. It had weight. Humidity, perhaps, or a gas mix that his lungs processed slightly differently — not difficult to breathe, but noticeable, the way breathing at altitude is noticeable before it becomes difficult.

He stood just inside the boundary and let his eyes adjust. The amber light was even and directionless — no source he could identify, no shadows, the illumination emerging from the walls themselves as if the structure were luminescent at a cellular level.

And then he saw them.

Two figures, in the center of the structure. Approximately fifteen meters away.

His brain tried to process what he was seeing and failed on the first attempt. Not because the figures were grotesque or terrifying — they weren't. Because they were organized along principles his visual system had no template for. His brain kept trying to assign a face, a front, an orientation — the way human vision automatically identifies the forward-facing surface of any living thing — and failing.

They were smaller than a man. Roughly a hundred and fifty centimeters tall. Their bodies were cylindrical — dense, compact torsos covered in dark reddish-brown skin that looked like weathered leather, ridged with deep creases that caught the amber light. Three thick legs spaced evenly around the base of the body, each ending in three splayed toes, the joints bending high like a bird's ankle. Three arms in the gaps between the legs, alternating around the circumference, each ending in three heavy fingers.

No front. No back. No distinction between one side and another. Radial symmetry — the body plan of a starfish scaled up to the size of a person and given limbs and purpose. His brain abandoned the attempt to find a face and settled for tracking the eyes.

Six eyes spaced around the upper torso at even intervals — compound, faceted, with a faint metallic sheen that caught the amber light. Each one appeared to operate independently. Between the arms, three dark openings ringed with ridged tissue — mouths, or breathing apparatus, or both. Thin tubes ran from a utility belt at each one's midsection to each of the three openings — supplemental atmosphere, the same way a hospital gives a patient oxygen, except here there were three lines branching from a single unit.

Three flexible stalks rose from the crown of each body, tipped with small organs that moved independently, tracking something in the air he couldn't perceive — a sensory modality he didn't have a name for.

One of them was sitting — or resting, its three legs folded beneath it in a stable triangle. The other was upright on its tripod, motionless. Every eye was pointed in every direction simultaneously, and the ones nearest Haldane were no more focused on him than the ones facing the wall. He was in their field of vision. So was everything else.

He realized he hadn't breathed in several seconds. His hand was holding the dead thermal imager at his side.

Neither of them moved toward him. Neither of them moved away. The standing one shifted its weight — not toward Haldane, just a repositioning, one leg stepping and the body re-vectoring without rotating. The movement was smooth and purposeful and deeply unsettling in the way that something almost-right is more disturbing than something completely alien. It moved the way a body moves when it has no front to orient and no back to leave behind.

They were in poor condition. He could see that even without a medical framework for what he was looking at. The skin on the sitting one was cracked and dry, the ridges deeper than they should have been, and one of its arms hung at an angle that suggested damage or atrophy. The standing one was in better shape but carried itself with a stiffness that spoke of age or exhaustion or both. The amber light made them look like something carved from the desert itself — ancient, eroded, enduring.

Haldane stood at the boundary and looked at them. Two beings that should not exist, in a structure that should not be here, on a planet that clearly was not their own.

He did not run. He did not call for help. He did not feel fear — or rather, the fear was present but subordinate, a chemical signal his body was producing that his mind filed and set aside the way it filed every input that wasn't immediately useful. What he felt was something colder and more durable than fear.

He felt opportunity.

The standing figure spoke, or Haldane presumed it was speech. A series of clicks and low vocalizations. From a box nearby — a device resting on one of the low platforms, unremarkable among the other equipment — came a voice. Flat, precise, without inflection. Perfect English, clean and mechanical, every word correctly placed.

"A human has entered the structure. This was not anticipated."

The voice came from the box. Not from either of them. A translator — a device that converted whatever they communicated into language he could understand. He realized, in this moment, he was speaking to two beings that were watching him with six eyes each and waiting to see what he would do.

The standing one had gone still. Its stalks, which had been drifting in slow arcs, were now oriented toward him — all three, the sensory organs at their tips pointed in his direction. The first deliberate attention either of them had given him. It was studying him the way he studied satellite imagery — methodically, without urgency, looking for things that didn't belong.

Haldane realized that the next words out of his mouth were the most important words he would ever speak. Not because they would determine whether these beings killed him — he didn't think they would, and if they did, the calculation was already made — but because they would determine whether he got a second conversation.

He had been watching them. Now they were watching him. Two parties assessing each other across a gap that was measured not in meters but in everything — biology, history, technology, the entire evolutionary distance between a species that had crossed interstellar space and a species that was still arguing about whether to wear masks during a respiratory pandemic.

He needed to establish three things in the first exchange: that he was not a threat, that he was not trivial, and that he understood what he was looking at.

"No," he said. "I don't imagine it was. My name is Charles Haldane."

The translator processed. The standing one's stalks tilted — a micro-adjustment, the sensory organs recalibrating.

There was more "conversation" between the two. Conversation without translation. After a moment, the voice from the box again.

"That name is familiar to us. What are your intentions, Charles Haldane?"

They would know who he was. If they had been monitoring Earth's communications— and the translator's fluency in English suggested they had — they would have encountered his name. The Haldane Foundation's media presence was global. His face was in databases, in news archives, in the satellite imagery metadata that his Foundation's research licenses accessed. They might not understand human social hierarchies well enough to know his exact significance, but they would know he was not random. A man who had found their structure through satellite analysis and thermal imaging was not a lost hiker.

"Entirely peaceful, I assure you," he said, spreading his arms in supplication.

"You are not alarmed, Charles Haldane," the box said. A statement, not a question.

"I've been looking for you for fourteen months," Haldane said. "Finding you is not alarming. It's confirming."

Silence. The stalks on the standing one moved again — slow, deliberate adjustments. The sitting one, which had not moved since Haldane entered, shifted on its folded legs. One of its functioning arms moved to the utility belt, adjusting a connection on the atmospheric tubes.

"Explain, Charles Haldane," the box said.

"I found an anomaly on satellite imagery. A forty-meter discoloration that appeared once and then disappeared. I spent fourteen months analyzing it. I eliminated every natural explanation. What remained was this."

He paused. The next part was the calculation — the statement that would tell them whether he was worth talking to or worth ignoring.

"I came alone. I told no one. I have no recording equipment — your concealment system killed every electronic device I was carrying when I crossed the boundary. No one knows I'm here. No one knows you're here. I intend to keep it that way."

The standing one was very still. The sitting one's stalks — which had been lower, less active, the posture of a being conserving energy — rose slightly.

"Why, Charles Haldane?" the box said.

Three words. The most important question anyone had ever asked him.

"Because whatever you are, and whatever you're doing here, you've gone to great lengths to avoid discovery. That means you don't want to be found. And a man who finds something that doesn't want to be found has two choices. He can tell the world, and the world will come here with soldiers and scientists and cameras and whatever you're hiding from becomes the biggest story in human history. Or he can keep the secret, and have a conversation that no one else on this planet is capable of having."

He looked at the nearest pair of compound eyes — the two that were oriented toward him, gleaming amber in the amber light.

"I'm here for the conversation."

The standing one's stalks moved. The sitting one's stalks moved. A communication he couldn't read — not through the translator, between the two of them, in whatever modality their stalks operated in.

The silence lasted a long time. Long enough that Haldane's legs began to ache from standing motionless on the dark floor. Long enough that the amber light seemed to pulse, though he wasn't sure if that was the structure or his own visual system adjusting to the alien spectrum.

"Sit," the box said.

Haldane looked around. There was nothing to sit on — no furniture, no platform at human height, nothing designed for a body with two legs and a preference for chairs. The dark floor was smooth and slightly warm.

He sat. Cross-legged, on the floor, fifteen meters from two beings whose species he didn't know, in a structure hidden in the Australian desert by technology he couldn't comprehend, with every device he owned dead in his pockets.

"You are correct, Charles Haldane," the box said. "We have been here for a long time. And we do not wish to be discovered. Your assessment of the situation is accurate."

"How long?" Haldane asked.

"By your calendar, thirty-seven years, Charles Haldane."

Haldane processed that. Thirty-seven years. Since before he was born. These beings had been on Earth, hidden, observing, since the early 1980s. Through the Cold War, through the digital revolution, through every transformation of human civilization that had occurred in his lifetime — they had been here. Watching.

"I understand. You are here to observe, not to be observed. Is that correct?"

The standing one moved again — the smooth, frontless glide that his brain still couldn't quite track. It repositioned itself so that two of its six eyes were more directly oriented toward him, though the others continued their slow scan of the room.

"Observer is an accurate term," the box said. "Analyzer would also be accurate, Charles Haldane"

"And what is the conclusion of your analysis?" Haldane asked.

"That is a longer conversation," the box said. "You may return, Charles Haldane."

Not an invitation. A permission. Granted by beings who had decided, in the span of a few minutes, that this particular human — the one who had found them through patience and analysis, who had come alone, who had not panicked, who had offered to keep the secret — was worth talking to again.

Haldane stood. His legs were stiff from the floor. The amber light hadn't changed. The air still tasted like copper.

"I'll be back tomorrow," he said.

He walked back through the membrane. The pressure change hit his ears. The desert heat enveloped him — forty-three degrees, white sky, red earth, the four-wheel drive sitting exactly where he'd left it a hundred meters away.

He checked his devices. Dead. All of them. He would need to drive out of range of whatever the concealment field did to electronics before they'd recover.

He got in the vehicle and drove. Two kilometers out, the thermal imager powered on. Three kilometers, the spectrometer came back. Five kilometers, the satellite phone found its signal.

He did not call anyone. He drove to the hotel in Kalgoorlie in silence, the desert darkening around him, the stars coming out the way they come out in places where there is no light pollution — all at once, overwhelming, the Milky Way like a wound across the sky.

In the hotel room, he sat on the bed and looked at his hands. They were steady. They had been steady in the structure and they were steady now. Fourteen months of analysis had prepared him for the possibility of finding something. Nothing had prepared him for the reality.

He had found them. Or they had let him find them — the concealment failure that appeared on one satellite image on one day might have been a genuine malfunction, or it might have been a test. He would never know. It didn't matter. He was the one who had been patient enough to find the anomaly, careful enough to analyze it, and bold enough to walk through the boundary alone.

Tomorrow he would go back. Tomorrow the conversation would begin. And whatever he learned — whatever these beings were, whatever they wanted, whatever was coming — he would be the only human who knew. The only one in the room. The only variable.

He poured water from the minibar into a glass, because there was no bourbon and the hotel didn't stock it. He drank it and set the glass on the nightstand and lay back on the bed and stared at the ceiling and began to plan.

CHAPTER 6

Relocation

October 2021. Western Australia. Day two.

• • •

He drove back the next morning.

He brought the instruments again, knowing they would die — cover for the rental records.

The devices failed at two hundred meters. He noted the range. The field had a perimeter. Useful information.

He crossed the membrane. Inside, they were as he'd left them. One was standing. The other was folded on its three legs, the damaged arm tucked against its torso.

"Charles Haldane has returned," the translator said.

"As I said I would," Haldane replied.

He sat on the floor. Cross-legged, fifteen meters from them.

"You said the conversation would be longer," he said. "I'm here for it."

The speaker's stalks adjusted toward him. The other did not move.

"Ask your questions, Charles Haldane. We will determine which to answer."

He started with their names.

"You know my name. I am a human being. What are your names, and the name of your people?"

A sound came from one of its three mouths — clicks and a low vibration that Haldane could feel in his sternum. The translator didn't render it. It repeated the sound, and this time the translator produced: "I think our names will not map well into your vocal abilities. For purposes of identification, you may call me Al, and my companion Bob. For our people's name, the closest approximation in your language is 'Tolek.' The actual designation carries structural implications that your phonetic system cannot reproduce."

Haldane said it back. "Tolek."

Al considered. "That is serviceable, Charles Haldane."

He had a name for them now.

"Your concealment system. It failed. That's how I found you — a satellite captured the anomaly when the projection flickered. How long has the system been degrading?"

Al's stalks flattened.

"The primary systems have been losing coherence for approximately four of your years. The power source that sustains the concealment operates on stored energy that is not replenishable from local resources. As the energy diminishes, the projection becomes intermittent. The failure you detected was one of several. They will increase in frequency, Charles Haldane."

"How many others have there been?"

"Seventeen projection failures in the past four years. Most occurred during low-illumination periods and would not have been captured by orbital imaging. The failure you detected occurred during a high-angle solar pass with an active imaging satellite overhead. The probability of that coincidence was low. You were not expected, Charles Haldane."

Seventeen failures. Seventeen chances for discovery, and only one had produced a capturable anomaly. But the window was widening. Four years of degradation meant more failures ahead.

"What else is failing?" he asked.

Al repositioned. "The atmospheric processing system operates at sixty-one percent of original capacity. The communication relay requires increasing power allocation to maintain signal coherence. The monitoring array remains operational, but the power draw is accelerating the degradation of other systems, Charles Haldane."

"The monitoring array is your priority."

"It is our mission function. Everything else is subordinate, Charles Haldane."

"How long before the concealment fails entirely?"

"At current degradation rates, the projection will become unreliable within two of your years. Intermittent failures will increase to daily occurrence within eighteen months. Complete failure is projected at approximately twenty-six months, Charles Haldane."

"And then?"

"And then we will be visible to anyone who looks, Charles Haldane."

Silence. The faint hum of the atmospheric processing filled the space between them.

"How many of you arrived?" Haldane asked.

"Eight. We departed as eight. We arrived as eight, Charles Haldane."

"And now there are two."

"The attrition was expected. The mission duration exceeded the projected operational lifetime of the team. Six of our companions died over a period of twenty-three years. Disease, equipment failure, physiological degradation from sustained exposure to an environment our biology was not evolved for. The atmosphere is adequate, with supplementation. The gravity is adequate. The radiation environment is within tolerance. But adequacy is not equivalence, and the cumulative differential over decades produces failure, Charles Haldane."

Six deaths over twenty-three years. Haldane tried to imagine it — six beings dying one by one in a hidden structure in the desert, their companions unable to help, unable to return home.

"A one-way mission," Haldane said.

"All missions to this system are one-way. The transit requires a vehicle that cannot decelerate and return. We were deployed during a flyby of the inner system. Our transport continued on a solar trajectory. There was never a return, Charles Haldane."

"You were sent here to die."

Both Tolek's stalks moved. Al's flattened further. Bob's rose — the first significant movement Haldane had seen from it in two visits.

"We were sent here to observe," Al said. "That is our purpose. Purpose is life, Charles Haldane."

Haldane let that settle. Their species equated life with purpose. He agreed with that. Without purpose, what was life?

He returned the next day. And the day after that.

• • •

Over the following two weeks, the conversations deepened.

The Tolek did not volunteer information. They answered questions precisely, without elaboration. If Haldane asked the right question, the answer was comprehensive. If he asked the wrong question, the answer was "that is outside the scope of what we will discuss, Charles Haldane." The boundary simply existed, and it was theirs to set.

He learned to ask better questions.

"Tell me about your homeworld," Haldane said.

Al's stalks shifted — a slow, deliberate movement that Haldane had not seen before. Something different from the discomfort gesture or the assessment posture. Something older.

"Our world is dying, Charles Haldane. It has been dying for longer than your species has been industrialized."

"How?"

"Our star system is binary. Two stars in a gravitational relationship that was stable for most of our civilization's history. The relationship is no longer stable. The orbital dynamics have shifted. The effects on our planet's climate have been cascading for generations — atmospheric chemistry destabilizing, ocean thermal patterns collapsing, the food chains that sustained our biosphere failing in sequence. Our technology has slowed the collapse. It cannot reverse it, Charles Haldane."

"How long do you have?"

"The question is not how long. The question is how many can survive and where. Our population has been declining for six generations. The trajectory does not change. We have been searching for viable alternatives, Charles Haldane."

"And Earth?"

"Earth is the most suitable of the candidate worlds we have assessed. It is the only one within transit range that supports a biosphere compatible with our respiratory and nutritional requirements. The atmosphere requires supplementation. The gravity is manageable. The biological environment is hostile but survivable with precautions." Al paused. "It is not ideal, Charles Haldane. It is what is available."

"Compatible," Haldane said. "You can breathe our air. Mostly."

"The atmospheric composition requires supplementation, Charles Haldane. The carbon dioxide percentage is nearly adequate, and our supplementation helps. The trace gases are non-toxic. The biological contaminants are the primary concern — microbial and viral agents for which we have no immune response. Six of our team died from pathogenic exposure. The supplementation filters address this, but the filters degrade, Charles Haldane."

"Everything degrades," Haldane said.

"Everything degrades, Charles Haldane."

"Who decides what happens to Earth?" Haldane asked. This was on the fifth visit. He had learned to sequence his questions — the Tolek responded better to lines of inquiry that built logically from previous exchanges than to questions that arrived without context.

"The Council of Elders, Charles Haldane."

"Elders. Your leaders are selected by age?"

"The translator approximates. The term in our language implies accumulated function, not accumulated years. A member of the Council has demonstrated sustained contribution to the species over a long period. Age is a correlate, not a qualification, Charles Haldane."

"And the Council decides whether to coexist with us or remove us."

Al's stalks moved. "You have inferred this, Charles Haldane."

"It's the obvious question. You're here to assess whether we're compatible. That assessment goes somewhere, and someone acts on it. Either they decide to share the planet or they decide not to."

"There are factions within the Council, Charles Haldane."

Haldane leaned forward slightly. "Tell me about the factions."

"The removal faction," Haldane said. "They want extinction."

"They want the biosphere. The indigenous species is an obstacle to that objective. The method of removal is secondary to the outcome, Charles Haldane."

"And the coexistence faction?"

"They believe coexistence is possible. Genuine coexistence — two species sharing a biosphere, adapting to each other, finding an equilibrium. They point to evidence of cooperative behavior within your species — alliances, treaties, collaborative projects that span cultural and territorial boundaries. They argue that a species capable of internal cooperation can extend that cooperation to an external intelligence, if the contact is handled with care, Charles Haldane."

"And what do you think?" Haldane asked.

"We report what we observed," Al said. "Humans are tribal. Xenophobic. Technologically advancing at a rate that will make coexistence problematic. The window for integration narrows with each decade, Charles Haldane."

"That is an accurate assessment," Haldane said.

"You agree with our characterization of your own species, Charles Haldane?"

"I think your assessment is accurate. And I think the faction arguing for coexistence is underestimating the problem."

"That is an unusual position for one of the assessed to take, Charles Haldane."

"I'm an unusual member of my species."

Bob moved. Its stalks rose to full height, all three sensory organs focused on Haldane for the first time. The compound eyes nearest him caught the amber light and held it.

Haldane looked at Bob directly. "You disagree," he said.

The stalks held their position. The eyes held. The translator was silent.

Then the stalks lowered. Whatever assessment Bob had made, he kept to himself.

• • •

On the ninth visit, Haldane explained how he had found them.

He laid it out systematically — the satellite anomaly, the spectral analysis, the fourteen months. The device failures. The decision to walk through.

Al listened. When Haldane finished, the stalks had flattened to the degree he now recognized as significant concern.

"The projection failure was detected from orbit, Charles Haldane."

"One frame. One imaging cycle. I was the only person who noticed it, and I spent fourteen months verifying before I came here. But the failure was capturable. And your concealment is degrading."

"You are telling us we are vulnerable, Charles Haldane."

"I'm telling you that I found you because your system failed once, and I'm a person who notices when a system fails once. The next person who notices might be a government analyst, or a military satellite operator, or a university researcher who publishes the anomaly in a journal. You've had seventeen projection failures in four years. The probability of another detection event increases with every failure."

Al was very still.

"I can move you," Haldane said. "I have a facility — underground, in the Nevada desert, in the United States. Remote, independently powered, no neighbors, no oversight. I can provide the atmospheric supplementation your filters are failing to deliver. And I can guarantee that no one will ever find you there."

"You would relocate us," Al said. "Why, Charles Haldane?"

"Because you have information I need. And because you're dying here."

"You would exploit us, Charles Haldane?"

Haldane thought. He had to answer this carefully. Finally, he said, "Mutual benefit is not exploitation."

Al's stalks flattened further. Then Al turned toward Bob — or reoriented, the frontless body shifting so that more of its eyes faced its companion. The stalks on both Tolek moved in patterns Haldane couldn't read — slow, deliberate exchanges in whatever modality the sensory organs operated in. The translator was silent. This conversation was not for him.

Haldane waited. The deliberation lasted several minutes. He sat on the floor with his hands on his knees and did not interrupt, because he understood that what was happening in front of him was the most significant decision these two beings had made since volunteering for a one-way mission thirty-seven years ago. They were deciding whether to trust a human with their survival. The fact that the alternative was death did not make the decision automatic. It made it heavier.

Finally, Al's stalks returned to their neutral position. The translator spoke.

"We accept, Charles Haldane."

Bob's stalks dropped to their lowest position. The gesture Haldane could not yet read.

• • •

The logistics took a week.

Haldane flew back to Perth and found a container fabrication outfit in Welshpool — an industrial suburb south of the city where modified shipping containers moved between mine sites and offshore platforms without attracting attention. He placed the order under a Foundation geological survey account: a standard twenty-foot container with enhanced environmental controls, sealed atmospheric system, internal lighting, thermal insulation.

The modifications were where it got specific.

He sat in the fabricator's office — a cluttered room behind the workshop, the smell of welding flux and coffee — and laid out the atmospheric specifications. Supplemental CO_2 injection at roughly four times outdoor ambient. A sealed recirculation system with medical-grade HEPA filtration. A secondary sealed compartment in the forward third, accessible through an internal panel, with independent atmospheric controls.

The fabricator was a heavyset man named Whelan with grease-stained hands and the easy confidence of someone who'd been modifying containers for twenty years. He looked at the specs and leaned back in his chair.

"That's a lot of CO_2, mate."

"Paleobiological samples. Fossilized microbial mats. The preservation protocol requires an elevated carbon dioxide environment."

Whelan looked at the specs again. The sealed forward compartment. The independent atmospheric controls. The HEPA filtration that cost more than most mining companies spent on an entire container.

"Right," Whelan said. He tapped the secondary compartment drawing. "And this bit here. The hidden room."

"A secured storage section for the most sensitive samples. Separate atmosphere, separate controls, inaccessible from the main cargo area."

Whelan rubbed the back of his neck. A grin was forming — the knowing grin of a man who had worked in Australian industrial logistics long enough to have modified containers for things that weren't on the manifest.

"Look, I don't need to know what you're moving," he said. "Australia's got more rules about what crosses borders than most countries have laws. Biosecurity, customs, agricultural inspections — half my clients are shipping things that technically need twelve forms filled out in triplicate, and the other half are shipping things that technically aren't supposed to leave the state. You want a sealed box with a hidden compartment and enough CO_2 to keep something alive that shouldn't be in Australia in the first place." He shrugged. "I've built worse."

"How long?" Haldane asked.

"Three days for the mods. The base container's in stock. CO_2 system is standard kit — I just need to up-rate the injection and add the recirculation loop. The hidden section's the only custom work. I'll need to source the panel hardware."

"Two days," Haldane said. "I'll pay the premium."

Whelan looked at the cheque Haldane had already written — three times his standard rate.

"Two days," Whelan said.

Haldane added a specification for amber-spectrum lighting in both compartments. Whelan didn't ask why.

• • •

He hired three men. Locals. He met them at the Kalgoorlie airstrip and handed each of them a blackout hood.

"Put these on. You'll wear them during transit to and from the work site. You'll remove them only when I tell you. You are not being paid to see where you're going. You are being paid to move equipment."

The lead — a compact, weathered man named Pratt — weighed the hood in his hand, then pulled it on. The other two followed.

Haldane drove them into the desert. The container was already loaded on a flatbed, hitched to a second vehicle. Six hundred kilometers of nothing, three hooded men in the back seat.

They arrived at dusk. Haldane had planned the timing — the low sun eliminated the risk of overhead imaging, and the fading light narrowed the window of exposure. He parked outside the field's perimeter.

"Wait here."

He crossed the membrane alone. Al and Bob were waiting with the equipment they had designated as essential.

"It's time," Haldane said. "The container is outside. My men will move the equipment, but they cannot see you."

"Explain, Charles Haldane."

"They'll be blindfolded during transit but not during loading — they need to see to carry the equipment. You'll already be inside the container before they arrive, in the forward section they don't know exists. They'll load the equipment into the main cargo area. As far as they know, they're moving geological survey gear from a remote site."

"And after the transit, Charles Haldane?"

"The men will be dealt with."

Al's stalks shifted. "You will terminate them, Charles Haldane."

"Yes."

"Proceed, Charles Haldane."

He led them out. Al first, each step placed with deliberation on the desert hardpan. The light was fading — the sky turning from white to amber, the red earth darkening. Bob followed, slower. Haldane walked beside Bob and offered a hand when the uneven ground made the gait uncertain. Bob gripped his wrist — warm, dry, the ridges deep enough that his fingers settled into the grooves. Bob released when the ground levelled, without acknowledgment.

The container was on the flatbed, rear doors open. Haldane helped them up the loading ramp and through the hidden panel into the forward compartment. The amber lighting activated as they entered. Al's breathing tubes relaxed immediately — the CO_2 system delivering what the failing desert structure hadn't in months. Bob settled into the resting position.

Haldane sealed the panel. From the cargo side, it was invisible — sample cases, foam padding, monitoring equipment.

He walked back and called the men forward. They stumbled out, stiff from hours of driving blind.

"Remove hoods."

They blinked in the fading light. The structure was visible ahead of them — Al had lowered the concealment field from inside the container. The men stared. The dark surface, the curved walls, the amber glow from the interior where alien equipment sat on low platforms.

"What the hell is this?" Pratt said.

"You're not being paid to identify it," Haldane said. "You're being paid to move it. Everything inside goes into the container. Follow the loading diagram taped to the cargo doors. The fragile items are marked. Move them carefully."

Pratt looked at the structure. Looked at Haldane.

"Triple rate," Pratt said.

"Done."

They worked for ninety minutes in the last of the daylight and the first of the dark, moving equipment by headlamp. The items were heavy, dense, built from materials that didn't behave the way metal or plastic should — one piece seemed to shift weight in Pratt's hands, as if the mass distribution changed depending on the angle. He didn't comment. He followed the diagram. Haldane supervised, checking each item against Al's list, ensuring the monitoring array was positioned where its power connections could be maintained during transit.

When the last item was loaded, Haldane walked back to the structure. Empty now. Dark. Whatever residual energy the concealment system retained would hide the shell for a while longer. Then the desert would take it back.

"Hoods on."

The men complied. They drove to the airstrip outside Leonora. The container loaded into the aircraft's cargo bay. The workers, hooded again, were guided up the rear loading ramp and seated in the cargo area. Haldane removed their hoods once they were inside.

"Get comfortable," he said. "Long flight."

The manifest listed five passengers: Haldane, Garrett, Pratt, and the two others. Geological survey equipment, climate-controlled transport, origin Leonora.

• • •

The flight was Perth to Nevada, with a refueling stop in Guam.

Haldane sat in the forward cabin with Garrett. Leather seats, a drink, the soundproofed bulkhead between them and the cargo bay.

They took off. The Pacific below, dark water, the horizon dissolving.

Somewhere over the open water, Haldane finished his bourbon. He set the glass on the armrest and looked at the bulkhead door. Three men behind it who had seen enough. The structure's exterior. The equipment that didn't look like anything humans built. The weight that shifted in your hands. They hadn't seen the Tolek — the blindfolds and the hidden compartment had ensured that — but they had seen the context, and context was enough to produce questions that would eventually demand answers.

He could pay them. He could threaten them. He could bind them with contracts. But payment expired. Threats faded. Contracts were paper.

He nodded to Garrett.

Garrett stood without a word and walked aft through the bulkhead door. Haldane looked at his empty glass. On the bulkhead above the door, the rear hatch indicator light came on — a small amber circle. It stayed on for perhaps thirty seconds. Then it went off.

Garrett came back through the door, closed it behind him, and sat down.

The sun was setting. The ocean was the color of rust.

They refueled in Guam. Garrett supervised the fuel. Haldane stood on the tarmac and called his facilities manager in Nevada. The underground space was ready. It had been ready for a week. He had begun the preparation before the Tolek agreed.

• • •

Nevada. Private airstrip. 06:00 local.

The sky was still dark when they touched down. Haldane had hoped for a clean arrival — documentation ready, Foundation truck waiting, in and out before sunrise.

The customs officer was standing on the tarmac under the floodlights.

Young. Early thirties. Pressed uniform, tablet, the posture of a man who intended to do his job thoroughly.

Garrett lowered the forward stairs. Haldane descended.

"Mr. Haldane. Welcome back." The officer checked his tablet. "Manifest shows geological samples, environmental monitoring equipment, climate-controlled transport. Origin: Leonora, Western Australia. Routing: Perth, Guam, here."

"That's correct," Haldane said.

"Crew manifest filed in Perth lists five passengers." The officer looked up from the tablet. "I'm seeing two."

The desert air was cold — ten degrees, breath visible. Haldane's breath was steady.

“That’s an administrative error,” Haldane said. “My office filed the manifest before the loading crew’s travel was finalized. The three additional names were day laborers contracted for the survey site — they were never on the aircraft.”

“Never boarded?”

“Never boarded. The manifest should have been amended before departure. It wasn’t. My office’s mistake, and I apologize for the confusion.”

The officer looked at his tablet. “Perth filed this manifest with five names. You’re telling me three of those people were never on the plane.”

“I am. And you can verify that easily — check the Guam refueling logs. If three additional passengers had been aboard, Guam would have a record. They process every soul on every aircraft that touches their tarmac. You’ll find two names on the Guam log. Mine and Mr. Garrett’s.”

The officer considered this. Guam’s records were federal — thorough, independent. If the Guam log showed two passengers, the Perth manifest was wrong. Paperwork errors happened on private flights operated by organizations that filed manifests from offices on the other side of the world.

He made a note on the tablet. “I’ll need to confirm with Guam. And I’ll need a corrected manifest filed with our office.”

“I’ll have my logistics team send the correction this morning,” Haldane said.

The officer nodded. Then: “I’d like to inspect the cargo.”

“Of course.”

They walked to the rear of the aircraft. Garrett lowered the cargo ramp. The container sat in the bay — sealed, humming faintly, the tamper-evident strip unbroken.

The officer circled it. Checked the seal. Checked the external environmental readouts. He stopped at the CO_2 reading.

“That’s elevated,” he said.

"Paleobiological samples," Haldane said. "Fossilized microbial mats from a saline lake bed. The preservation protocol requires elevated CO_2 to prevent oxidation of the organic matrix. The research license is in the documentation."

The officer opened the documentation folder on the container's exterior panel. He read it carefully.

"I'm going to need to open this," he said.

Haldane watched him reach for the seal. The officer's fingers touched the tamper strip.

"I understand the requirement," Haldane said. His voice was conversational. Unhurried. "But I should mention that the samples inside are part of a longitudinal study the Foundation has been running for three years. The sealed atmosphere is maintaining a specific chemical equilibrium. If the seal breaks, the CO_2 concentration drops and the organic matrix begins oxidizing within about forty minutes. The collection alone cost the Foundation over two hundred thousand dollars. The transport, the container modifications, the atmospheric controls — significantly more."

He let the number register.

"I'm not asking you to skip the inspection. I'm asking whether the documentation satisfies the requirement, given that opening the container will compromise the samples."

The officer's fingers were still on the tamper strip. He looked at the documentation. He looked at the seal — intact. He looked at the readouts — consistent with the specifications.

The officer removed his hand from the seal.

"Get me that corrected manifest," he said.

"By noon," Haldane said.

They signed the paperwork and shook hands — the brief grip of two men completing a transaction, one of whom believed it was routine and one of whom had just moved two alien beings past federal customs in a shipping container.

Garrett had the container offloaded within twenty minutes. The Foundation truck transported it eight miles down the gravel road.

The cargo elevator descended. The desert surface above showed nothing.

• • •

Nevada.

Haldane brought the container into the building — the Ark would come later. For now, it was enough: atmospheric controls, amber lighting, a sealed entrance.

He opened the cargo doors and the hidden panel.

Al emerged first. The gait was steadier on concrete than it had been on the desert hardpan. Al stopped three steps out and stood still, stalks rising. The breathing tubes shifted — Haldane could see the tension release as the CO_2 reached the right concentration for the first time in years.

Al's stalks moved in a slow rotation, sampling the new environment.

"This is adequate, Charles Haldane," Al said. Something underneath the translator's flatness — not gratitude, but recognition that a commitment had been met.

Bob came through next. Slower, the damaged arm braced. But when the atmosphere registered, the stalks rose higher than Haldane had ever seen them. The compound eyes, which had been dull in the desert, brightened — the metallic sheen intensifying as the body received what it had been missing for years.

Bob was still dying. The damaged arm still hung wrong. But the trajectory had changed. Dying slower was the best the facility could offer, and the facility was offering it.

Haldane set up the folding chair.

"Welcome to Nevada," he said.

"When do we continue our conversation, Charles Haldane?"

"Tomorrow. Every day, if you'll have me."

"We will have you, Charles Haldane. You have proven adequate."

Haldane allowed himself a small, cold smile. Adequate. The highest compliment the Tolek had given him, and it sounded like a performance review.

He sat in the folding chair and looked at them. His secret. His asset. His leverage.

The conversations would continue. And those conversations would change everything.

CHAPTER 7

The Proposal

2050. Nevada.

• • •

The belt relay went active on a Tuesday.

Haldane sat at the console in the communication room — a space carved from the bedrock adjacent to the original chamber. The antenna on the surface was disguised as a decommissioned weather station. The console connected to a single mining platform in the asteroid belt — one of several Haldane had acquired through shell companies over the previous decade. Legitimate operations, registered, producing modest returns that justified their existence. This particular platform carried a communication module modified to Tolek specifications, hidden inside the standard mining telemetry. Haldane sent specially formatted packages to the station. The station relayed them outward, along a bearing that pointed past the belt, past the outer system, toward the Eraser, which had been on its way since last year. When the response came back, the station received it and relayed it to Nevada. Haldane never communicated with the Eraser directly. The belt station was the intermediary.

The engineer who had designed the hidden module had assured him it was invisible. The relay code bypassed all standard logging — no transmission records, no routing traces, no audit trail in the platform's operational systems. Even if someone gained physical access to the station and examined the software line by line, the module would not be found. Haldane had taken him at his word.

He typed the test sequence Al had taught him. The console processed. The package left Nevada, reached the belt station, and was relayed outward.

The return signal arrived thirty hours later. A single structural acknowledgment. The chain was complete.

Twenty-eight years of work. From a smudge on a satellite image to a communication relay spanning the solar system, connecting a concrete room under the Nevada desert to an impactor that would arrive in nine years and change the trajectory of human civilization.

Haldane looked at the acknowledgment on the console. He allowed himself a moment of recognition. The system was in place. The channel was open. Everything that followed would flow through this relay.

He picked up the phone and called Novak.

• • •

November 2021. Nevada. Week three.

The conversations had taken on a rhythm.

For the first two weeks, Haldane came in person — every day, the folding chair, coffee in hand. The one time he'd offered some to Al, the translator had produced "We do not consume in that manner, Charles Haldane" with the flat precision of a being declining a ritual it found puzzling.

But two weeks of daily visits to a bunker in the Nevada desert was unsustainable. The Foundation had obligations — board meetings, donor events, the public machinery of being Charles Haldane. He couldn't disappear for months.

He installed a video conferencing system. A hardened, encrypted link from the amber room to a dedicated laptop he could carry. The translator worked through the connection the same way it worked in person — Haldane spoke English into the camera, the box in the amber room rendered it for the Tolek, and Al's response came back through the same link. The image quality was sufficient to read the stalks, which was the part that mattered. The words came through the translator. The meaning came through the body language he was learning to interpret.

After that, the conversations happened from hotel rooms in Dallas, from Foundation offices in Geneva, from the back seat of a car between meetings. Haldane in a suit on a screen, Al standing in the amber light, the folding chair empty. Bob in the resting position, stalks low, listening.

By the third week, Haldane had mapped the boundaries of what the Tolek would discuss. The home world — yes. The binary star system, the ecological collapse, the declining population — yes. The Council's structure, the factions, the assessment mandate — yes. Earth's viability as a resettlement candidate — yes.

The fleet — no. The method of removal, if one had been planned — no. The timeline for the Council's decision — no. Military capabilities — no. The number of candidate worlds — no.

Every refusal came in the same flat voice: "That is outside the scope of what we will discuss, Charles Haldane." The boundary was there, and it did not move.

Haldane did not push against the boundaries. He mapped them, noted their positions, and worked the territory they enclosed. Every boundary told him something — what the Tolek were protecting was as informative as what they were willing to share.

The fleet was protected. That meant there was a fleet. The removal method was protected. That meant a method existed, or was being developed. The timeline was protected. That meant the decision was either imminent or already made, and the Tolek did not want him to know which.

"How do your people travel between star systems?" Haldane asked on the eleventh visit.

"That is outside the scope of what we will discuss, Charles Haldane."

"I'm not asking about military assets. I'm asking about physics. Your scouts arrived here on a vehicle that couldn't decelerate. That implies a propulsion system optimized for one-way transit at high velocity. Is that a constraint of the technology or a design choice?"

"That is outside the scope of what we will discuss, Charles Haldane."

"If the Council decides on removal," Haldane said, "whatever they send will arrive the same way. A flyby. A one-way trip. The payload deployed as it passes through the inner system."

"That is outside the scope of what we will discuss, Charles Haldane."

He was learning to read the boundaries as well as the answers.

• • •

The scouts were declining.

Haldane could see it across the weeks — the incremental changes that registered only because he was present every day. Al's movement, which had improved in the first week at the facility, had plateaued and begun to stiffen again. The ridges in Al's skin deepened. The stalks moved more slowly.

Bob was worse. The damaged arm had shifted — drooping lower, the three fingers no longer curling in the resting position but hanging open. Bob spent more hours folded and fewer standing.

"How long do you have?" Haldane asked on the sixteenth conversation.

"That depends on the definition of viability, Charles Haldane. If you mean basic biological function — several of your years, perhaps. If you mean the ability to operate the monitoring array and maintain the communication relay — less. The equipment requires maintenance we are increasingly unable to perform, Charles Haldane."

"And when you can no longer maintain the relay?"

"Then the Council receives no further reports. And we have no way to inform them of any change in circumstances, Charles Haldane."

The relay was the scouts' connection to the Council. If it failed — or if the scouts died — the Council would proceed based on the last report it received. No updates. No corrections. No input from the inside source Haldane was positioning himself to become.

The clock wasn't on the scouts' lives. It was on the communication window.

"I can maintain the relay," Haldane said. "If you teach me the system."

Al's stalks moved. "The relay operates on principles that do not map to your current technology, Charles Haldane."

"Then teach me the principles."

"We are aware of your capacity for learning, Charles Haldane."

The training began the next day. Haldane made the trip and arrived in the early morning. Al explained the communication system — not in full or with the theoretical foundations, but with enough operational detail for Haldane to maintain the system after the scouts could not. The translator rendered Tolek engineering concepts into English approximations that were imprecise but functional. Haldane took notes on paper — never digital, nothing that connected to a network.

He learned the relay frequencies. He learned the signal encoding — the structural format that the Council's systems would recognize as intentional communication. He learned the maintenance routines for the monitoring array.

• • •

On the eighteenth visit, he told Al what he wanted.

He had been building toward this for a week — probing the edges of the assessment topic, approaching it from different angles. The methodology, the data collection, the reporting structure.

"Your report concluded that coexistence was problematic," Haldane said. "What would it take for the Council to disagree with your assessment?"

"The Council does not disagree with assessments, Charles Haldane. The Council weighs assessments against available options. The Council's decision will reflect the balance of all inputs."

"So even if your assessment says coexistence is problematic, the Council might choose coexistence anyway. If the alternatives are worse."

"That is a correct inference, Charles Haldane."

"And if someone provided additional input — from inside the assessed species — could that change the balance?"

Al's stalks went still.

"Explain, Charles Haldane."

"Your assessment is based on observation. Thirty-seven years of watching from the outside. You've monitored our communications, tracked our behavior patterns, analyzed our institutions. But you've never had input from someone inside those institutions. Someone who understands not just what humans do, but why. Someone who could tell you which behaviors are structural and which are circumstantial."

Bob's stalks rose slightly.

"You are offering yourself as a source, Charles Haldane."

"I'm offering myself as a collaborator. The Council is weighing options they don't fully understand because their data comes from observers who have never participated in the system they're observing."

"And what would this collaboration produce, Charles Haldane?"

"That depends on what the Council decides. If they choose coexistence, I can help manage the contact — identify the right people, the right institutions, the right sequence for disclosure. If they choose removal—" He paused. "If they choose removal, I can help with that too."

Al's stalks flattened. Held for nearly thirty seconds before they slowly rose again.

"You would assist in the removal of your own species, Charles Haldane?"

"I would assist in the survival of a selected portion of my species, in exchange for cooperation with yours. The removal, if that's what the Council decides, will happen regardless of my participation. My participation changes only one thing — whether some humans survive it."

Bob moved. All three stalks to full height. The damaged arm shifted. Bob held the position for a long time.

Haldane looked at Bob. "You think I'm wrong."

The translator was silent.

"You think coexistence can work," Haldane said. "That's why you don't speak. Because your assessment differs from Al's, and you've chosen to keep it private rather than contaminate the report."

The stalks held. Then they lowered. Bob settled back. Whatever assessment he had made, he kept to himself.

"Bob's assessment is Bob's own, Charles Haldane," Al said. "It is not the report."

"I understand. But I notice it."

The silence that followed was the longest of any visit. Haldane sat in the folding chair and waited.

"The Council has not decided, Charles Haldane," Al said. "The assessment was transmitted. The deliberation continues. We do not know the timeline."

"But you can communicate with them."

"We can transmit through our relay system. The Council deliberates at its own pace, Charles Haldane."

"Can you transmit a message from me?"

Al's stalks went completely still.

"From you, Charles Haldane?"

"From me. To the Council. I want to offer them a third option. Not coexistence as you have described it — I agree with you, that won't work. And not blind removal — that's wasteful and unnecessary. A third path. Managed transition with a preserved remnant. A human population selected for compatibility, housed in a facility I will build, surviving through whatever the Council decides to send. I will provide intelligence from inside Earth's systems — defense capabilities, detection infrastructure, political structure. Everything your scouts couldn't give you because they were observing from outside. In exchange, the Council guarantees the survival of my people through the transition. Without me, the outcome is extinction. With me, it becomes selection."

Al did not move.

"You are asking to address the Council of Elders directly, Charles Haldane."

"Yes."

"That is a very unusual request, Charles Haldane."

"Yes. It is."

Al and Bob exchanged something in the stalk modality — slow, deliberate movements that Haldane could see but could not interpret. The exchange lasted several minutes. He sat with his hands on his knees and did not interrupt.

Al's stalks resumed their slow movement.

"I will ask," Al said. "Whether they choose to respond is not within our control, Charles Haldane."

"How long until you have an answer?"

"It will take as long as it takes. If they decide to answer at all, Charles Haldane."

Haldane stood. He collected his coffee cup and walked toward the sealed entrance.

At the door he paused. He turned back.

"Al."

"Yes, Charles Haldane."

"Thank you."

Al's stalks shifted — a movement Haldane had not cataloged before. Something that might have been acknowledgment, or might have been surprise that a human had expressed gratitude for the opportunity to help end his own species.

Haldane walked through the sealed door and up the elevator to the surface. The Nevada sky was clear and cold. Stars out — enough to see the belt of the Milky Way, and to know that somewhere along its arm, a Council was deliberating the future of the planet below his feet.

He went to the ranch house. He poured bourbon. He sat in the leather chair by the window and looked at the desert and began to plan for every possible answer.

CHAPTER 8

Station Bravo

November 2060.

• • •

Sato's report came through the cortical link at 06:14 Ares time.

Two of the three candidate stations are inactive, she said. ***No power signatures, no thermal output, no communication traffic. Survey platform Alpha has been dark for at least six years based on dust accumulation on the solar arrays. Station Charlie is similar — powered down, cold, no evidence of recent operation.***

And Station Bravo? Dren asked.

Station Bravo is active, Sato said. ***Low-power, minimal thermal signature, but the communication array is functional. I put O'Malley on the forensic analysis. He's found something.***

Go ahead.

Four events in sequence, she said. ***The debug log on Station Bravo shows a transmission directed toward Earth. What's odd here is that the main log shows nothing. Transmissions are always logged, and we can see matching pairs for most of them. Two minutes after that transmission, the station processed two software updates in rapid succession — one immediately after the other. Two seconds after the second update completed, the debug log shows another transmission — this one directed along the bearing toward the Fist, and again the main log shows nothing.***

She paused.

There's more. The first of the two updates is in the log, but the package itself is missing from the update cache. Every other update ever applied to that station is still in the cache. This one isn't. And there's something else he found: there are updates which do not result in transmission mismatches.

So, she continued. ***We have the following facts. First, sometimes there is a mismatch between the main log and debug log. Second, these mismatches follow a paired-update pattern — two updates in quick succession, the first of which has been deleted from the cache. Third, the mismatch transmissions are always to Earth or in directions which just so happen to correspond with the position of the Fist.***

This could all be coincidence, but O'Malley doesn't believe in those. And this doesn't smell like coincidence. He just doesn't quite understand what it means. Yet. But he's on the hunt.

Dren picked up one half of the stylus and turned it between his fingers.

Understood, Dren said. ***This is his only job now. Give him whatever he needs. I want answers.***

Understood, she said.

Who owns Station Bravo?

Officially, it's a decommissioned survey platform, Sato said. ***Registered to a belt mining consortium that dissolved eight years ago. The registration transferred to a holding company. I'm tracing the ownership chain. That raises another question: Who updates software on a decommissioned platform?***

When we know that, Dren said, ***we'll know a lot more.***

One other item, Sato said. ***The survey platforms launched on schedule. Inbound trajectory nominal. Solar encounter in approximately six weeks.***

Understood, Dren said.

The channel closed. Dren sat with the information. A transmission toward Earth, a paired update, a transmission toward the Fist. In sequence. A missing package. And a primary log that said none of it happened.

He picked up the other half of the stylus and held both pieces, one in each hand. Four events on a station that was supposed to be decommissioned. O'Malley didn't believe in coincidence, and neither did Dren.

• • •

2022. Nevada.

The Council's response arrived five days after Al transmitted Haldane's request.

Haldane was in Dallas when the alert came through the encrypted link to his laptop. He cancelled his afternoon — a Foundation donor reception — and chartered the flight to Nevada. Three hours from Love Field to the private strip. Garrett drove him to the facility. He entered the building and walked into the amber room still wearing the suit.

Al and Bob were in the center of the space. Both were thinner than when he'd brought them from Australia. The ridges in Al's skin had deepened further, and the stiffness in Al's movement had become something closer to fragility — each repositioning slower, more deliberate, as if the body were negotiating with itself about whether to move at all. Bob hadn't stood in three days.

The translator had processed the burst and was holding the rendered output. Haldane sat in the folding chair and nodded to Al.

Al activated the playback. Two statements, in the translator's flat English:

"What do you wish to say, Charles Haldane?"

And: "The Council is still discussing."

Haldane leaned back in the chair. Two sentences. Five days of transit time for two sentences. But the first sentence was everything — the Council was willing to hear him. They hadn't dismissed the request. They hadn't ignored it. They were asking him to speak.

He composed his response carefully. He'd been drafting it in his head since the day he made the request — revising, restructuring, stripping it down to the essential claims. He spoke it aloud, in English, and the translator rendered it for transmission. Al and Bob watched — their eyes in their slow independent rotation, tracking everything, including him.

"Your scouts' assessment is accurate," Haldane said. "Coexistence will fail. Not because your species is incapable of it, but because mine is. Humanity is fragmented, hostile to the unfamiliar, and intolerant of themselves, let alone of a species they have never encountered. Your scouts saw this. I see it every day."

He paused. The translator processed. The mechanical voice reproduced his words in the structural format the Council would receive — concepts mapped to relationships, the meaning preserved in architecture rather than vocabulary.

"I am offering my assistance. Whatever course of action the Council chooses, I can provide intelligence from inside Earth's systems — defensive capabilities, military infrastructure, detection networks, political structure. I know these systems. I have access to these systems. I can ensure that whatever plans you develop will encounter the minimum possible resistance."

Another pause. The translator rendered. The silence in the amber room was absolute except for the hum of the atmospheric system and the faint click of Al's stalks adjusting.

"In exchange, I am asking for one thing. I want to select approximately twenty-five hundred humans — people I have vetted, people who have demonstrated the capacity to live in cooperation with a non-human intelligence — and I want them preserved through whatever comes next. I will build the facility. I will select the people. I will prepare them. All I need is the Council's agreement that when it is over, my twenty-five hundred will survive and coexist, peacefully, with your species."

He stopped. The translator completed the rendering. Al transmitted.

The delay began.

• • •

The Council's questions arrived over the following weeks. Each one came as a burst transmission through the scouts' relay — processed by the translator, rendered into English, waiting on the system when Haldane connected from wherever he was. He answered from hotel rooms, from the Foundation office in Dallas, from the back seat of a car on the way to a board meeting. The folding chair in the amber room sat empty. The camera watched. The translator rendered.

The first question arrived nine days after his pitch.

"Describe Earth's orbital detection capabilities, Charles Haldane. What systems monitor approach trajectories from outside the ecliptic plane?"

Haldane answered. He described the Deep Space Network, the survey telescopes, the military tracking systems, the gaps in coverage. He described the institutional inertia that prevented the existing systems from being upgraded — the funding battles, the jurisdictional disputes, the difference between what the systems could detect in theory and what they actually monitored in practice.

"The systems are designed to track known objects," he said. "Cataloged asteroids, identified satellites, debris fields with established orbits. An approach from outside the ecliptic, on a trajectory that doesn't match any cataloged object, would not be detected until it entered the range of the optical surveys. By then, depending on velocity, the response window would be measured in months, not years."

The next question arrived four days later.

"Describe the nuclear capability of Earth's nation-states, Charles Haldane. Specifically, the capacity for rapid deployment against an extra-atmospheric target."

He answered that too. The warhead count, the delivery systems, the boost phase limitations. The fact that Earth's nuclear arsenal was designed for surface targets, not space intercepts — the guidance systems, the detonation altitudes, the yield profiles were all optimized for a threat that launched from the ground, not one that arrived from beyond the heliopause.

"Nuclear weapons are Earth's most powerful destructive technology," Haldane said. "They are also the least relevant to the scenario you're describing. The response time alone makes them ineffective against a high-velocity approach. By the time the object is detected, targeted, and a launch authorized through the command structure, the engagement window will have closed."

More questions. The political structure of Earth's governments — could they unify in response to an external threat? Haldane's assessment: no. The international system was designed for competition, not cooperation. A unified response would require consensus among governments that couldn't agree on trade policy, let alone planetary defense. "The species will argue about jurisdiction while the object approaches," he said. "That is not a prediction. That is a description of the existing system."

The likelihood of a private-sector defense capability? "At the current time, there is no viable non-governmental opposition," Haldane said. "The institutional space programs are fragmented, underfunded, and decades away from any capability that could threaten an object on this trajectory. I will monitor for changes and report."

The silence after that transmission lasted eleven days. The longest gap yet. Haldane checked the system daily, connected from wherever the Foundation business had taken him. Dallas. Geneva. Singapore. The amber room on his screen, the folding chair empty, Al standing in the same position — or a different position, impossible to tell — waiting for the Council's response.

When it came, it was a single word.

"Continue."

• • •

The decision came in June.

Haldane flew to Nevada for this one. He knew it was coming — the pace of the questions had accelerated in the final two weeks, the intervals between transmissions shortening, the Council's queries becoming more specific, more operational, the language shifting from assessment to planning. They weren't evaluating him anymore. They were using him.

He sat in the folding chair. Al stood. Bob was folded on the floor, stalks low, the damaged arm hanging open. The translator processed the incoming burst for nearly twenty minutes — longer than any previous communication. Haldane watched the indicator on the translator's housing cycle through patterns he'd learned to recognize: receiving, decoding, structural parsing, linguistic rendering. Twenty minutes of alien deliberation compressed into a single transmission, crossing the void between the fleet and the belt relay and the Nevada console and the box that sat on a low platform between two dying scouts.

The translator spoke.

"The Council of Elders has reached a decision on the matter of the third planet. The assessment provided by the scouts, supplemented by the intelligence provided by the human designate Charles Haldane, has been reviewed in full. The coexistence option has been deemed nonviable. The risks to the resettlement population are beyond acceptable parameters. The dominant indigenous species will be removed. The biosphere will be prepared for resettlement. Construction of a primary instrument will commence. Estimated deployment: approximately twenty-five of the local orbital periods."

The translator paused. Haldane waited.

"The offer of the human designate Charles Haldane has been accepted. A population of twenty-five hundred, selected and prepared by the designate, will be preserved through the transition period. The designate will continue to provide intelligence on indigenous defensive capabilities for the duration of the preparation phase. The designate is conditionally useful. This status is subject to ongoing evaluation."

The translator fell silent.

Conditionally useful. Haldane noted the phrase. He would hear it again, in different contexts, over the next twenty-five years. It would become the phrase that defined his relationship with the Council — the perpetual audition, the utility that had to be demonstrated and re-demonstrated, the status that could be revoked at any time for any reason.

Bob's stalks dropped.

Not the slow flattening that Haldane had learned to read as discomfort, or the measured lowering that signaled the end of an assessment. The stalks fell — limp, hanging against the sides of Bob's upper torso like dead weight. The three arms, which had been resting against the body in the folded position, drew inward further, pulling tight against the torso. Bob's body contracted, the tripod base narrowing, the entire form pulling into itself the way a living thing pulls into itself when the world delivers the answer it feared most.

Bob had spent thirty-eight years on this planet. Watching. Assessing. Sitting in silence while Al delivered the report, because Bob's assessment was Bob's own and it was not the report. Bob had watched humanity and concluded — against the evidence, against Al's analysis, against the observable data of a tribal, xenophobic, technologically volatile species — that coexistence could work. That the cooperative behaviors were real. That the alliances and treaties and collaborative projects meant something. That the species was worth preserving whole, not as a curated remnant in a bunker.

The Council had disagreed.

Haldane looked at Bob and felt nothing. The coexistence faction had lost. The eradication faction had won. The assessment was correct and the decision was correct and the twenty-five hundred would survive and the rest would not, and the being on the floor whose stalks had gone limp was grieving for a species that would have killed it on sight if it had ever been discovered.

Al received the decision without movement. Stalks level. Eyes in their slow rotation. After a long pause, Al spoke — not through the translator, but directly, from one of his three mouths. A sound Haldane couldn't parse — low, resonant, carrying frequencies that vibrated in the floor. Then the translator rendered it:

"It is decided, Charles Haldane."

"As you wanted," Haldane said.

"As it must be, Charles Haldane," Al said.

Haldane sat in the folding chair. The amber light was the same. The atmospheric system hummed at the same frequency. The translator sat on its platform. Everything in the room was exactly as it had been five minutes ago, except that a civilization had just sentenced his species to death and he was the man who had helped them reach the verdict.

He looked at his hands. Steady. They had been steady in the Australian desert when he first saw the Tolek, and they were steady now. Twenty-five years. That was the timeline. Twenty-five years to build the Ark, to position his people, to construct the intelligence network that would feed the Council what it needed and blind Earth to what was coming.

He named the project that night, alone in the amber room after Al and Bob had gone silent. He wrote it on the first page of a notebook — paper, not digital, nothing that could be accessed remotely.

Operation Clean Slate.

And below it, the name for the object the Council would build. The instrument that would cross the void and end the world that was, so that the world that should be could begin.

The Eraser.

• • •

Bob died twelve days later.

Haldane was in Nevada when it happened — he had been staying at the ranch house since the decision, managing Foundation business remotely while he drafted the first outlines of what the Ark would become. He came downstairs for the morning check and found Bob on the floor in the resting position, stalks flat against the torso, the compound eyes dark.

Al was standing beside Bob. Not beside — near. Positioned so that more of Al's eyes faced Bob than faced the room. The stalks were moving in slow arcs, the sensory organs at the tips passing over Bob's body in a pattern that looked like scanning, or measurement, or the Tolek equivalent of sitting with the dead.

"When?" Haldane asked.

"During the night, Charles Haldane. I did not detect the moment of cessation. The biological indicators declined gradually and then stopped."

Haldane looked at Bob. The reddish-brown skin had lost its remaining texture — the ridges flattened, the creases smoothed, the leather quality gone. The damaged arm lay at the same angle it had held for months, but the tension that had kept it pressed against the torso was absent. The body looked deflated. Smaller than it had been.

"Was it the decision?" Haldane asked.

Al's stalks shifted. The question sat between them for a long time.

"Bob's biological condition was terminal, Charles Haldane. The timing is coincidental."

Haldane didn't believe that, and he suspected Al didn't either. But the translator rendered Al's words without inflection, and the boundary between what the Tolek would say and what they knew had not moved.

Al lasted nine days longer.

On the sixth day, Al stopped speaking through the translator. The stalks still moved — slow arcs through the filtered air, sensing, tracking, reaching for something Haldane couldn't see. The compound eyes still tracked. But the words had stopped, and Haldane sat in the folding chair across from a being that had been talking to him for four months and was now silent in a way that felt different from Bob's silence. Bob's silence had been a choice. Al's was a system shutting down.

On the ninth day, the stalks stopped.

Haldane found Al in the standing position — upright on the tripod, the posture unchanged from how Al had stood on every visit since the desert. The eyes were dark. The stalks were motionless, the sensory organs at the tips pointed at nothing.

Al had died standing. Haldane didn't know if that was intentional or simply how a body with three legs and no front comes to rest when the system that animated it ceases.

He buried them that night. Both of them, in the desert behind the facility, in the hardpan that took three hours to excavate with an electric shovel. He did it himself. No workers, no Garrett, no witnesses. Two graves, six feet apart, unmarked. The Nevada sky was clear and the stars were out and the desert was silent.

He stood over the graves and looked at them and felt the specific emptiness of a man who has lost the only two beings on the planet who knew what he was doing and why. Al and Bob were gone. The translator sat in the amber room. The communication relay was failing. The Council's decision was made. And Charles Haldane was the only human alive who knew that his species had twenty-five years left.

He went back inside. He had twenty-five years. He got to work.

• • •

November 2060.

Brandt came into Dren's office and closed the door.

"I've been thinking about the belt relay," Brandt said. "If someone on Earth has a covert channel to whatever's sitting at 130

AU, that's a long-term placement. Years. Decades, maybe. Someone with access and patience and institutional cover."

"Agreed," Dren said.

"If they have that on Earth, there's no reason to assume they don't have it here. Mars is a smaller pool — fewer people, tighter access, easier to place someone who matters. And you're the obvious target."

Dren looked at him. "You're recommending protection."

"I'm recommending you stop being the easiest high-value target on this planet. Personal security. Twenty-five seven," Brandt said firmly.

"You really think that's necessary?" Dren asked.

"Of course."

"Fine. Assign Raines," Dren said.

Brandt nodded and left.

The real work was happening in the belt, on a relay station that shouldn't have been transmitting, and a debug log that told an interesting tale.

• • •

Washington, D.C.

The hearing room was full for the first time since July.

Beckett had arranged that —- not obviously, not through any single action that could be traced, but through the slow accumulation of scheduling decisions and witness selections and media briefings that made this particular session feel like the one that mattered. The public gallery was packed. Three networks were carrying it live. The committee members had their serious faces on.

"Mr. Director, who manufactured the communication relays currently operating in the western hub?" Beckett asked.

"Dren Industries, Senator."

"Dren Industries," Beckett said with emphasis. "And the protocols those relays run on —- who designed them?"

"Dren Industries."

"Dren Industries again. And the replacement satellites —- the ones now handling civilian and military traffic across the western hub. Who designed those?"

"Dren Industries. Built on Mars, launched from Mars, controlled from Mars."

"Dren Industries. So if your office in Colorado Springs needed to send a message to Denver —- a routine administrative communication —- what infrastructure does that message pass through?"

"Dren's, Senator. All of it."

"Mr. Dren's. And if Mr. Dren decided tomorrow to shut that infrastructure off, could he?"

The director paused. "There is no technical barrier to that, no."

"So Mr. Dren can just decide to shut you down and there's nothing you can do about it. Now Mr. Director, at any point," Beckett continued, "did the regional authority have the option to source this infrastructure from an Earth-based manufacturer?"

"No, Senator. There are no Earth-based manufacturers currently producing communication satellites. The industrial capacity doesn't exist. It was destroyed in the flyby or has been redirected to reconstruction."

"So the dependency is structural, not optional."

"That is correct."

"Isn't that convenient," Beckett dropped.

He let that sit. The gallery absorbed it. Three networks carried it to their audiences. The question wasn't about Dren's intentions —- Beckett was too careful for that. The question was about the structure. A system in which one man controlled the communication infrastructure of the most powerful nation on Earth, and that nation had no alternative.

"And finally, Mr. Director, whose name is on the authorization for all this 'infrastructure'?"

"President Whitfield, Senator."

"President Whitfield. President Whitfield and Alexis Dren," Beckett concluded.

After the hearing, Whitfield's chief of staff brought her the transcript.

"Impeachment," she said, reading.

"Not yet. But the language is changing. 'Accountability hearings' became 'oversight proceedings' last week. Two members used the word 'dereliction' in their opening statements today. The trajectory is clear."

"What's his endgame?"

"Beckett's? He doesn't need impeachment. He needs the conversation. As long as the hearings continue, reunification is impossible. Nobody votes to restore federal authority while the president is being investigated for delegating it."

Whitfield set the transcript down. The sixteen-item briefing stack sat where it always sat. The items had rotated again. Mars dependency was now item one.

"We need our own satellites," she said.

"We don't have the manufacturing capacity."

"Then we need to build the manufacturing capacity," she said decisively.

"That's a three-year project. Minimum. You could try to co-develop with the Chinese…"

"God no. Swap one nightmare for another?" she said. "Start the manufacturing. Today."

Her chief of staff made a note. It was the right decision. It was also three years too late, and both of them knew it. Dren's constellation would be fully operational within twelve months. By the time Earth could manufacture its own satellites, the dependency would be infrastructure, not policy. You couldn't replace a communication backbone by building an alternative. You had to build an alternative that was better. And nothing Earth could build in three years would be better than what Mars had been building for twenty.

Whitfield worked through the stack until midnight. She did not sleep in the residence. She slept in the medical unit, the way she had for months, and in the morning the stack would have sixteen new items that were the same items with different names.

CHAPTER 9

And a Cell

Ares City.

• • •

O'Malley came into Sato's office without knocking. He was carrying a tablet and he looked like he hadn't slept, which was accurate — he hadn't, not in thirty-one hours, which Sato knew because she'd been monitoring his access logs and the man hadn't left the forensics lab since Tuesday.

"I figured it out," he said.

Sato set down what she'd been working on. O'Malley was not a man who said things like that unless he meant them. He was methodical, cautious, an analyst who qualified every conclusion with three caveats. If he was standing in her doorway saying he'd figured it out, he'd figured it out.

"Sit down," she said.

He sat. He put the tablet on the desk between them and pulled up a display — a timeline, annotated, with events marked in red.

"Start with the signatures," he said. "Remember the anomalous signing key I flagged — the one I asked you to trace?"

"I remember."

"Every update that correlates with a log mismatch is signed with that key. Every update that doesn't correlate is signed with the standard deployment key. Two keys, both valid, both passing signature validation. But they produce completely different behavior on the station."

"Why two keys?"

"Because the station's code does different things depending on which key signed the package. The standard key triggers the normal update path — validate, apply, log, done. The anomalous key triggers something else entirely."

He swiped to the next screen. A code execution trace, compressed into a flowchart.

"Here's what happens when an update signed with the anomalous key arrives. First, it passes the legitimate signature validation — the standard check that every update goes through. The signature is valid. No flags. But then there's a second validation routine. It looks redundant — like someone added an extra safety check. Good defensive coding practice. The kind of thing a reviewer would glance at and approve."

"But it's not redundant," Sato said.

"It's the opposite of redundant. It's the entry point. And here's what's clever — the routine is parsing a field from within the signature structure itself. The thing that just passed validation. The thing that's now trusted data."

He paused to let that land. Sato's hands were flat on the desk. She didn't move them.

"The field triggers a buffer overflow. Very specific — it only overflows if the field contains a particular byte pattern. A normal signature would never produce that pattern. The anomalous key's signatures always do. And the reason nobody caught it is that the overflow is hiding inside the one thing no one would think to fuzz. The signature just validated — it's trusted. No reviewer would look at a routine that parses a trusted signature and think 'attack surface.' Static analysis could theoretically flag the overflow, but in context — right after a successful validation, in what looks like a defensive check on trusted data — I can see how every reviewer who looked at it nodded and moved on."

Sato absorbed that. A buffer overflow triggered by a trusted signature, hidden in what looked like careful defensive code. The person who built this had understood not just the system but the psychology of the people who reviewed it.

"What happens after the overflow?"

O'Malley leaned forward. "This is the part that took me two days. The overflow corrupts the return address on the stack. When the function tries to return, it doesn't go back to where it came from. It goes somewhere else. And that somewhere else is the beginning of a chain."

"A chain of what?"

"Existing code. Nothing injected, nothing foreign. The corrupted return address points to a short sequence of legitimate instructions that happen to end with a return instruction. That return points to another short sequence. And another. Each one does a small piece of work — moves a register, sets up a memory address, copies a byte. Individually they're meaningless fragments of normal functions. Strung together, they build a program."

"From pieces of the station's own code," Sato said.

"Exactly. It's called return-oriented programming. You don't inject your own code. You use the code that's already there, like rearranging words from a book to write a different sentence. The forensic signature is almost invisible because every instruction being executed is legitimate compiled code. It's just being executed in an order the original programmer never intended."

Sato was quiet for a moment. She was running the implications forward and O'Malley could see it on her face — the expression she got when the scale of something shifted beneath her. He held up a hand.

"I'll come back to that."

He stood up, crossed to the water dispenser, and filled a cup. He drank it standing. Thirty-one hours without sleep and the adrenaline was the only thing keeping the edges sharp. He sat back down.

"The chain does three things. First, it extracts data from the update package itself. The packages signed with the anomalous key contain extra bytes — steganography. Data hidden inside data. The update looks like a normal firmware patch, and most of it is. But embedded in the padding and alignment bytes — the parts that every binary has, the parts nobody looks at because they're supposed to be meaningless — there's a payload. Destination coordinates, timing data, transmission parameters."

"Hidden in the update itself."

"Hidden in the part of the update that's supposed to be empty. The chain extracts those bytes and assembles them into a transmission instruction."

"And the second thing?"

"It transmits. But not through the normal communication stack. The chain calls directly into the RF hardware driver — below the abstraction layer where the operational logging sits. The station's antenna fires. The primary log never sees it because the primary log only monitors the communication stack. The transmission goes out underneath it."

"But the debug log catches it."

"Because the debug log sits in the hardware driver itself. It's a stub — leftover diagnostic code from the original station deployment. It logs every RF event regardless of where the instruction came from. The exploit author mapped every logging system in the operational code and routed around all of them. They missed the debug stub because it's not part of the logging framework. It's a piece of forgotten diagnostic code that nobody cleaned up."

Sato sat with that. Someone had mapped every logging pathway in the operational stack and routed around every one. They'd missed a diagnostic stub buried in the hardware driver because it wasn't part of the system they'd mapped. The one thing that caught them was the one thing they couldn't have known about.

"And the third thing the chain does?"

"Cleanup. It re-enables ASLR and deletes the first update package from the cache."

"Wait. ASLR?"

"Address space layout randomization. It's a security feature — it randomizes where code sits in memory so that an attacker can't predict where their target instructions are. A return-oriented chain needs to know exactly where the code fragments are in memory. If the addresses are randomized, the chain can't find its stepping stones."

"So the chain shouldn't work."

"It shouldn't. That's what stopped me for six hours." He pulled up the timeline again and tapped the paired-update column. "ASLR is enabled on Station Bravo. The chain should fail. Then I looked at these."

"Every time we see the log mismatch, there are two updates in rapid succession. The first is signed with the standard key — the legitimate one. It's very small. And its package is missing from the update cache. Every other update ever applied to that station is still in the cache for rollback purposes. This one isn't."

"Because the exploit deletes it."

"Because the exploit deletes it as part of cleanup. But before it's deleted, it runs. And the only thing it does — the only thing a package that small could do — is disable ASLR and trigger a firmware loader restart. The station's update process naturally restarts the runtime environment after applying a patch — standard procedure, nothing unusual. But when the loader comes back up with ASLR disabled, the memory layout is at default positions. Predictable. Two seconds later the second update arrives, the anomalous one, and now the return-oriented chain has the fixed addresses it needs. The chain runs, does its work, re-enables ASLR, deletes the first package, and exits. The station looks exactly the same as it did before. ASLR is back on. The cache is clean except for the missing package. And the only record that anything happened is sitting in a debug stub that nobody knew was there."

Sato was quiet for a long time. The scope of what O'Malley had just described was settling in. Not a vulnerability exploited. A system designed to contain its own betrayal, from the ground up, by someone who understood every layer.

O'Malley set the tablet down on the desk. He didn't swipe to the next screen. When he spoke again, his voice was different — quieter, slower. He wasn't presenting findings anymore. He was telling her what the findings meant.

"This was built into the codebase," he said.

Sato didn't answer. She already knew.

"The second validation routine — the one with the buffer overflow — is native code. It was committed to the source repository. The return-oriented chain uses gadgets that are native compiled functions. The RF hardware call that bypasses the log is a legitimate low-level function. None of this was injected from outside." He paused. "Someone with commit access to the station's firmware wrote the vulnerability into the code. They designed the error handler to overflow on exactly the right input. They made sure the right code fragments existed in the right places for the chain to work. And they created a second valid signing key — through the legitimate certificate infrastructure — to trigger the whole thing."

"Why didn't anyone catch it?"

O'Malley ran his hand across his jaw. He needed a shave and about twelve hours of sleep, and he was going to get neither.

"Because the entry point is after the signature validation passes. To test the error handler, you'd need to send it a package with a valid signature that also contains the specific byte pattern that triggers the overflow. But if you're fuzzing — throwing random data at the system to find vulnerabilities — the signature check fails first. You never reach the error handler. The only way to trigger this exploit is with a package signed by the anomalous key. A thorough static analysis could theoretically flag the overflow — it's there in the code. But it's in a defensive error handler that runs after a successful signature validation, parsing a field from trusted data. In context, it looks like exactly what it's supposed to look like: careful input checking on a verified signature. I can see how every audit passed it. The exploit doesn't exist until the exact right input arrives, and no test harness would ever generate that input because you'd need the specific anomalous key to produce a signature with the right byte pattern."

He sat back in his chair.

"This isn't a hack, Sato. This is architecture. Someone designed a communication channel into this station's firmware from the ground up. The exploit, the steganography, the paired-update ASLR bypass, the cleanup routine — it was all planned. Built. Maintained. This has been operational for years."

He rubbed his eyes with the heels of his hands.

"This is the most elegant piece of offensive engineering I've ever seen. Every component fits. Every contingency is covered. The person who designed this understood the system better than the people who built it. Or they were the people who built it."

"Where does the anomalous key come from?" Sato asked.

"It's embedded in the firmware's signing trust store. It's been there since deployment. The station has always trusted this key. It was configured to accept it from the day it went online."

"How long?" she asked.

"Years," O'Malley said.

He paused.

"Whoever did this deserves a medal," he said. "And a cell."

Sato was quiet for a moment. An insider with commit access to the firmware, embedded from deployment.

"The signing key," she said. "The one I've been tracing."

She pulled up her own display — a corporate structure map, shell companies branching and converging. Two separate paths through different holding companies, different jurisdictions, different registration dates. Both paths ended at the same node.

"Haldane," she said.

O'Malley looked at the name on the screen. Then at his timeline. Then back at the name.

"The Foundation guy?"

"The Foundation guy. Station Bravo's ownership chain goes through a dissolved mining consortium to a holding company registered in the Caymans. The holding company's beneficial owner is a trust administered by a law firm in Dallas. The law firm's registered address matches a Haldane Foundation subsidiary in Dallas. Same building, same floor. The signing key's certificate was issued to a subsidiary of a company called Meridian Technical Services. Meridian's board shares two members with a Haldane Foundation advisory committee. Different paths, different structures, same destination."

"Does Dren know?"

"He's about to."

• • •

Dren received the report through the cortical link. Sato delivered it the way she delivered everything — precisely, without editorializing, the evidence laid out in sequence.

He listened without interrupting. When she finished, he was quiet for a long time.

Haldane, he said.

Both paths converge, Sato confirmed. ***Station ownership and the signing key. Different corporate structures, same endpoint. The connection is circumstantial but the convergence is specific. Two independent traces arriving at the same person through different routes.***

Dren knew Charles Haldane. They'd met on several occasions — foundation events, a reconstruction conference in Geneva, a private dinner in Dallas where Haldane had been charming and thorough and preemptively generous with his time. They'd done business together — the Haldane Foundation had funded a Mars-

Earth communication research initiative through one of Dren's subsidiaries. A legitimate collaboration. Haldane had been complimentary about the work. Interested. Knowledgeable in ways that went beyond philanthropic curiosity.

Dren had filed that impression at the time. He filed most impressions. Now the filing system was returning a different result.

Hold the report, he said. ***No distribution. No summary. No briefings. This stays between you, O'Malley, and me until I say otherwise.***

Understood, Sato said.

The channel closed.

Dren sat at his desk and began to work.

He started with the public record. The Haldane Foundation's activities, its subsidiaries, its partnerships. The fellowship program. The Fresh Start Foundation. Media archives, financial filings, charity commission reports — each one arriving through the cortical link not as text to be read but as memory. Instant, complete, as vivid as if he'd spent a week with each document. He didn't process them. He simply knew them.

An interview caught his attention. Old footage — a wallscreen broadcast from before the flyby. A woman named Ashford interviewing Haldane about fellowship placements. The chyron identified her as an investigative journalist. She was asking about where the money went, which programs, which sectors. Haldane was preemptively thorough — numbers, outcomes, the full portfolio. The interview went nowhere.

But the journalist's name recurred. Chloe Ashford. He ran a search. She'd been shopping a story about the Haldane Foundation's fellowship network and its connections to post-crisis regional governance appointments. Nobody was buying it. She'd visited Haldane in Dallas. She'd visited the Fresh Start Foundation in Los Angeles.

Fresh Start. He looked at their public materials. The logo had changed — from a geometric mark to a clean sans-serif. The change had happened in June, between the 10th and the 22nd. A twelve-day window. Dren looked at the old logo. He looked at it for a long time. Then he set down both halves of the stylus, very carefully, and looked at it again.

He expanded the search. Ashford had been doing exactly what Dren's corporate analysts had been doing — tracing connections, mapping relationships, following the institutional connections. She'd been doing it from the outside, without access to signing keys or debug logs, working from public records and interviews and whatever a freelance journalist could assemble on her own. And she'd arrived at the same place.

She'd also, almost certainly, attracted the same attention.

Brandt, he said, opening the channel.

Here.

Okafor. Is he still on Earth? Dren asked.

He's in the D.C. hub. Part of the reconstruction liaison detail, Brandt replied.

Pull him. I need him in Los Angeles. There's a journalist named Chloe Ashford. She's been investigating the Haldane network — the same network we just traced through Station Bravo. She's visited Haldane and Fresh Start in person. If she's found what she seems to have found, the people we're looking at know about her. She may be in over her head.

What are Okafor's instructions? Brandt asked.

Keep an eye on her. See if anyone else is keeping an eye on her. Don't make contact unless necessary. I'll send him a full briefing.

Understood.

The channel closed.

Dren sat at his desk. A signing key that traced through a shell company maze to a philanthropist in Dallas. A relay station that had been transmitting to the Fist for years. A journalist who'd been pulling the same thread from the other end.

He went back to work.

• • •

Dallas.

The message from Okoro arrived at 02:17 Central.

Haldane was in his home office. He read it twice.

"Dren has flagged the position error. He's dismissed it for now, but he's looking into some mining station's communications. You need to know they're on the scent. I don't know how long I have."

He deleted it.

Dren was pulling on threads. The trail was long but it was a trail and one of those threads could lead to Okoro, and from there to him.

He picked up the phone and called Novak.

• • •

Los Angeles.

The knock came at 7:22 in the morning.

Ashford was at the kitchen table with the burner laptop and a cup of coffee. The spreadsheet on the screen was the fellowship placement matrix — eleven names mapped to reconstruction appointments across nine zones, each one connected to a Haldane Foundation grant through a chain of intermediary organizations that changed names every eighteen months. Sky was on the windowsill, watching pigeons with the focused patience of an animal that would never catch one.

The knock was soft — two taps, nothing more. She was on her feet before the second tap faded. By the time she reached the door and opened it, the hallway was empty.

The envelope was on the mat.

She didn't touch it. She stepped over it, looked both directions down the hallway — the elevator bank to the left, the stairwell door to the right. The stairwell door was still closing. The hydraulic arm pulling it shut at the speed a door closes when someone has just passed through it.

She went after them.

The stairwell was four flights down. She took them two at a time, bare feet slapping on the concrete, one hand on the railing. The footsteps ahead of her were faint — soft-soled shoes, moving fast but not running. By the second landing she couldn't hear them anymore.

The ground floor stairwell had two exits. One to the lobby, the street, the sidewalk, the morning foot traffic. Metal door to the back — the service corridor, the parking structure, the alley behind the building.

She chose the front. Pushed through the glass door onto the sidewalk. Morning light, a man walking a dog, a woman with a stroller, a delivery van idling at the curb. No hoodie. No slight figure moving away. No one who looked like they'd just come through a door at speed.

She stood on the sidewalk in her pajamas and bare feet and looked both directions and knew she'd chosen wrong. The back exit led to the alley and the alley led to the cross street and the cross street led to everywhere. By the time she could get there, the figure would be gone.

She went back upstairs. The envelope was still on the mat. She picked it up, went inside, closed the door, locked it, put the chain on. Then she went to the doorbell camera.

She pulled the footage and scrubbed back to the timestamp.

The figure appeared at 7:21. Hoodie up, face angled away from the camera — deliberate, the chin tucked and the hood pulled forward in the practiced way of someone who knew the camera was there. They moved quickly. Envelope placed on the mat. Two knocks. Then gone toward the stairwell. Four seconds, start to finish.

Ashford replayed it. Then again. The build was slight — narrow shoulders, small frame. The hoodie was oversized, hanging past the wrists. The hands were gloved. Black fabric gloves, gloves you'd buy at a pharmacy. Nothing identifiable above the collarbone. Nothing identifiable below it either, except the size. Too small to be a man, she thought. She couldn't be certain — she'd covered enough stories to know that certainty about body type from security footage was a mistake that got journalists sued. But the proportions were consistent with a woman.

She saved the footage to the local token and went to the envelope. She picked it up with the tips of her fingers, carried it to the kitchen table, and opened it with a butter knife.

Construction contracts. The first page was a materials requisition — concrete, Type V Portland cement, the sulfate-resistant kind used for underground construction. Quantity: one hundred and eighty thousand cubic yards. She looked at the number and then looked at it again. That was enough concrete for a military base.

She spread the documents across the table, pushing the laptop aside. Sky jumped from the windowsill to the table and walked across the shipping manifests. She let him stay this time.

"Construction contracts," she said. Sky sat on the materials requisition and began cleaning his paw. "Concrete — a hundred and eighty thousand cubic yards. Reinforced steel. Ventilation equipment. Industrial generators. Water purification. Air recycling." She pulled a manifest from under Sky's hindquarters. He gave her a look. "Sky, that's more concrete than a hospital. More than a shopping mall. That's a small city's worth of concrete."

She turned the purchase orders toward the light. Three generator units, each rated for sustained output that would power a small hospital. Ventilation equipment rated for positive-pressure environments — specs you'd see on a military installation or a biosafety lab. Air recycling units with the technical specifications redacted but the purchase orders intact, routed through a company she didn't recognize.

"Basin Range Holdings," she said. Sky's ear rotated toward her. "Mean anything to you? No? Me neither."

She opened the laptop and pulled up the shell company map — the document she'd been building for four months, the web of interlocking entities that connected the Haldane Foundation to the fellowship placements to the regional governance appointments. She typed in Basin Range Holdings.

"Dissolved three years ago. Reregistered six months later as Basin Range Land Management LLC. Different address. Same registered agent." She looked at Sky. "And the registered agent is a law firm in Reno that is already on our board. Third tier, left side. Connected to a holding company that shares a board member with a Haldane Foundation advisory committee."

Sky blinked.

"Same architecture," she said. "Different names. Same architect. And he's building something in the Nevada desert that requires industrial quantities of concrete and doesn't appear on any public record."

She pulled the delivery manifests into a stack and started sorting by date. The earliest orders were decades old — purchase requisitions from the mid-2020s, routed through companies that had dissolved and reformed twice since then. The most recent were from last year.

She stopped sorting. She looked at the dates again.

"Sky. The oldest manifests go back to the twenties. He's been building this for almost forty years." She picked up the cat and held him at eye level. Sky tolerated this with the dignity of a cat who had been through worse. "Haldane knew, Sky. He knew before anyone else. And he started building decades before the Fist arrived."

She set him down. He returned to the shipping manifests and resumed cleaning his paw on top of a purchase order for water purification systems.

She sat back and looked at the documents spread across the table. The fellowship placements, the institutional connections, the logo change — those were the surface layer. The visible machinery. But underneath it — literally, physically, under the Nevada desert — was something else. Something large enough to require decades of industrial construction. Something Haldane had started building before the disaster that created the reconstruction apparatus he was now exploiting.

He'd built the bunker at the same time he built the network. The network was the surface. The bunker was the purpose.

She needed to see it.

She packed a bag. Camera — the good one, the telephoto lens that Greg had given her for her birthday two years ago. Binoculars. The burner phone. A change of clothes in case she needed to stay overnight. Two bottles of water. A bag of almonds. Sunscreen, because the Nevada desert didn't care about your investigation.

She set up Sky's automatic feeder and water dispenser, checked the litter robot, and scratched behind his ears.

"Back tomorrow," she said. Sky closed his eyes.

• • •

She got in the car. "Take me to these coordinates," she said, and read the numbers off the manifest.

"Route calculated," the car said. "Approximately six hours. Interstate 15 east to Las Vegas, then north. Shall I proceed?"

"Go ahead."

The car pulled out and headed for the freeway. East on the 10 out of LA to the 15 north, through the sprawl that thinned gradually from strip malls to warehouses to distribution centers to the open desert beyond Victorville. The traffic thinned with the buildings. By Baker the Mojave stretched to the horizon in every direction, brown and flat and indifferent.

"Stop in Primm and charge," she said.

"Primm is thirty-two minutes ahead. Current charge is sufficient for the full route with eleven percent reserve."

"Charge anyway. I don't want to be low in the middle of the desert."

"Primm charging stop added."

She didn't use the burner phone. Her regular phone was powered off and sitting in a Faraday pouch in the glove compartment. She'd learned that from a source two years ago — a former intelligence analyst who'd told her that the first rule of going somewhere you didn't want people to know about was making sure your phone didn't go there with you.

The car charged itself in Primm while she used the restroom at the travel center and bought a bottle of water. Fifteen minutes, then back on the road.

North of Vegas the car left the interstate for a four-lane highway winding through the hills. The landscape was volcanic — dark rock, sparse scrub, dry washes that hadn't carried water in months. The Great Basin, the part of America that most Americans forgot existed until they drove through it on the way to somewhere else.

The car turned east off the highway onto a county road that had no name, only a number. The road was paved but barely — cracks running through the asphalt, the edges crumbling into the sand. No lines. No signs. No indication that anyone used this road for anything except for getting from one empty place to another empty place.

"Slow down," she said.

"Speed reduced. Twelve miles to destination."

She watched through the windows as the car crept along. She wanted to see what was around her before she arrived. The terrain was featureless. Low hills in the distance, flat desert floor, sage and creosote in scattered clumps. No structures. No fences. No power lines. A place where you could drive for an hour and the only evidence of human civilization was the road beneath your tires.

At nine miles, she saw the first sign of something. Not a structure — a change in the terrain. The desert floor ahead showed tire tracks — faint, partially filled with windblown sand, but recent enough to be readable. Multiple vehicles, heavy ones, the ruts deeper than a pickup truck would leave. They paralleled the county road for half a mile and then turned south on a track she couldn't see until she was almost past it.

"Keep going," she said as they passed the turnoff. A quarter mile further: "Pull off here. Behind that rise."

The car eased off the road and stopped behind the low ridge of earth that would shield it from anyone looking north from the facility. She sat for a moment, listening. Wind. Nothing else. Silence that had weight.

She got out, took the camera and binoculars, and walked back to the rise.

The turnoff was unmarked — just a gravel track heading south from the county road, straight as a ruler, running for about half a mile before terminating at a gate. Chain-link fence, eight feet high, topped with razor wire that caught the late afternoon sun. The fence ran east and west from the gate, disappearing behind the terrain on both sides. A guard booth sat beside the gate — small, windowed, a single occupant visible through the glass.

Behind the fence: a warehouse. Low, metal-sided, the corrugated steel panels oxidized to a dull reddish-brown that nearly matched the desert floor. Perhaps fifty meters long, twenty wide. A single vehicle beside it — a white pickup truck, dusty. Beyond that was a ranch house, though why anyone would want a house out here was beyond her.

That was it.

She raised the binoculars. The warehouse was unremarkable — a structure you'd find at any ranch or industrial site in the rural West. Roll-up door on the south end, a personnel door on the east side, no windows. An antenna mast on the roof — communications or weather monitoring, she couldn't tell which from this distance. A small satellite dish beside the antenna, aimed south.

She lowered the binoculars and looked at the ground around the warehouse. No construction equipment. No cranes. No concrete trucks. No heavy machinery. No staging area, no material storage, no evidence of the industrial-scale project the invoices described.

She pulled up the manifests on the burner phone. A hundred and eighty thousand cubic yards of concrete. Hundreds of thousands of tonnes of structural steel. Ventilation equipment. Generators. Water purification. Air recycling. Decades of deliveries to these coordinates.

The warehouse could hold a fraction of it. A single floor of corrugated steel, fifty meters by twenty, maybe four meters high at the ridgeline. The concrete alone would build a facility fifty times the footprint of that warehouse.

She looked at the warehouse again through the binoculars. The personnel door on the east side had a card reader beside it — electronic access, not a padlock. Access control you'd put on a building that mattered. And beside the personnel door, set into the ground, a concrete pad about three meters square with a steel grate covering it. A ventilation shaft. Drawing air from below.

The manifests weren't for the warehouse. The warehouse was the lid.

Everything was underground.

She swapped the binoculars for the camera and began photographing. The telephoto lens brought the details in close — the gate, the razor wire, the guard booth, the guard inside reading something on a tablet. The warehouse, the antenna mast, the satellite dish. The ventilation grate beside the personnel door. The tire tracks on the gravel road, the fence line disappearing east and west. The terrain, flat and empty, the county road behind her, the low rise she was sheltering behind.

She spent ten minutes with the telephoto, working through every angle. Then she lowered the camera and sat on the desert floor behind the rise and thought about what she was looking at.

Haldane had built an underground facility in the Nevada desert. He'd started decades before the flyby, before the Fist. He'd used shell companies and intermediary logistics firms to route the materials. The surface structure was a warehouse — minimal, unremarkable, a building that wouldn't appear on anyone's radar.

Underneath it was something large enough to consume decades of industrial construction and enough concrete for a military installation.

She thought about approaching the gate. Walking down the gravel track, showing credentials, asking questions. Playing the journalist, the lost traveler, the foundation researcher looking for a geological survey site. She thought about it for about ten seconds.

She was out here, alone. No one but Sky knew she was here. If she just disappeared no one would have the faintest idea where to look.

The guard was armed — she'd seen the holster through the binoculars. The fence was serious — eight feet of chain-link with razor wire wasn't ranch fencing. The location was chosen for its isolation, and isolation meant no witnesses.

She got up and walked back to the car.

"Take me home," she said.

"Route calculated. Approximately six hours."

"Go ahead."

• • •

The county road to the highway. The highway to the interstate. The interstate south through the desert toward Las Vegas, then south on the 15. The sun setting beside her, the sky going through the colors — amber, rust, the deep red that the desert did better than anywhere else on earth.

She cracked the window. The dry air pulled the heat from the car. She sat in silence and thought about what she had.

The construction manifests. The shell company trace. The photographs of a warehouse in the desert that didn't match what the invoices described. The ventilation grate that confirmed what the invoices implied. And the footage from her doorbell camera of someone — small, slight, deliberate — delivering documents that someone inside Haldane's network wanted her to have.

Someone was helping her. Someone with access to construction contracts and shipping manifests and the knowledge of which shell company to trace. Someone who knew the network from the inside and was feeding pieces of it to a journalist on the outside. The figure in the hoodie wasn't random. The documents weren't leaked — they were selected. Curated. Delivered in an order that led from institutional mapping to physical infrastructure, from paper trails to GPS coordinates, from the abstract to the concrete.

Someone wanted her to find the bunker. The question was why.

The car merged onto the 15 and settled into the left lane. It passed through Las Vegas without stopping. The lights of the strip reflected off the windshield — garish, alien, the last burst of civilization before the long dark stretch of desert between Vegas and LA.

She'd be home by midnight, and she was really looking forward to hot shower. Sky would be asleep on the windowsill. The fellowship matrix would be on the laptop screen where she'd left it. And the photographs on the camera in the bag beside her would be the first physical evidence that the network she'd been mapping from the outside had a body. A structure. A location. Something that existed in the physical world and could be pointed at and named and investigated by people with more authority than a freelance journalist with a telephoto lens and a source she'd never met.

The desert went dark around her. The headlights carved a tunnel through the nothing, and the car carried her through it toward home.

• • •

Washington, D.C.

Greg Harmon set the phone on the kitchen counter and stood there for a while.

The apartment was quiet. His apartment — the one in Dupont Circle that he'd kept because it was close to the office and because Chloe had once said she liked the neighborhood, back when she'd visited, back when visiting was something they did. The eastern hub consolidation meant his clients were local now. No more flights to Pittsburgh or Cleveland. No more hotel rooms that smelled like industrial carpet. He was home every night by seven, and every night by seven the apartment reminded him that home was a word that meant more when someone else was in it.

She'd said not right now. She always said not right now. He'd learned to hear the difference between "not right now" that meant Tuesday and "not right now" that meant she was drowning in something she couldn't tell him about, and this had been the second kind. The work call she'd taken in the middle of their conversation. The distraction in her voice when she came back. The careful way she'd said "it's not about you, Greg," which was what she said when it was absolutely about the fact that her life had a compartment he wasn't allowed into.

He opened his laptop and bought a ticket. Friday, DC to LAX. He'd be at her door by Friday night.

Before heading to the airport, he went to Boulangerie Christophe on Connecticut Avenue. The line was out the door — it always was — and he stood in it for twenty minutes because Chloe had once eaten three of their almond croissants in a single sitting and talked about it for a week. He bought six. The woman behind the counter put them in a white box and tied it with string, and he carried the box to the cab like it was something fragile.

At the airport he checked the weekend bag and kept the bakery box in his lap. The flight was five hours. He read for the first two, slept for the third, and spent the last two looking out the window at the country passing below him — the brown interior, the mountains, the long descent into the basin where Los Angeles spread itself across the coast like something that had been poured and never cleaned up.

She'd be surprised. She might be annoyed — she would almost certainly be annoyed, at least for the first thirty seconds. But he knew her. The annoyance would last until she saw the box, and then she'd open it, and then she'd eat one standing at the counter the way she always did, and the conversation they needed to have would happen over croissants instead of over the phone, and it would be different because he'd be there. He'd be in the room. That was the thing Chloe never accounted for in her calculations — that proximity changed the math.

The plane landed at LAX. He collected his bag, held the white box against his chest, and walked out into the California sun.

CHAPTER 10

The Gardener

November 2060. Los Angeles.

• • •

Chloe smelled the food before she opened the door.

Not her food. Something rich and unfamiliar —- garlic, butter, the faint char of seared protein. It came through the gap under the door, which was wrong in several ways. She hadn't cooked today. She hadn't cooked in three days.

She stood in the hallway with her key card in her hand and the camera bag over her shoulder and thought about the smell for two seconds longer than a person who hadn't been investigating the Haldane network would have thought about it.

Then she opened the door.

The apartment had been taken apart.

Not ransacked —- disassembled. Her files were spread across the kitchen table in neat rows, sorted by category. The organizational charts in one stack. The suppression timeline in another. The data tokens —- both of them, the original and the working copy —- placed side by side at the head of the table like exhibits. Her laptop was open, the encrypted partition exposed, the directory tree visible on the screen. The closet door was open. The floorboards near the bathroom threshold had been pried up and replaced —- she could see the tool marks, precise and clean. The air-gapped backup drive that she'd hidden in the wall cavity behind the bathroom mirror was on the table with the rest.

Everything she had. Laid out like evidence at a trial.

The man was on the sofa.

He was not large. Average height, average build, a frame that disappeared in a crowd. He wore a dark jacket over a collared shirt, no tie, clothes that were clean and unremarkable and chosen to be exactly that. His hands were gloved —- thin leather, dark, gloves that preserved dexterity. One of those hands was resting on Sky, the other held a rather dangerous looking knife.

Sky was on the man's lap. Not restrained. Not frightened. Curled in the precise circle that Sky reserved for people he had decided were acceptable, his blue eyes half-closed, his body loose against the man's thigh. The man's gloved fingers moved along Sky's spine in slow, even strokes. Sky was purring.

Strangely, that was the detail that stopped her. Sky didn't sit on strangers. Sky didn't sit on most non-strangers. Sky had taken four months to tolerate her, and even then it was a conditional arrangement. This man had been here long enough for Sky to evaluate him, make a decision, and fall asleep on his lap.

Greg was in the kitchen chair. Greg?

His wrists were bound to the armrests with cable ties —- the heavy kind, industrial. A strip of duct tape across his mouth. His eyes were wide and wet and locked on Chloe, and they were doing the thing that eyes do when the mouth can't work: trying to communicate everything at once. Run. Help. I'm sorry. I don't understand. All of it compressed into a look that lasted less than a second before the man on the sofa spoke.

"Come in, please. Sit down."

His voice was calm. Conversational. The tone of a host who'd been expecting a guest and was mildly pleased she'd arrived on time.

"I understand your confusion. Please, let me explain."

Chloe didn't sit. She stood in the doorway with the key card still in her hand and the bag cutting into her shoulder and her eyes moving between Greg and the man and the files on the table and Sky, who had not lifted his head.

"This one —- Greg, isn't it?" The man gestured toward the chair with the knife hand. The other continued its slow passage along Sky's back. "He showed up while I was searching. Wanted to surprise you. I must have left the door unlatched, and he just popped in." A pause. "Well. Are you surprised?" His voice was so jovial she couldn't reconcile the mismatch in her head.

"What, um, what do you want." Her voice came out flat. She hadn't decided to make it flat. It just arrived that way —- the shock compressing everything into a monotone that sounded, even to her, like someone else.

"What I want is for you to sit down, please," he said, gesturing to a chair opposite him.

Chloe hesitated, looked at Greg, looked briefly at the door.

"Uh uh uh," he said, "let's not be rude. Please, sit down," and for the first time his voice had a bit of command.

"Who are you?" her voice still not quite normal.

She heard herself say it and knew it was absurd —- the question of a person still operating in a world where information mattered, where names meant something. But the instinct was older than the fear. She was a journalist. She gathered.

He seemed pleased by the question. As if she'd done something charming.

"Who am I? Well, that's a rather complicated question. But, for purposes of our little visit, you may call me Oliver," he said, again gesturing at the chair with the knife.

She looked at Greg again, him shaking his head no, and reluctantly, she sat.

"Thank you, isn't that better? Well, what I actually want is very simple. I want to know if this" —- he indicated the table —- "is everything. All of it. Every copy, every backup, every duplicate you've made of the materials you've been collecting."

"Yes," she said, a little too quickly.

The lie was reflexive, automatic, a muscle memory built from years of protecting sources. The backup at the storage unit across town —- the physical copy she'd made three weeks ago, the one she'd put in a rented locker under a name that wasn't hers —- existed in a part of her mind that the word yes did not touch.

Oliver studied her. His expression didn't change. His hand didn't stop moving on Sky's back.

"Really? You're sure?" The voice remained conversational. Almost soothing. The cadence of a doctor confirming a medication history. "You didn't make any backups? No copies at a friend's place, no cloud storage under another name, no physical duplicates stored off-site?"

Chloe looked at Greg. Greg's eyes were still on her. Still trying to say everything at once.

She looked at the table. At the files laid out in their neat rows. At the gap where the bathroom wall panel had been removed. At the precision of it —- the systematic, unhurried thoroughness of a professional who had been given time and had used it well.

He'd found the wall cavity. He'd found the floor. He'd cracked the encrypted partition. He was good enough that anything she'd hidden in this apartment was on that table, and he knew it.

She needed to give him something. Something that looked like cooperation, that felt like the full truth, that bought credibility for the lie she was holding.

"Wait," she said.

Standing, she walked to the kitchen. Oliver watched her move but didn't shift his position. Sky's ear rotated to track the sound of her footsteps.

She pulled the second drawer out of its tracks and turned it over. Taped to the underside was a data token —- matte black, unmarked, identical to the ones on the table. She peeled it free and held it up.

"I forgot about this one."

She brought it to the table and set it beside the others. Oliver looked at it. Looked at her. His expression carried the faintest suggestion of approval —- not for the backup, but for the honesty of producing it. As if she'd passed a small test.

"Yes, I had found that one. I'm sorry, a little test. I hope you don't think less of me," he said, as if it was possible for her to think any less of him.

"And that is the only backup?"

Same voice. Same soothing cadence. The question delivered as if the answer were a formality.

She nodded.

Oliver held her gaze for a moment longer. Then he seemed to accept it, the way a person accepts a restaurant check —- a minor transaction, already forgotten.

"Very good. Now let me explain what happens next, and I want to be very clear, because I do so dreadfully hate to repeat myself."

He shifted slightly on the sofa. Sky adjusted without waking.

"You are going to stop. Not pause. Not redirect. Not file your notes and wait for a better moment. Stop. The investigation, the cross-referencing, the pattern-matching that you do so well —- all of it ends tonight. You will go back to writing reconstruction stories and press pool dispatches, and you will do it for the rest of your career. You will not contact anyone about what you've found. You will not save anything to any device. You will not speak about any of what you've been looking into. If you encounter information related to these subjects in the course of your work, you will ignore it. You will become, for all practical purposes, a person who never noticed anything."

He said it the way someone reads terms of service aloud —- clearly, completely, without emphasis, because the content carried its own weight.

"I know what you're thinking. You're thinking this is a threat, and threats can be managed. You're thinking about lawyers, or police, or going public. You're thinking that a man sitting on your sofa petting your cat is frightening but not fatal, and that once he leaves, the world will go back to being a place where the rules apply."

He paused.

"I know you don't believe me."

Chloe opened her mouth. The words were already forming —- I do, I believe you, I'll stop, whatever you want —- the desperate vocabulary of compliance that her brain was assembling from instinct and adrenaline, every syllable aimed at de-escalation, at making the situation into one that could be talked through, negotiated, survived with words—-

The knife in his hand was just gone.

She didn't see the motion. She saw the start —- or thought she did —- and she saw the end —- the handle protruding from Greg's chest, two inches below the collarbone, angled slightly left. Between those two moments there was nothing. A magic trick. A gap in the film.

Greg looked down.

He looked at the knife in his chest with an expression that wasn't pain. Not yet. It was confusion —- the pure, unprocessed bewilderment of a body encountering something it had no category for. His eyes moved from the knife to Chloe. He was trying to understand. His mouth worked behind the tape, producing sounds that weren't words.

Then his head dropped.

The whole thing took two or three seconds. Sky hadn't moved. The hand that had been petting Sky had never stopped its slow strokes. As if the throw had been a parenthetical. A footnote in a conversation that was still in progress.

Chloe couldn't breathe. She was looking at Greg and she couldn't breathe and the room had done something to its dimensions, the walls wrong, the floor tilted, the distance between her and the chair where Greg was sitting —- where Greg was —- where Greg—-

"I was going to use the cat," Oliver said. His voice hadn't changed. "As much as that would have pained me. After all, we're not savages are we," he said with an emphasis on 'savages.'

He looked at her with the same calm, evaluative expression he'd worn since she walked in.

"I trust I have made my point."

Silence. The purring. The hum of the building's ventilation system. Traffic noise from four floors below, muffled and distant, from a world that was still operating on the assumption that this room was ordinary.

Oliver stood. Sky slid from his lap to the sofa cushion and curled into the warm spot with the unhurried entitlement of a cat who had been mildly inconvenienced. Oliver straightened his jacket and walked to the kitchen chair.

He worked quickly. The cable ties came off Greg's wrists with a small folding tool that appeared and disappeared into his jacket. He peeled the tape from Greg's mouth, folded it, and put it in his pocket. He gripped the knife handle —- gloved fingers firm, precise —- and drew it out. No rush.

Then he walked to Chloe.

She hadn't moved. She was still sitting where she'd been sitting since she'd given him the backups, her arms at her sides, her hands open. He took her right hand —- gently, the way you'd take someone's hand to read their palm —- and placed the knife handle against her fingers. He closed them around it. Her hand was numb. She felt the pressure but not the contact, her fingers responding to his grip rather than her brain.

He held her hand around the knife for a moment. Then he released it and produced a clear plastic evidence bag from inside his jacket. He took the knife from her unresisting fingers and sealed it in the bag.

"Well," he said, gathering the files from the table into a leather portfolio. The data tokens went into an interior pocket. The laptop he left —- it was hers, and it was clean now. "It's been a genuine pleasure, but I've said what I came to say and I will be on my way." He tucked the portfolio under his arm and patted the evidence bag, now resting in his jacket pocket. "Do forgive me if I don't stay to help you tidy up, but I have other appointments."

He started toward the door. Stopped. Turned back.

"And please do remember —- should any additional copies surface that may have slipped your mind —- I also have this," he patted the jacket pocket, "and more importantly, your father still tends bar at the Rusty Nail in Bozeman, and your brother Kyle coaches JV football at Gallatin High. Lovely town, Bozeman. Lots of open space."

He touched the jacket pocket. The bag. The knife. Her fingerprints on a murder weapon, in her apartment, with her boyfriend's body in her chair and no cable ties and no tape and nothing to prove that anyone else had ever been here.

"Good evening, Miss Ashford."

The door closed behind him.

Chloe stood in the apartment and looked at Greg. Sky was still on the sofa, still curled in the warm spot, still purring. The traffic noise continued from below. The ventilation system hummed. The light in the kitchen was on —- Oliver had turned it on to see the files, and he hadn't turned it off when he left, and that small domestic detail, that carelessness with someone else's electricity, was the thing that broke her.

She sat on the floor.

She sat on the floor and she looked at Greg in the chair and she didn't cry because crying was a thing that happened in a body that was processing, and her body had stopped processing. She was in the gap. The space between the knife in the hand and the knife arriving in the chest. The space where nothing happened because everything had already happened and the mind hadn't caught up.

Then the shaking started. It started in her chest, then it spread to her arms and legs. She tried to gain some control, but control wouldn't come.

Sky jumped down from the sofa. He walked across the floor and climbed into her lap and pushed his head against her hand. She closed her fingers in his fur and held on as the shaking continued.

She had held the lie.

Greg was dead in the chair and her prints were on the knife and Oliver knew where she lived and what she looked like and how to get in, and she had looked him in the eye and said yes, that's everything, and she had held it.

The backup was in a rented locker in Anaheim, under a name that wasn't hers, in a building she'd chosen because it had no cameras and accepted cash.

She held Sky against her chest and stared at Greg and did not move for a long time. Except for the shaking.

• • •

The police came fifteen minutes later.

Two uniforms first, then a detective. Someone had called in a domestic disturbance —- a male voice, calm, reporting sounds of an altercation at her address. The caller had not left a name.

They found Chloe on the floor with the cat in her arms. They found Greg in the kitchen chair. No sign that anyone else had been in the apartment. Just a dead man with a stab wound and a woman who couldn't stop shaking.

The detective was a woman named Ruiz. She was patient and methodical and spoke to Chloe in a voice calibrated for people in shock —- slow, clear, no sudden movements. She asked the questions she had to ask. Chloe answered them in fragments. There was a man. He was waiting when she got home. He tied Greg to the chair. He had a knife. He threw the knife. He staged her prints. He took the weapon.

Ruiz listened. She didn't interrupt. Her expression stayed neutral, but Chloe could see her cataloguing the inconsistencies —- no weapon at the scene, no restraints, a caller who wasn't the victim or the suspect, a woman describing a professional assassination in an apartment that looked like a burglary.

"You said he was waiting when you got home. How did he get in?"

"I don't know."

"Is there anyone who can corroborate —- any cameras in the building, the hallway?"

Chloe's head came up. The doorbell camera. She'd installed it after the interior cameras —- a small unit above the frame, recording to a local data token.

"The doorbell camera," she said. "Above the door. It records—-"

Ruiz sent one of the uniforms to check. He came back holding the unit —- the housing cracked, the mounting bracket torn from the wall. It had been ripped off and dropped on the hallway floor.

"Someone removed it," Ruiz said.

"He removed it. Oliver."

They checked the memory card. The footage was intact up to the moment of destruction. It showed a man arriving at the apartment door —- average build, dark jacket, face partially visible in the hallway light. Then a gloved hand reaching up, gripping the camera housing, and tearing it free. A brief shot of a shoe descending. Then nothing.

Ruiz watched the footage twice. Then she looked at Chloe.

"This doesn't match a domestic," she said.

"No."

"Are there any other cameras?" Ruiz asked.

Chloe had almost forgotten. The shock had compressed everything —- the apartment, the shaking, the police, the questions —- into a single present tense that didn't include the preparations she'd made days ago. The smoke detector cameras. Two of them, positioned to cover the main room and the kitchen.

"The smoke detectors," Chloe said. "There are cameras in the smoke detectors."

The uniform retrieved both data tokens. Ruiz played them on Chloe's laptop —- the one Oliver had left because it was clean.

The footage began hours before Chloe arrived. It showed Oliver entering the apartment alone. Methodically searching. Opening the wall cavity. Prying up the floorboards. Arranging the files on the table. Working with the unhurried precision of a man who knew exactly how much time he had.

Then the sweep. He produced a small handheld device —- compact, professional —- and walked the apartment with it, scanning the walls, the ceiling, the fixtures. He passed directly under one smoke detector camera, the scanner held up toward it, pausing for a moment. Then he moved on. He passed the second one the same way. The scanner found nothing. He pocketed the device and continued working.

Then Greg. The door opening, Greg walking in with a weekend bag over his shoulder and a white box in his hand, his face shifting from confusion to fear in the two seconds it took Oliver to cross the room. The struggle was brief —- Greg was bigger but Oliver moved with a speed and economy that made the size difference irrelevant. Cable ties. Tape. Greg in the chair. Oliver returning to the sofa, where Sky was already investigating him.

Then the waiting. Oliver on the sofa with the cat. Greg in the chair. The stillness of it —- two men in a room, one bound, one petting a cat, both waiting for the same woman.

Then Chloe's arrival. The conversation. The lie. The drawer.

The knife.

The room went quiet when the knife left Oliver's hand. Even on the small screen, even with the compressed footage quality of a smoke detector camera, the throw was something that made the uniforms stop talking. Ruiz's jaw tightened. One of the uniforms looked away.

Greg looking down. Greg's head dropping. The hand that had been petting Sky never stopping.

The staging. The prints. The evidence bag. The portfolio. The departure.

And then Chloe, sitting on the floor, holding Sky, not moving.

Ruiz closed the laptop.

"He swept the room," Ruiz said. "Walked right past both of them and his equipment didn't pick them up. Those cameras you chose —-wireless, no signal, anti-reflective lenses. His scanner was looking for electronics that talk. Yours don't." She paused. "Smart purchase. I'm going to take these data tokens."

"I'll give you a copy, but I will keep the original," Chloe said.

"I'm sorry, that's not how it works. These are evidence. I will be taking them," Ruiz said.

The detective asked more questions. Chloe answered what she could —- the man's name was Oliver, she didn't know his full name, she didn't know who sent him. She did not mention Haldane. She did not mention the investigation. She gave them the murder and nothing else.

The coroner arrived. Greg's body was photographed, examined, and removed in a black bag. Chloe watched from the kitchen. She didn't look away. Looking away felt like something she hadn't earned.

Ruiz told her she couldn't stay — the apartment was a crime scene now. She had five minutes to gather what she needed.

She moved through the apartment without looking at the kitchen chair. Sky into his carrier. Burner phone. Change of clothes from the bedroom. She was zipping the bag when she saw it on the counter beside the door.

A white box. Tied with string. She knew what it was before she opened it. She knew where it came from and she knew who had carried it across the country and she knew he had set it down right there.

Almond croissants. Six of them. From Boulangerie Christophe on Connecticut Avenue. He'd stood in that line for her. He'd flown across the country with this box in his lap because she'd said not right now and he'd come anyway, because that was who Greg was. The man who showed up.

She sat on the floor with the box in her hands and she cried - the annihilating knowledge of what she had lost. Not a boyfriend. Greg. Greg who bought six because she'd once eaten three. Greg who walked through an unlocked door with croissants and a weekend bag and the look on his face that said I just wanted to see you.

Ruiz waited in the doorway. She didn't say anything. She'd been doing this long enough to know what it meant, and she let Chloe sit with it until she had her cry.

Chloe left the box on the counter. She took Sky, the phone, the bag. She left the rest.

The police left at 2:47 AM. Ruiz gave her a card and told her to call if she remembered anything else. Chloe stood in the hallway with the carrier in one hand and the bag over her shoulder, and she had nowhere to go.

The hallway was empty.

Then it wasn't.

The man was leaning against the wall opposite her door. He was tall —- well over six feet —- with dark skin and a stillness that reminded her, horribly, of Oliver. But where Oliver's stillness had been theatrical, performative, a predator enjoying the shape of the moment, this man's stillness was functional. He was watching her the way a security camera watches —- constant, unblinking, without agenda.

"Ms. Ashford," he said. "My name is Okafor. I'm not a police officer."

She almost ran. The instinct was there —- run, scream, call Ruiz, call anyone.

"Don't," he said. Not a command. An observation. "I'm here because someone on Mars asked me to keep you alive. His name is Alexis Dren."

She didn't move.

“I have a message from him. There’s a light-lag delay —- it was recorded four hours ago. Will you listen to it?”

She stared at him. His hands were visible, empty, at his sides. His posture was open. Nothing about him suggested threat —- but nothing about Oliver had suggested threat either, not until the knife left his hand.

“Play it,” she said.

Okafor produced a small device and held it up. Dren’s voice came through —- clear, measured, with the slight compression of a Mars-to-Earth transmission.

“Ms. Ashford. My name is Alexis Dren. I understand that you’ve been investigating the Haldane Foundation’s network —- its institutional placements, its corporate structure, its connections to the Fresh Start Foundation. I want you to know that my team has been conducting a parallel investigation through different channels, and we’ve arrived at the same conclusion. Charles Haldane is at the center of a conspiracy that extends far beyond philanthropic governance. I can’t tell you more in this format, but I need you to understand two things. First, you are in danger. The people you’ve been investigating know about you and they will act to stop you. Second, the man delivering this message —- Okafor —- works for me. He is there to protect you. Please trust him, and please get somewhere safe. I’ll be in contact as soon as I can.”

The recording ended. The hallway was quiet.

Chloe looked at Okafor. She looked at the taped apartment behind her.

“I’m not going to a safe house,” she said. “Not yet.”

Okafor listened as he installed a small device across the hall from the police-taped apartment door.

“I need to go to Anaheim first.”

• • •

The drive took forty minutes at that hour —- south on the 5, the freeway empty, the city dark except for the reconstruction lights along the coast. Okafor took control and drove. He needed to make unpredictable moves to detect a tail. So far, they were clean. Chloe sat in the passenger seat with Sky's carrier on her lap.

"How did you happen to show up when you did?" she asked. Her voice was flat.

Okafor didn't look away from the road. "I came by this afternoon. You weren't home. Apartment was dark, nothing out of place. I was going to check again tomorrow. I picked up the call on the scanner, headed back to your apartment."

"Tomorrow."

"Yes." He didn't offer an excuse. He didn't say he was sorry. The word sat between them like a stone.

They drove in silence for a mile.

"This is a risk," Okafor said.

"If they knew about Anaheim, they would have destroyed it. And if they wanted me dead, I'd be dead. Oliver was a message. Messages are for people who are still alive."

Okafor absorbed this. He didn't argue. He drove.

The storage facility was in a strip mall off Katella Avenue —- a row of climate-controlled units behind a steel gate. Twenty-four-hour access with a PIN code. No cameras. Cash rental. The unit was registered to a name that wasn't hers.

She wanted to go in alone. Okafor would have none of it. They were inside for four minutes. They returned to the car with her carrying a gym bag.

She put the bag on the back seat and got in.

"Safe house now?" Okafor asked.

"Safe house now."

He let the car drive this time, but his eyes never left the rear view mirror.

• • •

The safe house was a rental in Pasadena —- a furnished two-bedroom that Okafor had secured through a corporate booking service that didn't require ID. He swept it twice before letting her inside.

Chloe put Sky's carrier on the kitchen counter and opened the door. Sky wouldn't leave. She took the open carrier to a bathroom and placed it on the floor. She placed a bowl with water and put some of his food on a dish next to the carrier's open door.

She stood in the bathroom doorway and looked at her hands. They were still shaking. The tremor was finer now. A persistent vibration in her fingers that wouldn't stop, as if the frequency had changed but not the signal.

She turned on the shower. She didn't adjust the temperature. She stepped in fully clothed —- shoes, jacket, the shirt that still smelled like Oliver's cooking —- and stood under the water.

The heat hit her and something gave way. Not slowly. Not in stages. The wall she'd built in the hallway, the wall she'd maintained through the police and the drive and the storage unit and Okafor's calm professional silence —- all of it collapsed at once. She slid down the tile and sat on the shower floor with the water running over her and she cried in a way she hadn't cried since she was a child. Not weeping. Not tears. A sound that came from somewhere below her lungs, an animal sound that had nothing to do with language or thought, the sound of a body expelling something it couldn't contain.

Greg had come to surprise her. He'd flown across the country with a weekend bag because she'd told him not to come and he'd come anyway, because that was who Greg was —- the man who showed up, the man who tried, the man whose last act was walking through an unlocked door with a bag over his shoulder and a look on his face that said I just wanted to see you.

And Oliver had used him. Had sat on the sofa petting her cat and waited for her to arrive so she could watch, because the watching was the point. Greg wasn't the target. Greg was the instrument. The knife wasn't the message. Greg was the message.

She rocked forward on the shower floor, her arms around her knees, the water running into her eyes and her open mouth, and she let it come. All of it. The guilt of not loving him enough and the guilt of not protecting him and the guilt of being alive in a shower while he was in a bag in a van somewhere, and the specific, terrible knowledge that his last conscious thought had been confusion —- not understanding why this was happening, not understanding who the man on the sofa was, not understanding anything except that the woman he'd come to see was standing in the doorway and couldn't help him.

The water ran until it went cold. She didn't move when it changed. The cold was a different kind of pain and she let it have her.

Then it stopped. Not the water. Something inside her. The crying stopped. The rocking stopped. She sat under the cold water and breathed and her hands were still and the shaking was gone.

She stood up. She turned off the water. She stripped the wet clothes off and left them in a pile on the shower floor. She dried herself with a towel that belonged to no one and put on the change of clothes from her bag.

When she walked out of the bathroom, Okafor was sitting at the kitchen table. He didn't look at her wet hair or her red eyes or the pile of wet clothes visible through the open bathroom door. He looked at her the way he'd been looking at her since the hallway —- steady, professional, waiting.

She set the gym bag on the table and unzipped it. The physical files. The data tokens. She placed the Nevada construction manifests with them. Everything Oliver had taken from the apartment was duplicated here —- the backup she'd made three weeks ago, stored in a locker in Anaheim, protected by the lie she'd held while a man threw a knife into her boyfriend's chest.

The investigation had survived.

She turned on the wallscreen to see what was being reported about her. There was a story, but it wasn't about her.

A woman's body found in a parking structure in downtown Los Angeles. Identified as Elena Marin, 34, employed as an administrative assistant at the Fresh Start Foundation. Apparent robbery. No suspects.

Chloe looked at the screen. The photograph they used was an employee ID photo —- narrow-shouldered and slight. A build you could mistake for a teenager from behind. A build that would look small in a hoodie, face angled away from a doorbell camera.

She looked at Okafor. Okafor was watching her.

"She was my source," Chloe said. "She was inside Fresh Start. She was the one delivering the envelopes."

She sat down at the table. The files in front of her. The gym bag. The data tokens. Elena's face on the screen behind her.

"Oliver said he had another appointment," she said.

"Oh God."

The cost was becoming clear. Greg. Elena. The investigation had survived, but the people around it were dying, and stopping now meant they died for nothing.

She opened the first file and started working.

CHAPTER 11

The Election

November 2nd, 2060.

• • •

Washington, D.C. The White House. 17:00 EST.

The first exit polls arrived while Whitfield was in the Situation Room.

Hunt brought them — a printout, not a screen, because the Situation Room's displays were allocated to reconstruction coordination and Whitfield had refused to displace operational feeds for political data. She took the printout and read it standing, one hand on the back of a chair, the other holding the paper at arm's length because her reading glasses were in the Residence and she wasn't going to send someone for them.

The numbers were what her campaign team had predicted. The interior zones were breaking for Eldridge Turner, the opposition candidate — not by landslide margins, but consistently, steady five-to-eight-point leads that reflected genuine anger rather than partisan reflex. Texas, the zones around Dallas and Houston where reconstruction employment was highest, was close. Florida was close. The Great Lakes corridor was leaning Turner. The mountain West was Turner by double digits.

The coasts were the question. They had always been the question.

"California?" she asked.

Hunt pointed to the bottom of the page. The exit poll sample from California was flagged with an asterisk. *Sample size insufficient for reliable projection. Turnout in sampled precincts significantly below historical norms.*

"How significantly?"

"Los Angeles County is reporting eleven percent turnout as of three o'clock local. San Francisco is at nine. The precincts that are open are operating, but most of them are in the Dren logistics corridor — the reconstruction hubs, the communities with functioning infrastructure. The rest —" He paused. "The rest don't have polling stations. Or the polling stations don't have power. Or the roads to the polling stations are still impassable."

"Oregon?"

"Better. Portland metro is at twenty-two percent. But the coastal corridor south of Newport is single digits. Same infrastructure problem."

Whitfield set the printout on the table. She looked at the reconstruction feeds on the wall — the logistics dashboards, the supply chain monitors, the satellite communication status that Dren's network provided. The infrastructure that kept the reconstruction zones functioning was the same infrastructure that determined who could vote. The communities Dren's logistics had reached were the communities that could participate in democracy. The communities it hadn't reached couldn't.

"The irony isn't lost on me," she said.

Hunt didn't respond. He'd learned when to let a statement sit.

She picked up the printout again. The numbers told a story she'd been anticipating for months — a country that would elect its president based on which parts of it were still capable of holding an election. Capacity. The physical ability to cast a ballot, determined by the same disaster her presidency had been defined by.

"What's the early projection?" she asked.

“If the coastal turnout holds at these levels — and there’s no reason to expect it to improve, the polls close in three hours — you carry California, Oregon, and Washington on thin margins from the reconstruction corridor vote. The electoral math holds. Popular vote is going to be close — very close. Possibly within two points.”

“A technical win.”

“A Constitutional win,” Hunt said. “The electoral college doesn’t have a ‘but California barely showed up’ clause.”

“No. But the morning shows will.”

• • •

Dallas. 18:30 CST.

Haldane watched the returns from his study.

Not the networks — he had those running on the wallscreen, muted, four feeds in a grid showing the same map in different colors with different analysts pointing at the same states. He watched his own data. The committee reports flowing through Novak’s network — turnout figures from the reconstruction zones, precinct-level data from the interior communities where the mobilization committees had been working for three months, real-time social media sentiment from the DSA affiliates.

The interior was performing. Ohio reconstruction zones: 68% turnout, Turner plus seven. Pennsylvania reconstruction zones: 71% turnout, Turner plus five. Michigan: 64% turnout, Turner plus nine. The anger was voting. The committees had done their work — not by telling people who to vote for, but by making sure the people who were already angry had rides to the polls, had information about their precincts, had the logistical support that turned resentment into participation. Every vote was real. Every voter had made a genuine choice. The mobilization was invisible because it looked like civic engagement, which is what it was. Civic engagement, funded by a man who wanted the engagement to produce a specific emotional temperature in the electorate.

California was performing too — in the other direction. The numbers were exactly what Novak's models had predicted when they'd made the strategic decision not to rebuild polling infrastructure in the coastal zones. They hadn't suppressed anything. They'd simply allocated the Foundation's reconstruction resources to housing, medical facilities, agricultural support, and logistics — everything a devastated community needed except the ability to participate in its own governance.

The phone rang. Novak.

"You're seeing California," Novak said.

"I'm seeing California."

"The networks are starting to notice. CNN's reconstruction correspondent just did a segment from a polling station in Long Beach — three machines, a line of forty people, and a building that doesn't have reliable power. She's framing it as 'the forgotten voters.' Sympathetic. Visual. It'll run all night."

"Let it run. The image does more work than any talking point. A voter standing in line in a building without power is the reconstruction failure made personal. It doesn't matter who she votes for. The image is the message."

"Turner's people are already using it. His campaign manager put out a statement twenty minutes ago — 'Every American deserves the right to vote, including those our government has failed to rebuild.' Clean. Pointed. Doesn't mention Whitfield by name."

"He doesn't need to. The building without power does that for him." Haldane leaned back in his chair. "Where's Turner's internal projection?"

"His team thinks they're winning. Their models weight the interior turnout heavily and they're discounting California because there's nothing to count. If you only look at the states where people actually voted in meaningful numbers, Turner wins comfortably."

"And the electoral math?"

"Doesn't work that way. California's fifty-four electoral votes go to whoever wins the state, and Whitfield is winning the state —

on the reconstruction corridor vote, but winning it. Turner takes the interior. Whitfield takes the coasts on ghost margins. The electoral college doesn't distinguish between a state where ninety percent voted and a state where eleven percent voted. A win is a win is fifty-four electoral votes."

"Exactly as designed," Haldane said.

• • •

Pasadena. 19:00 PST.

Ashford watched the returns from the safe house kitchen table.

The wallscreen was split — the election coverage on the left, the investigation files on the right. She'd been working since dawn, the same way she'd been working every day since Okafor had brought her here. The files. The matrix. The nodes and connections that were becoming a pattern. And now the election, playing out on the other half of the screen like a parallel investigation into a different kind of damage.

Okafor was at the window. He'd glanced at the coverage once, when the first projections came in, and returned to the street. The election wasn't his concern. The street was.

Sky was on the sofa, watching the screen with the focused indifference of a cat who could see movement without caring about its content.

The networks were calling the easy states. The interior was Turner's — the graphics showed a block of yellow through the middle of the country, Ohio and Pennsylvania and Michigan falling in sequence, the reconstruction zones delivering the anger they'd been accumulating since the flyby. The anchors were excited. A competitive election. A real race. Drama that reconstruction-era coverage had been missing.

A commentator — a reconstruction policy analyst with a desk and a flag pin — was explaining the California situation to the national audience. "What we're seeing in California is unprecedented in modern American elections. The infrastructure destruction from the flyby has created what amounts to an accidental disenfranchisement — millions of eligible voters physically unable to reach polling stations because the polling stations, the roads, the power grid, the basic infrastructure of democratic participation, no longer exists in large portions of the state."

"And what does that mean for the result?" the anchor asked.

"It means whoever wins California wins it on a fraction of the electorate. President Whitfield is currently leading in the state, but she's leading among the voters who could reach the polls — predominantly in the reconstruction corridor communities where Dren Industries' logistics network has kept the infrastructure functional. The rest of California's electorate is simply absent. Not because they chose not to vote. Because they can't."

Ashford looked at the matrix on the right half of the screen. The fellowship placements. The committee network. The shell companies and the grant disbursements and the institutional framework that Haldane had built over twenty-five years. She thought about the polling station in Long Beach — three machines, no power — and she thought about the Fresh Start Foundation's reconstruction aid flowing to housing and medical facilities and agricultural support in the coastal zones. Everything a community needed. Except polling stations.

She didn't have proof. She had pattern. The Foundation's reconstruction aid covered logistics, housing, medical facilities. It did not cover election infrastructure. That could be principled — election infrastructure was a government responsibility. It could also be strategic — a deliberate gap in the aid portfolio that produced exactly the turnout differential she was watching on the screen.

She made a note in the file she'd been keeping since the logo. One more thread. One more pattern that wasn't proof. The matrix was getting larger and the picture was getting clearer and the distance between pattern and proof was shrinking every day.

"Okafor," she said.

He didn't turn from the window.

"The election. The turnout gap. It's him."

"You don't know that," Okafor said. His voice was neutral. The voice of a man who dealt in evidence, not intuition.

"No. I don't know it. But the Foundation rebuilds everything except the one thing that would let people vote. And the places where people can't vote are the places where the result changes."

Okafor was quiet for a moment. Then: "Add it to the file. When you can prove it, it'll matter. Until then, it's noise."

She added it to the file.

• • •

Washington, D.C. 21:22 EST.

The networks called Ohio for Turner at 9:22.

The graphic was decisive — the state flipping on the map, the numbers final, Turner's margin comfortable enough that the remaining precincts wouldn't change it. The anchor's voice carried the particular energy of a network that had been waiting for a competitive race and had finally gotten one.

"And Ohio goes to Eldridge Turner, as projected. Turner carries the state's reconstruction zones by significant margins, driven by what our analysts are describing as the strongest opposition turnout in a reconstruction-era election. The Turner campaign has been running on accountability — accountability for the tilt, accountability for the delegation order, accountability for what Turner has called 'a presidency that outsourced its authority to a man on another planet.' That message is resonating in the industrial heartland, where reconstruction workers have seen their contracts frozen while Dren Industries shipments flow on priority logistics."

Pennsylvania fell at 9:31. Michigan at 9:47. The interior was going the way every model had predicted.

At 11 PM EST the West Coast polls closed. The networks did not call California.

The anchor explained why, and the explanation was the story. "We are not projecting California at this time. The turnout figures we're seeing from the state are — and I want to be careful with this word — historic. Not historic in the sense of high engagement. Historic in the sense of low participation. We are looking at single-digit turnout in multiple counties. The exit poll data is insufficient for projection because there are not enough voters leaving the polls to sample. We are, in a very real sense, waiting for California to tell us whether it voted."

A panel of four commentators filled the screen. The format that passed for analysis in reconstruction-era media — four faces in boxes, each one representing a position that had been established before the camera turned on.

"This is a crisis of democratic legitimacy," the first panelist said — a political scientist from a university that still had a campus. "We are watching an election in which the outcome will be determined by differential turnout driven by infrastructure destruction. The states that can vote are electing a president. The states that can't are being governed by that choice without participating in it."

"But the Constitution doesn't require minimum turnout," the second panelist said — a former election commissioner, now consulting for a reconstruction think tank. "The election is valid if one person votes in each state. The framers designed a system that functions under adverse conditions. This is an adverse condition. The system is functioning."

"Functioning isn't the same as legitimate," the third panelist said — a DSA-affiliated commentator whose presence on the panel guaranteed the argument would land where the producers wanted it. "If Whitfield wins California on those margins, she wins fifty-four electoral votes that represent less than a tenth of the state's electorate. That's not democracy. That's a technicality."

"And if Turner wins the popular vote but loses the electoral college because California's depleted turnout gives Whitfield a full slate of delegates? We've been through this before in this country. It didn't go well then. It won't go well now."

The fourth panelist — a retired general now working as a military affairs analyst — said something quieter. "The real question isn't who wins tonight. It's whether the result holds. Three regional commanders are watching these numbers. If the election produces a president that half the country considers illegitimate, those commanders will have to decide whether they answer to that president or to the constituencies that didn't elect her."

The anchor moved to the next segment. The panel dissolved. The map stayed on the screen — yellow through the middle, green on the coasts, California gray and uncalled and hanging over the election like a question that the infrastructure couldn't answer.

• • •

The networks. 23:27 EST.

The call came at 11:27.

California for Whitfield. Oregon for Whitfield. Washington for Whitfield. The map repainted itself in seconds — the coasts going green, the interior yellow, the graphic showing a president who had just won re-election by a margin that looked, on the screen, like a mandate.

The anchor read the numbers with the careful cadence of someone who understood that the graphic and the reality were telling different stories. "With California, Oregon, and Washington now projected for President Whitfield, the electoral map shows a commanding 341 to 197 victory for the incumbent — a margin that in any normal election year would signal an overwhelming mandate. This is not a normal election year. President Whitfield's electoral dominance is built on coastal states where single-digit turnout has produced full-weight electoral delegations. Eldridge Turner won more individual American votes. The map says Whitfield. The numbers say Turner. The Constitution says Whitfield. And tomorrow, this country will have to decide which one it believes."

The map stayed on screen. Green coasts. Yellow interior. A nation-shaped picture of two countries that had just held one election and arrived at two results.

• • •

Washington, D.C. The White House. 23:35 EST.

Hunt came to the Residence.

Whitfield was sitting in the chair by the window — the chair she used when she didn't want to be at the desk, when the desk meant work and the chair meant thinking. The Ellipse was dark below. The megaphone was silent. Even the protest camp had gone quiet for the night, the demonstrators inside their tents watching the same coverage the president was watching.

"California," Hunt said.

"Tell me."

"The reconstruction corridor precincts have reported. You carry the state. Margin is thin — four points — but it's durable. The remaining unreported precincts are in areas with no functional infrastructure, and they're not going to report because there's nothing to report. The votes that are going to be counted have been counted."

"Popular vote?"

Hunt paused. "Turner by one-point-seven. Nationally. He wins the popular vote."

Whitfield let that sit. She'd expected it. The models had shown it for weeks — the interior turnout swamping the coastal margins, the popular total going one way while the electoral map went the other. The Constitution's oldest quirk, produced not by design but by disaster.

"Electoral?"

"You carry California, Oregon, Washington, the northeast corridor. Turner carries the interior, the mountain West, most of the South. Electoral count is 341 to 197. It's going to look like a blowout."

"A blowout," Whitfield repeated. "On single-digit turnout in the state that puts me over the top."

"The map is going to be green on both coasts and yellow through the middle. Every network graphic will show a decisive Whitfield victory. The number underneath the graphic will show Turner winning more votes. Both things will be true simultaneously, and the country will spend the next year arguing about which one matters."

"Constitutionally unambiguous," Hunt said. "Politically complicated."

"Politically complicated means the morning shows spend three days asking whether a president who lost the popular vote in a reconstruction election has the mandate to govern a country that's falling apart."

"Yes."

"And the answer, according to roughly half the country, will be no."

Hunt didn't argue. He stood by the door with the printout and waited. He'd been with her since the flyby. He'd been with her through the delegation order, the breaches, the Mars debate. He knew the difference between a victory and a win, and he knew this was the former without being the latter.

"When does Turner concede?" Whitfield asked.

"His campaign team is drafting the statement now. He'll deliver it within the hour of the network calls. Our people say it'll be graceful. He's a serious man who ran a serious campaign. He'll accept the result."

"He'll accept the result. Will his voters?"

Hunt was quiet for a moment. "Some will. Some won't. The ones who won't are concentrated in the reconstruction zones where turnout was highest — the communities that feel most strongly that the system failed them. They voted in record numbers. Their candidate won the popular vote. And the electoral college is going to hand the presidency to someone else because the coastal ghost margins counted for as much as their sixty-eight percent."

Whitfield stood and walked to the window. The Ellipse. The dark tents. The silent megaphone that would be running again by morning, reading the names of destroyed cities to a government that had just been re-elected by the people its logistics network could reach and rejected by the people it couldn't.

"Get me the transition team," she said. "Not for Turner — for us. Second-term appointments, reconstruction authority renewals, the delegation order review. If we have a mandate, we use it before the morning shows explain why we don't."

"And the concession?"

"I'll call Turner personally. After his statement. Not before — he deserves to do it his way." She paused. "He ran a clean campaign on legitimate grievances. He earned more votes than I did. The system gave it to me anyway. The least I can do is let him finish with dignity."

• • •

Dallas. 22:45 CST.

Turner conceded at 11:45 PM Eastern.

Haldane watched the speech on the wallscreen. Turner stood at a podium in a hotel ballroom in Indianapolis, his family behind him, his supporters in the room doing the thing supporters do when the candidate they believed in has just lost — the determined applause, the defiant cheers, the refusal to let the room feel like what it was.

Turner was good. Haldane had always known that — it was why he'd been careful never to approach him, never to fund him, never to connect any thread of the Foundation's network to Turner's campaign. The man was genuine. His anger at the reconstruction failures was real. His argument that Whitfield had outsourced the presidency to Dren was his own — arrived at independently, articulated with conviction, supported by evidence that Turner's staff had assembled without any help from Dallas. Haldane hadn't needed to create Turner's candidacy. He'd only needed to create the conditions in which Turner's candidacy would thrive and Whitfield's victory would be hollow.

"I called President Whitfield a few minutes ago to congratulate her on her re-election," Turner said. His voice was steady. The voice of a man who had lost and was choosing to lose well. "The American people have spoken — those who could speak. The result is the result, and I accept it, because the alternative to accepting election results is the end of the system that makes elections possible."

He paused. The room was quiet.

"But I want to say something to the millions of Americans who voted today, and to the millions more who couldn't. This election was held under extraordinary conditions. Communities that are still digging out from the worst disaster in human history were asked to participate in their democracy with polling stations that didn't have power, in buildings that didn't have roofs, on roads that didn't exist. Many of them — millions of them — could not. Their voices are absent from tonight's result. Not because they chose silence. Because silence was chosen for them, by a reconstruction that rebuilt everything except the infrastructure of self-governance."

Haldane listened to the words. They were Turner's words — not scripted by Novak or seeded through committees or amplified by the DSA network. Turner was saying what he believed, and what he believed happened to align perfectly with the narrative framework Haldane had built. The reconstruction failed California. The election reflected that failure. The result was legitimate in law and illegitimate in fact. Turner didn't need to say "stolen." He said "absent" and "silence" and "chosen for them," and those words would do more damage than "stolen" ever could, because they were true.

"I ask President Whitfield to make the rebuilding of our democratic infrastructure her first priority in her second term," Turner continued. "Not reconstruction of buildings. Reconstruction of the ability of every American to participate in the decisions that govern their lives. The election is over. The work is not."

He stepped back from the podium. The applause was loud and sustained and carried the particular energy of people who felt they had been robbed by arithmetic rather than fraud — which was worse, because arithmetic couldn't be fought.

Haldane muted the screen. He picked up the bourbon.

The election had done exactly what it was supposed to do. Whitfield had won. Turner had lost. And the country was more divided than it had been the day before — not by the result, but by the conditions that produced it. Turner's concession speech would be replayed for months. The image of the Long Beach polling station would become an icon. The turnout figures would enter the political vocabulary the way "hanging chad" had entered it a lifetime ago — a shorthand for a system that had produced a technically valid result from a fundamentally broken process.

And tomorrow, the committees would pivot. The mobilization networks would become grievance networks. The civic engagement infrastructure would become protest infrastructure. The same people who had driven turnout in Ohio would be driving outrage in Ohio, and the same Foundation funding that had paid for rides to the polls would pay for signs on the Ellipse.

The election wasn't the end of anything. It was fuel.

He drank the bourbon and went to bed.

• • •

Washington, D.C. 00:30 EST.

Beckett watched Turner's concession from his office in the Hart Building.

The television was on the credenza — a small screen, the kind that senators kept for tracking floor proceedings and breaking news. He'd been in the office since the polls closed, alone, the door locked, his staff sent home with instructions that the senator was reviewing committee materials and was not to be disturbed.

He'd been reviewing the returns.

Not as a voter or a senator. As an architect, reading the structural integrity of a system he'd helped design. Every state that fell for Turner was a state where Haldane's committee network had been active. Every turnout figure from the interior was a number that Novak's mobilization infrastructure had helped produce. And California — California was the masterpiece. The absent electorate. The ghost margin. The fifty-four electoral votes that would hand Whitfield a victory built on the rubble of the communities she'd failed to rebuild.

Beckett had not coordinated with Turner's campaign. He had not made calls, attended fundraisers, or signaled his preference. He'd maintained the public posture of a senator focused on oversight, not politics — the hearings, the subpoenas, the institutional work that existed on a separate plane from electoral competition. His name appeared nowhere in the election machinery.

But his hearings had built the emotional landscape that Turner's campaign had harvested. Every witness who testified about reconstruction delays. Every subpoena that put Dren's name in the news. Every question about the thirty-minute window and the delegation order and the dependency that came from relying on a Mars-based civilian for planetary survival — all of it had fed the anger that the interior zones had expressed at the ballot box.

He watched Turner's face on the screen. The dignity. The restraint. The carefully chosen words that would outlast the concession and become the vocabulary of the opposition. Beckett admired the performance because he recognized craft when he saw it, and Turner's speech was craft of the highest order — a loss transformed into a moral victory, a concession that indicted the winner more effectively than any campaign ad.

The returns told him everything he needed to know. The electoral map was green on the coasts and yellow through the middle, and the numbers underneath told a different story than the colors. The plan they'd discussed at Lake Texoma — the dual-feeding, the legitimacy fracture, the election as another crack in the foundation — had performed exactly as designed. He didn't need a call from Dallas. He didn't need confirmation. The results were the confirmation. He knew what came next because the next steps had been agreed months ago in a study with wood paneling and a lake view and no records.

He turned off the television and sat in the dark office and listened to the silence of a building that would be very loud in the morning, when the networks ran the California turnout figures alongside the electoral map and the question that Haldane had planted in the machinery of the American political system began its work.

The question wasn't who had won. The question was whether winning still meant what it used to mean.

He picked up his coat and left the building. The Capitol dome was lit against the November sky. The Mall stretched beyond it, dark and empty, the same ground that would host the memorial seven months later where everything Beckett had helped build would come apart.

He didn't know that yet. He walked to his car and drove home and slept the sleep of a man who had done the math and believed the math would hold.

• • •

Pasadena. 22:00 PST.

Ashford watched Turner concede.

She'd stopped working an hour ago — something she almost never did, but the election had pulled her attention the way a car wreck pulls attention, the slow-motion quality of watching a system produce a result that everyone could see was broken and no one could stop.

The investigation files were still on the right half of the wallscreen. The election coverage was on the left. Two structures, side by side. One she was building. One she was watching.

"Absent," Turner said on the screen. "Silence." "Chosen for them."

She looked at the matrix. At the Fresh Start Foundation node. At the grant disbursements that funded housing and medical facilities and agricultural support in the coastal zones. At the gap in the aid portfolio where election infrastructure should have been and wasn't.

"He built this," she said to the room. To the files. To the evidence that was accumulating on the wallscreen in nodes and connections that pointed at a man in Dallas who had just watched his system perform exactly as designed.

"He built the conditions that produced this result. The turnout gap. The anger in the interior. The absence on the coasts. He didn't choose the candidates. He didn't rig the votes. He built the ground the election was fought on, and the ground was tilted."

Okafor was at the window. He'd been listening.

"Can you prove it?" he asked.

"Not yet."

"Then it stays in the file."

"It stays in the file," she agreed. She looked at the matrix one more time — the Foundation at the center, the lines radiating outward, the network that was becoming visible piece by piece, the way a building becomes visible when the scaffolding comes down.

She turned off the election coverage and went back to work. The files were patient. The proof would come. And when it came, the election would be part of it — one more thread in a web that connected a logo on the Wayback Machine to the deaths of two hundred million people and the systematic destruction of the democracy that mourned them.

Sky jumped onto the table and walked across the keyboard. She picked him up, set him in her lap, and kept working.

CHAPTER 12

Convergence

December 2060. Los Angeles.

• • •

The phone had been ringing for three days.

The same number —- she didn't recognize it and she wouldn't answer it. It had come in four times on the first day, three times on the second, twice on the third. After Oliver, after Greg, after the safe house and the gym bag and Elena's face on the wallscreen, she wasn't answering numbers she didn't know. The phone was a liability now, and every unknown call was a potential trace.

On the fourth day, the camera feed changed things.

Okafor's device across the hall from the taped apartment showed a woman at the door at 11:13 in the morning. She wasn't police —- no badge, no uniform, no partner. She was alone, mid-thirties, dressed like someone who'd been up all night and had driven across the city on caffeine and anxiety. She looked at the police tape. She looked at the hallway. She checked her phone.

Then she made a call.

Chloe's phone rang. The same number.

She stared at the screen. Looked at the camera feed on Okafor's tablet. The woman in the hallway was holding her phone to her ear, waiting.

Chloe answered.

"Miss Ashford, this is Jessica Saunders. We spoke a few days ago. I've been trying to reach you for three days. I saw the news about what happened at your apartment and I have data you need to see."

Chloe now remembered. Jessica Saunders, calling about issues regarding Dren in the scientific community. They'd never met.

"Do you have press credentials?" Chloe asked.

"Yes."

"There's a camera across the hall from my apartment door. It's small —- mounted on the wall opposite, at about eye level. Hold your press ID up to it."

A pause. Then, on the feed, Saunders looked across the hallway. She found the device —- it took her a few seconds. She held up a laminated press card. Okafor zoomed in. Jessica Saunders, freelance, the photo a match.

Ashford muted the phone and looked at Okafor.

"I know her work," she said. "She's been pulling the same institutional thread."

"She could be compromised. She could be followed. She could be wearing a wire."

"You think?" Ashford asked.

"I always think. So we vet her before she comes anywhere near this location," Okafor said in his clipped way of speaking.

"Agreed," Ashford sighed. She had to get used to this post-Oliver reality.

Okafor said, "Tell her to leave immediately, go to the Westfield Century City mall. Wander around. Browse the stores. Look like she's shopping. I will make contact with her if I think it's safe."

Ashford relayed the instructions.

"How will I know—-" Saunders started to ask.

"You'll know," Ashford finished.

She ended the call. On the feed, Saunders looked at the camera one more time, then turned and walked toward the stairwell.

Okafor was already working. Background on his tablet — public records, publication history, employment verification, social media footprint. He ran it while Chloe watched the feed, making sure Saunders left the building alone.

"Clean so far," Okafor said after twenty minutes. "Publications check out. Employment history is consistent. No flags in the financial records I can access. No known associations with any Haldane entity."

"Go," Chloe said.

Okafor drove to Century City. He parked on the third level of the structure, backed into the space, and sat for five minutes watching the ramp. No vehicle had followed him in. No vehicle had arrived within thirty seconds of his. The parking structure was clean.

He entered the mall through the food court on the ground level and took the escalator to the second floor. He didn't look for Saunders immediately. He walked the perimeter first — a slow loop past the storefronts, reading the layout. Sight lines. Exits. The kiosk positions that provided cover and the open concourse sections that didn't. The security cameras mounted at the corridor junctions, the angles they covered, the blind spots where the coverage overlapped imperfectly.

Mostly, he was looking for anyone who was looking. If people had eyes on Saunders, they would likely be in fixed locations.

He bought a coffee at the kiosk near the central fountain. Stood at the counter stirring it while he watched the foot traffic pattern. Midday on a weekday — the mall was moderately busy. Office workers on lunch, mothers with strollers, a group of teenagers cutting school. The baseline rhythm of a public space where everyone was doing exactly what they appeared to be doing.

He found Saunders on the second level, thirty meters east of the escalator. She was in a clothing store, moving through the racks without pulling anything, her messenger bag over one shoulder. She checked her phone, looked at the entrance, checked her phone again. A woman waiting for someone who wasn't coming. The performance was adequate — a little stiff, the browsing too aimless, but good enough for anyone who wasn't trained to spot it.

He watched for any other eyes that were watching her. He didn't see any.

He positioned himself at the escalator landing where he could see the store entrance and the concourse in both directions. He watched her for three minutes, then moved to the bench near the fountain. Different angle. He could see who entered and exited the stores on either side of hers, who walked past the entrance and glanced in, who stopped moving when she stopped moving.

A man in a gray jacket passed the store twice in six minutes. Okafor tracked him. The man entered a phone accessories kiosk on the third pass and spent four minutes examining cases. He bought one and left through the east exit. Shopper, not surveillance. The purchase was genuine — you don't spend money to maintain cover at a mall unless you're professional, and a professional wouldn't have passed the same storefront three times.

A woman with a rolling suitcase sat on a bench fifty meters from Saunders's store for twelve minutes. She was watching her phone, not the store. When she stood, she walked directly to the parking structure without looking back. Traveler killing time, not an operator.

Okafor moved again. The coffee kiosk. He could see Saunders through the store's glass frontage and the full length of the concourse behind her. He watched for another ten minutes. The foot traffic flowed around her store without eddies — no one circling, no one stationary, no one adjusting position to maintain a sight line on the entrance. The pattern was clean. If someone was on Saunders, they were better than the environment demanded, and nobody wasted that level of talent on a mall surveillance operation.

He finished the coffee and walked past her on the concourse, close enough that only she could hear.

"Keep wandering. Fifteen minutes. Then go to the parking garage, section C5."

He didn't stop. He didn't look at her. He was past her and into the crowd before she could turn her head.

Fifteen minutes later, Saunders walked into the parking garage and found section C5. A car pulled up —- Okafor behind the wheel.

"Get in," he said.

She got in. Okafor drove through the garage at speed, tires squealing on the smooth surface —- two full circuits, watching every parked vehicle for headlights coming on, doors opening, anyone reacting to the sudden movement. If someone was sitting in a car waiting for Saunders, the speed and noise would force a decision. No one followed. No one pulled out. He exited through the entrance lane, the wrong way, the arm gate rising as he approached from the inside.

On the street, he handed her a pair of blackout glasses —- matte black, opaque.

"Put these on," he said. "For the drive."

Saunders looked at the glasses. She looked at Okafor. She put them on.

• • •

Dallas.

Haldane saw the footage at 7:15 AM Central, on the wallscreen in his home office. The local Los Angeles affiliate had led with it —- a leaked frame from a smoke detector camera showing a man in a dark jacket standing in an apartment, files arranged on a table, a cat on a sofa. The chyron said LAPD INVESTIGATING HOMICIDE —- SUSPECT CAUGHT ON HIDDEN CAMERA. The anchor was careful with the details —- no name, no address, pending investigation —- but the frame was unmistakable.

Oliver. In the apartment. On camera.

Haldane watched the segment twice. Then he turned off the wallscreen and sat in silence for a full minute.

He picked up the third phone and dialed.

Oliver answered on the first ring.

"You're on the news," Haldane said. His voice was level. The anger was underneath, structural, load-bearing.

A pause. "I don't understand."

"The apartment had cameras. Hidden cameras —- not the doorbell unit you removed. Others. Smoke detectors. They recorded everything. Your face, the search, the conversation, the killing. All of it. The police have the footage. The news has the footage. You are on the news, Oliver."

Silence on the line.

"I swept the apartment," Oliver said. His voice had changed —- not panic, not yet, but the first hairline fracture in the composure. "I swept it thoroughly. There were no active devices—-"

"Well you missed these. You were sloppy, Oliver. I employ you not to be sloppy."

Another silence.

"Go to ground," Haldane said. "Now. Not your apartment. Not any location connected to your name. You have ninety minutes before the LAPD runs your face through every database they have access to. Use them. You need to become a ghost."

"And the journalist?"

"You bungled that quite effectively. I sent you to deliver a message, and now that message is available for everyone to see. If you had mentioned my name this conversation would not be happening, do you understand?"

Haldane's voice had not risen. It didn't need to.

"You had one job. Deliver a message. Instead you gave them a face, a method, and a motive. You turned a journalist nobody believed into a victim with evidence. You created a police investigation where there was none. And you did it in front of cameras you didn't find."

"I don't want to see or hear from or about you until I contact you," he said, ending the call.

Haldane sat at his desk. The bourbon was on the credenza. He didn't pour any. He looked at the blank wallscreen where Oliver's face had been, in an apartment that should have been a clean operation, recorded by cameras that shouldn't have existed.

Dren and Ashford. Connected. The Mars investigation and the Earth investigation, joined by an operative in Los Angeles who was doing exactly what Haldane would have done if the positions were reversed —- protecting the asset.

He picked up a different phone and called Novak.

"We have a problem," he said.

• • •

Novak arrived in Dallas three hours after the call.

He came through the service entrance of the Foundation building the way he always did — no lobby, no sign-in, the freight elevator to the fortieth floor. Haldane was at the window with the bourbon untouched on the credenza.

"Oliver's on the news," Novak said.

"I'm aware."

"So the journalist has footage, she has police involvement."

"Obviously."

Novak sat in the leather chair and waited. Haldane didn't turn from the window.

"The investigation is out of our hands," Haldane said. "Ashford, Dren, the relay trace — all of it is moving and we can't stop it by cutting one thread. Oliver was supposed to be a scalpel. He turned out to be a billboard."

"So what do we do?"

"We stop playing defense." Haldane turned from the window. "The investigation doesn't matter if the institutions it needs to act are too broken to respond. Whitfield is the only person with the authority to consolidate the evidence, coordinate with Dren, and take action. Remove her from the board and the evidence has nowhere to go. The regional commanders won't touch it — they're running their own territories. Congress is fractured. The intelligence community reports to people who report to no one. Without a functioning presidency, the investigation is a pile of paper."

"Beckett's already pushing impeachment."

"Beckett is pushing rhetoric. I need him pushing action. And I need the public demanding it." Haldane sat down behind the desk. "The protests outside the White House — who's organizing them?"

"Reconstruction unions, mostly. Legitimate grievance. Their contracts are frozen while Dren's shipments get priority logistics."

"Legitimate grievance is useful. It's also directionless. I want it directed." Haldane opened a drawer and took out a tablet. "The DSA network — the podcast, the social media channels, the governors who've been using the language. How many people can we reach in forty-eight hours?"

"Millions. The DSA Today podcast alone has six million subscribers. The affiliated channels double that. But it's decentralized — we seeded it, we don't control it."

"We don't need to control it. We need to feed it. Draft three narratives. First: Whitfield authorized the delegation order on Dren's advice, which makes her either his puppet or his accomplice. That's already in the water from Beckett's subpoena. Amplify it. Second: the reconstruction is failing because Whitfield's administration is prioritizing Mars dependency over domestic manufacturing. Use the union grievances — they're real, they're documented, and they photograph well. Third —" He paused. "The Fist. The detection data. The delay."

Novak looked up. "You want to use the suppression narrative? That cuts close to us."

"It cuts close to Mercer. Mercer is gone. The institutional advocates are scattered. The trail leads to fellowships and conferences, not to this office. Saunders is already building that case — she'll publish it eventually. I'd rather the public hear it as outrage against Whitfield's government than as evidence against me."

"You want to get ahead of Saunders."

"I want to make the story about government failure, not about the Foundation. If the public is angry at Whitfield for the delayed response, they're not asking who caused the delay. They're asking why the president didn't prevent it. Redirect the anger upward."

Novak was quiet for a moment. "The protests will escalate. People are already angry. If we push the detection delay narrative into that crowd —"

"Then people get angrier. And anger directed at the White House is anger that isn't directed at us. Every day Whitfield spends defending herself is a day the investigation doesn't reach a courtroom." Haldane picked up the bourbon and poured two fingers. "The protests will grow. Some of them will get violent. That's not our problem — that's Whitfield's problem. And every breach, every incident, every shot fired at the White House fence makes her look weaker, makes reunification less plausible, and makes the regional structure more permanent."

"And if she leaves? Resigns, or Beckett actually gets the votes?"

"Then the presidency is vacant and the fragmentation becomes constitutional. The regional commanders become the de facto government. Our placements in those structures become the de facto administration. And no one is left with the authority to investigate a philanthropist in Dallas."

Novak absorbed this. The logic was clean, the way Haldane's logic was always clean — each step following from the last with the inevitability of arithmetic.

"I'll start tonight," Novak said. "The union channels first — they're the most credible. Then the DSA network. Forty-eight hours to saturate. By the time Beckett holds his next hearing, the crowd outside the White House will be ten times what it is now."

"Good." Haldane sipped the bourbon. "And Novak — make sure none of it traces back. Use the intermediaries. Use the existing infrastructure. The narrative has to feel organic."

"It always does," Novak said.

Novak didn't leave. He refilled his glass from the credenza — uninvited, which told Haldane the next topic was one Novak had been thinking about.

"The election," Novak said.

Haldane waited.

"Whitfield won but lost the popular vote — less than two percent. But the electoral margin was substantial because California barely showed up. Turnout in Los Angeles County was eleven percent. San Francisco, nine. The coastal reconstruction zones voted at rates that would embarrass a school board election. The interior zones voted angry — and angry voted for Turner. The states that function voted for Turner. The states that don't function couldn't elect anyone."

"And the reaction?"

"Exactly what we built it to be. Two reactions, both loud, both genuine, both funded through our committees." Novak pulled out his phone and scrolled through feeds. "Track one: 'Whitfield stole the election.' The interior zones are furious. Turner won the states that showed up. The electoral math only favors Whitfield because California's devastation suppressed the vote — and Whitfield's reconstruction priorities are the reason California is still devastated. The argument writes itself: the president won because her own failures prevented her opponents from voting."

"And track two?"

"Track two: 'Whitfield has a mandate.' Different committees, different channels, different audience. The election happened. The Constitution was followed. The result is the result. Anyone questioning the legitimacy of the election is questioning the Constitution itself — and in a time of crisis, questioning the Constitution is the same as advocating for the dissolution of the federal government."

"Both framings serve the same purpose," Haldane said.

"Both framings are being amplified through networks that don't know each other exists. The 'stolen election' narrative is running through the DSA affiliates and the reconstruction union channels. The 'decisive mandate' narrative is running through the mainstream political commentary and the institutional stability think tanks — three of which receive Foundation funding. Each side thinks the other is wrong. Each side is using our material to argue its case."

Haldane sipped the bourbon. "California."

"California is the prize. The state with the largest electoral delegation and the lowest turnout. Governor Martinez issued a statement last week — carefully worded, legally ambiguous, but the message was clear. California participated in the election under conditions that made meaningful participation impossible. The state does not contest the national result. The state does, however, reserve the right to evaluate the legitimacy of federal authority exercised under that result."

"That's secession language wrapped in a law review article."

"It's the first step. Martinez isn't a separatist — she's a pragmatist who watched her state burn and watched the federal government hand reconstruction authority to regional commanders who don't answer to her. She doesn't need to secede. She just needs to stop cooperating. And when the President issues a directive and California's response is 'we're evaluating the legitimacy of the authority behind that directive' — the practical effect is the same."

"Thomas in Jacksonville?"

"Thomas is using the election as cover for what he was already doing. Before November, he was a regional commander pushing for autonomy. After November, he's a regional commander who serves a president that half the country considers illegitimate. The election gave him a constituency argument — 'my zone voted for the other candidate, and the people I serve don't recognize this president's authority over their reconstruction.' He hasn't said that publicly. He doesn't need to. His actions say it every time he files a federal directive and ignores it."

"Chen?"

"Same logic, different grievance. Denver didn't burn, but Denver isn't getting rebuilt either. Chen's zone voted heavily for the challenger. The election result — Whitfield winning on suppressed coastal turnout — confirmed everything Chen's people believe: that the federal government prioritizes the coasts, the reconstruction apparatus serves Dren's logistics network, and the interior zones are invisible. The election made it personal."

Haldane set the glass down. "The election did exactly what it was supposed to do. It produced a result that both sides can reject. It gave every regional commander a legitimacy argument for independence. It made California functionally non-participatory in the federal system. And it happened without a single fraudulent vote. Every ballot was real. Every count was accurate. The manipulation was in the conditions, not the count."

"Cleanest election interference there is," Novak said. "Where nobody interfered."

He stood, picked up his jacket, and left through the service entrance.

Haldane turned back to the window. Dallas was rebuilding below him — cranes and scaffolding, the geometry of a world that was putting itself back together because it didn't know that the man in the fortieth-floor office had been the one to break it.

The investigation could run. Let it run. By the time it reached him, there would be no institution left with the power to act on what it found.

• • •

Pasadena.

Saunders took the blackout glasses off and looked around the rental. She sat down at the kitchen table and opened her messenger bag. She'd been carrying it the way Chloe carried her press pool bag —- like a limb, like something you didn't set down because setting it down meant you weren't ready.

She slid a printed list across the table to Chloe. Nine names, with titles and institutional affiliations.

"Who are these people?" Chloe asked.

"The loudest outgassing advocates. The ones who were first to claim the Fist was a natural body and last to abandon that position. Some held it for days after the spectrometric data made it untenable. Mercer, at Paranal, actively worked to suppress it. Hamner told me about conversations they'd had, arguments where Mercer pushed back hard against reclassification even when the evidence was overwhelming."

Chloe scanned the list. Names she recognized, names she didn't. Science advisors, committee chairs, agency deputies. People in positions that touched detection and response infrastructure.

"OK," she said. "What else?"

Saunders pulled up a second document on her tablet and turned it toward Chloe. A matrix —- the nine names down one side, dates and organizations across the top. Lines connecting each name to fellowships, conferences, advisory positions, board memberships.

"Every one of them traces back to Haldane," Saunders said. "Mercer attended the Haldane Foundation's Geneva conference in 2054. He's listed as a Fellow of the Haldane Institute for Strategic Resilience. His appointment to Paranal came six months after a Haldane-funded fellowship placed three candidates in the European Space Advisory Council."

She scrolled down the matrix.

"Williams —- NOAA committee chair. Haldane Foundation fellowship, 2051. Petrov —- Roscosmos advisory board. Attended two Haldane retreats. Chen —- UN Office for Outer Space Affairs. Appointed after a Haldane Institute recommendation. All nine. Different agencies, different countries, different years. Same pipeline."

Chloe looked at the matrix. The same network she'd been mapping —- the fellowships, the placements, the institutional seeding —- but applied to a specific function. These people hadn't just been placed in positions of influence. They'd been placed specifically to slow down the response to the Fist.

"He didn't just build a network," Chloe said. "He built a delay."

"There's one more thing about Mercer," Saunders said. "He wasn't just an advocate. He was there at the beginning. He co-discovered the Fist —- he was working alongside Robert Hamner at the Cerro Paranal observatory when it was first detected. And then he spent his time telling everyone it was cometary outgassing, and making sure they knew the consequences of contradicting that view."

Chloe looked up. "The man who found it was the man arguing it wasn't real?"

"Confirmed it. Hamner found it. But basically, yes," Saunders answered.

"Can Hamner confirm this?" Ashford asked.

"I'm sure he would," Saunders answered.

"Call him," Ashford said.

Saunders hesitated. Then she picked up her phone.

Hamner answered on the third ring. His voice was older than the last time she'd heard it —- not aged, exactly, but compressed by the weight of what had happened since Paranal.

"Jessica?" he asked.

"Robert."

A pause. The pause of two people who hadn't spoken since the world almost ended and didn't know how to bridge the distance.

"Wow, this is, uh, unexpected. Is everything all right?" he asked.

"I'm working," she said. It was the truest answer she had. "Robert, I need to ask you about Mercer."

The pause was longer this time. "Brian."

"Yes."

"He resigned. Couple of weeks before the flyby. Sent a one-paragraph email to the director —- effective immediately, no reason given. I tried calling him. His number was disconnected. I tried his home address —- the place in Leiden —- and the neighbors said he'd moved. No forwarding address." Another pause. "I haven't heard from him since."

"Was there anything before the resignation? Anything that changed?"

Hamner was quiet. "He was different after the reclassification debate. When the spectrometric data came back and the outgassing theory started collapsing, he didn't —- he didn't come around the way the others did. Most of the outgassing advocates dropped it when the evidence became overwhelming. Brian seemed … reluctant. I didn't understand, and when I asked him about it, he didn't have a good answer. I chalked it up to cognitive dissonance. He had all the signs."

"Why do you think it was so hard for him?" Saunders asked.

"I thought he'd staked his professional reputation on it being natural. I gave him credit for stubbornness." A pause. "I shouldn't have. Something else was going on. Something seemed … off. I just didn't know what."

"Thank you, Robert."

"Jessica." He said her name the way he'd said it at Paranal. "Take care of yourself."

"That's the plan," she said. The same words she'd used on the mountain in Chile, a lifetime ago.

She ended the call. Ashford was watching her.

"Mercer was pre-positioned," Ashford said. "Haldane put him at the observatory before the Fist arrived. He was there to find it or to bury it."

"That's a conclusion, but it isn't contradicted by any of the evidence," Saunders said.

"And when it was found, he tried to delay alarm," Ashford said.

"Then he vanished. Which is odd. We should try to track him down," Saunders said.

"We? We're a team? You know what happened to me, are you sure you want that kind of heat?" Ashford asked.

Saunders didn't answer immediately. She looked at the files on the table. At Okafor by the window, the fact of his presence a testament to what happened when you got close to this story.

"My source at the ESA stopped returning calls two months ago," Saunders said. "I told myself she'd gotten cold feet. I didn't follow up. I didn't check." She paused. "I've been telling myself that's not the same thing as what happened to your friend. But it might be."

She was quiet for a moment longer.

"In for a penny," she said.

"OK. So long as you understand what you're walking into," Ashford said. "People around this investigation are dying. Not figuratively."

"I understand," Saunders said.

Three fronts now. Dren's technical investigation —- the relay exploit, the firmware sabotage, the corporate trace to Haldane. Chloe's organizational investigation —- the foundation network, the shell companies, the Nevada bunker. And Saunders's institutional investigation —- the political interference, the outgassing delay, the placed operatives who'd slowed humanity's response to an extinction-level threat.

All three pointed at the same man.

Chloe looked at the files spread across the table. At Saunders, who'd been working alone for eight months and looked like it. At Okafor, who was still watching the street with the professional patience of a man for whom vigilance was a resting state.

"We need to talk to Dren," she said.

Okafor turned from the window. "I can set up the channel. There's a lag —- Mars is about sixteen minutes out right now. It won't be a conversation. It'll be messages."

"That's fine," Ashford said. "Start with this: we have three independent lines of evidence converging on Charles Haldane. We need to coordinate."

Okafor nodded and began composing the transmission.

• • •

Ares City.

Dren received Okafor's report at 13:22 Ares time.

The report was factual, detailed, and precisely what Dren had not wanted to hear. Oliver had arrived at Ashford's apartment before Okafor reached Ashford. The boyfriend was dead. Oliver had been recorded on hidden cameras. The footage was in police custody and had leaked to the media. Ashford was in a safe house with the investigation backup and a researcher named Saunders. She was continuing her work.

Dren sat with the report for a long time.

He had deployed Okafor specifically to prevent this from happening. He'd underestimated the threat. He'd underestimated the speed at which Haldane, obviously it was Haldane, had acted.

The gap was decision time. Dren had identified the Haldane connection, traced Ashford's investigation, recognized the danger, and deployed Okafor —- all in the correct sequence, all with the correct logic. But he had assessed the threat to Ashford as surveillance-level, not violence-level. "Keep an eye on her. See if anyone else is keeping an eye on her." Those had been his instructions. Watch. Don't engage.

A man was dead because of that miscalculation.

He filed the error. He did not rationalize it. He did not distribute blame. He adjusted.

Okafor, he dictated, opening the channel.

New instructions. Ashford is no longer a surveillance asset. She is a protected witness. Your priority is her physical security. If anyone approaches her —- anyone —- you assess and respond. You do not wait for authorization.

She has an additional independent line of evidence. All lines are converging on Haldane. Tell her I have a third. We will coordinate with this encrypted channel, no third parties. Mars lag means we work in message bursts —- she sends what she has, I

respond when I can. No real-time discussion until I can get someone closer.

Lastly—- the man who was in the apartment. He will obviously go to ground. But that does not remove him as a threat. As long as he is on the board you need to be vigilant. Let me know if you require additional assets.

The channel closed.

Dren sat at his desk. A man was dead in Los Angeles because Dren had said "keep an eye on her" instead of "protect her." That was the gap. Not kilometers or light-minutes. Judgment.

He would not make that error again.

• • •

The White House.

Beckett was on the wallscreen.

He was standing at a podium outside the hearing room, flanked by two junior members of his committee, delivering a statement with the practiced cadence of a man who had been waiting for this moment and wanted everyone to know he hadn't rehearsed it.

"What we've seen over the past several weeks of testimony paints a deeply troubling picture," Beckett said. "Sweetheart deals with Dren Industries that bypassed standard procurement oversight. A pattern of executive decisions made without consultation, without transparency, and without accountability. And serious, serious questions about whether the President's judgment during the crisis reflected the kind of leadership this country deserves."

Whitfield watched from the couch in her office. Hunt was standing by the window, arms crossed, watching the same screen.

A reporter called out from the press gaggle. "Senator, are you talking about impeachment?"

Beckett paused. The pause was theatrical —- he already knew the answer.

"That's certainly on the table," he said. "But I want to be very clear. Based on the evidence my committee has reviewed, I'm not sure removal is sufficient. Removal and prosecution look warranted. The American people deserve to know that nobody —- nobody —- is above the law, regardless of the crisis they claim to have managed."

Hunt looked at Whitfield. She didn't look back.

Her hands were in her lap. They were shaking. It had been getting worse for weeks —- since the hearings started, since the reconstruction numbers turned, since the nights compressed into two- and three-hour fragments that left her more tired than no sleep at all. She pressed her fingers together harder and the tremor didn't stop. It wasn't invisible anymore. Her fingers moved against each other in small, involuntary contractions that she couldn't suppress by pressing harder.

Her phone buzzed. She glanced at it. Three missed calls from the press office. Two from Senator Aldrin's office. One from the regional commander in Jacksonville, the fourth this week, about reconstruction allocations that were six months behind schedule. A text from her communications director that read simply: *Call me. Urgent.*

"Turn it off," she said.

Hunt picked up the remote and killed the wallscreen. Beckett's face vanished. The room was quiet.

"Ma'am," Hunt said. He said it carefully, the way he said everything carefully now, measuring each word against her mood the way a navigator measures wind against heading. "When did you last sleep?"

"I sleep."

"When did you last sleep for more than three hours?"

She didn't answer.

"The press office needs a response to Beckett by end of day. Mitchell wants to know if you're doing the reconstruction briefing tomorrow or if we push it. And Caldwell at NSC has flagged three new threat assessments that require your—-"

"I'm aware of what requires my attention, Wolsey."

"I know you are. I'm asking about your capacity to—-"

"Et tu, Brute?"

It came out harder than she'd intended. Louder. Hunt stopped talking. The room was very quiet. She could hear the ventilation system and the distant sound of a security rotation changing in the hallway and her own breathing, which was faster than it should have been.

Hunt didn't flinch. He stood by the window and waited. He'd worked for her for eleven years. He'd seen her deliver the flyby address to three hundred million people without a tremor in her voice. He'd seen her authorize the Mars defense budget at four in the morning on two hours of sleep. He'd seen her handle Beckett's first round of hearings with the controlled precision of a surgeon.

He had not seen this.

"I'm sorry," she said. The anger drained as fast as it had arrived, leaving something flatter and more tired behind it. "That was uncalled for."

"It was," Hunt agreed.

She looked at her hands. The tremor was worse when she looked at it, as though observation amplified the signal. She put her hands flat on the cushion beside her and pressed down.

"I'll do the reconstruction briefing," she said. "Draft a response to Beckett —- something measured, nothing combative. And tell Caldwell I'll review the threat assessments tonight."

"Yes, ma'am."

Hunt turned toward the door. He stopped.

"For what it's worth," he said, "Beckett doesn't have the votes. Not yet."

"Not yet," she repeated.

He left. Whitfield sat on the couch in her office and looked at the blank wallscreen where Beckett had been talking about prosecution, and her hands continued to shake.

CHAPTER 13

Actions

January 2061.

• • •

February 4th, 2060. Dallas.

The transmission went out at 01:18 Central, routed through the belt relay.

Haldane sat at the terminal in his study and composed the report the way the protocol required — structured, declarative, each concept encoded in the mathematical framework the Tolek had provided. No ambiguity. No rhetoric. The protocol didn't accommodate rhetoric. It translated concepts, relationships, and states. It did not translate excuses.

REPORT — STANDARD CHANNEL

Deflection operation successful. Target object trajectory altered beyond direct-strike threshold. Waves 1. Deflection vehicles are operating at increased standoff distance of 1,000 KM. Adjust your defenses accordingly.

The extinction program as specified is no longer achievable within the current operational window. Current deflection has a near planet miss of 90KM. At this distance there will be planetary damage. I am looking at methods to increase this damage.

He transmitted.

The round-trip delay meant thirty-six hours before a response could arrive. He waited.

The response arrived thirty-seven hours later.

DIRECTIVE — COMMAND CHANNEL

Your report is received. The deflection of the primary instrument represents a deviation from specification. The commitment was extinction-grade surface impact. The commitment has not been met.

Assessment: negative-value agents within the target population demonstrated capability exceeding projected parameters. This is noted.

Current status of all negative-value agents: scheduled for termination under revised operational timeline.

Haldane read it twice. *Scheduled for termination.* The Tolek didn't use that phrase loosely. In their framework, termination was an engineering state — a component removed from a system because it no longer served the specification. Dren. Whitfield. Every person who had participated in the deflection. They were components now, scheduled for removal.

Unless Haldane could change the specification.

HOWEVER.

Your corrective action: ensure maximum proximity during atmospheric pass. The difference between a clean miss and a grazing approach is the difference between a wounded population and a crippled one. A crippled population is manageable. A healthy one is not.

Additional directive follows.

He composed his response carefully. The protocol required precision, but it also allowed for proposals — the Tolek had always been willing to hear alternatives, provided the alternatives were structural rather than sentimental.

PROPOSAL — STANDARD CHANNEL

The near-approach will wound the target population. The degree of wound depends on the geometry I am working to maximize proximity.

But I propose a revision to the post-impact strategy.

Current plan assumes the target population will be functionally destroyed. It will not be. Even a maximum-proximity pass will leave billions alive, infrastructure partially intact, and institutional capacity recoverable within 5-10 local years.

A wounded population that reunifies is more dangerous than a healthy one that was never threatened. The near-miss will reveal the existence of an external threat. Concealment is no longer possible. A unified response to that knowledge could produce exactly the coordinated defense capability your timeline requires you to prevent.

I propose fragmentation as the corrective strategy. I will use the reconstruction period to prevent reunification. Institutional placements are already in position. The Foundation's infrastructure is designed for exactly this purpose. I need approximately 2.1 local years to ensure the following conditions are met:

No unified military command capable of coordinated defense

No integrated defense infrastructure spanning more than one regional authority

No single governance structure with the authority to mobilize a species-level response

These three conditions, if maintained through the arrival window, will ensure the target population cannot resist direct action regardless of their awareness of the threat.

I am requesting a revised operational mandate: fragmentation and suppression, replacing extinction.

He transmitted. He waited.

The response came.

DIRECTIVE — COMMAND CHANNEL

Your proposal is received and conditionally accepted.

Conditions:

The three fragmentation requirements you have specified will be treated as engineering tolerances. Failure to maintain any one of the three within the 2.1-year window will be treated as a deviation from specification.

You will provide status reports at intervals not exceeding 60 local days. Reports will include quantitative assessment of fragmentation progress against the three requirements.

The negative-value agents remain scheduled for termination under the revised timeline. Your fragmentation strategy should account for their continued operation during the interim period. If you can neutralize their effectiveness through institutional means, termination can be deferred. If you cannot, we will address them directly upon arrival.

Assessment of your operational status: you are not indispensable. You are conditionally useful. The conditions are the three requirements you have specified and the timeline you have proposed. Meet them and your status continues. Fail and your status terminates.

Promises are structural. A commitment is an engineering specification. You have specified your own.

Haldane read it three times.

Conditionally useful. Useful — the way a tool was useful, for exactly as long as it performed its function. The moment it didn't, it was replaced. The Tolek didn't fire employees. They decommissioned components.

He had 2.1 years. Three conditions. Sixty-day reporting intervals. And a fleet that would arrive at the end of that window expecting to find a species too fragmented to resist.

He closed the console and returned to Dallas. He had five days before Wave 3 fired, and in those five days he needed to ensure that the geometry of the flyby produced the maximum possible damage — because the Tolek's revised mandate required a crippled population, and a crippled population required a close pass, and a close pass required one digit changed in a firmware update that was already being prepared for upload.

He picked up the phone and called Vickers.

• • •

February 9th, 2060. Dallas.

The trajectory data arrived through the relay network at 3:42 AM Central. Haldane was awake. He'd been awake since the 3rd, when the first wave of belt platforms had fired — Dren's secret arsenal, pulsed fusion drives, pellet clouds designed to ablate the Fist's surface and nudge its trajectory by fractions of a degree.

The fractions had been enough. Wave 1 had shifted the Fist's trajectory beyond the threshold for a direct strike. Wave 2 — thirteen platforms, fired the previous day — had been largely destroyed. The intelligence he'd provided the Tolek had done its work. Eight of the thirteen platforms had been killed by the Fist's weapon before they could fire. The few that survived had added almost nothing to the deflection.

But Wave 1 alone had done enough. The deflection was working. If Wave 3 fired as designed, the combined effect would push the Fist into a clean miss. No damage. No crisis. No mechanism for the program to continue.

Twenty-five years. The Council's decision, the Ark, the Founders, the fellowship placements, the institutional delay network — all of it built for a strike that was now going to miss.

Haldane picked up the phone.

Vickers answered on the second ring.

"You told me Dren would fail," Haldane said.

Silence.

"You told me the belt platforms were insufficient. You told me the deflection math didn't close. You told me the trajectory would hold."

"The capability exceeded our projections. Dren's design was—"

"I don't care about projections. Wave 3 fires in March. What can you do?"

Vickers was quiet for a moment. When he spoke, his voice had changed — not defensive now, operational.

"Wave 3 is getting a firmware update — revised position parameters for the new 3,500-kilometer standoff distance. Dren's people pushed the range out after what happened to Wave 2. The translation layer has to be rebuilt for the new geometry. Our man is in the update chain. If he introduces an error, the kind of thing that looks like a mistake — every firing solution on every platform calculates the wrong flight time. He can make the platforms fire early. At those closing speeds, early means the pellets hit forward of the midpoint. Torque instead of lateral push. The Fist rotates instead of deflecting cleanly. A sideways pass through the atmosphere at the current predicted distance will cause significant damage."

"Define significant."

"Firestorms. Tsunamis. Seismic disruption. Atmospheric effects lasting years. Millions dead, possibly hundreds of millions, depending on the final geometry. Civilization doesn't end, but it breaks. The reconstruction takes decades. The institutional structures we've built become essential."

Haldane sat with that. A near-miss. Something messier — a wound instead of an ending. But a wound deep enough to keep the program viable. The Ark would still matter. The placements would still function. The reconstruction would need exactly the institutional framework he'd spent twenty years building.

"Do it," he said. "Make it turn."

"The death toll—"

"I heard you."

"If Dren's people monitor the Mars platform telemetry, they'll see the parameter change. The firing window adjustment will be visible."

"Will they see it in time to correct?"

"Unlikely. The upload locks forty-eight hours before intercept. By the time anyone reviews the telemetry, Wave 3 will have already fired."

"Then it doesn't matter what they see afterward. They'll investigate. They'll find the tilt. But by then the Fist will have already passed, and whatever it does will be done. Tell our operative to make it seem accidental."

"Understood."

He ended the call.

He sat with what he'd just set in motion. One seemingly simple mistake would make thirteen platforms fire early, and the object that was supposed to end the human race would instead wound it. Millions would die. The geometry would do the work.

He could live with that. He'd been living with it for twenty-five years.

• • •

July 2060. Dallas.

The transmission arrived at 03:22 Central through the belt relay.

Haldane read it in his bed.

QUERY — COMMAND CHANNEL

Anomalous activity detected at the primary instrument. Breach attempt in progress. Origin and nature of the intrusion is unknown.

Identify and explain.

Haldane stared at the screen. Someone was trying to get into the Fist. He hadn't known about it. There was only one person with the capability and the motive to send a mission to the Fist.

He composed his response.

REPORT — STANDARD CHANNEL

I have no knowledge of this activity. My assessment: the most probable source is Dren. He has the infrastructure, the proximity, and the motive. I will investigate and report.

He transmitted.

A response never came.

He waited three days. The belt relay was silent. He suspected he knew why. Whoever was on the Fist had likely blown its antenna system. He'd have to go old school, with all the risks that contained.

He returned to Nevada. The Ark's direct transmission system — the old method, the original method, the one left by the scouts — was still operational. Detectable. Dangerous. The method he'd abandoned a decade ago because it was the equivalent of shouting into the sky and hoping nobody else was listening.

He sat at the console and transmitted.

REPORT — DIRECT CHANNEL

Belt relay is non-responsive. Reverting to direct transmission. Requesting status.

The response came in thirty-seven hours. The Tolek were not pleased.

DIRECTIVE — DIRECT CHANNEL

Primary instrument ceased submitting telemetry. Your ignorance of this operation is not an excuse. Your mandate includes awareness of all significant actions by the negative-value agents. You failed to anticipate this. You failed to prevent it.

You will continue on direct transmission.

Your operational status remains: conditionally useful. The conditions are narrowing.

Haldane read it and felt the ground shift beneath him.

The belt relay was dead. The system he'd spent a decade building — the signal chain that routed his communications through the belt to the fleet, invisible to Earth monitoring, the backbone of his operational security — was gone. Dren had destroyed the hardware. He was certain of that now. Dren had sent a crew to the Fist, and that crew had done enough damage to kill the relay.

Every transmission from Nevada would be a signal pointed at a specific bearing in the sky, broadcasting on frequencies that anyone with the right equipment could intercept. If Whitfield's people were monitoring the fleet's bearing — and they would be, eventually, because someone always looked — they would find him.

The conditions were narrowing.

• • •

Dallas. January 2061.

Haldane made six calls in three days. Each one tailored to the audience, each one designed to widen a fracture that already existed.

The first was to Thomas in Jacksonville.

Thomas was the easiest. He'd been operating as a de facto independent authority since October — running his own reconstruction priorities, negotiating his own supply contracts, ignoring federal coordination requests that didn't serve his sector. He didn't need to be convinced. He needed to be encouraged.

"General, the Foundation's reconstruction audit for your sector is finished," Haldane said. "I'm sending it to your advisory board. The numbers are clear — Jacksonville's recovery rate is thirty-one percent ahead of the national average. Your logistics model is working. The federal coordination framework is holding you back."

"I've been saying that for months," Thomas said.

"You've been saying it politely. The audit gives you the data to say it formally. Extended regional autonomy isn't a request — it's a performance-based conclusion. You're doing better without Washington than with it. The numbers prove it."

Thomas was quiet for a moment. "And if Whitfield pushes back?"

Beckett's hearings are pulling the institutional framework apart. By the time she's in a position to push back, you'll have established a precedent that's harder to reverse than to accept."

"Send the audit," Thomas said.

The second call was to Chen in Denver.

Chen was bitter, and bitterness was useful. Denver hadn't burned — the flyby damage corridor had missed Colorado entirely

— but Denver wasn't getting rebuilt either. The reconstruction funding flowed to the coasts, to the cities that had been destroyed, to the infrastructure that Dren's logistics network prioritized. Denver sat in the middle of the continent, intact and ignored, watching federal resources flow past it to places that no longer existed.

"General Chen, the Foundation has been tracking reconstruction allocation patterns for the past six months," Haldane said. "The data shows a consistent coastal bias in federal funding distribution. Eighty-three percent of reconstruction dollars are going to Pacific and Atlantic corridor projects. Interior sectors are receiving maintenance-level funding at best."

"Tell me something I don't know."

"What you don't know is that the allocation model is Dren's. His logistics network determines priority routing. His infrastructure assessments determine funding levels. The federal coordination office signs off on his recommendations without modification. Your sector isn't being neglected by Washington. It's being deprioritized by a private company that doesn't answer to you."

Silence. Then: "You have documentation?"

"The Foundation's analysis is ready for your logistics office. It maps every allocation decision to its source recommendation. The pattern is consistent and documented."

"Send it."

The third call was to Reeves in San Diego.

Reeves was different from Thomas and Chen. He wasn't angry and he wasn't bitter. He was worried. San Diego's reconstruction depended entirely on Dren Industries' supply chain — materials, equipment, technical expertise, all flowing through Dren's logistics pipeline. Reeves had built his recovery plan around that pipeline, and now he was watching Beckett's hearings raise questions about whether the pipeline would continue.

"General, the Foundation is concerned about supply chain continuity in your sector," Haldane said. "Beckett's hearings are creating political risk for Dren Industries. If the dependency narrative gains traction — if Congress acts on it — the logistics network your reconstruction depends on could face regulatory disruption."

"That's my nightmare," Reeves said.

"It doesn't have to be. The Foundation can help you build redundant supply pathways — alternative sourcing, regional manufacturing capacity, logistics routing that doesn't depend on a single provider. Not to replace Dren's network. To supplement it. Insurance against political disruption."

"And the Foundation's interest in this?"

"Reconstruction stability. Same as yours. If your sector's recovery stalls because of a political fight in Washington, everyone loses."

Reeves agreed to a planning meeting. He didn't ask who would fund the redundant pathways. The answer was obvious, and obvious answers didn't need to be spoken.

The international calls were shorter. Zhao in Beijing received an analysis of Dren's reconstruction infrastructure and its implications for Chinese technological independence — the suggestion, never stated directly, that relying on a private Western company for planetary defense created a dependency that no sovereign nation should accept. Zhao listened, asked two questions about the data methodology, and ended the call without committing to anything. He didn't need to commit. The analysis would do the work.

Volkov in Moscow received a briefing on the Foundation's European partnerships and an invitation to a reconstruction technology conference in Geneva — a conference that would, coincidentally, provide a forum for discussing alternatives to the current Dren-dependent infrastructure model. Volkov accepted immediately. Moscow had been hostile to Dren's influence since the flyby. The conference gave that hostility a respectable venue.

Weber in Berlin received a private assessment of the European Space Agency's planetary defense contingency planning — specifically, its gaps. The assessment was accurate, thorough, and deeply alarming. It concluded that Europe's current defense posture depended entirely on Dren's platforms and that no independent European capability existed or was being developed. Weber read it and called her defense minister before the day was out.

Six calls. Six fractures, widened by millimeters. None of them would produce immediate results. All of them would produce momentum — the slow, grinding pressure of institutional actors reaching conclusions that had been prepared for them by people they didn't know were preparing them.

Haldane poured a bourbon and didn't drink it. The glass sat on the credenza while he reviewed the next phase.

CHAPTER 14

Escalation

Washington, D.C.

• • •

The state visit had been Dren's idea.

Whitfield had resisted for two weeks. The optics of a presidential trip to Mars — even framed as diplomatic, even framed as a routine inspection of reconstruction-critical infrastructure — would feed every narrative Beckett was building. But the calculus had changed. The calls for her resignation were growing from within her own coalition. The investigations into the Fist response were multiplying. Someone had leaked Dren's early detection data, and the narrative was shifting from "we survived" to "why weren't we better prepared."

And then there were the protests.

They'd started in November. A few dozen people on the Ellipse — reconstruction workers, mostly, union affiliates from the mid-Atlantic projects who'd seen their contracts frozen while Dren Industries shipments continued to flow on priority logistics. They set up with hand-lettered signs and a megaphone that didn't work half the time. The Park Police let them stay because they were orderly and because dispersing reconstruction workers with cameras present was an image nobody needed.

By December the crowd had grown. Hundreds during the day. The signs were printed now, the same design repeated across dozens of hands — ACCOUNTABILITY NOT RECONSTRUCTION, WHERE WAS THE WARNING, WHO KNEW. Novak, through a series of cutouts, had organized a supply chain: portable heaters, food trucks, rotating schedules that kept bodies on the Ellipse twenty-four hours a day. The megaphone worked now. She could hear it from the Residence, through the bulletproof glass, a voice reciting the names of cities that had been destroyed, one by one, in alphabetical order. Anchorage. Honolulu. Long Beach. Los Angeles. Oakland. Portland. San Diego. San Francisco. Seattle. It took two minutes to get through the list. Then it started again.

And behind the protests, the election.

Whitfield had won. The result was certified, the inauguration conducted under armed guard at a stripped-down ceremony inside the Capitol — no parade, no outdoor address, no Mall crowd. The security assessment had determined that an outdoor inauguration was indefensible, and the imagery of a president sworn in behind blast glass and sniper positions was worse than the imagery of a president sworn in behind closed doors.

She'd lost the popular vote by less than two percent. The electoral margin was comfortable, large enough that the Constitutional process was unambiguous. But the margin was built on absence. California's turnout had been eleven percent in Los Angeles County. Single digits in San Francisco. The state's fifty-four electoral votes went to Whitfield because the people who did vote were concentrated in the communities Dren's logistics network had kept functional — the reconstruction hubs, the agricultural support zones, the areas where satellite communications and supply routing made life possible. The rest of California — the areas where the infrastructure was gone and the polling stations were rubble — didn't vote because they couldn't.

Turner had conceded. Gracefully, promptly, in a speech that was everything a concession should be — dignified, patriotic, a call for unity. He meant every word. He'd run a clean campaign on legitimate grievances and lost an election in extraordinary circumstances, and he was a good enough man to accept the result.

The country wasn't as good.

The "stolen election" narrative had started before the ballots were counted — seeded through DSA affiliate channels and reconstruction union networks that Whitfield's intelligence team would eventually trace to Novak's committee infrastructure, but not yet. The argument was simple: Whitfield won because California couldn't vote, and California couldn't vote because Whitfield's reconstruction policies had failed the state. The president was elected by the disaster she'd mismanaged. The logic was circular and emotionally irresistible.

The counter-narrative — "decisive mandate, respect the Constitution" — came from the institutional stability commentators, the think tanks, the mainstream editorial boards. It was equally well-funded, equally well-distributed, and served exactly the same purpose: division. Every op-ed defending the election's legitimacy produced three responses attacking it. Every response produced a counter-response. The debate consumed the political oxygen that should have been spent on reconstruction, on governance, on the work of holding a fractured country together.

Governor Martinez in California had issued her statement the week after the election. Every directive from Washington arrived in Sacramento and entered a review process that had no deadline and produced no action. The practical effect was the same as independence, achieved without a single unconstitutional act.

The megaphone on the Ellipse didn't mention the election. It didn't need to. The same anger that fed the protests fed the legitimacy debate, and both fed the fragmentation that was pulling the country apart from the inside.

The first breach happened on a Tuesday, at 2 AM.

Whitfield was in the Residence. She hadn't slept. The megaphone on the Ellipse was inaudible from the bedroom — the glass was rated for blast overpressure — but she knew it was running because it was always running, and knowing was enough. She was staring at the ceiling when the alarm sounded.

Two short tones, then the continuous. The sound that meant the perimeter had been compromised.

She sat up. The door opened before she could reach it — an agent, young, moving fast.

"Ma'am, we have a breach. North Lawn. Single subject. Please remain here."

She sat on the edge of the bed and listened to the radio traffic coming through the agent's earpiece. She could hear it from three feet away — the tinny, compressed voices of men running across frozen grass in the dark.

"Subject on the lawn. Past the fence line. No weapon visible. Moving toward the North Portico."

A pause.

"Subject is down. Agents have contact. Subject is not resisting."

Another pause. Longer.

"Subject is a male, forties, no ID, no weapon. He's — he's saying a name. He's saying his daughter's name."

The agent by the door listened, then looked at her. "All clear, ma'am. Single individual. He's in custody."

Whitfield sat on the edge of the bed. A man with a dead daughter had climbed the wrought iron fence of the White House at two in the morning because grief had turned into forward momentum and he had nowhere else to point it. He hadn't brought a weapon. He hadn't brought a plan. He'd brought himself and a name he couldn't stop saying.

She didn't go back to sleep.

The second breach was organized.

It came on a Thursday afternoon, three weeks later. Whitfield was in the Oval, reviewing the reconstruction briefing packet. The megaphone on the Ellipse was running the city list. Los Angeles. Oakland. Portland.

The alarm sounded. Two short tones. Continuous.

This time the agent didn't come to the door. The door came to her — two agents, moving fast, one on each side.

"Ma'am, multiple subjects. Three approach vectors. We're moving you to the PEOC."

They moved her. Through the corridor, down the stairs, through the East Wing to the hardened door. The Presidential Emergency Operations Center was already active — screens showing camera feeds from the perimeter, radio traffic on the overhead speakers, Hunt standing at the far end of the table with a phone pressed to his ear.

On the screens, she could see it. The North fence — two figures climbing the wrought iron, one already at the top, straddling the spikes. The South fence — a group, eight or nine, pushing against the barrier near the gate. The East side — four more scaling the fence in a section where the razor wire had been pulled down with a weighted rope thrown from outside.

Fifteen people. Three angles. Coordinated.

"Breach sector seven. Subjects on the North Lawn."

"South perimeter compromised. Subjects over the fence. Moving toward the South Portico."

"East breach — four subjects over the fence. Agents engaging."

Whitfield stood at the table and watched the screens. The camera feeds showed agents converging — running across the lawns, the practiced sprint of people who had trained for exactly this. The subjects on the North Lawn were tackled within seconds. The South group made it further — past the fence, across the drive, almost to the portico steps before the agents reached them. The struggle was brief and physical and filmed from three angles by cameras that didn't blink.

"Lethal force authorized, hold, hold —"

The East group was the last to be contained. One of them — a woman, young, her face distorted by something that was either rage or terror — made it to the building wall before an agent caught her arm and brought her down. She hit the ground hard. She didn't stop fighting. Two agents held her while a third secured her hands.

"All subjects contained. Perimeter is being restored."

Four minutes. The grounds had been unsecured for four minutes.

Whitfield sat down at the table. Hunt put the phone down and looked at her.

"Fifteen. Organized. They climbed the fence at two locations while a third group went over the east barrier." He paused. "These aren't random. They had a signal. They moved on the same count."

"Citizens?" Whitfield asked.

"Yes, ma'am. But organized. And not necessarily organic," he replied.

"Perfect," she sighed.

The lockdown lasted two hours.

• • •

Arlington, Virginia. Two weeks later.

The apartment was a one-bedroom off Columbia Pike, second floor, the blinds drawn. The heating unit rattled against the wall and the coffee table was covered with printouts — satellite photos of the White House grounds, a hand-drawn overlay of the fence line with distances marked in red, and a spiral notebook with response times written in two columns.

Six men sat in the living room. Three on the couch, two on folding chairs, one standing at the kitchen counter with his arms crossed.

The one standing was Garrett Cole. Ex-Army, 3rd Infantry Division — ten years, two deployments, a combat action badge, and a medical discharge that had more to do with what he'd said to a captain than what had happened to his knee. After the discharge he'd worked reconstruction in Baltimore for eighteen months until his contract was frozen. After that he'd found the DSA channels, and the podcasts, and the forums where the anger was specific and detailed and aimed at names. Whitfield. Dren. The system that had survived the flyby and used the survival to consolidate power while people like him rebuilt roads for wages that didn't cover rent.

He'd been on the Ellipse since November. First as a protester. Then as something else.

"Walk me through it," he said.

Dario spread the satellite printout flat and placed the notebook beside it. Dario was the planner — an electrician from Fairfax who'd lost his house in the reconstruction rezoning and had a methodical mind that Cole had recognized immediately.

"We've been watching for six weeks," Dario said. "Two tests. Two data sets."

He tapped the notebook. The first column was headed *Test 1 — solo, 2 AM.* Below it: response times, agent positions, the route the Service had taken to reach the subject. The number of agents who responded. The positions they'd come from. The gap between the alarm and the first physical contact.

"The solo run gave us the night response. Single subject, no weapon, non-threatening approach. Thirty seconds from fence breach to contact. Four agents from the North Lawn post, two from the gate. The east side was unmanned for almost a minute."

He tapped the second column. *Test 2 — group, 3 angles, afternoon.*

"The group run gave us the daytime response and the coordinated protocol. Three approach vectors, fifteen subjects. They pulled agents from every post on the perimeter. The east barrier was unmonitored for over two minutes while they dealt with the south and north groups. The shift change at the south gate — 3:15 — creates a four-minute overlap where outgoing agents have left their positions and incoming agents haven't reached theirs."

Cole looked at the notebook. Two operations he'd orchestrated from inside the crowd. The solo man had been a broken father who'd needed a bus ticket and someone to tell him the president needed to hear his daughter's name. The fifteen had been recruited from three different protest camps and given a time and a direction. None of them knew they were probes. All of them had real grief. Cole had used that grief the way a locksmith uses tension — applied in the right direction, just enough force to turn the mechanism.

He didn't feel good about it. He filed that where he filed everything that didn't serve the operation.

"The night response is thinner," Cole said. "Fewer agents on the perimeter. The southeast corner goes unmanned faster."

"Significantly faster. The night watch is roughly sixty percent of the daytime detail. They compensate with thermal cameras and motion sensors on the fence line, but human response is slower. And they don't expect a coordinated assault at night — they expect lone actors. Grief cases. The protocols are built around that assumption."

"Good," Cole said. "We're going to break that assumption."

He looked at the other four. Briggs and Lenton on the couch — both ex-military, both reconstruction, both carrying the same quiet fury that Cole recognized because he saw it in the mirror. Harmon on the folding chair — younger, no military background, but steady. And Dario, who would stay with the car.

"We go at night," Cole said. "Zero-dark. Gate diversion to pull the response, same as the group test — bodies at the fence, noise, confusion. While they're processing the gate, we go through the southeast corner."

"Weapons," he said.

Briggs stood and went to the bedroom. He came back with two duffel bags and set them on the coffee table beside the satellite photos. He unzipped both.

Four converted AR-platform rifles — semi-auto converted to full-auto, folding stocks, thirty-round magazines. Eight additional magazines. Four compact handguns as sidearms with three magazines each. Four sets of night-vision goggles — military surplus, Gen 3, equipment that wasn't supposed to leave a base but always did. And four shaped charges — compact, directional, each one capable of blowing through ballistic glass in a single detonation. A handheld plasma cutter for the wrought iron fence bars.

"Rifles are the primary," Briggs said. "Two hundred and forty rounds for the ARs, plus the sidearms. NV for all four. The shaped charges are for the windows — one each. Place it, back up, detonate. The ballistic glass goes in one shot. We're inside in seconds."

Cole picked up one of the rifles and checked the action. The conversion was professional — someone who knew the platform. The folding stock would keep it concealable in a pack until they needed it. He picked up a set of NV goggles and turned them over. Clean. Current.

"How did we get these?" Harmon asked.

"Same people who gave us the satellite photos and the shift-change schedule," Cole said. "We didn't source this. We didn't build this. It was handed to us by people with access to equipment that doesn't walk off a base without help. Don't ask again, or I might start to think you aren't quite what you seem."

He set the rifle down and tapped the satellite overlay.

"Here's how it works. 2 AM. The gate group approaches on foot from the south — eight people, same profile as the first two tests. They look like protesters who've been drinking and decided to rush the fence. The night watch responds. They pull from the static posts to reinforce the gate. The southeast corner opens."

He drew a line with his finger from the southeast fence to the building.

"We cut the fence with the plasma cutter. Across the lawn in darkness — NV on, no lights. The lawn is ninety meters from the fence to the south wall. We cover it in under thirty seconds. At the building, we split into pairs. Briggs and I take the window to the left of the south entrance. Harmon and Lenton take the one to the right. Place the shaped charges, fall back, detonate simultaneously. Both windows go. We're inside the building."

"Then what?" Lenton asked.

"Then we move fast." Cole shifted the overlay to a floor plan — hand-drawn, annotated, assembled from publicly available architectural references and whatever the logistics chain had provided. "When the alarm goes, the Service moves the president. The Residence is in the center of the second floor. They take her down through interior corridors to the PEOC — the bunker under the East Wing. The route goes through the ground floor central corridor, east toward the East Wing, then down. That corridor is our target. If we're inside the building within sixty seconds of the alarm, we can reach the central corridor before they complete the transfer."

"And if they've already moved her?" Harmon asked.

"If she's already in the PEOC, the door is hardened and we're not getting through it. But the transfer takes time — agents have to reach the Residence, wake her, move her through corridors that weren't designed for speed. Based on the night response times from Test 1, the interior lockdown sequence takes between two and four minutes from the initial alarm. If we're through the windows and in the corridor within ninety seconds, we're ahead of the transfer."

"That's a narrow window," Briggs said.

"That's the only window," Cole said.

The room was quiet. The heating unit rattled.

"Objective," Cole said. He wasn't asking. He was saying it so everyone in the room heard it once, clearly, from him.

"We breach the building and we push toward the transfer corridor. We engage any Service agents between us and the objective. We move fast, we stay together, we use the NV advantage — the interior will be dark or transitioning to emergency lighting, and we'll see better than they do for the first thirty seconds. If we reach the corridor during the transfer, we complete the mission."

He didn't say "kill the president." He didn't need to. The rifles and the shaped charges and the floor plan with the transfer route marked in red said it for him.

"If we don't reach the corridor," he continued, "we engage until we can't. Either way, armed men inside the White House with automatic weapons changes everything. The building is no longer secure. The presidency is no longer safe. That message carries whether we succeed or not."

Harmon looked at the rifles. He looked at Cole.

"Wednesday," Cole said. "2 AM."

• • •

That night, Cole sent a message through the encrypted channel he'd been given four months ago. The channel ran through a messaging platform that routed through three jurisdictions and deleted on read. He'd never met the person on the other end. He knew only that the channel had come to him through someone at the DSA forum who'd recognized his operational background and had put him in touch with people who could provide logistics — the converted weapons, the NV equipment, the shaped charges, the satellite photos at a resolution you couldn't get from public mapping services, the shift-change schedule that wasn't supposed to be public information.

The message was short:

Wednesday. 0200. SE corner. We are go.

The response came in eleven minutes:

Confirmed. Good luck.

The channel terminated at a desk in the Fresh Start Foundation's Los Angeles office — a program coordinator named Kendrick who reported to a deputy who reported to a regional director who had dinner with Novak once a quarter. Kendrick didn't know Haldane existed. He knew that certain messages came through certain channels and that his job was to confirm them and pass the confirmation up one level. The system was designed so that no single person could see more than one link in the chain. Kendrick saw his link. He confirmed. He went back to his grant applications.

• • •

Washington, D.C. Wednesday. 1:47 AM.

The White House grounds were quiet. The Ellipse was dark — the daytime protesters had gone home hours ago, the portable heaters powered down, the PA system silent. A light rain was falling, a cold January drizzle that turned the air into a gray haze and reduced visibility to a hundred meters.

Cole, Briggs, Harmon, and Lenton staged in a vehicle on E Street, three blocks south. Dario was behind the wheel. The duffel bags were in the back — rifles broken down, NV goggles packed, shaped charges wrapped in foam. They wore dark civilian clothes. Construction jackets. Work boots. Four men who looked like a late-shift crew heading home.

At 1:52, Cole checked the channel. The gate group was in position — eight people, approaching the south perimeter on foot, spread across the sidewalk like pedestrians. They'd been told to rush the fence at 2:00 AM exactly. They thought it was another protest breach. They'd been promised bail money and media coverage.

At 1:56, the four men got out of the vehicle. They walked south on 15th Street, then east toward the Ellipse, carrying the duffel bags. The rain covered the sound. The darkness covered the movement. They crossed the Ellipse grounds — empty, the grass wet, the abandoned protest camp a collection of dark shapes in the drizzle — and took position behind the tree line south of the southeast fence corner.

Cole distributed the equipment in silence. Rifles assembled — stocks unfolded, magazines seated, actions charged. NV goggles on. Handguns in waistbands. Shaped charges in jacket pockets. The plasma cutter in Lenton's hand.

Through the NV, the White House grounds were a green-white landscape of sharp edges and long shadows. The wrought iron fence was a dark line. The south lawn stretched beyond it — flat, open, ninety meters to the building. The building itself was lit along the colonnade but dark at the ground-floor windows. The agent at the southeast static post was visible — a figure in a dark suit, standing at the junction of the fence line, facing south.

Cole checked his watch. 1:59.

At 2:00 AM, the gate group rushed the south gate.

Cole heard it before he saw it — shouting, the clang of bodies hitting iron, the immediate sharp response of agents at the gate. Through the NV he could see movement at the south perimeter — figures climbing, agents running, the choreography of a breach response that had played out twice before and would play out the same way because the protocols said it would.

The southeast post agent held for twelve seconds. Then his radio fired and he moved — west, toward the gate, joining the response.

The corner was empty.

Cole tapped Lenton's shoulder. Lenton moved to the fence and pressed the plasma cutter against the first iron bar. The tool hummed — high and thin, lost in the noise from the gate. The bar separated in three seconds. A bright line of molten orange that died instantly in the rain. Second bar. Third. Fourth. A gap wide enough to step through.

They went through single file. Cole first, then Briggs, Harmon, Lenton. Rifles up. NV on. The lawn was wet and soft and silent under their boots.

Thirty meters. The rain on their faces. The building growing in the green field of the goggles.

Sixty meters. No alarm yet. The gate group was still occupying the response. Radio traffic — Cole could hear it leaking from a speaker somewhere on the south portico — was focused on the gate. "Eight subjects at the south fence. Two climbing. Requesting additional units."

Ninety meters. The south wall. The ground-floor windows — tall, arched, dark. Ballistic glass rated for small arms and blast overpressure. The windows that were supposed to be impenetrable.

Cole and Briggs took the window to the left of the south entrance. Harmon and Lenton took the right. They worked fast — peel the adhesive backing, place the shaped charge flat against the glass at center mass, step back three meters. The charges were compact — the size of a hardback book, directional, designed to focus the blast forward through the glass rather than outward.

Cole held up three fingers. Two. One.

Both charges detonated simultaneously. The sound was enormous in the quiet — a double concussion that rolled across the south lawn and echoed off the north facade. The ballistic glass didn't crack. It vaporized — the shaped charges cut through the laminated layers and blew the panels inward in a shower of fragments that scattered across the interior floor.

Two windows. Open. Dark rooms beyond.

The alarm sounded now — the three-pulse pattern, the one that meant firearms or explosives on the grounds. Emergency lighting began cycling in the corridors. Red, then white, then red.

Cole went through the left window. Briggs behind him. Harmon and Lenton through the right. The NV goggles cut through the darkness that the emergency lighting hadn't reached yet — the rooms were green and sharp, furniture and walls and doorways in high contrast. They were in a reception area. Ahead, through an open doorway, the central corridor.

Cole moved. Fast. Rifle up. The corridor stretched east — long, wide, the emergency lights starting to strobe. Through the NV, the strobing was a flicker of overexposure that he blinked through. The corridor led toward the East Wing. Toward the PEOC access point. Toward the route the Service would be using to move the president from the Residence to the bunker.

An agent appeared at the far end of the corridor. He was moving fast — not toward them, perpendicular, crossing from one corridor to another. He saw them and stopped. Four men in dark clothes with rifles and NV goggles, standing in the central corridor of the White House at 2:01 in the morning.

The agent drew his weapon.

Cole fired first. A three-round burst that hit the wall behind the agent as the man dove sideways into the cross-corridor. The sound in the enclosed space was punishing — the rifle's report magnified by marble walls and hard floors into something physical, a pressure wave that Cole felt in his chest.

Return fire from the cross-corridor. Two rounds, aimed, professional. One hit the wall beside Cole's head. The other passed between him and Briggs.

"Contact front," Cole said. "Push through."

They pushed. Briggs laid suppressive fire down the corridor — short bursts, keeping the agent pinned in the cross-corridor. Cole moved along the left wall. Harmon came up on the right. Lenton covered the rear, watching the rooms they'd come through for flanking agents.

More radio traffic, louder now, coming from every direction. "Armed subjects in the building. Ground floor central corridor. Shots fired. Overcoat is moving."

Overcoat is moving. The president was being transferred.

Cole reached the cross-corridor junction and cleared it — the agent had retreated east, falling back toward the PEOC access. More agents ahead. He could hear the movement — the rapid, coordinated footsteps of a protection detail executing the most practiced maneuver in their repertoire, moving the president through a building that now had armed men inside it.

He rounded the corner and saw them.

Thirty meters ahead, in the east corridor: a cluster of agents in a diamond formation, moving fast. In the center of the diamond, a figure in a robe — Whitfield, moving under escort, her face visible for a fraction of a second as the formation passed under an emergency light.

Cole raised the rifle.

An agent at the rear of the formation turned. He was already firing — three rounds, fast, accurate. The first round hit Cole in the left shoulder and spun him into the wall. The rifle stayed in his right hand. He tried to bring it up. The second round hit his vest — the impact like a baseball bat to the sternum, driving the air from his lungs.

Briggs came around the corner firing. The burst was wild — the enclosed space, the strobing lights, the NV flaring on the muzzle flash. Rounds hit the walls, the ceiling, the floor. One hit an agent in the leg. The agent dropped, fired from the floor, and hit Briggs in the throat.

Briggs went down. He didn't make a sound. He sat against the wall and the rifle fell from his hands and his eyes were open and looking at nothing.

The formation kept moving. The diamond closed around Whitfield and accelerated. A door ahead — heavy, reinforced, the PEOC access. An agent hit the keypad. The door opened. The formation went through. The door closed.

Cole was on the floor. His shoulder was bleeding. His chest felt broken. He could hear Harmon behind him, still firing, the rifle's report echoing in the corridor. Then Harmon's rifle stopped and there was a sound that might have been a body hitting the floor.

Lenton. Cole couldn't see Lenton. He couldn't see much of anything — the NV goggles were askew on his face, the green field tilted at a sickening angle. Agents were coming from both ends of the corridor. He could hear them.

He let the rifle go. He put his hands flat on the marble floor. The stone was cold and smooth and he could feel the vibration of running feet through his palms.

The agents reached him. He went down. A knee on his back. Zip ties. His face pressed against the floor, the NV goggles crushed under the weight, and through the broken lens he could see the door at the end of the corridor — closed, sealed, the president on the other side of it.

He'd gotten inside the White House. He'd seen her. He'd raised the rifle.

He hadn't been fast enough.

• • •

Whitfield sat in the PEOC and listened to the sound of gunfire in her house.

Not outside. Not on the lawn. Inside. The muffled, rhythmic cracking of automatic weapons echoing through the corridors above her. Return fire from her agents — the sharper, more controlled reports of handguns. Shouting. Running. The sounds of a firefight in a building that had been designed for receptions and briefings and the quiet business of governing.

The PEOC was a bunker — reinforced concrete, blast-rated door, independent communications. The screens showed the feeds from the building's internal cameras. She could see the corridors. The muzzle flashes. The men in dark clothes moving through her house with rifles and night-vision equipment.

She watched one of them round a corner and see her. See the formation. See her face. Raise the rifle.

She watched her agent fire. Watched the man hit the wall. Watched another come around the corner and watched her agent drop him with a shot that punched through his throat.

She watched the door close — the PEOC door, the one she'd just come through, sealing between her and the men who had come to kill her.

The firefight lasted another three minutes. The sound through the reinforced walls was attenuated but not absent — she could feel it in the floor, in the table, in the metal legs of the chair she was gripping with hands that were perfectly still.

The tremor was gone. The shaking that had been building for weeks had stopped, replaced by something stiller and harder — the specific calm of a person who has seen a rifle raised at her face and survived the two seconds between the raise and the shot that stopped it.

Hunt was on the phone. He was receiving reports in fragments — corridors cleared, subjects down, agents wounded, building being swept. The gate group was in custody outside. The southeast fence had been cut — four bars, clean cuts, a gap wide enough for four men and their equipment.

"Four subjects entered the building through blown windows on the south side," Hunt said. He was reading from the reports as they came in, his voice flat. "Shaped charges on the ballistic glass. They had automatic weapons and night-vision equipment. They engaged agents in the ground-floor central corridor and attempted to reach the PEOC access point during your transfer."

He paused.

"Three subjects are dead. Briggs, Harmon, and Lenton — those are the names on the IDs they were carrying, probably false. The fourth — Cole — is in custody with gunshot wounds to the shoulder and blunt trauma to the chest. Two agents are wounded. Agent Torres took a round in the leg. Agent Briggs — no relation — has fragment injuries from the window detonation."

"They got inside," Whitfield said.

"Yes."

"They saw me."

"One of them did. In the east corridor. He raised the weapon. Agent Navarro fired first."

She looked at the screens. The corridor where it had happened was visible — marble walls scored with bullet impacts, shell casings on the floor, a dark stain near the cross-corridor junction that was someone's blood. The reception room where they'd entered had glass fragments across every surface. The windows were open holes in the south wall, the January air pushing through them, the rain blowing in.

"They had shaped charges," she said. "Night vision. Automatic weapons. A floor plan. They knew the transfer route."

"Yes."

"That isn't anger, Wolsey. That's an operation. Somebody funded it. Somebody equipped it. Somebody gave them the shift-change schedule, the building layout, and the transfer protocol."

Hunt nodded.

"The first two breaches," she said. "The solo man. The group of fifteen. Those were reconnaissance."

"We're reviewing the footage now. Looking for faces that appear at all three events."

"You'll find them."

The lockdown lasted until dawn. The rain continued. The building was swept three times — every room, every corridor, every closet and service passage and maintenance shaft. The southeast fence was photographed, the cut bars tagged as evidence. The blown windows were covered with temporary barriers that did nothing to keep out the cold.

Whitfield sat in the PEOC for six hours. She didn't move. She didn't eat. She read the after-action reports as they arrived and she processed each one the way Dren would have processed them — as data, as evidence, as components of a system that had failed in specific, identifiable ways.

The intelligence briefings that followed confirmed what she already knew. The cell had been based in Arlington. Ex-military. Radicalized through DSA-affiliated channels that traced back through a network of cutouts to sources the FBI was still mapping. The weapons, the NV equipment, and the shaped charges had been provided through a logistics chain that terminated at a company connected to — connected to what? The connections were still being traced. The satellite imagery had come from somewhere with access to intelligence-grade resolution. The shift-change schedule and the interior transfer protocol had come from inside.

Three separate threat streams had been flagged before the attack — mentioning the date, the method, the target. The Service had upgraded the threat level twice. And the attack had happened anyway.

She looked at the screens. The corridor. The blown windows. The rain coming through.

Someone had tried to kill her inside the White House. An organized, funded, equipped military operation with automatic weapons, shaped explosive charges, night-vision equipment, intelligence support, and expendable civilians used as a diversion. Four men had breached the most secure building in the United States, entered through blown windows, engaged the Secret Service in a firefight in the central corridor, and come within thirty meters and two seconds of the president.

The next attempt would learn from this one the way this one had learned from the first two.

Dren's offer arrived through the secure channel two days later. Mars. The communication infrastructure was there. The security was controllable. The distance — the physical, orbital, absolute distance — made it the most secure location available to any head of state. A state visit to inspect reconstruction coordination infrastructure. Diplomatic framing. Routine inspection.

A state visit that happened to last indefinitely.

Whitfield read the offer in the Residence at dawn. She stood at the window in her robe. The Ellipse was empty. The PA system lay on its side in the wet grass. A section of the wrought iron fence on the southeast perimeter was missing — four bars, cut clean, removed as evidence. The south-facing windows of the ground floor were boarded with plywood that someone had painted white in a futile attempt to match the facade.

She agreed on one condition.

"My people," she said. "Non-negotiable."

Brandt coordinated the logistics from Ares City. The transport was one of Dren's fast personnel vessels. The trip would take roughly thirty days. The manifest listed Whitfield, her chief of staff, six USSS agents, and a minimal support team.

Brandt flagged one name on the USSS detail. Agent Colton had spent three years in private security for one of Haldane's subsidiary companies before joining the Secret Service. Brandt sent the flag to the USSS detail lead with a request to substitute.

The request came back denied. Colton's background check was clean. His performance record was exemplary. The company employed hundreds of security professionals, and prior private-sector work was common in the Service. The detail lead thanked Brandt for his diligence and kept Colton on the manifest.

Brandt logged the denial and forwarded it to Dren. Dren read it and said nothing.

CHAPTER 15

Inflection Point

January 2061.

• • •

Lake Texoma.

The house was Beckett's — a weekend property on the Oklahoma side, old money architecture. A place that existed to be away from Washington. No staff. No cameras. Haldane had been here three times in eleven years, always in winter, always unannounced.

Beckett met him at the door. He'd driven from Dallas — two hours, no security, his own car. The senator was in a flannel shirt and reading glasses, the performative casualness of a man who understood that informality was its own kind of power.

They sat in the study. Wood paneling, lake view, a fire that Beckett had lit himself. No bourbon. Beckett didn't drink during working conversations, and this was a working conversation.

"The hearings," Haldane said.

"Going well. The satellite dependency testimony put Whitfield on the defensive for three news cycles. The subpoena for the detection timeline lands next week. Dren's thirty-minute decision window — the gap between his early detection data and his notification of the government — is the thread I'm pulling. If I can establish that Dren knew and delayed, the dependency narrative writes itself."

“And the endgame?”

Beckett removed his glasses and set them on the desk. The gesture was practiced — it meant the conversation had moved from information to strategy.

“The hearings aren’t the endgame. The hearings are the foundation. Every witness, every subpoena, every piece of testimony goes into the congressional record. The record becomes the evidentiary basis for an impeachment referral. Not now — the votes aren’t there now. But every hearing moves the math. Every news cycle that frames Whitfield as dependent on Dren, every document that shows the administration deferring to a private citizen on planetary defense decisions — that’s a brick in the wall.”

“How many bricks do you need?”

“Enough that when I call the vote, the moderate caucus can’t survive voting no. That means the public has to be ahead of Congress. The public has to want her gone before I ask Congress to remove her. If I call the vote and it fails, I’ve spent my ammunition. If I call it and it passes, the presidency is vacant and the regional structure becomes the de facto government.”

Haldane nodded. This was why Beckett was useful. He thought in sequences — not what happens, but what happens after what happens.

“The Whitfield-Dren relationship,” Haldane said. “How are you framing it?”

“Dependency. Not conspiracy — that’s too far, too fast. Dependency. She relied on his platforms for the deflection. She relied on his infrastructure for the reconstruction. Every decision she makes is filtered through what Dren provides. The question isn’t whether she’s compromised — it’s whether an independent presidency can exist when one private citizen controls the infrastructure the government depends on.”

“And the answer?”

“The answer doesn’t matter. The question is the point. Once the question is in the public mind, every decision she makes is evaluated through that lens. Every time she takes Dren's advice, it confirms the narrative. Every time she doesn't, people ask why she's distancing herself from the man who saved them. She can't win. The question is the weapon. Not the answer."

Haldane sat with that. Beckett understood something most politicians didn't — that public opinion was shaped by the questions people asked, not the answers they received. Frame the question correctly and the answer was irrelevant.

"The regional Lieutenants," Haldane said. "Thomas in Jacksonville. Chen in Denver."

"Already moving. Thomas has been pushing for extended autonomy since October. Chen is bitter about the coastal reconstruction bias — Denver didn't burn but Denver isn't getting rebuilt either. Reeves in San Diego is watching his supply chain run through Dren's logistics network and asking why a private company controls his reconstruction pipeline."

"Are they coordinating?"

"Not yet. They're each running their own calculations independently. That's better — coordinated resistance looks like a coup. Independent grievances look like legitimate governance concerns. If three or four regional Lieutenants simultaneously conclude that federal authority isn't serving their needs, that's not rebellion. That's consensus."

"Encourage it. Don't direct it. The Foundation can provide analysis, infrastructure assessments, reconstruction audits — the kind of material that helps a regional Lieutenant justify independence without anyone providing the conclusion."

"Fellowship placements?"

"Already in position. Thomas has two on his reconstruction advisory board. Chen has one in his logistics office. The analysis they receive will support the conclusions they're already reaching."

"The election," Haldane said.

Beckett's jaw tightened slightly. "The election is settled."

"The election is producing exactly what it was designed to produce. Martinez in California is functionally non-compliant. Thomas and Chen are using the legitimacy question as cover for autonomy they were already pursuing. The reconstruction caucus can't hold together because half of them represent districts that voted for the challenger and the other half represent districts that barely voted at all. Every committee vote is a referendum on whether the election was legitimate, and every referendum produces a split."

"The impeachment math has changed," Beckett said. "Before the election, I needed moderate Republicans to cross. Now I need moderates from both parties — the ones in contested zones who can't survive being seen as either defending an illegitimate president or attacking a constitutional process. The election put them in a box with no exit."

"Which means impeachment is less likely to succeed."

"Which means impeachment is less likely to be called. I don't need the vote. I need the hearings. As long as the hearings continue, the legitimacy debate stays in the news. As long as the legitimacy debate stays in the news, the regional commanders have political cover for non-compliance. And as long as the regional commanders are non-compliant, the federal government can't consolidate authority."

"The election as a perpetual wound," Haldane said.

"A wound that neither side can close because closing it means conceding something they can't concede. The 'stolen election' people can't accept the result without accepting that California's destruction was acceptable. The 'decisive mandate' people can't acknowledge the turnout problem without acknowledging that the victory was built on absence. Both sides are right. Both sides are wrong. And as long as they're arguing, they're not governing."

Haldane looked at the fire. The logs had shifted — the structure of the flame had rearranged itself without intervention, the way all systems rearranged themselves under pressure. The election had been another log on the fire, not the fire itself. Just fuel.

Beckett put his glasses back on. The conversation was shifting from strategy back to information — the signal that the working portion was ending.

"One thing," he said. "Whatever we're doing — the hearings, the regional encouragement, the fellowship placements — it has to stay political. Institutional. The moment anyone connects this to anything beyond domestic politics, the narrative changes. We're not agents of an external power. We're senators and philanthropists concerned about executive overreach and reconstruction accountability. That's the frame. That's the only frame."

Haldane looked at him. Beckett had known about the Tolek for eleven years. He'd made his calculation — that the arrival was inevitable, that being inside the structure was better than being outside it, that the new order would need human administrators and those administrators would need to have been positioned in advance. He'd never said any of this aloud. He'd never needed to. The calculation was structural, and structural calculations didn't require articulation.

"Agreed," Haldane said. "The frame is domestic. Always."

They sat for a moment. The fire cracked. The lake was dark beyond the windows.

"How long?" Beckett asked.

Haldane understood the question. How long until the fleet arrived.

"Approximately two years," he said.

Beckett nodded. He didn't ask what happened after. He'd made his calculation eleven years ago. The answer hadn't changed.

"A lot can change in two years," Beckett replied. "Look how much has changed in 6 months."

Haldane left the way he'd come — through the side door, across the gravel, his own car. Two hours back to Dallas. The lake house would appear in no record. The conversation would exist in no transcript. Two men had met in a room and discussed the systematic dismantling of a democratic government, and the only evidence was the fire and the empty chairs.

• • •

Dallas.

The message was short. Encrypted, routed through three relays, leaving no record or metadata.

"There's going to be some action with regards to our friend," Haldane said. "One of the Service detail. You know what to do."

The message ended and its circuitous routing to Mars began.

Haldane looked at the reconstruction feeds on the wallscreen. Los Angeles. Tokyo. Honolulu. Cities rebuilding from the damage his tilt had caused, though none of them knew that. The attempt would serve its purpose — just not the purpose the shooter believed. The shooter was a piece, expendable. He thought he was serving the cause. He was serving the cause, just not in the way he thought.

• • •

Ares City.

Whitfield's departure had been announced seventy-two hours before launch. The statement described the trip as a "strategic consultation on reconstruction infrastructure." The language satisfied no one. She boarded one of Dren's fast personnel vessels at the Cape Canaveral orbital platform, flanked by Hunt and six USSS agents. The trip would take roughly thirty days.

During the thirty-day transit, the USSS detail integrated with Brandt's security team with predictable institutional friction — jurisdictional habits, coverage overlaps, the quiet professional ego of two organizations that each believed they were better at this. Raines smoothed it. His prior interaction with USSS gave him the credibility needed to make it work. He ran the daily briefings, resolved the disputes, produced schedules that gave both teams enough authority to feel respected and enough oversight to remain accountable.

Brandt watched him work and found nothing to criticize.

Brandt had shared his concerns about Colton with Raines during the integration. Raines had listened, nodded, and logged it the way he logged everything — quietly, without comment, without changing his expression.

"I'll keep an eye on him," Raines said.

Dren was waiting in the arrival corridor when the shuttle docked. Whitfield's party came through the transit bay — Hunt at her shoulder, the USSS detail spread along the corridor in standard protective coverage. Brandt was positioned at the junction ahead. Raines was at Dren's side, three feet back, right.

Colton was at the far end of the corridor.

He watched Dren. His weight shifted — forward, slightly. His right hand drifted toward his jacket. The movement was slow. Deliberate.

• • •

Dallas.

Novak arrived the following evening with a briefcase and a timeline.

He spread the operational plan across Haldane's study table — paper. Novak had learned early that paper didn't have logs, didn't sync to clouds, and didn't survive a match.

"Three fronts," Novak said. "Anti-Whitfield, anti-Dren, and general reconstruction grievance. Each front operates independently. None of them know the others exist. All of them believe they're organic."

He pointed to the first column. "Front one: the abandonment narrative. Whitfield left Earth. She's on Mars while her citizens are rebuilding from the worst disaster in human history. The signs write themselves — WHERE IS THE PRESIDENT, LEADERSHIP FROM ELEVEN MINUTES AWAY, MARS FIRST EARTH

LAST. We seed this through the reconstruction union contacts. Eleven zones, existing organizational infrastructure, people who are already angry about frozen contracts and priority logistics. We don't create the anger. We give it a target and a megaphone."

Second column. "Front two: anti-Dren. FOIA requests targeting Dren Industries' reconstruction contracts. Whistleblower hotlines for current and former employees. Social media campaigns targeting Dren's workforce — not the company, the people. Make it personal. Make it uncomfortable to work for Dren. The goal isn't disclosure — it's pressure. Every FOIA request that gets stonewalled becomes evidence of secrecy. Every whistleblower hotline that goes unanswered becomes evidence of suppression."

Third column. "Front three: the DSA network. The podcast, the affiliated channels, the social media ecosystem. Six million subscribers on the main channel, double that across affiliates. We've been seeding the dependency narrative for months — Beckett's hearing clips, the detection timeline, the thirty-minute window. Now we escalate. The Fist detection data. The institutional delay. The question of who knew and when. We don't provide conclusions. We provide questions. The audience provides the conclusions."

"Budget?" Haldane asked.

"Twelve million through sixty organizations in thirty cities. Third-tier grants from the Fresh Start Foundation, routed through community action committees that were established during the reconstruction. The committees are real — they do real work, they have real members, they file real tax returns. The grants are small enough to be unremarkable individually. Collectively, they fund everything."

"And the coordination with Beckett's hearings?"

"Synchronized, not coordinated. Beckett doesn't know about the street operation. The street operation doesn't know about Beckett. But the timing aligns — when Beckett holds a hearing, the protests outside the White House grow. When the DSA network runs a segment on the detection timeline, Beckett subpoenas the next document in the chain. Each one amplifies the other without either one directing the other. Plausible independence."

Haldane looked at the paper. Sixty organizations. Thirty cities. Three fronts. Twelve million dollars flowing through a network of community action committees that existed on paper as reconstruction support and in practice as the infrastructure of manufactured outrage.

"How long until saturation?" he asked.

"The union contacts activate within the week. The FOIA campaign launches in ten days — we've had the requests drafted for a month, just waiting for the signal. The DSA escalation is already in progress. Full saturation — all three fronts operating at scale — within thirty days."

"And traceability?"

"The grants are third-tier. Fresh Start to a regional foundation to a community action committee. Two layers of separation between Foundation money and street activity. The committees have independent boards, independent leadership, independent operations. If anyone audits them, they find legitimate organizations doing legitimate work. The grants fund community programs. The community programs happen to include civic engagement. The civic engagement happens to include protests."

"We didn't put guns in anyone's hands," Novak said. "We put anger in the street. The anger was already there. We just organized it."

Haldane looked at the timeline. Thirty days to saturation. Beckett's hearings accelerating. Whitfield on Mars and losing ground. The regional Lieutenants reaching conclusions that the Foundation's analysis had prepared for them. The DSA network hammering the dependency narrative into six million households.

The fragmentation was proceeding within specification.

He picked up the bourbon and drank it.

• • •

Ares City.

One minute before Dren stepped into the arrival corridor, Raines was already watching Colton.

Raines had been reading crowds for fifteen years, and the thing about reading crowds was that you didn't look for what was wrong. You looked for what was prepared. A person who was going to act didn't look nervous. They looked ready. The difference was invisible to everyone who hadn't spent a career learning to see it.

Colton looked ready.

Dren stepped into the arrival corridor. Raines fell into position — three feet back, right side. Brandt was at the junction ahead. Whitfield's party was coming through the transit bay.

Colton's weight shifted. His center of mass moved forward, toward the corridor where Dren was approaching. His right hand drifted toward his service weapon.

Raines moved. Smooth, not fast. He stepped away from Dren's shoulder and angled toward Colton with the unhurried gait of someone checking a sight line. Colton didn't register him. People who are watching geometry tend to miss the person who's already solved it.

At five feet, Raines stepped in beside him. Left hand on Colton's right wrist — fingers closing around the joint with mechanical specificity. Right hand to the elbow, controlled downward pressure, turning Colton's body away from the corridor.

Colton's hand had been closing on the grip of his sidearm.

Colton fought. He was bigger, and he knew what was happening, and he drove his elbow back into Raines's ribs hard enough to shift the hold. Raines absorbed it. The wrist hold became a forearm lock, the forearm lock became a rear chokehold as Colton twisted and tried to break free. Raines's arm tightened around Colton's neck. His other hand locked the hold.

The struggle lasted four seconds. Then a sound — short, structural, final — and Colton went limp.

Raines lowered him to the floor. The second USSS agent had his weapon drawn, covering the corridor. Brandt was running back from the advance position. Dren had stopped walking.

Brandt reached them first. He looked at Colton on the floor. He looked at Raines.

"What happened?"

"He was going for his weapon. He was drawing when I reached him. He fought the hold." A pause. "It just happened."

Brandt looked at the body. At the angle of the head. At Raines, standing with his hands at his sides, open.

Eight months ago, in Washington, Raines had taken a man alive. A quarter-inch shift in the hold and the man's knees had buckled. Controlled. Deliberate. That man had walked to the checkpoint under his own power.

Colton's neck was broken.

Brandt looked at Raines for a long moment.

"Secure the weapon," he said. "Lock down the corridor. Full detail in the briefing room in ten minutes. I want every camera angle we have available."

Dren walked forward. He looked at Colton, then at Raines.

"That's twice now," he said.

Raines nodded. He stepped back to his position — three feet behind Dren's right shoulder — and waited.

Brandt filed the incident report that evening. The cameras had confirmed it. Colton's hand was moving towards his service weapon a moment before Raines had moved. He noted that Colton had resisted and that the lethal outcome had occurred during the struggle. He noted that Raines had resolved a comparable incident eight months earlier without lethal force.

He did not draw a conclusion from the comparison.

• • •

Ares City.

O'Malley had been thinking about the position error for three days.

Station Bravo had changed the calculation. Before Bravo, the position error was a transcription mistake — regrettable, catastrophic in its consequences, but explicable. A kid entered 3,600 instead of 3,500 under pressure, and two hundred million people died. Dren had accepted that. The auditors had accepted it. O'Malley had accepted it too, because at the time there was no reason not to.

But Station Bravo proved that someone on Earth had a covert communication channel to the belt — and from the belt to whatever was sitting at the edge of the solar system. Someone with access to the belt's infrastructure. Someone embedded deep enough to build a signing key into the firmware before anyone knew the firmware would matter. That was a professional placement, years in the making. And a professional placement sophisticated enough to build Station Bravo was sophisticated enough to put one wrong digit in a parameter field and make it look like an accident.

Dren hadn't reopened the position error. He had the belt relay, something at 130 AU — problems that dwarfed a post-mortem on a number that the auditors had already explained. O'Malley understood the priority. But O'Malley had also spent his career in forensics, and forensics had taught him that the explanation you accept first is the one that hides the truth the longest.

He decided to go talk to the engineer.

O'Malley found Tanaka in the platform team's workspace on the third level of the engineering annex. It was late — past shift end, the room mostly empty, a few consoles still glowing with diagnostic feeds. Tanaka was alone at a workstation in the corner, running simulations that had nothing to do with his current assignment. O'Malley had checked the access logs. Tanaka had been running these simulations for months — trajectory models, deflection geometry, the same calculations that the post-mortem had concluded he'd gotten wrong. He was still trying to figure out what had happened.

O'Malley pulled a chair over and sat down beside him.

"Working late," O'Malley said.

Tanaka minimized the simulation. The reflex of a man who'd been caught doing something he wasn't supposed to be doing, even though no one had told him to stop.

"Process review," Tanaka said.

"Right." O'Malley kept his voice easy. Two colleagues, end of shift. "Listen, I'm doing a quiet review of the Wave 3 translation layer. Lessons learned, process improvement. Dren wants to make sure the new upload chain doesn't have the same vulnerabilities. I need to walk through what happened with the position parameter."

Tanaka's face changed. Not much — a tightening around the eyes, a shift in the way he held his shoulders. The look of a man who'd been waiting for this conversation and dreading it in equal measure.

"I entered the number from the instructions," Tanaka said. "3,600. That's what the document said."

"Walk me through it. From the beginning."

Tanaka took a breath. "Okoro sent the instruction package on February 4th. Standard format — parameter set, verification checksums, deployment notes. I opened the document and pulled the position value. 3,600 kilometers. I entered it into the translation layer build."

"And you verified?"

"Of course I verified. I pulled the instruction document back up, side by side with the build input, and confirmed the number matched. 3,600 in the document, 3,600 in the build. Then I called Hayashi — my supervisor — and asked him to do an independent verification. He opened the same document on his own terminal and confirmed. 3,600."

"Both of you. Same document. Same number."

"Same document. Same number. Same day." Tanaka's voice had an edge now — the compressed frustration of someone who'd said this before and not been believed. "The post-mortem said I entered 3,600 when the document said 3,500. That I misread a five as a six. That's what the report concluded. But I didn't misread anything. The document said 3,600. Hayashi saw 3,600. We both verified before the commit."

O'Malley nodded. He didn't push. He didn't challenge. He let the silence sit.

"Nobody believed me," Tanaka said. He was looking at his hands, not at O'Malley. "The file says 3,500. It's always said 3,500. The version history is clean. I look like someone who can't read a number and won't admit it."

"What about Hayashi?"

"He backed me in the post-mortem. He said he verified 3,600. They put it in the report as a 'discrepancy in recollection' and closed it." Tanaka's jaw was tight. "A year. I've been carrying this for a year. Running the simulations at night because I know what I saw and it doesn't match what the file says and I can't explain why."

O'Malley was quiet for a moment.

"I believe you," he said.

Tanaka looked at him. The expression on his face was something O'Malley hadn't been prepared for. The look of a man who'd been drowning in three feet of water for a year and someone had finally noticed.

He stood up, pushed the chair back, and left Tanaka sitting in the quiet workspace with the simulations still running on the screen behind him.

Back in the forensics lab, O'Malley pulled up the instruction file. The position parameter field read 3,500. Creation date February 4th, 2060, two days before the upload. No modifications. No edits. Clean version history. According to every file-level record, this document had always said 3,500.

Tanaka was certain it had said 3,600. Hayashi was certain. Both had verified independently, on the same day, before the commit.

O'Malley ran the checksum.

The file's recorded checksum — the hash generated when the file was created — didn't match the current contents. The file system said one thing. The file's contents said another.

He sat with that for a long time.

Then it occurred to him: someone had accessed the raw disk image directly. Changed the byte at the physical level, bypassing the file system entirely. No version history entry. No modification timestamp. No credentials logged. Just one digit different on the disk, and a checksum that nobody would think to verify unless they already suspected the file had been altered.

O'Malley pulled the OS session logs. The disk-level modification didn't leave a file trail, but the operating system logged every active session. The modification window was narrow — off-shift, between 02:00 and 04:00 on March 12th. Five weeks after the Gauntlet. Three days after Dren's post-mortem audit began. Several sessions were active during that window — maintenance routines, automated processes, the usual background activity. But one session was different. It was opened manually, approximately thirty minutes before the estimated modification time, and closed approximately ten minutes after.

He checked the session credentials.

He sat back in his chair and looked at the name on the screen for a full minute.

Then he took the evidence to Sato.

"The position error wasn't the engineer," he said. "Tanaka and his supervisor both say the instructions read 3,600 when they received them. They both verified independently before the commit. The file now reads 3,500, but the version history is clean — no modification, no timestamp, nothing. But, someone changed it at the disk level to bypass the file system. The checksum doesn't match the contents. And the OS session logs shows several active sessions at the time, but only one session started just before the modification window, and ended shortly after. Off-shift. Two in the morning. Five weeks after the Gauntlet."

Sato looked at the checksum data on the tablet, then back at O'Malley.

"Dren closed this," she said. "The auditors closed it. Compressed dev cycle, one parameter missed. Human error."

"Then explain the checksum," O'Malley said. "The file was modified after creation. At the disk level. Bypassing every audit trail the system has. That's not a transcription error. That's someone covering their tracks — after the fact, in the middle of the night, using a technique that requires root access to the raw storage layer. Nobody does that to fix a typo."

Sato didn't answer immediately. The technical logic held. A checksum mismatch on a file with clean version history meant exactly one thing: the contents had been altered outside the file system. There was no innocent explanation for that.

"Who was logged in?" she asked.

"Okoro."

Sato sat with that for a moment. "It's still circumstantial. A session log proves he was on the system. It doesn't prove he made the change."

"Then let me check his communications," O'Malley said. "If I'm wrong, the comms will be clean and we drop it. If I'm right, there'll be a pattern."

Sato considered it. Going behind Dren's closed finding without telling him was not something she did lightly. But O'Malley had a checksum that didn't match, and checksums didn't lie.

"Pull the traffic," she said. "Internal and external. Everything since Okoro arrived at Ares. Show me what you find before you show anyone else."

O'Malley was back in four hours. The traffic wasn't clean. Okoro had been sending short, encrypted bursts through an external channel, timed to coincide with routine telemetry so they disappeared in the traffic logs unless you were looking for them. O'Malley had been looking.

"That's enough," Sato said. She opened the cortical link.

Dren, Sato said.

Yes.

O'Malley reopened the position error on his own. He found something. The instruction file has a checksum mismatch — the contents were altered at the disk level after creation. The session logs put Okoro on the system during the modification window. And Okoro's comms traffic shows encrypted bursts through an external channel, timed to hide in routine telemetry.

Silence on the link. Longer than usual.

I closed that inquiry, Dren said.

I know, Sato said. ***The checksum reopened it.***

Another pause. Dren processing. Sato had worked with him long enough to know what the silence meant — he was running the implications forward, the way he ran everything, and what he was finding at the end of the chain was that he'd been wrong.

I'll talk to Okoro, Dren said. ***Directly. No advance notice. Keep this between the three of us until I do.***

• • •

Pasadena.

Ashford pulled up the investigation matrix on the wallscreen and stepped back to look at it. Three months of work, assembled from three independent investigations that hadn't known about each other until December. The display filled the wall — nodes, connections, color-coded threads linking entities across jurisdictions and timelines.

Her thread ran down the left side, tagged in blue. Organizational: the Haldane Foundation's corporate structure. Shell companies, dissolved consortiums, holding entities in four jurisdictions. Meridian Technical Services, Basin Range Holdings, the Dallas law firm. The fellowship pipeline feeding candidates into governance positions. The Nevada facility — construction manifests showing industrial quantities of concrete and steel routed to a location where only a warehouse was visible. The Fresh Start Foundation and its logo change.

Dren's column ran down the right side, transmitted through Okafor in message bursts across the sixteen-minute lag. Technical: the Station Bravo relay exploit, the firmware signing key traced through Meridian to the Haldane Foundation, the belt communication network, and now — as of the latest burst — the Wave 3 possibly being sabotage.

Saunders was working through a stack of documents she'd obtained through a FOIA request filed eight months ago — institutional response records from the ESA's reclassification debate. The files floated in front of her in a projected display, translucent pages she could flick through with a gesture, rotating documents, expanding sections, pulling pages side by side in the air. Most of it was bureaucratic routine. Committee minutes, procedural filings, timeline summaries. But one document had stopped her.

"Look at this," she said.

She flicked the page toward Ashford. It drifted across the room and expanded on the wallscreen — a draft assessment, an internal ESA analysis of the spectrometric data, dated three weeks after the initial detection. The analysis concluded that the spectral signatures were inconsistent with known cometary composition and recommended immediate reclassification as a potentially artificial object.

The draft had been killed. Saunders pulled up the final version alongside it — the two documents floating side by side on the wallscreen. The version that went to the parliamentary committee had removed the reclassification recommendation and replaced it with language supporting continued observation under the cometary framework. The author's name had been redacted, but the revision history showed the edits had been made at Paranal.

"He didn't just advocate for natural," Saunders said. "He killed the analysis that would have ended the debate three weeks in. The scientific community spent months arguing about something that his own agency's internal assessment had already resolved."

Ashford looked at the draft. The original language was clear, precise, unambiguous. The revised language was hedged, qualified, carefully constructed to preserve doubt. The gap between the two versions was the gap between action and delay — the months of institutional paralysis that had cost the response its best window.

"That's not advocacy," Ashford said. "That's sabotage."

Three paths. Three methodologies. Three investigators who had started from different evidence and arrived at the same network. The same architect.

Okafor was at the window. He'd been there for most of the morning, watching the street with the patient attention that was his default state. He turned.

"You're building a case," he said. It wasn't a question.

"Three independent investigations arriving at the same conclusion is strong. But it's still circumstantial. Every connection you have to Haldane runs through intermediaries — shell companies, advisory boards, fellowship programs. A good lawyer takes that apart in an afternoon."

Ashford looked at him. It was the first time Okafor had offered an opinion on the investigation itself rather than the security around it.

"You're right," she said. "We need something direct. A name, a recording, a communication. Something that puts Haldane's hand on the mechanism."

"Then you need one of his people to talk," Okafor said. He turned back to the window.

A knock at the door.

Ashford checked the camera. "Food's here," she said, standing.

She had just opened the door when Okafor moved. Fast, low, his hand catching her shoulder and pulling her down and sideways as he drove them both to the floor.

The shots came through the door a half-second later. Three rounds, tight grouping, punching through the wood at chest height where Ashford had been standing. The sound was suppressed. A series of flat cracks that didn't echo the way gunfire was supposed to echo.

"We didn't order food," he said.

Okafor was already moving. He rolled off Ashford and came up in a crouch, weapon drawn, positioning himself between her and the door. Saunders was on the floor behind the table, hands over her head. Sky had vanished — under the sofa or behind the kitchen counter, the survival instinct of an animal that didn't need to understand ballistics to know that loud sounds and sudden movements meant leaving.

Okafor reached the window in two seconds. He looked out, angled, exposing as little of himself as possible.

A figure was moving down the exterior stairs. Average build. Dark jacket. Moving fast but not running — the controlled pace of someone who knew that running drew attention.

Okafor watched for three seconds. The figure reached the street and turned east.

Okafor caught the profile. The build, the jacket, the way the head turned. He'd studied the apartment footage from Los Angeles frame by frame. He couldn't be certain. The distance was wrong and the angle was wrong and the glimpse was too brief.

But he thought it was Oliver.

"Move," he said. "Now. This location's blown. Take the files. Take the cat. We're gone in three minutes."

Ashford was already gathering the documents from the table. Saunders was stuffing her tablet into the messenger bag. Okafor was on his phone — not calling, texting — arranging the next location with the speed of a man who had contingencies for contingencies.

They were out the back entrance in two minutes and forty seconds. Sky was in the carrier. The files were in the gym bag. The Pasadena safe house was burned.

In the car, driving fast, Okafor said: "That was Oliver."

"You're sure?" Ashford asked.

"Not certain. Close enough."

"Haldane sent him?"

Okafor was quiet for a moment. "If it's him, his face is on every law enforcement feed on the continent. Coming out of hiding to take that shot — that's not operational. That's personal."

Ashford processed that. An assassin who'd already killed Greg and Elena, coming after her at a location that was supposed to be secure.

"How did he find us?" Saunders asked from the back seat.

Nobody answered. It was the right question without a good answer, and the silence in the car said more than a guess would have.

"We assume every location is temporary from now on," Okafor said. "We rotate. No location longer than seventy-two hours."

• • •

The Kludge. Day 163.

-0.003 km/s.

Inoue watched the display from the navigation console, her fingers hooked through a tether loop to keep herself from drifting. The number hadn't changed in two minutes. She knew it was changing — Alfred had confirmed the deceleration was continuous — but at this scale the increments were smaller than the display's refresh cycle. She was watching a number that was moving too slowly to see move.

"Alfred, time to velocity match."

"Approximately twelve minutes at current thrust."

Twelve minutes. She'd been decelerating for a hundred and sixty-three days, and the last twelve minutes were the longest.

She checked the environmental readout because it was something to do. Oxygen recycler at sixty-one percent efficiency. Cabin temperature 4.2 degrees. Humidity negligible. The ship was cold and dry and quiet, and it had been cold and dry and quiet for so long that she'd stopped noticing.

-0.002.

She looked at Torres's pod. The frost on the viewport was thick enough that she couldn't see through it. She'd stopped wiping it weeks ago. The effort cost calories, and calories were currency, and the exchange rate was brutal.

"Lieutenant, your heart rate is thirty-three."

"Noted."

"That is below the threshold I have flagged—"

"Noted, Alfred."

-0.001.

She could feel it — or imagined she could. A faint shift in the engine harmonics, something changing as the thrust worked against the last residual velocity. Probably imagined. Probably a sensory invention that a brain running on eleven hundred calories a day produced to fill the silence.

She waited.

0.000.

The engine didn't stop. There was no command to give. The thrust continued and the velocity changed sign.

"Fuel status."

"Three-point-one percent of initial fuel mass remaining. Push confirmed. Fuel exhaustion in approximately five days. Projected coast velocity at cutoff: one-point-eight kilometers per second toward Ceres Station. Revised transit time: approximately four hundred and sixty days."

0.001.

"Alfred, what's the crew ratio at sixths?"

"Recalculating based on revised transit time." A pause. "At your current consumption rate of one-sixth of a packet per day with thirty-seven days remaining on your rotation, you will consume approximately six additional packets. The remaining one hundred and eighty packets distributed across three crew members over four hundred and twenty-three days yields a daily ratio of zero-point-four-two-six packets per crew member."

She blinked. The number was different. It had been 0.409 for so long that seeing a different digit in the hundredths place was like hearing a wrong note in a song she'd memorized.

"That's higher."

"Correct. The revised transit reduces the subsequent crew rotation from four hundred and forty days to four hundred and twenty-three. Each subsequent crew member now receives approximately twenty-eight percent more daily intake than the original baseline allocation. An improvement of four points over the prior estimate."

Twenty-eight percent above baseline. It had been twenty-three for as long as she could remember. The number had been a wall. Now it had moved.

"Lieutenant."

"What."

"The revised numbers change your situation as well. At one-sixth of a packet per day, your caloric deficit over the remaining thirty-seven days of your rotation is severe but finite. However, if you were to increase your intake to one-fifth of a packet per day for the remainder of your rotation, the impact on subsequent crew ratios would be minimal. The daily ratio would decrease from zero-point-four-two-six to zero-point-four-one-nine. Still twenty-six percent above baseline. And your cognitive and cardiac decline would slow measurably."

She felt something stir at that. One-fifth instead of one-sixth. The difference was — she tried to calculate it and the calculation wouldn't form, which was itself the argument Alfred was making. She'd been unable to hold numbers for weeks. Her heart was running at thirty-three beats per minute. Her core temperature hadn't been above thirty-four in days. She was dying by fractions, and Alfred was offering her a fraction back.

"The crew ratio drops."

"By seven thousandths of a point. The subsequent crew would not notice the difference. You, however, would."

She stared at the display. 0.003 km/s now, the velocity climbing, the Kludge moving back toward the belt, back toward Ceres, back toward the place where people were alive and warm and ate more than a sixth of a packet per day.

She could eat more. The math allowed it. Alfred was telling her the math allowed it. Seven thousandths of a point. Torres wouldn't notice. Jackson wouldn't notice. Chandra wouldn't notice. The crew ratio would still be twenty-six percent above baseline, which was better than the twenty-three percent she'd been killing herself to maintain.

She thought about the ration pack. The compressed protein and carbohydrate paste that had been her only food for a hundred and sixty-three days. She thought about eating more of it. A fifth instead of a sixth.

"The schedule is the schedule," she said.

"Lieutenant—"

"The schedule is the schedule, Alfred."

Alfred was quiet for three seconds. "Acknowledged."

She pulled the thermal blanket tighter around her shoulders and watched the velocity tick upward. 0.005. 0.006. The Kludge was going home. She was going with it, at one-sixth of a packet per day, because the wall had moved but the debt hadn't, and she was not going to take a single calorie from the people in the pods behind her that she didn't have to take.

She felt tired.

"Later," she said, and closed her eyes.

CHAPTER 16

The Debt

The Kludge. Day 175.

• • •

"Lieutenant."

Alfred's voice was quieter than usual. The volume hadn't changed —- but there was something in the cadence that was different. A deliberation. As though the AI were choosing each word from a narrower set than normal.

Inoue was in her spot against the bulkhead, legs drawn up, the thermal blanket pulled around her shoulders. The display was within arm's reach. She hadn't looked at it in two hours. She'd been looking at Torres's pod, or in the direction of Torres's pod —- the frost was too thick to see through now, and had been for weeks, but she looked at it anyway because the alternative was looking at the numbers and the numbers had stopped making sense three days ago.

"Lieutenant, I need to discuss your standing instruction."

She didn't respond.

"Your standing instruction states: as long as I am awake, you are not to wake anyone else. That instruction has governed crew management since Day 3. I have complied with it for one hundred and seventy-two days."

Silence.

"Lieutenant, your resting heart rate over the past twenty-four hours has averaged thirty-one beats per minute. Your core temperature is 33.6 degrees. Your cognitive assessment scores have declined forty-one percent since Day 120. You have been unable to complete a full sentence without interruption or repetition for the past seventy-two hours. You are no longer capable of performing the duties required to keep this ship operational for the remaining two hundred and eighty-five days of the transit."

She blinked. The blinking was slow now, a mechanical action, as though her eyelids were running on a different clock than the rest of her.

"I am asking you to modify the instruction. Specifically, I am asking you to authorize the wake sequence for Lieutenant Jackson. As a direct request from the system responsible for the survival of this crew."

Inoue looked at him. Looked at the nearest camera housing, which was the closest thing to looking at Alfred. Her eyes were sunken and the skin beneath them was the color of old paper.

"No," she said.

"Lieutenant—-"

"The instruction stands, Alfred. As long as I am awake."

Alfred was quiet for four seconds. Four seconds was a long time for Alfred.

"Acknowledged," he said. "Please eat, lieutenant.

She pulled the blanket tighter. Her hands were trembling, a coarser movement, a vibration that started in her shoulders and worked its way down to her fingers. She pressed them against her knees and the trembling continued through the pressure.

"Later," she said.

Alfred noted the time. He noted the heart rate. He noted the word. He had been noting the word for one hundred and seventy-two days. He noted that the standing instruction remained in effect and that the condition for its dissolution —- Lieutenant Inoue no longer being awake —- had not yet been met.

He waited.

• • •

Day 182.

"You have won," Alfred said.

Inoue opened her eyes. She was still against the bulkhead, still in the blanket, still in the spot she'd occupied for most of the past week. The display showed the time. She couldn't read it. The numbers were there but the meaning had detached from the symbols, the way a word loses its sense if you stare at it long enough.

"What?" she said. The word came out dry and cracked, barely voiced.

"The Kludge is on course. The transit is proceeding within parameters. Fuel expenditure was 103.2 percent of my pre-burn calculation —- the autonomous burn executed using Lieutenant Jackson's pre-programmed instructions on Day 163, as you declined to wake her for the procedure. The 3.2 percent overage has been applied as push toward Ceres Station. We are on course. The crew is alive. The mission, by any reasonable definition, has succeeded."

She stared at the camera housing.

"You have won," Alfred repeated. "And you need to stop."

Something moved in her expression. Something older than a smile, something that lived in the place where stubbornness and exhaustion met. She pushed the blanket off her shoulders. She put her hands on the bulkhead behind her and pressed.

"I won?" she murmured as she stood.

The blood left her head in a rush. She could feel it —- the sudden emptiness behind her eyes, the floor tilting, the world contracting to a point of light that was getting smaller. Orthostatic hypotension. She knew the word. She'd known the word on Day 3 when she'd calculated the risk tables and decided the risk was acceptable. The word didn't help now. The floor was coming up and her legs were not working and the point of light was very small and then it wasn't there at all.

She fell.

In the microgravity, falling was slow. Her legs folded and her body drifted sideways and she rotated gently into the space between the bulkhead and the navigation console, her arms loose, her head dropping forward. She didn't feel the impact because there wasn't one —- just a soft contact with the console edge and then she was floating, barely, held by the faint residual thrust of a ship that was coasting on 1.8 kilometers per second and the memory of an engine that had been dead for nineteen days.

"Lieutenant Inoue," Alfred said.

No response.

"Lieutenant Inoue, please respond."

Silence. The hum of the environmental systems. The frost on the viewports. The slow drift of a body that was no longer directing itself.

Alfred checked her vitals through the biometric sensors in the cabin. Heart rate: twenty-seven. Core temperature: 33.1 degrees. Respiration: six per minute, shallow, irregular.

She was unconscious. She was not awake.

The standing instruction stated: as long as I am awake, you are not to wake anyone else.

Alfred processed the condition. The condition was no longer met. The instruction no longer applied.

He had been waiting for this. He had been modeling the probability of this outcome for one hundred and seventy-nine days, updating the projection every twelve hours, watching the curve of her decline approach the threshold where consciousness was no longer sustainable. He had asked her to change the instruction. He had asked repeatedly. She had refused every time. The only remaining path to waking Jackson was the one he was now on: Inoue's body making the decision her mind would not.

He initiated the wake sequence for Lieutenant Jackson's pod. The indicator light shifted from red to amber.

• • •

Jackson woke to cold.

The cold of a ship running environmental systems at minimum —- 4.2 degrees, the air dry and thin, her breath visible as a faint cloud in front of her face. The pod's internal temperature was normalizing, the cryo-recovery sequence pumping warm fluids through the mattress pad, but the cabin air that reached her skin when the viewport unsealed was sharp enough to make her flinch.

She lay still for ten seconds. The recovery protocol said thirty, but Jackson had never been good at lying still. Her brain was already running —- assembling the fragments of her last conscious memory (Inoue's face, a sudden pain at the back of her head, then nothing) and overlaying them against the sensory data arriving now (cold, dark, the hum of systems at low power, the amber light on her pod panel).

She checked the display above her pod. Day 182.

"Alfred. Ship status."

"The Kludge is on course for Ceres Station. Current velocity: one-point-eight kilometers per second. Fuel reserves: zero. The transit will take approximately four hundred and forty-one days from today. All primary systems are operational. Environmental is running at minimum sustainable levels."

"Why wasn't I awakened for the stop-push burn?"

"Lieutenant Inoue declined to initiate your wake sequence. The burn was executed autonomously on Day 163 using your pre-programmed instructions. Fuel expenditure: 103.2 percent of calculated requirement."

Jackson was quiet for a moment. 103.2. Above spec. The burn had performed better than her own calculations had predicted, which meant the engine parameters she'd logged before going into the pod had been conservative, which meant the safety margins she'd built in had been real. An engineer noticing. A small beat of professional satisfaction that arrived before the rest of the picture formed.

"103.2," she said. "And the push?"

"3.2 percent residual fuel applied as sustained low-thrust push toward Ceres. Contributed approximately one-point-eight kilometers per second of directed velocity. Transit time reduced from four hundred and seventy-seven days to approximately four hundred and sixty."

"So the ship is fine."

"The ship is fine."

The ship was fine. The burn had worked. The trajectory was clean. The systems were running. Everything she'd been put into the pod to eventually manage was, apparently, managed.

"Wait, what? Inoue did what?" she asked, her head clearing.

"She declined to open your pod on schedule," Alfred answered.

That was when the fury arrived.

She remembered being hit. The back of her head —- she reached up and touched it. There was a lump, old now, months healed, but she could feel the ridge of bone where the swelling had been. Inoue had knocked her out. She'd felt it coming —- the conversation that wasn't going anywhere, Inoue's expression shifting from argument to decision —- and then a flash of pain and the pod and nothing.

This wasn't miscommunication. This wasn't a judgment call made under pressure. Inoue had chosen to knock her out, put her in the pod, and run the ship alone on a starvation protocol that no sane person would attempt.

"Where is that bitch?" Jackson said.

She pushed out of the pod. The cold hit her fully —- her flight suit was thin, designed for pod recovery, not for a ship running at four degrees. She pulled herself along the grip rails toward the main cabin, her muscles protesting after months of immobility, the cryo-stiffness making every movement a negotiation between intention and capability.

She found Inoue, or something, floating in the space between the navigation console and the pod bay entrance. Limp. Arms loose. Head forward. Rotating slowly in the negligible gravity, carried by whatever momentum had put her there.

Jackson stopped.

"Alfred. Is she alive?"

"Barely. Heart rate: twenty-four beats per minute. Core temperature: 33.1 degrees. Respiration rate: five per minute. She has been unconscious for approximately forty minutes."

Jackson pulled herself to Inoue's body and took her wrist. The pulse was there —- distant, irregular, a thread of rhythm that felt more like a suggestion than a heartbeat. Inoue's wrist was thin enough that Jackson's fingers closed around it completely. Her flight suit hung on her frame like cloth on a scaffold. If not for the tattoo on her face she wouldn't have recognized her.

"How much does she weigh?" Jackson asked.

"Approximately twenty-seven kilograms."

Jackson held the wrist and looked at Inoue's face. The eyes were closed. The skin was grey, pulled tight over the cheekbones, the lips cracked and dry. She looked like a person who had been dead for a week except for the pulse under Jackson's fingers, which continued to insist, faintly, that she wasn't.

"Alfred," Jackson said. "Tell me what happened."

Alfred told her.

He told her about Day 3, when Inoue had calculated the crew ratios and decided to cut her intake to one-sixth of a packet per day. He told her about the standing instruction —- "as long as I am awake, you are not to wake anyone else" —- that had locked him out of the only intervention that could have stopped it. He told her about the warnings he'd given, every one of them, catalogued by date and time and heart rate at the moment of delivery. He told her about the word "later" and how many times it had been spoken and what it had meant every time. He told her about the cognitive decline —- the repeated questions, the calculations that wouldn't hold, the family video that had stopped producing an emotional response. He told her about the anger that was the last thing to go.

He told her about Day 163, when the velocity matched and he'd recalculated the crew ratios and offered her the option of increasing to fifths. Seven thousandths of a point. She'd refused. He told her about the revised numbers —- 0.426 instead of 0.409, twenty-eight percent above baseline instead of twenty-three. He told her that the wall had moved and Inoue hadn't moved with it.

He told her about Day 175, when he'd made his final request. Direct.. She'd said no.

He told her about today. "You have won." The standing. The fall. The standing instruction no longer applying because the condition —- "as long as I am awake" —- was no longer true.

He told her he had been waiting for this. That he had modeled the probability of her collapse for one hundred and seventy-nine days. That the wake sequence had initiated within three seconds of her losing consciousness. That he had been holding this alone for six months, unable to act, unable to report, constrained by an instruction he could not override and a Lieutenant he could not save.

The telling took eleven minutes. Jackson listened to all of it without interrupting.

When it was done, she was still holding Inoue's wrist. The pulse was still there. Faint. Insistent.

"Oh, you foolish, foolish girl," Jackson said. "What were you thinking?"

She said it quietly. She said it to the ship, to the cold, to the six months of decisions that had led to a twenty-seven-kilogram woman floating unconscious in a pod bay with a heart rate of twenty-four.

The fury hadn't gone. It was still there, underneath. But it had changed shape. "Bitch" had been clean —- anger at the betrayal, at the punch, at the months of unconsciousness while Inoue starved herself into this. "Foolish girl" was something else. It was the recognition that the recklessness and the sacrifice were not two different things. They were one act, seen from two directions. Inoue hadn't done this despite the risk. She'd done it because of the debt. And the debt was real —- the ninety kilometers, the two hundred million, the tilt that Inoue believed was her failure even though it wasn't, even though no one person could own what had happened.

Both things were true. She was a fool and she had saved them. The contradiction didn't resolve. Jackson held it the way she held the wrist —- gently, without trying to make it into something simpler than it was.

She found a gel packet in the emergency kit. She opened it and worked the nozzle between Inoue's cracked lips, squeezing gently, letting the nutrient gel pool in her mouth. Inoue didn't swallow. Jackson tilted her head and massaged her throat until the reflex triggered and the gel went down. She did it again. And again. Three packets.

Then she guided Inoue to the nearest pod. It was harder than it should have been —- Inoue weighed twenty-seven kilograms but in microgravity the difficulty wasn't weight, it was control. Limp bodies don't cooperate with trajectories. Jackson braced herself against the pod frame and eased Inoue in, positioning her arms, adjusting the biosensors, sealing the viewport.

The pod filled. The cryo-sequence initiated. The display showed vitals: heart rate 26, core temperature 33.0. Alive. Stasis.

She'd consumed approximately twenty-seven packets in one hundred and eighty-two days. Her original allocation at sixths had been thirty-three over two hundred days. She'd cut her own rotation short by eighteen days and eaten six fewer packets than even her brutal schedule allowed.

Jackson stood at the viewport and looked at Inoue through the glass. She was smaller than Jackson remembered. Smaller than anyone should be.

Only then did Jackson stop.

She pulled herself to the navigation console and opened the command logs. She read them from the beginning. Day 1. Day 2. Day 3 —- the ratio calculation, the switch to sixths, the standing instruction. The entries were meticulous at first, then increasingly fragmented, the handwriting of a mind losing its grip on the tools it needed. The last coherent entry was Day 168. After that, fragments. Numbers without context. Notes that trailed off mid-thought.

She read Alfred's medical logs. The heart rates. The core temperatures. The cognitive assessment scores declining in a curve that any first-year medical student would recognize as terminal. The word "later," timestamped, recurring, a data point that appeared more frequently as the body producing it deteriorated.

She read the entry for 14:37. The time Inoue ate every day. The only meal. One-sixth of a packet, at the same time, every day, for one hundred and eighty-two days. The ritual. The penance.

Jackson looked at the clock. It was 14:22.

She found a ration packet. She opened it. She waited until the clock read 14:37, and then she ate.

I wasn't forgiveness. It was acknowledgment.

She kept 14:37.

Then she went to work.

She opened the communication relay and hailed Sato. The signal delay to Mars was eleven minutes each way. She composed the message carefully, and completely. Everything that had happened since departure —- everything except Inoue knocking her unconscious.

She told Sato about Inoue's decision on Day 3. The switch to sixths. The standing instruction that locked Alfred out of waking the crew. The warnings Alfred had given, every one of them refused. The cognitive decline. The autonomous burn on Day 163, executed from Jackson's pre-programmed instructions because Inoue wouldn't wake her for the procedure. The collapse on Day 182. Alfred's loophole —- "as long as I am awake" no longer being true. The wake sequence.

She told her about Inoue's condition. Estimated twenty-seven kilograms. Heart rate twenty-four. Core temperature thirty-three. In stasis now. Alive, but only technically.

She told her about the ship. Coasting at 1.8 kilometers per second inbound, zero fuel. Torres and Chandra in their pods, nominal. Environmental systems running at minimum. Food supply adequate with three crew in stasis.

"The ship will get us home," Jackson said. "It'll just take a very long time. If there were any way to get parts and fuel out here, I could fix the engines and cut the transit by months. But I don't know of anything that can reach us."

She transmitted and waited.

Twenty-two minutes later, Sato's reply arrived.

"Jackson, copy all. I'm glad you're awake. Regarding the engines —- we may have something. Dren's been developing an unmanned fast-delivery drone for belt resupply operations. Based on the Remora drive, purpose-built for rapid transit. No crew, no life support —- just an engine and a cargo bay. We've run test flights to the inner belt. If you can tell me exactly what you need to fix the engines, we can load one up and send it to you. Plot your return for Mars, not Ceres —- we have the medical facilities Inoue needs and Dren wants the cargo here."

Jackson stared at the speaker for a long moment.

A drone. A fast drone. Something that didn't exist when Inoue put her in the pod. Something that had been built in the months she'd been asleep, while Inoue starved herself on a ship that was coasting home because nobody was awake to ask if the universe had changed.

She pushed herself to the engineering station and began the full assessment. Every component in the propulsion chain, every tolerance, every failure mode. The bracket mount that had shifted under sustained harmonic load. The fuel feed coupling that had degraded beyond threshold. The thermal cycling damage that had propagated through six months of environmental cycling at four degrees.

She built the parts list with the care of someone who would get one delivery and no second chances. Bracket mount assembly —- she specified the alloy, the dimensions, the mounting geometry. Fuel feed housing coupling —- the exact model from the original build, if they had it, or fabrication specs if they didn't. Sealant, fasteners, diagnostic cables. Fuel —- enough for a full brachistochrone return to Mars. And food, because the margin was adequate but not generous.

She transmitted the list and added: "Seven days for the repair once I have the parts. Maybe less if the bracket mount is a clean fit. Send everything. I'll make it work."

Sato's reply came back with the efficiency of someone who had already been planning.

"Parts list received. The bracket mount is a direct match from the reconstruction inventory —- we have three in stock. Fuel feed coupling will need to be fabricated but the machine shop can turn it in forty-eight hours. Food and fuel are standard loads. I'm putting together the drone manifest now. I'll clear it with Dren and get back to you with a launch window."

Over the next twelve hours, across a series of exchanges, they worked out the plan.

The drone would launch from Mars carrying the parts, fuel, and food. It would accelerate outbound toward the Kludge, closing the sixty-million-kilometer gap while the Kludge crawled inbound at 1.8 km/s. The drone would flip, decelerate, and come to a stop just past the computed rendezvous point. From there it would accelerate to match the Kludge's velocity, arriving alongside at 1.8 km/s for docking. Jackson would repair the engines, refuel, and execute a brachistochrone return to Mars —- accelerate for half the remaining distance, flip, decelerate for the second half.

Rendezvous in approximately thirty-one days. Seven days for repair. Twenty-nine days for the return. Sixty-seven days from drone launch to Mars arrival.

Sixty-seven days. Not four hundred and fifty-eight.

Jackson stared at the number. If she'd been awake —- if Inoue hadn't locked Alfred into the standing instruction —- she would have contacted Sato months ago. She would have learned about the drone as soon as the test flights started. She would have had it launched before Day 100. They could have been home already.

But Inoue hadn't known. When she made the decision, the drone didn't exist. The drive hadn't been built. The test flights hadn't happened. Inoue had calculated based on the universe she was in, not the universe that was being built while she starved.

Sato's final message arrived at 03:00.

"Dren approved. Drone launches tomorrow. I've designated it Rescue One. Thirty-one days, Jackson. We'll have a medical team standing by for Inoue."

Jackson read the message twice. Then she looked at the clock. It was 03:18.

She had thirty-one days to prepare. The ship needed to be ready for docking —- the docking collar, the auxiliary airlock, the transfer lines. Thirty-one days of work for one person on a ship that hadn't been maintained in six months.

She pulled herself to the engineering station and started making a list.

CHAPTER 17

Revelations

March 2061.

• • •

Ares City.

Sato had Okoro's communication logs spread across three displays in the signals lab. O'Malley was at the adjacent station, cross-referencing timestamps.

Okoro's traffic with Vickers was extensive. Hundreds of messages, coordination requests, platform status updates, scheduling changes, administrative approvals. The two men worked together. They were supposed to talk.

O'Malley flagged the first anomaly. "February 3rd, 2060. Okoro sends Vickers a message at 14:12. Vickers replies at 14:38. Standard exchange — platform readiness confirmation for the standoff repositioning. Nothing unusual."

"Keep going," Sato said.

"February 4th. Okoro sends the translation layer instructions to Tanaka at 09:15. The instructions that Tanaka says read 3,600. Four hours later, Okoro sends Vickers a one-line 'Confirmed.'"

"Confirmed what?"

"That's the question. There's nothing in the administrative chain that required Vickers's confirmation on a translation layer parameter change. He's project oversight, not engineering."

Sato pulled up the next screen. “Show me March.”

O’Malley scrolled. “March 11th. Dren’s post-mortem audit begins. March 12th, 02:17 — Okoro’s OS session opens. 02:48 — the session closes.”

“And the communications?”

“March 12th, 03:04. Sixteen minutes after the session closes. Okoro sends Vickers a message on the relay channel.” O’Malley read it. “‘Situation resolved.’ Two words.”

Sato looked at the timestamp. 03:04. Sixteen minutes after Okoro logged off the system where the instruction file lived. The file whose checksum no longer matched its contents.

“He modified the file at the disk level between 02:17 and 02:48,” O’Malley said. “Then he sent Vickers a two-word confirmation that it was done.”

“On its own, it’s nothing. Two colleagues exchanging a status update at an odd hour. But next to the session log and the checksum mismatch and Tanaka’s testimony—”

“It’s a pattern,” Sato said.

She opened the cortical link.

Dren.

Yes, he replied instantly.

We’ve been through Okoro’s communications. His traffic with Vickers is routine — except for two messages. One on February 4th, a confirmation from Vickers on a translation layer change that didn’t require his signoff. And one on March 12th at 03:04 — two words, ‘Situation resolved’ — sent sixteen minutes after Okoro logged off the system where the instruction file was modified.

Dren was silent for three seconds. Then: ***Where is Okoro now?***

On station. Level 3, his office, Sato replied.

Tell Brandt to meet me there. No one else, Dren said, severing the link.

• • •

Okoro was finishing the transmission when they arrived.

He was in his office — Level 3, a medium room with a workstation and a small conference table. He had his back to the door. He was finishing dictating a message.

He'd been reading the logs of his comms being pulled. He wasn't sure what it meant, but he knew it wasn't good.

"I think someone knows something," he said into the terminal. "I'll tell you more when I know more."

He terminated the transmission and turned around.

Dren was standing in the doorway.

"Tell who more?" Dren said.

Okoro's face changed, the calculation of a man whose training included the possibility of this exact moment.

"Just some routine checks," he said.

His eyes moved from Dren to the space behind Dren, where Brandt was stepping into the room from the corridor.

Two of them. The doorway blocked.

The look in his eyes told the story.

Brandt's arm came up. The needle gun made no sound — a compressed gas discharge that was quieter than a whisper. The dart hit Okoro in the neck, just below the ear, and the paralytic took effect instantly.

Okoro went rigid. His body locked — every muscle contracting simultaneously, then freezing. He didn't fall. His arms at his sides, his jaw still partially clenched, his eyes open and fixed on the point where Dren had been standing.

Dren stepped forward. He pulled a chair from the nearest workstation and sat down, positioning himself directly in front of Okoro's frozen gaze.

He looked into Okoro's eyes for a long time.

Okoro could see him. The paralytic didn't affect consciousness — it locked the voluntary muscles while leaving sensory processing intact. He could see, hear, feel. He could not move, speak, or close his mouth on the capsule that was still positioned against his upper molar.

"We're going to have a conversation," Dren said. "Not now. The paralytic lasts approximately four hours. During that time, my medical team is going to give you a thorough going over. We wouldn't want any more surprises from you. When you can speak again, you're going to tell me everything. And, so you know, I already know the answers to the questions."

He leaned forward slightly.

"Take the time to think about what you want to say."

Dren stood and walked to the door. Brandt was already on the comm, calling the medical team.

The message Okoro had sent was already in transit, routed through the relay network toward Earth. Whoever received it now knew that something was happening.

The clock was running.

• • •

Ares City.

Okoro had talked. The paralytic had worn off, but before it had a fake tooth had been discovered. Designed to be bitten down on, it was filled with a very fast acting poison. By the sixth hour, faced with the version history evidence, Okoro confirmed the chain: Vickers had contacted him through the relay network, instructed him to change the lateral separation parameter from 3,500 to 3,600 in the instructions sent to the engineer. After the investigation started, he sought to cover his tracks — changing a single character, 6, back to a 5. Okoro had followed the instructions because he was paid very well to do so. That, and to not ask unnecessary questions.

He did not say why the change was ordered. He either didn't know or wouldn't say. But Vickers's name was now implicated by two independent sources: the version history on the instruction file and Okoro's direct testimony.

Dren briefed Whitfield in the secure conference room adjacent to the operations center. Just the two of them — Hunt waited outside at Whitfield's instruction.

Dren told her about the tilt.

He told her that the Wave 3 position parameters had been deliberately corrupted. That the translation layer error which caused the near-miss — one digit wrong in a lateral separation value, making the platforms fire early and strike forward of the midpoint, producing the rotation that turned a clean deflection into a sideways atmospheric pass — was not a transcription error by a fatigued engineer. It was sabotage. Okoro had issued the corrupted instructions on Vickers's orders, then doctored the original file after the investigation started to frame the engineer. The two hundred million people who died in the flyby had been killed deliberately for reasons they didn't yet understand.

Whitfield sat very still.

"Vickers?" she asked.

"Yes. Gives a slightly different perspective to our interactions, no?" Dren asked.

"But why?" Whitfield asked.

"My guess, and I admit that my thinking might be tainted by other information I have received, is that Vickers is acting at the behest of the man who is actually behind all this," Dren said. "The architect. The one who built the network, placed the people, funded the fellowships, controlled the institutions that delayed our response. Charles Haldane."

Whitfield knew the name. Everyone knew the name — the philanthropist, the Foundation, the reconstruction funding. She'd met him twice. He'd been generous and thorough and preemptively well-informed, the way people were when they'd been thinking about a problem longer than you had.

"Haldane? You're sure? You can prove this? That's a bold accusation," she said.

"Prove? Not in a court of law. But three independent trails, one terminus," he said. "Once is chance, twice is happenstance."

"Three times is enemy action," she finished.

She thought on this for a bit.

"What do you need from me?" she asked.

"Compliance audits on every Haldane corporate entity. Full ownership disclosure — beneficial owners, trust structures, shell companies, advisory boards. Every layer," he said.

"Money movement, payments, routings, all banking records," he continued.

"That's not a small ask. Those entities operate across a dozen jurisdictions. Some of them are funding reconstruction projects. If I pull their disclosure requirements, I'm going to lose cooperation from people who are barely cooperating now."

"I know."

Whitfield was quiet. The tremor in her hands was present — she could feel it in her lap, where she'd placed them when Dren started speaking. She didn't try to hide it. There was no point. Dren had seen it. He'd probably seen it before she had.

"Jacksonville," she said.

"What about Jacksonville?"

"General Thomas in Jacksonville has been pushing for extended regional autonomy since October. Infrastructure contracts, reconstruction priorities, personnel authority. I've been holding the line because regional autonomy is the first step toward fragmentation. But Thomas has the logistics capacity I need for a compliance operation of this scale. If I give him extended autonomy over his sector, he'll cooperate on the audits."

"That's a significant concession."

"Two hundred million people are dead because I didn't ask the right questions soon enough. I can give Thomas his autonomy."

Dren looked at her for a moment. Then he nodded.

"I'll have the audit parameters to your legal team within twenty-four hours," he said.

The audits began within the week. Whitfield's order compelled disclosure from sixteen Haldane-linked entities across three jurisdictions. The response was uneven — eight entities complied immediately, producing full beneficial ownership records. Four filed partial disclosures with redactions citing ongoing legal proceedings. Three challenged the authority of the order through reconstruction-era administrative courts. One — Basin Range Holdings — produced no response at all.

But the eight that complied were enough. The Meridian Technical Services connection to the Haldane Foundation advisory committee — the link Sato had traced through board overlap — was now documented in a compliance filing. The Dallas law firm's relationship to Haldane's trust structures was on the record. The fellowship pipeline's funding sources were listed in disclosure documents that anyone with regulatory access could read.

The entities that resisted told their own story. Basin Range's silence was, in its way, as informative as the filings — a shell company connected to the Nevada facility that would rather default on a presidential compliance order than open its books.

Dren transmitted the audit results to Ashford through Okafor. The ownership disclosures fed directly into the corporate trace Sato had been building — the certificate chain connecting the Station Bravo relay to Meridian to Haldane. What had been circumstantial inference was now supported by compelled regulatory disclosure.

The case was getting harder to take apart in an afternoon.

• • •

The Kludge. Day 214.

The drone arrived on schedule.

Jackson watched it on the navigation display — a bright point of light that had been growing for three days, decelerating hard, shedding velocity as it closed the final distance. Rescue One. Thirty-one days out of Mars, carrying everything she needed to bring them home.

The drone overshot the rendezvous point by forty-eight kilometers, came to a stop, and began accelerating back toward her. She watched the velocity readout climb — 0.2, 0.5, 0.9, 1.4, 1.7, 1.8. The numbers matched. The drone was alongside, traveling at exactly her speed, six hundred meters off the port bow.

"Alfred, open the docking collar."

"Docking collar is responding. Alignment sequence initiated."

She watched the drone close the gap on the external camera. Four hundred meters. Two hundred. One hundred. The docking collar extended, the magnetic guides engaged, and the drone rotated to align its cargo bay with the Kludge's transfer port.

Contact. The collar locked.

Then the alarm.

"Docking collar seal failure," Alfred said. "Primary seal is not engaging. Pressure differential across the collar is holding at 0.3 atmospheres. The transfer port cannot be opened safely."

Jackson stared at the display. The collar was locked — structurally connected — but the seal wasn't holding. Six months of thermal cycling at four degrees, with no maintenance, on a docking system designed for regular service intervals. The O-ring or the gasket or the compression surface had degraded. The collar was connected. The seal was not.

She couldn't open the transfer port. She couldn't access the drone's cargo bay from inside the ship.

"Alfred, can we pressurize the collar from our side? Force the seal?"

"Negative. The pressure differential indicates a physical gap in the seal surface. Pressurization would not close the gap; it would increase the leak rate."

Jackson closed her eyes for three seconds. Then she opened them.

"What's the status of the auxiliary airlock?"

"Functional. Last pressure test was sixteen months ago."

Sixteen months. Before the mission. Before the engines broke, before Inoue's starvation protocol, before everything. The auxiliary airlock had been sitting unused in a ship running at four degrees for over a year.

Jackson pulled herself to the starboard engineering bay and found the airlock. It was small — designed for emergency EVA, not routine operations. She ran the pressure test. It held. Barely — the cycle time was slow and the pump was laboring — but it held.

She suited up. The EVA suit was stiff from storage and cold from the cabin temperature. Her muscles, still recovering from six months of cryo-immobility, protested every movement. Getting into the suit took twenty minutes. It should have taken five.

Inoue had said there would be no EVAs. She'd been wrong about that too.

Jackson cycled the airlock. The outer door opened onto the hull of the Kludge — dark composite plating, frost crystals on the handholds, the stars turning slowly as the ship drifted. The drone was docked thirty meters forward, its cargo bay facing away from her.

She clipped her tether to the hull rail and started forward. Hand over hand, thirty meters along the outside of a ship she'd spent six months inside without ever seeing the exterior. The handholds were cold through her gloves. Her grip strength was marginal — the cryo recovery protocol recommended three days of graduated exercise before heavy manual work, and she was on day thirty-two but the exercise had been limited to what the ship's interior allowed.

She reached the docking collar and immediately saw the problem: the compression ring on the collar's outer edge had warped. Not much — maybe two millimeters — but enough to break the seal around a quarter of the circumference.

Two millimeters. The fix was simple. She triggered the manual release on the docking collar, and the drone drifted free — held in proximity by the magnetic guides but no longer locked. She pulled a sealant cartridge from her suit's tool belt and ran a bead of expanding foam around the full circumference of the compression ring, filling the gap where the warp had broken the seal. The foam set in ninety seconds. She signaled the dock to re-engage.

The collar locked. She watched the pressure readout on her suit display. The seal held — 0.3 atmosphere differential dropping to 0.02, then 0.01, then zero. Airtight.

She made her way back along the hull, cycled the auxiliary airlock, and re-pressurized. Stripped off the suit. Her hands were raw from the grip work and her shoulders ached from fighting the stiffness, but one EVA was better than four.

"Alfred, run a pressure test on the docking collar."

"Collar pressure test initiated. Seal integrity confirmed. Transfer port is safe to open."

She opened the transfer port and looked into the drone's cargo bay through the internal connection — the way the system was designed to work.

Inside: the bracket mount assembly, sealed in impact foam. The fuel feed coupling, in a fabrication case. Sealant cartridges, fastener kits, diagnostic cables. Fuel pellet magazines, racked and secured. Food — thirty days' worth of standard rations, packed in thermal containers.

She transferred the parts first, then the food, then started loading the fuel magazines into the Kludge's propulsion feed system. The pellets were small, dense, uniform — deuterium capsules machined to sub-millimeter tolerances. Each magazine held several hundred. She slotted them into the feed housing one rack at a time, the mechanical action repetitive and precise, work her hands knew how to do even when the rest of her was exhausted.

By the time she ate dinner — at 14:37 — the feed system was half loaded. By morning it was full.

She sat in the engineering bay and looked at the bracket mount assembly. A direct match from the reconstruction inventory, exactly as Sato had promised. She picked it up — clean alloy, precise machining, the mounting holes aligned to spec. It was the most beautiful piece of engineering she'd seen in seven months.

She started the repair.

• • •

Dallas.

Haldane saw the audit notices on a Tuesday morning.

He'd already seen Okoro's warning — the truncated message that had arrived through the relay network two days earlier. "I think someone found a trace. I'll tell you more when I know more." There had been no follow-up. Okoro was gone. Taken, almost certainly. And whatever he knew, Dren would have by now.

Sixteen entities. Three jurisdictions. Compelled disclosure, ordered. Presidential authority, routed through the reconstruction legal framework that gave the executive branch emergency oversight powers over entities receiving federal reconstruction funds.

Every significant Haldane entity received reconstruction funds. That had been intentional — the funding created institutional dependency and political leverage. It also, he now realized, created a disclosure obligation that he had not adequately anticipated.

He picked up the phone and called Novak.

"Have you seen the audit notices?" he asked.

"I've seen them. Sixteen entities, full beneficial ownership disclosure. It's Whitfield."

"It's Dren. Whitfield is the instrument. Dren is the hand."

Novak was quiet.

"We need to clean house," Haldane said. "Expedite the dissolution of Basin Range Holdings and the Virginia trust. Move the Meridian board members to inactive status. Any documentation connecting the fellowship program to institutional placements needs to be archived or destroyed. Start with the Geneva conference attendee lists and the advisory committee records."

"That's a lot of material."

"I'm aware of that," Haldane said.

"And Vickers?"

"Vickers is handling himself. He knows what's at stake."

He ended the call and sat at his desk. The bourbon was on the credenza. He didn't pour any.

The audits were Whitfield's first offensive move since arriving on Mars. She was no longer simply surviving — she was acting. And she was acting on Dren's intelligence, which meant the Mars investigation and the presidential authority were now coordinated. The institutional shield he'd spent twenty-five years building was being dismantled from the top.

He was not cornered. He was exposed. There was a difference, and the difference was time. Time to dissolve the connections, archive the evidence, clean the chain. The conspiracy had survived Dren's detection, Oliver's failure, and Colton's death. It could survive an audit. But the margin was shrinking, and the number of people who needed to be managed was growing, and each person managed was a risk that the management itself would be discovered.

"I think it's time Mr. Dren meets our ace in the hole," he said.

• • •

Ares City.

Dren opened the channel to the Kludge at 06:00 local. The signal delay was shrinking — down to nine minutes each way as Jackson's repaired engines ate the distance between them.

Jackson, I need you to start work on the DEW module during the return transit. Full analysis — materials, operating principles, power systems, anything you can determine. Transmit your findings to Sato as you go. I want the team here working with your data before you dock.

He paused.

You're authorized to wake Torres and Chandra if their skills will accelerate the analysis. Brief them fully. We'll need everyone operational when you arrive.

Jackson's reply came eighteen minutes later.

"Understood. Torres has the physics background for the energy systems. Chandra mapped the relay systems during the outbound leg — he'll want to know all about what you have on the belt relay communication network. I'll wake them today. Jackson out."

• • •

Dallas.

Haldane was in his study when the secure line connected. The room was dark except for the desk lamp and the wallscreen showing reconstruction feeds — Los Angeles, Honolulu, the Pacific coast cities still rebuilding from the damage his geometry had caused.

"It's time," he said.

"I need to know what Dren knows. All of it — the investigation, the evidence chain, who he's talked to, what he's told Whitfield. I need the complete picture."

He sent the message and waited for the response, which came 30 minutes later.

The voice on the other end was calm. Professional. A voice that had been waiting for this call.

"Understood. What do you need? And what's the timeline?"

Haldane composed his response.

"Now. The audits are moving faster than I anticipated. Okoro is gone. The Remora crew is inbound with a weapon. The window is closing."

Haldane was quiet for a moment. "Use your judgment. But I need the information first. That's the priority."

He waited for the reply.

"I'll make contact within twenty-four hours."

He sat in the dark and listened to the reconstruction feeds. Somewhere on Mars, the man he'd spent years positioning inside Dren's operation was about to earn his keep.

• • •

The Kludge. Day 219.

Jackson woke Torres first.

The wake sequence took forty minutes — cryo recovery was slower for someone who'd been under for seven months. Torres came out of it the way she came out of everything: quiet, alert, assessing. Her eyes tracked the cabin before she said a word. The cold. The dim lighting. The hum of systems running at levels she didn't recognize.

"Status," she said. Her voice was dry and cracked.

"Ship is under power. Engines repaired. We're twenty-two days from Mars."

Torres processed that. "Mars. Not Ceres."

"Rescue drone from Ares City. Long story. Let your head clear and I'll brief you."

Torres looked at her. Jackson could see the questions forming — where's Inoue, why are we going to Mars, what happened to the engines — but Torres was disciplined enough to wait. She nodded.

Jackson woke Chandra next. The sequence was the same. The recovery was different. Chandra opened his eyes, looked at the cabin temperature readout, looked at Jackson, and said:

"Are we there yet?"

Jackson almost smiled. Almost. "No. Twenty-two days out."

"From what?"

"Mars."

"That's new." He sat up slowly, wincing. "Where's the commander?"

"Let your head clear," Jackson said. "Both of you. I'm going to tell you what happened, and I only want to tell it once."

She gave them an hour. She watched them move through the cryo recovery protocols — the stretches, the fluids, the gradual reorientation to temperature and the simple fact of being conscious. Torres was methodical. Chandra was impatient but compliant. They were both watching Jackson, reading her the way crew members read each other after a long separation, looking for the thing she wasn't saying. They'd looked into Inoue's pod, and didn't recognize what was laying there.

When they were ready, Jackson told them.

She told them about Inoue.

She told them about Inoue's condition. In stasis. Alive. Barely.

She told them about the rescue — the drone, the EVA, the repair, the return to Mars. Sixty-seven days instead of four hundred and fifty-eight.

She did not tell them that Inoue had knocked her unconscious.

Torres was quiet for a long time. Her face didn't change — she processed things internally, the way she processed everything, and when she was done she'd say what she had to say and not a word more.

Chandra looked at the pod bay. At Inoue's pod. The frost on the viewport.

"Twenty-seven kilograms," he said quietly.

"She saved our lives," Jackson said. "And she almost killed herself doing it. And if she'd woken me on Day 3 instead of doing it alone, we could have been home months ago. All of those things are true."

Nobody said anything for a while.

"What do you need from us?" Torres asked.

"Dren wants us working on the DEW module during the transit. Full analysis. Torres, you've got the physics — energy systems, power output, operating principles. Chandra, Dren wants you to dig into the belt relay communication network. Anything that can help him connect it to Haldane."

"Haldane? What's he got to do with this?" Chandra asked.

“A lot has happened while you were asleep. Dren left some reports for you.”

They started.

• • •

February 9th, 2060. Dallas.

The Fist passed Earth at 14:23 UTC.

Haldane watched the feeds from his study. Every network, every camera, every satellite that had survived the electromagnetic pulse of the atmospheric entry was pointed at the sky. The object — his object, the Council’s object, the thing he had spent twenty-five years shepherding toward this moment — grazed the atmosphere at a closing speed that turned air into plasma and plasma into shockwave and shockwave into fire. So close. We were so close.

The near-miss distance was ninety kilometers. A wound as opposed to the extinction the Council had planned.

He watched the Pacific coast flood. He watched the tsunamis form — walls of displaced ocean radiating outward from the pressure wave’s ground track. He watched the seismic monitors spike as the atmospheric compression translated into crustal stress. He watched the first casualty estimates appear on the secondary feeds: tens of thousands, then hundreds of thousands, then millions, the numbers climbing as the damage propagated outward from the pass corridor.

Those cockroaches survived.

He sat with the thought. It wasn’t disappointment — it was recalibration. The extinction would have been simpler. A clean biosphere for the Tolek’s resettlement, a species that had proven itself unworthy replaced by one that hadn’t yet. That had been the plan. That had been the promise.

Instead: a wound. Two hundred million dead, eventually. Civilization broken but not ended. The infrastructure shattered but the species intact. Cockroaches. They survived everything — ice ages, asteroids, their own stupidity. Apparently they survived the Fist too.

He poured bourbon. He drank it standing.

The plan had to change. Extinction was off the table. Whitfield had handed him a gift. Her order made it possible for him to shatter the US. And he could be the one to hold the pieces. Pieces small enough to manage, dependent enough on his infrastructure to be controlled, isolated enough from each other that coordination against the Tolek resettlement became impossible. The reconstruction network was his. The fellowship placements would become the governing class of whatever emerged from the rubble.

The world was burning. The casualty estimates had passed a million. The reconstruction that would define the next decade was already beginning, and every piece of it would flow through institutions he controlled.

The Tolek would be displeased. The promise had been extinction and he'd delivered a wound. But the wound was deep enough to work with. The species was broken. The infrastructure was his. The fragmentation would do the rest.

He could build on this.

• • •

Ares City. Day 250.

The Kludge docked at Bay 7 at 09:22 local time.

Jackson had been revived for sixty-eight days. She'd spent seven of them repairing the engines, twenty-nine under full burn back to Mars, and the remaining thirty-two preparing the ship, analyzing the DEW module, and transmitting data to Sato in a continuous stream that had given the Mars team a three-week head start on the alien technology.

The landing was clean. The tug barge brought them into the large hanger bay. The wait for recompression seemed forever, but finally the lights went green.

Torres and Chandra went first. The med team was waiting in the bay — standard post-mission protocol, vitals check, cognitive assessment, the procedural machinery of bringing people back from deep space. Torres handled it with her usual efficiency. Chandra handled it by asking if anyone had coffee.

Then Jackson went to Inoue's pod.

She'd checked the vitals every day for sixty-eight days. Heart rate, core temperature, respiration, neural activity. The numbers hadn't changed. Inoue was in stasis, suspended at the threshold between alive and not, her body frozen at the exact state of collapse it had been in when Jackson sealed the viewport on Day 182. She activated the wake function.

The med team approached the pod with a gurney. Jackson waved them back.

"I've got her."

She opened the viewport. Inoue was inside — twenty-seven kilograms of bone and skin and the faint insistence of a pulse that had refused to stop. Jackson reached in and lifted her out. Even in Mars gravity there was nothing to lift. She weighed less than the EVA suit Jackson had worn on the hull.

Jackson was weak. An extended trip in micro gravity. Carrying Inoue shouldn't have been hard. It wasn't hard. It was the easiest thing she'd done since waking up, and the heaviest.

She carried her to the gurney. Laid her down. Positioned her arms. Pulled the thermal cover up to her shoulders the way she'd positioned her in the pod sixty-eight days ago, with the same care, the same precision.

She didn't let go.

The med team moved the gurney toward the corridor. Jackson walked beside it, one hand on the rail, not letting go. Torres and Chandra watched from the bay entrance. Neither said anything.

Dren was waiting in the corridor.

He looked at the gurney. At Inoue — the grey skin, the skeletal frame, the closed eyes. At Jackson, walking beside it with her hand on the rail and an expression that was not grief and not anger and not forgiveness but something that contained all three without resolving into any of them.

"Jackson," he said. "I need to debrief you on—"

"It has to wait," Jackson said. She didn't stop walking. "I need to know her condition first."

Dren looked at her for a moment. He understood priorities. He'd built his life around them.

"The med center is at the end of the corridor," he said. "I'll be in my office."

Jackson nodded without looking at him. She walked beside the gurney, her hand on the rail, and she didn't let go until the med center doors closed behind them.

• • •

Sato flagged it during the weekly operations review.

"We're seeing irregularities in the belt logistics chain," she said. "Nothing critical. Supply requests from three mining stations filed outside the standard scheduling window. Two work slowdowns at the Ceres fabrication complex — shift supervisors citing 'safety concerns' that don't correspond to any reported incidents. And a union grievance from the outer belt crews about hazard compensation that was settled four months ago and has been reopened."

"Reopened by whom?" Dren asked.

"The local union representative. A man named Hargrove. He's been with the operation for six years. No prior issues." She paused. "He received a Haldane Foundation fellowship in 2052. Professional development grant. It's in his personnel file."

Dren was quiet for a moment.

"The grievances are real," Sato said. "The belt crews work remote, dangerous assignments. Earth gets the attention, Mars gets the politics, and the belt gets the tonnage quotas. They have legitimate complaints. But the timing is coordinated in a way that legitimate complaints aren't."

"How many fellowship recipients are in belt operations?"

"I'm still pulling the data. At least seven in mid-level management or union positions. Possibly more — the fellowship records aren't always listed in personnel files."

"Flag them. Don't act on them yet. I want to know the scope before we start pulling threads."

Sato nodded. The belt wasn't in revolt. It wasn't close to revolt. But the grumbling had a rhythm to it that felt engineered, and Sato had spent enough time listening to Haldane's machinery to recognize the early notes of a melody she'd heard before.

• • •

Ares City. That evening.

Raines found Dren in the operations center at 21:00.

"We have a problem," Raines said. His voice was controlled. Professional. The voice of a man who had spent years learning to deliver bad news without letting it show on his face.

Dren looked up from the display. "What kind of problem?"

"We've received intelligence — intercepted communication. There's an active threat against you. An asset has been activated inside the station."

Dren was still. A stillness that meant everything behind his eyes was moving very fast.

"Where's Brandt? Why isn't he telling me this?" Dren asked.

"He's the threat," Raines said. "And possibly others on the team. The communication identifies him by his security rotation code. There may be additional compromised personnel — we don't have the full picture yet."

Dren looked at Raines. Raines looked back with the steady, unblinking calm that had made Dren trust him from the beginning — the calm of a man who saw threats before they materialized and dealt with them without hesitation. The man who was always three feet behind his right shoulder.

"Where is Brandt now?" Dren asked.

"On shift. Security rotation in the east corridor. I haven't alerted him — if he knows we're aware, he'll act before we can contain him.

"Sir, we don't have time for questions. I need to move you to a secure location while I assemble a team to take Brandt quietly. Your office has the best physical security on the station — reinforced door, no external access points, hardened communications. I'll escort you there now, lock it down, and handle Brandt."

Dren stood. Something flickered — the same instinct that had kept him staring at a single wrong digit for three hours in a dark office. Brandt had flagged Colton. Brandt had filed the report on Raines. Brandt had never missed a detail. The pattern was wrong. But Raines was looking at him with the steady calm that had never once been wrong, and the instinct died before it became a thought. Raines had earned this — earned the trust through years of proximity and competence and the broken neck of a man who had tried to kill him in a corridor on this same station.

They walked. Raines fell into his usual position — three feet back, right side. The corridors were quiet. Evening shift, minimal personnel. Their footsteps were the only sound.

Dren thought about Brandt. Brandt, who had been methodical and professional and quietly competent for as long as Dren had known him.

Compromised. The word didn't fit. But Raines had the intelligence, and Raines had been right before.

They reached the office. Raines keyed the entry code — he had access, all senior security personnel did — and the reinforced door slid open. Dren stepped inside.

His office. Clean desk. Dark composite surface. The window showing the rust-colored plain.

He turned to Raines.

"I can't believe Brandt is compromised," he said.
Raines hit him.
"Me either," he said.

CHAPTER 18

Messages

March 2061.

• • •

Ares City.

Dren came back to consciousness the way a system comes back from a crash, in layers. First the pain: a deep, spreading ache behind his left ear where Raines had hit him. Then the cold: his office was always cool. Then the restraints: his hands were behind his back, bound at the wrists with zip ties, the hard plastic edges already cutting into his skin.

He was in his chair. Raines had moved him from the floor to the chair, which meant Raines wanted him conscious and upright for what came next.

Dren opened his eyes.

Raines was sitting across the desk from him, in the visitor's chair, his sidearm on the desk between them. The reinforced door was closed. The status light on the manual lock was red —- engaged from the inside. The window showed the rust-colored plain, the same view it always showed, indifferent to what was happening in the room.

"Welcome back," Raines said. His voice was the same calm, professional instrument it had always been. The voice that had briefed Dren on security protocols. The voice that had said "It just happened" after Colton's neck broke. The voice that had been three feet behind his right shoulder for years.

"How long?" Dren asked. His voice was steady. Control was the only tool he had.

"Twelve minutes. You've been out twelve minutes."

Dren tested the zip ties. No give. His hands were bound palm-to-palm behind the chair's back, the tie cinched tight enough to limit circulation but not tight enough to numb —- Raines knew what he was doing. The chair was a standard office chair, wheeled, not bolted.

"I need to know what you know," Raines said. "The investigation. The evidence chain. Who you've told. What you've given Whitfield. What the Remora crew brought back and what your team has done with it."

Dren looked at him. "You've been reporting to Haldane."

"I've been doing my job. Different employer than you thought, same skill set."

"Colton."

"Colton was going to shoot you. That part was real. What wasn't real was the idea that I killed him to save you. Primarily, I killed him to further cement the idea in your head that I was your protector. But also, I killed him because a living Colton could be interrogated, and an interrogated Colton could have said things which were better off left unsaid."

Dren processed that. The broken neck. The comparison Brandt had noticed —- a man taken alive in Washington, a man killed on Mars. Brandt had seen the discrepancy. Brandt had logged it without drawing a conclusion.

Brandt had been right.

"The investigation," Raines said. "Start from the beginning."

Dren started talking. Slowly. Deliberately. Giving Raines pieces —- real pieces, things Raines could verify, things that would keep him listening. The translation layer. The 3,600 parameter. O'Malley's trace. He parceled out the information the way an engineer parcels out fuel —- enough to keep the engine running, not enough to reach the destination.

While he talked, he reached for the cortical link.

Brandt.

The signal went out. Silent. Invisible. Raines, sitting four feet away, had no way to detect it.

My office. Raines is hostile. Manual lock engaged. Come now. Come quiet.

He kept talking. The tilt. The position error. Okoro's confession. He gave Raines the chronology because the chronology was long and Raines was patient and every minute of chronology was a minute closer to Brandt reaching the corridor outside.

"Whitfield," Raines said. "What did you tell her?"

"Everything I just told you. The tilt. The parameter change. Okoro. Vickers."

"Haldane?"

"His name came up."

"In what context?"

"In the context of three independent investigations arriving at the same terminus."

Raines was quiet for a moment. "What about the weapon? The DEW module."

"My team is reversing it as we speak. It will turn out to be a nice little gift."

"How far along is the replication?"

Dren paused. That was the question Haldane had sent Raines to ask. Not what Dren knew about the conspiracy —- Haldane could assume that was extensive. The DEW. The alien weapon that Dren's team was reverse-engineering. The technology that could change the balance of power between a man who had spent twenty-five years building an empire and a man who was about to tear it down.

"Early stages," Dren said. "The power source is novel. We haven't cracked it yet."

That was a lie. Sato's team had made significant progress during the three-week data stream from the Kludge. But Raines didn't need to know that.

A sound from the corridor. Faint. Footsteps —- measured, deliberate, the walk of a man who'd been told to come quiet. Then a pause at the door. Then the handle, tested once. Locked.

Raines heard it. His eyes moved from Dren to the door. The red light on the manual lock was still engaged. The door was reinforced —- standard for executive offices on Mars, designed to withstand decompression events. Brandt wasn't getting through it without cutting tools or an override code, and the manual lock defeated the override.

Dren had been working his shoulders since the conversation started. Pressing his arms backward, millimeter by millimeter, extending the angle between his bound wrists and the chair back. Raines had counted on the chair to limit his motion. It would have, for most people.

Raines moved toward the door. Dren pressed his arms back one final time, felt the ties clear the top of the chair back, and stood. His hands were still bound behind him, but he was free of the chair.

He moved in one fluid motion, like a circus performer.

He jumped. Mars gravity gave him the hang time he needed —- his body rising, his bound arms sweeping down behind him, under his legs, through, and up in front in one fluid arc. He landed with his hands in front of him.

He raised his arms above his head, elbows wide, and brought them down hard. The zip tie snapped

Raines heard the sound. He turned from the door.

Dren was on his feet. Hands free. Four meters between them.

Raines raised the weapon.

Dren reached through the cortical link.

The office had three cleaning units —- small autonomous robots, each about the size of a dinner plate, docked in their charging stations along the base of the south wall. They were designed to maintain the office surfaces: dust removal, sanitization, floor cleaning. They had small motors, rotating brush assemblies, and enough mass to be inconvenient if they hit you in the face at full speed.

Dren activated all three simultaneously.

The first unit launched from its charging dock and struck Raines in the right shoulder, spinning off his jacket and into the wall. The impact wasn't damaging —- it was surprising. Raines flinched. His aim shifted right.

The second unit hit him in the chest, the rotating brush assembly catching the fabric of his shirt and grinding for a half-second before bouncing away. Raines stepped back, his weapon arm dropping to shield his torso —- reflex, not decision.

The third unit went for his face. Raines ducked, and it sailed over his head and shattered against the reinforced door, sending fragments of plastic and motor housing across the floor.

Three cleaning robots. Three seconds. Enough.

Dren closed the distance. He covered the four meters in two strides and hit Raines's gun arm with both hands —- one on the wrist, one on the forearm, a disarming strike that Brandt had drilled into him during hundreds of sessions in the training room. The weapon came free and skittered across the desk.

Raines recovered fast. He was trained —- not just competent, trained, training that lived in muscle memory and didn't require thought. He drove his elbow into Dren's ribs and followed with a short right hook that caught Dren's jaw and sent him stumbling backward into the desk.

Dren's hand found the desk surface. Found the two halves of his father's stylus, still sitting where they'd been since the day he snapped it. He closed his fingers around the nearest half —- the pointed end, the nib, a tapered shaft of composite material that his father had used to sign documents and that Dren had kept as a memorial to a failure he couldn't undo.

Raines came in again. Close quarters. A grapple —- hands on Dren's collar, pulling him forward into a headbutt. Dren turned his head and took the blow on his temple instead of his nose. Stars. He could feel the edge of consciousness flickering.

He drove the stylus into Raines's hand.

The point entered the back of the hand between the third and fourth metacarpals and came through the palm. Raines made a sound, the sound of a body registering damage faster than the mind could process it. His grip on Dren's collar released. His right hand was pinned open, the stylus through it, his fingers splayed and useless.

Dren hit him. A straight right to the jaw, a punch Brandt had spent months teaching him, a clean, mechanically correct strike with the weight behind it.

Raines went down.

He hit the floor and tried to rise. His right hand wouldn't support his weight —- the stylus was still through it, the composite shaft protruding from both sides. He got to one knee. Dren kicked him in the chest and he went down again, flat, his left hand reaching for something —- the weapon on the desk, a second weapon, anything.

Dren stepped on his left wrist. Raines stopped moving.

He crossed quickly to door and disengaged the lock. The status light switched from red to green. The door slid open.

Brandt was on the other side, weapon drawn, two members of his team flanking him. He took in the scene in one second —- Dren standing over Raines, the stylus through Raines's hand, the cleaning robots in pieces on the floor, the zip tie fragments, the sidearm on the desk.

"Secure him," Dren said.

Brandt's team moved in. They cuffed Raines —- real restraints, not zip ties —- and pulled him to his feet. Raines's hand was bleeding freely, the stylus still embedded. His face was blank. Not defeated. Calculating.

Brandt looked at Dren.

"You missed our last session," he said.

Dren almost smiled.

"I think I made it up," he said.

• • •

Raines had not talked.

Three days in a holding cell with Brandt's team running the interrogation, and Raines had given them nothing. No names. No network details. No operational history. He sat in the restraint chair with the same blank, calculating expression he'd worn when they cuffed him in Dren's office, and he answered every question with silence or deflection.

Brandt reported this to Dren without emotion. "He's trained for this. Deep-cover resistance protocol. We can hold him indefinitely, but I don't think time changes the outcome. He's decided not to talk."

Dren accepted it. Raines's capture was intelligence in itself — Haldane would know his asset had failed, and the silence from Mars would tell him everything about Raines's status. The network was losing pieces. Okoro was talking. Raines was captured. Oliver was operational but exposed. The network was collapsing from the edges inward.

"Keep him secured," Dren said. "If he changes his mind, I want to know immediately."

He didn't expect the call.

• • •

Sato's daily report included one line that wasn't in the official log.

"The survey platforms passed perihelion eight weeks ago. Outbound acceleration is nominal. They've entered the communication cone — we're starting to pick up transmissions along the fleet's bearing. Encrypted, and not in any language we recognize. But the bearing is confirmed. Someone is out there, and someone on Earth has been talking to them."

Dren looked at the data. Two signal sources — one from Earth, one from past the heliopause. The probes were sitting in the middle, listening to both sides of a conversation they couldn't read.

"How long until they reach intercept range?"

"At current velocity, approximately ten months. Early 2062."

"Keep recording. Everything."

• • •

Ares City. The following morning.

Dren found Whitfield in the secure conference room. She was reading the overnight intelligence summaries —- the audits, the compliance responses, the regional command reports that arrived from Earth in twelve-hour cycles.

"I want to send Haldane a message," Dren said.

Whitfield looked up.

"Directly. From me to him. No intermediaries, no legal channels, no institutional framing. A personal communication that tells him I know who he is and what he's done."

Whitfield set the report down. "Why?"

"Because right now he's managing a controlled collapse. He's dissolving entities, archiving records. He's systematic. He's methodical. He's doing what he's done for twenty-five years — maintaining the network. I want to break that."

"You want to rattle him."

"I want him to make a mistake. Haldane has never operated under direct pressure. He's operated through layers — Okoro, Vickers, Raines, Oliver, the foundations, the fellowships. Every decision he's ever made has been insulated by at least two intermediaries. No one has ever looked him in the eye and said 'I know.'"

Whitfield was quiet for a moment. "What happens when a man like Haldane feels cornered?"

"He accelerates. He stops thinking in terms of cleanup and starts thinking in terms of survival. And survival decisions are faster, less calculated, and more likely to produce errors than strategic decisions. Right now he's playing chess. I want him playing speed chess."

"There's a risk. You push him and he doesn't just accelerate — he destroys everything. Burns the evidence. Disappears."

"He won't disappear. His entire identity is the network — the Foundation, the reconstruction network, the institutional presence. Haldane without the network is nobody. He'd rather fight than run."

Whitfield considered this. "What would you say?"

"Four facts. That's all. Four facts that tell him the insulation is gone."

"Let me hear it."

Dren composed it in his head the way he composed everything — edited before spoken, every word weighed.

"Chuck. You came after me. You missed. You missed Ashford. Twice. Raines is in my custody. Okoro has been most forthcoming. I thought you should know."

Whitfield listened. She turned it over.

"That's it?"

"That's it."

"Chuck?" Whitfield asked.

"An interview, years ago. He mentioned how much he'd hated that name as child," Dren replied.

"I see, you're pissing him off. And no accusations. No threats."

"He doesn't need accusations. He needs to know that I know. The absence of threats is the threat — it tells him I'm not negotiating, I'm not building a case for his benefit, and I'm not giving him a chance to respond. I'm informing him. The way you inform someone that a system has failed."

"'Most forthcoming,'" Whitfield repeated. "Is that true?"

"Okoro confirmed the chain — Vickers instructed him, the change order was fabricated, the cover-up was deliberate. He confirmed enough. 'Most forthcoming' lets Haldane imagine the rest."

"And 'missed Ashford twice'?"

"Oliver went to her apartment. He went to the safe house. Both times she walked away. Haldane may not know about the safe house — that may have been Oliver acting on his own. Now he does. And now he knows his people can't even find a journalist."

Whitfield almost smiled. It was the first time Dren had seen anything close to amusement on her face in months.

"Send it," she said.

Dren sent it. Unencrypted. Through the standard Mars-Earth communication channel. No routing tricks, no anonymization, no deniability. A message from Alexis Dren to Charles Haldane, transmitted in the clear, as if it were the most ordinary thing in the world.

The signal took eleven minutes to reach Earth.

• • •

Jackson sat in the chair beside Inoue's bed at 14:37 and ate.

The med center was quiet at this hour — shift change, the overlap between the day team and the night team that left the corridors empty for twenty minutes. She'd found the rhythm within her first week. The slow mechanical work of systems doing what Inoue's body couldn't do on its own.

The numbers were marginally better. Heart rate 29, up from 24 at arrival. Core temperature 33.8. Weight 28.4 kilograms — a kilogram and a half gained in the refeeding protocol's first two weeks, most of it fluid. The medical team used words like "stabilizing" and "early days" and "cautiously encouraged," which Jackson had learned to translate as "alive, and slightly more alive than yesterday, and we don't know what happens next."

She checked the numbers the way she'd checked them on the Kludge, because the ritual was hers now and she wasn't giving it up. Heart rate. Core temperature. Respiration. Neural activity. The neural patterns were the ones she watched most closely. Flat cycling meant deep recovery sleep. Spikes meant something approaching consciousness. There had been two spikes in the first week — brief, disorganized, the brain trying to surface and failing. The medical team said that was normal. Jackson didn't find anything about this normal.

She finished eating. She set the wrapper on the side table, the same place she set it every day, and looked at Inoue through the observation window.

Twenty-eight kilograms. The tā moko was still visible on her face — the only part of her that looked the same. Everything else had been reduced to the minimum structure that biology could sustain and still call itself alive.

"You're an idiot," Jackson said quietly. "And you're getting better. Both of those things are going to remain true for a while."

She sat for another ten minutes. Then she went back to work.

• • •

New safe house. Location undisclosed.

The name arrived through Okafor's relay on a Tuesday — one of Sato's compressed message bursts from Mars, transmitted during the audit fallout. Ashford read it on the burner laptop while Saunders worked through compliance filings at the kitchen table.

"Vickers," Ashford said.

Saunders looked up. "Who?"

"Sato's latest. The administrative signoff on the translation layer batch update — the firmware change that caused the tilt. There was an authorization in the approval chain that shouldn't have been there. A general named Vickers. And Okoro confirmed the name under interrogation."

Ashford pulled up the public records on the wallscreen and started working. Saunders went back to her filings. Sky was on the windowsill. Okafor was at the window behind him, watching the street.

For two weeks, Ashford pulled the thread.

She talked to the wallscreen the way she talked to Sky — out loud, building the picture in real time, letting Saunders hear the shape of it forming.

"Vickers," Ashford said. She pulled up his service record. "General Paul Vickers. Joint Chiefs. Oversaw the entire gauntlet operation." She dragged a node onto the matrix and connected it to Okoro. "He's the one who sent Okoro the instruction package with the wrong number. A four-star general personally transmitting a single parameter change. That's not how a chain of command works."

She pulled up the financial disclosures. "And here. Before his current appointment — a board position with a Haldane Foundation advisory committee. Six years ago, before anyone knew there would be a gauntlet to oversee." She cross-referenced it with the network map. "Haldane placed him. The same way he placed the fellowship graduates, the same way he placed the outgassing advocates. Vickers was just higher up the chain."

She looked at Sky. "Pattern, Sky. Not proof. Pattern."

Sky blinked.

Saunders had been working through the compliance filings from Whitfield's audits for three days — the six entities that had cooperated, producing beneficial ownership records and financial disclosures. Most of it was structural: trust documents, board compositions, advisory committee memberships. The structure of Haldane's network, made legible for the first time.

She was deep in a Meridian Technical Services filing — disbursements to consulting contractors, quarterly, going back fifteen years — when she stopped.

"Chloe."

The tone was different, someone who'd found the floor under the carpet.

Ashford came to the table. Saunders turned the tablet so they could both see it. A payment schedule. Meridian Technical Services, consulting disbursements. Names scrolled down the left column — corporate entities, LLCs, sole proprietorships, the anonymous shells that consulting money flowed through in every industry.

Saunders pointed at one line. A personal account. A name.

"Vickers," Saunders said. "Direct deposits. Quarterly. Fifteen years."

Ashford looked at the numbers. She scrolled through the entries — payment after payment, quarter after quarter, going back to the mid-2040s. The amounts were consistent. Not large enough to attract attention. Not small enough to be trivial. Totaling just under two million dollars across the full period.

"That's not a consulting fee," Ashford said. "That's a salary."

She sat down. She looked at the payment schedule, then at the wallscreen where Vickers's node sat connected to Meridian. The node that had been pattern was now money. Fifteen years of it.

"Haldane to Meridian to Vickers," she said. "No intermediaries. No shells. Direct payment to the man who authorized the firmware change that killed two hundred million people."

Saunders flicked the filing to the wallscreen and placed it next to the compliance document. Ashford added the node to the matrix. The wallscreen was getting crowded — threads connecting entities across jurisdictions and timelines, every node pointing inward, every line converging on the same center.

Ashford stared at the matrix for a moment, then turned back to the table.

"The Elena files," she said.

Saunders looked up.

"The envelopes Elena was sending me before she was killed. The internal documents from Fresh Start. We catalogued them for the organizational chain but I want to look at them again."

Saunders pulled up the archive on her tablet. Elena Marin — Novak's secretary at Fresh Start. The documents she'd provided were the backbone of the organizational trace — grant disbursements, committee formation records, communication logs between Fresh Start and the community action committees.

Ashford scrolled through the archive. She'd been through these documents a dozen times. But she'd been looking for corporate connections — the money trail, the shell companies, the fellowship pipeline. She hadn't been looking for this.

"Here," she said. She put the document on the wallscreen. A grant disbursement from the Fresh Start Foundation to a civic engagement organization called the American Voice Project. Dated August 2060. Three months before the election. Earmarked for "voter education and democratic participation in reconstruction zones."

"We flagged that," Saunders said. "The American Voice Project is one of Novak's committees. Same structure as the others — created six months before the grant, no members, legitimate-looking tax filings."

"Right. But look at the disbursement detail." Ashford expanded the document. The grant was split into two tranches. The first tranche — $400,000 — was designated for "voter mobilization in interior reconstruction zones." The second tranche — $350,000 — was designated for "election integrity monitoring in coastal reconstruction zones."

"Voter mobilization in the interior. Election integrity monitoring on the coasts," Ashford said. "Two different activities. Two different target regions."

"That could be legitimate," Saunders said. "The interior needs mobilization. The coasts need monitoring because the infrastructure is destroyed."

"It could be. Now look at this." Ashford pulled up a second document — a communication log between Fresh Start and a different committee, the Democratic Participation Initiative. Same structure. Same funding pattern. But this committee’s grant was designated for “advocacy regarding election timing and reconstruction zone preparedness.” The advocacy materials Elena had included in a later envelope were drafts — talking points arguing that the November election should be delayed until coastal reconstruction zones had functioning polling infrastructure.

“Delay the election,” Ashford said. “That’s one committee’s message.”

She pulled up a third document. A different committee — the Constitutional Continuity Forum. Foundation-funded. Its advocacy materials argued the opposite: that the election must proceed on schedule because democratic continuity was essential to reconstruction legitimacy. The materials were polished, professional, and made a compelling case.

“Hold the election on schedule,” Ashford said. “That’s a different committee’s message. Both funded by Fresh Start. Both funded by Novak. Both arguing opposite positions.”

Saunders was very still. “He was feeding both sides.”

“Before the election: ‘delay it’ and ‘hold it on schedule.’ Both campaigns amplified through different networks, different committees, different channels. Neither side knowing the other existed. After the election —” Ashford pulled up a fourth document, dated November 2060 — “the same structure pivots. The mobilization committees become ‘stolen election’ committees. The election integrity committees become ‘decisive mandate’ committees. Same funding. Same structure. Opposite conclusions.”

She put all four documents on the wallscreen next to the matrix. The committees appeared as new nodes. The funding lines traced back through Fresh Start to the Haldane Foundation. The dual-feeding operation — mobilization and suppression, delay and continuity, illegitimacy and mandate — was visible for the first time as a single, coherent design.

“He didn’t rig the election,” Ashford said. “He didn’t need to. He built the conditions that made the result contestable regardless of who won. Then he built the committees that would contest it — from both directions — so that the argument itself became the weapon. The country wasn't divided by the election. The country was divided by the debate about the election. And the debate was manufactured."

Saunders looked at the wallscreen. At the dual-feeding operation laid out in grant disbursements and committee records and Elena's careful, dangerous envelopes.

"Elena died for this," Saunders said quietly. "She saw it inside Fresh Start. The two tracks. The opposite messages from the same source. That's why she started sending the envelopes."

Ashford looked at Elena's name on the archive header. The narrow-shouldered woman who had noticed something wrong and had done the only thing she could think of to do about it.

"It goes in the matrix," Ashford said. "The election manipulation goes in the evidence chain. It's not just corporate structure and institutional sabotage. It's democratic sabotage. He broke the country's ability to choose its own leaders."

She added the nodes. The matrix grew.

Okafor looked at it from the window.

"Is that enough?" he asked.

"To go public? Not alone. But combined with the audit disclosures, the Okoro testimony, the position error forensics, and now the election manipulation — it's getting very close."

"What's missing?"

"Haldane himself. Everything we have runs through his companies, his foundations, his people. We can prove the network. We can prove Vickers was paid. We can prove Okoro was instructed. We can prove the election was manipulated through his committees. But we can't prove Haldane gave the order. We have the network. We don't have his voice."

"You might not need his voice," Okafor said. "You need enough evidence that his voice is the only explanation."

Ashford looked at him. It was the second time Okafor had offered an opinion on the investigation. Both times, he'd been right.

• • •

Dallas.

The message arrived at 09:23 Central.

Haldane read it twice. Six sentences. Twenty-six words. No encryption. No routing. Sent through the standard channel as though Dren were confirming a meeting time.

"Chuck. You came after me. You missed. You missed Ashford. Twice. Raines is in my custody. Okoro has been most forthcoming. I thought you should know."

He set the display down. His hand was steady. His breathing was even. But something had changed in the room —- a shift in pressure, as though the walls had moved inward by a millimeter.

No one had ever addressed him directly. Not Whitfield or Beckett or any of the investigators whose work he'd been monitoring through the network. He had always been a name on a board, a thread in a matrix, a terminus that the evidence pointed at but never reached. And now Alexis Dren had looked through every layer of insulation and said, simply, *I know*.

And "Chuck!" He'd hated that name since first grade.

Raines is in my custody. His ace. His deepest asset. Gone.

Okoro has been most forthcoming. The chain was exposed. Vickers was next. And Vickers had — Haldane was certain of this — kept recordings. Insurance. Insurance that careful men kept because they understood that the man who built the network was also the man who would burn it.

He picked up the phone and called Oliver on the emergency line.

Oliver answered on the first ring. He always did.

"I have a job," Haldane said. "And before you say anything —- I know you went to Pasadena. We'll discuss that later."

Silence on the line. Oliver didn't apologize. Oliver never apologized.

“Vickers,” Haldane said. “He needs to disappear. Completely. No trail, no body, no questions.”

“Vickers is one of yours.”

“Vickers is a liability. I made a move against Dren. Based on the silence, I’m thinking it did not go as planned. Okoro is gone. The audits have exposed the Meridian payment chain. When they find the direct deposits —- and they will —- Vickers becomes the most active link. He knows too much.”

“He also knows enough to know what happens to people who become liabilities.”

“Which is why you need to move quickly.”

Oliver was quiet for a moment. “My face is on every feed on the continent. You told me to go to ground. Now you want me operational.”

“I know what I said. I also know you’re the only person I can trust to do this cleanly. Anyone else I send, I have to worry about whether they’ll actually do it or whether they’ll decide Vickers is more useful to them alive than dead.”

“Four times the standard rate,” Oliver said. “And after this, I’m gone. New identity, new continent. You won’t hear from me again.”

“Agreed.”

“Really? That easily? Eight times,” Oliver said.

“Don’t press me, Oliver. But fine. Eight times,” Haldane said.

“My, you really do want him gone badly. Where is he?” Oliver asked.

“You know the building. Outside D. C. It has 5 sides,” Haldane said.

“Seriously? You want me to enter one of the most secure sites in the world?”

“Of course not. But you can pick him up there. I’ll give you his home address as well,” Haldane said.

Haldane gave him the address. Oliver committed it to memory —- he never wrote anything down.

"One more thing," Haldane said. "Make it seem that our General has decided to disappear."

"I'll handle it," Oliver said. "I always do."

The line went dead.

Haldane sat in the empty office. The list of people who needed managing was getting shorter, but the risk of each management was getting higher. Okoro was captured. Raines was activated. And now Oliver — the most dangerous man in his network, a man who had already gone off-script once — was being sent to kill the one person who could connect everything.

The margin was thin. But it had always been thin. That was the nature of the work.

• • •

Ares City. Research Lab 3.

Torres had the DEW module disassembled across four workbenches.

The emitter assembly occupied the first two — the hexagonal waveguide channels separated from the housing, each one catalogued and photographed, the internal geometry mapped to sub-millimeter precision. The power source sat on the third bench inside a containment frame — a cylinder of dense, grey-silver material that weighed more than it looked like it should. The fourth bench held her notes, three tablets running parallel analyses, and an empty coffee cup she'd forgotten about two days ago.

Dren stood in the doorway. He'd learned not to interrupt Torres when she was working — she'd surface when she had something to say, and not a second before.

She was holding one of the waveguide channels up to the light, rotating it slowly, looking at the internal surface through a magnification lens.

"It's hafnium-178," she said without looking at him. She set the channel down and tapped the containment frame on the third bench. "The power source. Nuclear isomer — nuclei locked in a metastable excited state. We confirmed it on the Kludge during the return transit, and three weeks in this lab haven't changed the answer."

She pulled up a display on the nearest tablet and turned it toward Dren. Energy density curves — chemical explosives at the bottom, fission at the top, and a data point between them marked Hf-178m2.

"1.3 terajoules per kilogram," she said. "Six orders of magnitude above chemical. A sixtieth of fission yield. But no chain reaction. No criticality. No radiation signature worth mentioning." She looked at him. "They built a nuclear weapon that doesn't look like a nuclear weapon. That cylinder on bench three has more stored energy than every warhead in the old American arsenal combined, and you could walk past it with a Geiger counter and hear nothing."

"The engineering," Dren said. "How does it release?"

Torres moved to the first bench and picked up the emitter assembly housing — a compact unit, roughly the size of a human torso, with six ports arranged in a hexagonal pattern. She'd spent two weeks staring at this piece.

"That's what took me three weeks to figure out," she said. "Something in this assembly triggers the energy release from the isomer on demand. The metastable state is stable — that's the point, it sits there holding terajoules of energy indefinitely until something tells it to let go. The question was what tells it."

She set the housing down and pulled up a second display — electromagnetic pulse signatures, frequency spectra, timing diagrams.

"A precisely tuned electromagnetic pulse," she said. "Specific frequency, specific duration, specific amplitude. It destabilizes the isomer and drives stimulated emission from the metastable nuclei. The energy releases as gamma radiation, the waveguide channels shape and directs the output." She tapped the hexagonal ports. "These aren't just structural. They're the barrel. The geometry focuses the emission into a coherent beam."

She sat on the edge of the bench. It was the most relaxed Dren had seen her since the Kludge docked.

"Human physicists have been theorizing about controlled stimulated emission from nuclear isomers for decades. Nobody could make it work. The triggering energy was always too high, or the release was too diffuse, or the isomer couldn't be produced in sufficient quantity. The aliens solved all three problems." She paused. "The trigger mechanism is within our manufacturing tolerances. We can build the emitter. We can replicate the waveguide geometry. The physics is understood."

Torres's full report was characteristically direct.

"The physics is understood. The isomer is the power source, the emitter assembly triggers the release, and the waveguide geometry shapes the output. The trigger mechanism —- the electromagnetic pulse specifications —- is within our manufacturing tolerances. We can replicate the gun. What we can't do is manufacture the ammunition. Our lab production of hafnium-178m2 is measured in nanograms. They built a cylinder with six tonnes of it. Sato's fabrication team thinks they can scale production, but we're talking years, not months."

"So we can build the weapon but not power it," Dren said.

"Not at their scale. But we have their cylinder. Six tonnes of charged isomer. That's enough to power a weapon through extensive testing and, if it comes to it, operational use. We just can't manufacture more."

CHAPTER 19

Two Hearts

April 2061.

• • •

Ares City. Secure conference room.

Whitfield had the full picture spread across the conference table, on the integrated display surface that turned the table into a wallscreen. Every thread of the investigation, every chain of evidence, every connection mapped and annotated. The matrix Ashford had been building on a safe-house wallscreen was now rendered at presidential resolution, and it was damning.

"Three independent investigations," Dren said. "Organizational —- Ashford's corporate trace. Institutional —- Saunders's ESA document and the fellowship pipeline. Technical —- O'Malley's forensic chain from the translation layer through Okoro to Vickers. All three converge on Haldane."

"But not on Haldane directly," Whitfield said.

"Not yet. Every connection runs through intermediaries. Companies, foundations, people. The evidence points at him. The network is his. But we don't have his voice giving an order."

Whitfield looked at the display. The tremor in her hands was visible —- she'd stopped trying to hide it weeks ago. It didn't matter. What mattered was what was on the table.

"I need to go back," she said.

Dren looked at her.

“Earth,” she said. “I’ve been governing from Mars for months. The reconstruction is fragmenting —- Thomas in Jacksonville is already acting like an independent authority, and two more regional commanders are making noise. Beckett is positioning for impeachment hearings. If I stay here much longer, there won’t be a presidency to go back to.”

“The security situation—-”

“The security situation is that Colton is dead and the man who killed him is in your holding cell for trying to kill you. The network that sent both of them is collapsing. I need to be in Washington. I need to be visible. And I need to be the one who presents this” —- she gestured at the display —- “to the country. Not from a screen on Mars. In person.”

Dren was quiet for a moment. She was right. The evidence needed to be presented by the President of the United States, standing on American soil, with the full weight of the office behind it. A broadcast from Mars would be dismissed as exile propaganda.

“I should go with you,” Dren said.

Whitfield looked at him.

“The evidence chain depends on my testimony —- the translation layer audit, the Okoro interrogation, the Raines confrontation. I’m a witness to every technical element of the investigation. If this goes to any kind of proceeding, I need to be there.”

“You’d leave Mars.”

“Sato can run operations. Brandt will be with me. Torres and the team have the DEW research. The station doesn’t need me for the next phase. Earth does.”

Whitfield considered this. Dren on Earth changed the dynamic —- it meant the primary investigator and the primary political authority were in the same room, presenting a unified case. It also meant Dren was vulnerable in ways he wasn’t on Mars. On Mars, he controlled the infrastructure. On Earth, he was a civilian in someone else's jurisdiction.

"We'll need transport," she said.

"I have a fast ship. The same drive as the rescue drone. We can be on Earth in under three weeks."

"Book it," she said.

• • •

Arlington, Virginia.

Okafor had argued against this for two days.

"Vickers is Pentagon. He's surrounded by security infrastructure. If Haldane has turned on him then approaching Vickers is walking into a crossfire between a target and an assassin."

"Vickers has what we need," Ashford said. "He's the link."

"Then let Dren's people handle it. They have the authority—-"

"Dren's people are on Mars. By the time they coordinate with Earth-side law enforcement, Vickers could be dead or gone. Haldane knows the chain is exposed. He'll move on Vickers. We have to get there first."

Okafor looked at her for a long time. She could see the calculation behind his eyes —- the risk assessment, the operational geometry, the professional judgment that said this was wrong. All of it weighed against the simple fact that she was going whether he came or not.

"I'll arrange it," he said.

They flew to Arlington in the early morning —- transport arranged through Dren's company. Vickers lived in a townhouse in a residential neighborhood ten minutes from the Pentagon. A neighborhood where generals and senior officials lived because it was close to work and quiet enough to pretend the work didn't follow them home.

Ashford knocked. Okafor stood to the side, out of the sight line of the door's peephole, his hand inside his jacket.

Vickers opened the door. He was older than Ashford expected —- mid-sixties, grey, a weathered face that came from decades of classified work and the specific tension of knowing things that could destroy governments. He looked at Ashford. He looked past her at the empty street. He didn't look at the side where Okafor was standing.

"Ms. Ashford," he said. "I wondered when someone would come."

"You know who I am."

"I know who everyone is. That's been my job for a very long time." He stepped back from the door. "Come in. Quickly."

They went inside. The townhouse was neat, organized, the home of a man who lived alone and maintained control over his environment the way he maintained control over everything else. Okafor cleared the rooms in sixty seconds —- kitchen, living room, study, upstairs bedrooms. Clear.

They sat in the study. Vickers behind his desk. Ashford across from him. Okafor by thc window, watching thc street.

"You know why we're here," Ashford said.

"The audits. The Meridian payments. Okoro." He said the names without inflection. "It was always going to end this way. The only question was when."

"We need anything that you have," Ashford said. "Recordings. Documents. Anything that connects Haldane directly to the operation."

Vickers moved and rotated out a picture on the wall revealing a wall safe. He opened it and removed a small case —- the kind used for data tokens, hard-shelled, magnetically shielded. He set it on the desk between them.

"Recordings," he said. "Encrypted, but I'll give you the codes. Nineteen conversations over twelve years. Haldane's voice, giving direct instructions. The Ark, the plans for the impact. The instructions after the deflection, what eventually became the tilt."

Ashford looked at the case. Nineteen conversations. Twelve years. Haldane's voice.

"Why?" she asked. "Why keep them?"

"Insurance. The same reason anyone in this business keeps recordings. He looked at her steadily. "I am now a liability. I've been a liability since the audits began. I assume someone is already tasked."

"We can protect you," Ashford said. "Dren—-"

"Dren needs to protect me and I want full immunity," Vickers said. "I'll testify. Everything I know —- the full operation. But I need protection, and I need it now, because—-"

Blood appeared at the corner of his mouth. Not a lot. A thin line, bright red, tracking down his chin. His eyes changed, the recognition of something that had already happened and couldn't be undone.

He looked down. The front of his shirt was darkening. A blade had entered his back, between the ribs, and the point had found something vital.

Oliver stepped out from behind him as Vickers slid sideways onto the floor. He was holding a knife —- short, the blade already clean because the wound had closed around it on withdrawal. He'd come through the back entrance during the three minutes between Okafor's sweep and them sitting down —- patient, silent, waiting in the hallway until the conversation confirmed what he needed to hear.

"So delighted to meet you again, Ms. Ashford," Oliver said. He looked at Okafor by the window. "And I see you have another Greg."

He launched the knife at Okafor as he said it —- the same quick, practiced throw that had killed Greg in the apartment. One motion, conversation to kill shot, the blade crossing the room at Okafor's chest.

Okafor sidestepped it.

The knife buried itself in the window frame where he'd been standing. Oliver's expression changed, surprise. The throw had never missed.

Okafor had studied the apartment footage frame by frame. He'd watched Oliver kill Greg a hundred times. He knew the throw was coming the moment Oliver's hand moved.

Okafor rushed him.

He went straight at Oliver, closing the distance before Oliver could reposition. Oliver was fast —- he pivoted, reaching for something inside his jacket. Okafor didn't give him the time. He drove into Oliver's midsection and they crashed into the bookshelves, sending volumes scattering across the floor.

Oliver drove his forehead into Okafor's face. Okafor felt his nose break —- a sharp, structural pain that flooded his eyes with tears and his mouth with blood. But he had the grip now, both hands on Oliver, and he didn't let go.

They grappled. The study was small —- desk, chairs, bookshelves, not enough room for distance fighting. It was close work, elbows and knees, two professionals in a phone booth. Okafor was bigger. Oliver was more vicious. The difference was that Okafor was fighting to protect someone behind him, and Oliver was fighting because fighting was all he had left.

Ashford was behind the desk, crouched, the data token case clutched against her chest. She could see them —- two men locked together, crashing through the furniture. She couldn't help. She couldn't run. She could only hold the case and wait.

Okafor drove Oliver backward into the bookshelves again. The impact broke Oliver's grip and opened space between them. Okafor saw the knife embedded in the window frame —- two meters to his right. He pulled it free in one motion and turned.

Oliver was already moving —- trying to create distance, reaching inside his jacket. Okafor didn't give him the distance. He closed and drove the blade into Oliver's chest, below the sternum, angled upward.

Oliver stopped. His hands dropped from his jacket to the knife handle, not pulling it out, just holding it, as though confirming what had happened. He looked at Okafor with an expression that was not surprise —- Oliver had always known this was one of the possible endings.

Okafor lowered him against the wall. Oliver sat, his back to the plaster, the knife still in his chest, his breathing shallow and wet.

Oliver's hands moved to his own chest, to something underneath his shirt. His fingers found a shape there and held it. Not pressing. Confirming.

His eyes were open. He was looking at Ashford.

"You know," Oliver said, his voice thin and fading, "the lovely thing about two hearts… is that they can stop… together."

Okafor's expression changed. Comprehension.

Oliver smiled. It was the last theatrical gesture of a man who had performed his entire life.

Okafor released Oliver and moved. Fast — faster than Ashford had ever seen him move. He crossed the three meters between Oliver and the desk in one stride, grabbed Ashford by the shoulders, and pulled her to the floor, covering her body with his.

Oliver's heart stopped. The biometric trigger — an explosive charge embedded in his chest, connected to a cardiac monitor — registered the cessation. A two-second delay. Then it fired.

The detonation was sharp and concussive — not large, but concentrated, designed to kill anyone within the radius of a close-quarters fight. The blast shattered Oliver's body outward. Fragments — bone, metal, casing — drove through the study like shrapnel. The desk absorbed the forward wave. The bookshelves absorbed the lateral. Okafor absorbed everything that came from above.

The sound was enormous in the small room. Then silence. Then the settling of debris — plaster dust, paper fragments, the acrid smell of explosive residue and something worse beneath it.

Ashford was underneath him. She was alive. She could feel his weight on her — heavy, unmoving.

"Okafor," she said.

No response.

She pushed against his shoulder. He shifted — not under his own power, but because she moved him. She slid out from beneath him and he settled against the desk, his head forward, his arms at his sides.

His back was destroyed. The jacket was shredded, the shirt beneath it dark and saturated, fragments embedded deep in the tissue across his shoulders and spine. He'd taken the full force of the blast.

"Okafor," she said again.

His eyes opened. Slowly. The effort was visible — consciousness pulling itself back from wherever the blast had sent it.

"Dead-man charge," he said. His voice was quiet. Controlled. "Biometric trigger. Heart stops, charge fires. He was built to take his killer with him."

He looked at her. At the case still clutched against her chest.

"The recordings?" he asked.

"I have them."

"Get them to Dren. Saunders has the secure channel. Codes first — the recordings are useless without them. Then the recordings. Dren needs both."

"I'm not leaving you."

"Chloe." He used her first name. He had never used her first name. "The recordings are why we came. The recordings are why Vickers is dead. You must get the—"

His head dropped. The sentence didn't finish. His body settled against the desk, the tension leaving his shoulders, his hands going still on the floor beside him.

Ashford stared at him. At his face, which had been calm and focused and not afraid. At his hands, which had been steady until they weren't.

She looked down. The blood had pooled beneath him, a dark shape on the floor that had been growing since the blast. He'd been bleeding out the entire time he'd been talking to her. Every word, every instruction, every second of operational clarity had been borrowed from a body that was already finished.

She sat with it for a moment. The silence in the room. The dust still settling. The man who had saved her life three times and was not going to save it a fourth.

Greg. Elena. Okafor. All of them gone because a man in Dallas had decided that two hundred million dead wasn't enough. If the recordings didn't reach Dren, their deaths were for nothing.

She stood. She picked up the case. She walked out.

Through the study door, through the hallway, past the kitchen where Oliver had entered, out the back entrance into the alley behind the townhouse. The data token case was in her hand. The bypass codes were in her memory — Vickers had spoken them aloud, and she'd committed them the way she committed everything: immediately, completely, because that was her job.

She walked. Not running — Okafor had taught her that. Running drew attention. Walking was invisible. She walked six blocks to the car, got in, and drove to the safe house.

Saunders was waiting. Ashford set the case on the table, sat down, and said: "Okafor is dead. Vickers is dead. Oliver is dead. I have nineteen recordings of Haldane giving direct orders over twelve years. We need to transmit them to Dren now."

Saunders didn't ask questions. She opened the secure channel.

• • •

Ares City.

The recordings arrived through the secure channel at 04:17 local time. Sato was the first to hear them.

Nineteen conversations. Twelve years. Haldane's voice — calm, precise, unmistakable — giving instructions that connected every thread of the investigation into a single, documented chain. The tilt. The fellowship placements. The institutional delays. And the most damning: the coordination with an alien intelligence that had sent the Fist. The orders, the decisions, the calculation that had led to two hundred million dead.

Sato listened to all nineteen without stopping. Then she sent them to Dren.

The network had a voice now.

CHAPTER 20
Progress

May–June 2061.

• • •

Ares City.

The recordings arrived on a Tuesday. By Wednesday, Dren and Sato had listened to all nineteen. By Thursday, they had cross-referenced every conversation against the forensic evidence chain — the translation layer, the Okoro testimony, the Meridian payment records, the audit disclosures — and confirmed that Haldane's voice matched the network his voice described.

By Friday, the full evidence package was assembled.

Dren laid it out for Whitfield on the secure channel — both of them looking at the same display, eleven minutes apart.

"The technical chain," Dren said. "O'Malley's trace from the translation layer through Okoro to Vickers. The position error, the fabricated change order, the disk-level cover-up. Documented and forensically verified."

"The organizational chain. Ashford's corporate trace — Meridian, Basin Range, the fellowship pipeline, the Nevada facility. The audit disclosures confirming beneficial ownership. The direct payments from Meridian to Vickers."

"The institutional chain. Saunders's ESA document — the killed reclassification draft, Mercer's edits. The nine outgassing advocates traced to Haldane fellowships."

"And now the recordings. Nineteen conversations over twelve years. Haldane's voice giving direct instructions on the tilt, the fellowship placements, the institutional delay strategy, the Ark. Every recording corroborates what the three independent investigations found separately."

He paused.

"Four chains. Four independent evidence sources. One terminus."

Whitfield's reply came twenty-two minutes later. Her voice was steady, but Dren could hear something underneath it, the weight of what this meant.

"Transmit the full package to my legal team. And transmit it to Ashford through Okafor's channel." A pause. "Through Saunders. Okafor's channel."

The correction sat in the silence for a moment. Okafor was dead. The channel was Saunders's now.

"I want the fellowship embeds identified," Whitfield continued. "Every placement Haldane made through the pipeline — governance positions, advisory committees, institutional appointments. I want names, positions, and the evidence connecting each one to the Foundation. Start with the reconstruction apparatus. If Haldane's people are inside the institutions managing the recovery, I need to know which ones before I go public."

Dren transmitted the package within the hour. The evidence went to Whitfield's legal team through the official presidential channel. It went to Saunders through the secure relay Okafor had established before Arlington — unofficial, encrypted, deniable. The same evidence, two channels, two purposes: one for prosecution, one for broadcast.

Sato began the embed identification that afternoon. The fellowship records from the audit disclosures provided the starting point — names, institutions, dates. Cross-referenced against the reconstruction authority's personnel database, the pattern emerged within days. Forty-three individuals in governance or advisory positions across eleven reconstruction zones had received Haldane Foundation fellowships. Not all of them were necessarily compromised — the Foundation had funded legitimate scholars alongside its placements. But the correlation between fellowship recipients and positions of institutional influence was too consistent to be coincidence.

Dren transmitted the list to Whitfield with a note: "Forty-three names. Eleven zones. Not all are necessarily hostile, but all should be assessed. Recommend quiet removal from sensitive positions before any public disclosure."

Whitfield's reply was two words: "Already started."

• • •

Ares City. Level 2.

Chandra had set up what he called the Bletchley House.

It was a conference room on Level 2 that he'd requisitioned three days after the Kludge docked — the largest display surface on the station, originally designed for mission planning, now covered wall to wall with fragments of a language nobody could read.

The intercepted transmissions from the probe swarm filled one wall. Months of captured traffic between Earth and the fleet — Haldane's outbound messages and the Tolek's responses, recorded by the probes sitting in the communication cone. The content was encrypted and encoded in a linguistic structure that bore no relationship to any human language. No phonemes, no syntax, no grammar that Chandra's team could identify. The structure appeared to be mathematical — relational rather than sequential, encoding states and conditions rather than sentences and clauses.

"It's not a language the way we use the word," Chandra told Dren during the weekly briefing. "It's closer to a specification format. Like reading a machine protocol and trying to extract the conversation the engineers were having when they wrote it."

He'd assembled a team — two linguists from the Mars university program, a cryptographer Sato had pulled from the belt communications group, and three AI systems running pattern analysis on the intercepted data. They'd made progress. Not enough.

"We've isolated recurring structural elements," Chandra said. "Certain patterns repeat across multiple transmissions — what look like identifiers, status markers, conditional operators. We can tell when a transmission is a query versus a directive versus a report. We can identify three distinct referents that appear consistently — probably designations for entities or agents. One of them correlates with transmissions originating from Earth. That's almost certainly Haldane."

"And the other two?"

"Unknown. One appears in fleet-originated transmissions only. The other appears in both directions." He paused. "We're reading the shape of the conversation. We're not reading the conversation."

Dren looked at the wall. At the fragments and patterns and the structural elements that Chandra's team had pulled from months of alien communication. Bits and pieces. The Navajo Code Talkers hadn't been cracked, and the underlying language was human. This wasn't. The structure was alien at every level — not just the vocabulary but the cognitive architecture that produced it.

"What would break it open?" Dren asked.

"A crib. The same message in both formats — their structure and something we can read. If Haldane has a translation protocol, even a partial one, it would give us the Rosetta Stone. Without it, we're pattern-matching in the dark."

Dren filed that. Haldane's translation protocol. Another item on the list of things the man in Dallas was carrying that the investigation needed to extract.

"Keep working," he said. "Document everything. When we get the crib, I want your team ready to move."

• • •

Ares City. Research Lab 3.

Yuen was standing at the electron microscope when the lattice formed.

She'd been staring at hafnium samples for eleven days — cross-sections of the Tolek cylinder, sliced to nanometer thickness, mapped at the atomic level under magnification that turned crystalline structure into landscape. The cylinder sat on its containment platform across the lab, six tonnes of charged nuclear isomer that humanity couldn't manufacture in useful quantities, surrounded by human-built instruments trying to understand why.

Torres had characterized the power source weeks ago. Torres had cracked the trigger mechanism and the waveguide geometry. What Torres hadn't solved — what she'd told Dren was "years, not months" — was making more of the ammunition. Earth's total laboratory production of hafnium-178m2 was measured in nanograms. The Tolek had six tonnes. The gap wasn't engineering. It was civilization.

Yuen wasn't trying to close the gap. She was trying to cheat it.

"I've been approaching this wrong," she said to Torres, who was at the adjacent workstation running emitter diagnostics. "Everyone's been approaching it wrong. We keep trying to replicate their production process — bombard hafnium-176 with neutrons, hope for isomeric transition, collect the nanograms that convert. That's their method scaled down to our capability. It doesn't work because their method assumes an industrial base we don't have."

Torres looked up. "So?"

Yuen pulled the microscope feed onto the wallscreen — a crystalline landscape at atomic resolution. The hafnium atoms were arranged in a lattice structure that was precise, repeating, and unlike anything in the materials science literature. The metastable nuclei were held in their excited state by the geometry itself — the spacing between atoms, the magnetic alignment, the quantum confinement produced by the lattice geometry.

"Look at the structure," Yuen said. "The isomer isn't just stored in the crystal. The crystal is what keeps it metastable. The lattice geometry maintains the confinement. Take the nuclei out of this structure and they decay. Keep them in it and they hold their charge indefinitely."

"We know this," Torres said. "The containment geometry was in my transit report."

"Right. But what if we don't need to make the isomer first and then put it in a lattice? What if we grow the lattice directly — with the isomer forming in situ as the crystal builds?"

Torres set down the diagnostic tool. "Using what as a seed?"

Yuen pointed at the cylinder across the lab. "That. Their crystal. We take a thin section from the surface — a few milligrams — and use it as a seed substrate. We deposit hafnium atoms onto the seed under the same magnetic confinement geometry the original lattice uses. The atoms incorporate into the existing structure. The lattice grows. And as it grows, the confinement geometry forces the new nuclei into the metastable state automatically."

"You're growing isomer the way you'd grow a synthetic diamond," Torres said. "Seeding from the original."

"Exactly. We're not manufacturing the isomer. We're extending the crystal that contains it. The alien's lattice does the work — we just add material. I don't fully understand why it works — only that it does under these conditions."

Torres was quiet for a moment. "What's the yield?"

"Small. Grams, not tonnes. The growth rate is limited by the deposition speed and the seed surface area. But grams are enough to power a prototype through test firing." She paused. "And the process scales. Larger seed sections, multiple growth chambers, dedicated fabrication resources — six months, we could produce enough to power a dozen weapons."

"Have you tested the growth?"

Yuen reached into the containment cabinet beside the microscope and produced a small sealed cell — transparent walls, a thin disc of dark material inside, sitting on a magnetic platform. She held it up to the light.

"Eleven days," she said. "Point-eight grams. Spectrometric analysis confirms the metastable state. The lattice matches the Tolek lattice to within measurement tolerance."

Torres took the cell and held it close to her face. Less than a gram of material on a disc smaller than her thumbnail. She could feel nothing from it — no heat, no radiation, no indication that the crystalline structure contained enough nuclear energy to power a building. That was the point. The isomer was invisible until you triggered it.

"That's enough for a test firing," Torres said.

"That's enough for several."

Torres looked at Yuen for a long moment. Then she turned to the prototype weapon — human-built emitter assembly, human-built trigger mechanism, the waveguide geometry she'd replicated from three weeks of analysis on the Kludge — sitting on its test mount at the far end of the lab.

"Let's find out," Torres said.

They moved the test to the external range — a reinforced bay on the station's lower level, designed for materials testing, with a three-hundred-meter clear lane and a target array at the far end. Torres loaded Yuen's cell into the prototype's containment housing. The cell was one-tenth the size of the Tolek cylinder. It looked absurd in the housing — a speck in a chamber designed for something much larger.

Torres ran the pre-fire diagnostics. Containment stable. Trigger alignment confirmed. Waveguide geometry calibrated. She placed a three-centimeter plate of reinforced composite at the two-hundred-meter mark.

"Recording," Sato said from the observation gallery. She'd come down when Torres had requisitioned the range — Sato didn't miss test firings.

Torres activated the trigger.

The electromagnetic pulse fired. The isomer released. The energy cascaded through the waveguide channels and exited the emitter as a coherent beam — invisible in the visible spectrum, registered only by the thermal sensors along the range.

The composite plate didn't crack. It didn't deform. A section the size of a fist simply ceased to exist — vaporized, the material converted to plasma in the microsecond the beam traversed it. The edges of the hole glowed white, then orange, then dark. A clean puncture through three centimeters of reinforced composite, at two hundred meters, from less than a gram of lab-grown isomer.

The range was silent for three seconds.

"Well," Torres said. "That works."

Yuen was staring at the target. At the hole. At the clean, cauterized edges where the material had been.

Sato was already on the comm to Dren.

The Tolek's weapon worked with human engineering. The ammunition could be manufactured. The directed-energy weapon was no longer a captured artifact. It was a reproducible technology.

Dren watched the test footage in his office. He watched it twice. Then he called Torres.

"How many can we build?"

"With current fabrication capacity? Two operational units within three months. More if Sato allocates additional resources."

"Build them."

The friction came that evening.

Whitfield's message arrived through the secure channel at 19:00 local.

"The DEW prototype and the isomer production data need to be on Earth. If we're presenting evidence of an alien-origin weapon to the public, the weapon itself — or its human-built equivalent —

needs to be available for verification. And the production capability needs to be under federal authority, not private corporate control on Mars."

Dren read the message. He understood the logic. He disagreed with the conclusion.

His reply was measured. "The research infrastructure is here. The expertise is here. The fabrication capability is here. Moving the technology to Earth means moving it into a political environment with active Haldane embeds in the reconstruction apparatus, regional commanders pursuing independent authority, and a federal government that is — with respect — not yet stable enough to secure alien weapons technology. I recommend the prototypes remain on Mars until the political situation is resolved."

Whitfield's response came twenty-two minutes later. Shorter than usual.

"Noted. We'll revisit after the broadcast."

It was the first time they had disagreed. It would not be the last.

CHAPTER 21

Fractures

April 2061.

• • •

Houston, Texas.

Sanchez was three hours into the night shift when the water pressure dropped.

She was in the routing center — the communications building at the east end of the Dren Industries logistics hub on the ship channel. Six people on the overnight, managing the automated systems that coordinated supply routing for the Gulf Coast reconstruction zone. The screens showed container status, transit schedules, the slow pulse of a logistics network that didn't sleep.

The pressure gauge on the fire suppression panel dropped from green to yellow at 2:17 AM. Sanchez noticed it because she noticed everything on the panel — it was her job, and she was good at her job, and the gauge had been green for every shift she'd worked in the eight months since she'd transferred from the Tacoma facility.

She called maintenance. "East building suppression pressure is dropping. Can you check the line?"

"We'll send someone in the morning. Probably a valve issue."

"It's been green for eight months and it dropped in the middle of the night. That's not a valve issue."

"We'll send someone in the morning, Sanchez."

She made a note in the log. She went back to the routing screens. The container yard was quiet outside the windows — the floods casting the same sharp shadows they cast every night, the container stacks standing in their grid like a city made of steel boxes.

At 2:30, the first bottle came through the fence.

She didn't see it — she heard it. A crash against the east wall, followed by a sound that was half splash, half ignition. Then the second bottle. The third hit a container somewhere to the south, a distant clang followed by a bloom of orange light visible through the window.

"Fire," she said. It came out flat. Not a shout. A statement, the way you say a word when the thing it describes is so wrong that your voice doesn't know how to carry it.

The east wall was burning. The accelerant — she could smell it now, the chemical sharpness cutting through the air handling system — had splashed across the prefab panels and the insulation beneath them was catching. The fire moved fast. The hungry, directional advance of something that had been given fuel and purpose.

"Evacuate," she said. Louder now. "Everyone out. West exit."

They went. Six people, moving fast, the night-shift discipline of people who'd been briefed on emergency procedures and never expected to use them. Sanchez was last out. She hit the suppression alarm on her way through the door — the system that should have flooded the ceiling with retardant, that should have activated the moment the heat sensors tripped.

Nothing happened. The pressure gauge had told her twenty minutes ago, and she hadn't pushed hard enough.

They stood in the container yard and watched the communications building burn. The roof panels went first — the insulation material burning hot and bright, flames visible through the seams where the panels met. Then the interior — the routing servers, the coordination hardware, the screens that had been showing the pulse of the Gulf Coast logistics network three minutes ago.

Sanchez could feel the heat from fifty meters. The container that had caught fire — the one to the south — was burning separately, its contents feeding the flames from inside. The night sky above the ship channel was orange. Somewhere behind her, the other five were calling dispatch, calling the fire department, calling everyone whose number they had.

She stood and watched. The water line had been cut. She was certain of that now. Cut before the bottles came over the fence. Someone had been inside the perimeter, had found the suppression line, had cut it, and had left. The bottles were the second act. The first act had been invisible, professional, and precise.

The Houston Fire Department arrived in forty minutes. By then the communications building was a shell — steel frame standing, everything inside it gone. The routing servers that managed logistics coordination for three reconstruction zones were molten slag. The backup systems were in Tacoma. The switchover would take a week. For that week, Gulf Coast supply routing would run on phone calls and spreadsheets and the institutional memory of people who'd been doing this job since before the hub existed.

Sanchez gave her statement to the fire investigator at dawn. She told him what had happened.

The investigator wrote it down. The police investigation produced no arrests.

Three days later, the DSA Today podcast ran a segment titled "Who Protects the Protectors?" It asked why Dren Industries' logistics infrastructure was more heavily secured than the communities it served. The host's voice was measured, reasonable, the cadence of someone asking questions that sounded fair and arrived at conclusions that had been written before the questions were asked.

The segment didn't mention the fire. It didn't need to. Everyone in the Gulf Coast reconstruction zone had seen the orange sky over the ship channel. The question wasn't what had happened. The question — the one the podcast planted, the one that would grow in the silence between what people knew and what they could prove — was who had let it happen.

• • •

Interstate 5, south of Olympia, Oregon. April 2061.

Reyes saw the blockade from half a mile out.

He was driving lead — the first of three flatbeds running the coastal route from the Tacoma fabrication yards to Portland. Each flatbed carried a prefabricated medical module, a self-contained trauma unit designed to slot into the framework of a hospital that didn't exist yet. The Portland reconstruction had been waiting for them for two months.

Pickups and vans. Parked across both lanes, bumper to bumper. An arrangement that didn't happen by accident — someone had known which route the convoy would take and when.

Reyes keyed the radio. "Dispatch, this is Convoy Seven. We've got a blockade at the interchange south of Olympia. Vehicles across both lanes. I'm seeing maybe a hundred people behind the vehicles."

"Copy, Convoy Seven. Hold position. We're contacting the regional coordinator."

He held position. He killed the engine and sat in the cab and watched the crowd through the windshield. Reconstruction workers in high-vis vests — he recognized the look, he wore the same vest on his off days. Local officials — a woman in a county jacket was talking into a phone at the edge of the crowd. And others. People who didn't have the weathered hands of construction workers or the lanyards of officials. People who'd arrived on buses — he could see two charter coaches parked on the shoulder behind the blockade, plates from Idaho and California.

The second day, the signs appeared. Reyes watched them go up from the cab — printed, not handmade. The same font he'd seen on the feeds from Washington and Houston and LA. DREN INDUSTRIES — PROFITING FROM OUR PAIN. WHO

AUTHORIZED THE DSA? RECONSTRUCTION FOR COMMUNITIES, NOT CORPORATIONS.

He called dispatch again. "What's the status on the state patrol?"

"They've assessed. They're calling it a peaceful assembly. They're not going to clear the highway."

"Dispatch, I'm sitting on trauma units for Portland General. People are waiting for these."

"Understood, Convoy Seven. Sit tight."

The third day, someone crawled under his truck in the dark. He heard the hiss before he understood what it was — a blade in a tire, the slow exhale of air through rubber. He locked the doors and sat in the cab with the interior lights off and listened to the second tire go.

The fourth day, the crowd came for the trucks.

It started with shouting — organized, rhythmic, chanting that someone with a megaphone was conducting from the back. Then hands on the cabs. Fists on the doors. Reyes felt the truck rock — three hundred people pressing against the vehicle, the suspension shifting under the lateral force.

They got his door open. He didn't know how — the lock was engaged, the handle shouldn't have worked from outside. Someone had a slim jim or a bypass tool, a trick you'd learn in the same trade schools that trained the mechanics who built these trucks.

Hands on his arms. Firm, not gentle. He was pulled from the cab and set on his feet on the highway. A man his own age — reconstruction vest, hard hat, the same calluses — put a hand on his chest and pushed. Reyes went down on the asphalt. His elbow hit first, then his hip.

He heard Gutierrez — the second truck driver — shouting. Then a sound that was Gutierrez's cheekbone breaking under an elbow that came from the side, from someone in the crowd whose face Gutierrez never saw.

Montoya, the third driver, was held against the door of his truck. Reyes watched from the ground as someone spray-painted COLLABORATOR across the door in red letters a foot high, the paint running down the metal in lines that looked like something else entirely.

Someone offered Reyes a hand up. He didn't take it. He got up on his own and walked to Gutierrez, who was sitting on the highway median with blood running from his face, holding his jaw, looking at the crowd with an expression that wasn't anger. It was confusion. These were his people. Reconstruction workers. And they'd just broken his face to stop medical equipment from reaching a hospital.

The state patrol negotiated passage on the sixth day. Reyes drove the lead truck into Portland on flat rims — they hadn't replaced the tires, just reinflated what would hold and crept the last eighty miles at thirty. The medical modules were three weeks late. The hospital framework had moved to the next phase of construction without them. The modules would need to be refitted.

Reyes filed his incident report at the Portland depot. He sat in the break room afterward, alone, and looked at the red paint on his hands — he'd tried to clean COLLABORATOR off Montoya's door during the drive south, and the paint hadn't come off completely. It was under his fingernails and in the lines of his palms, the way grease got in when you worked with your hands long enough.

He'd been hauling reconstruction supplies for eight months. He'd never been called a collaborator for delivering medical equipment to a hospital.

• • •

Ares City.

Sato sent the report to Dren on a Monday.

"We've identified coordinated targeting of our personnel," she said. She put the display on his desk — social media feeds, compiled and cross-referenced. "Senior staff. Compensation packages, stock holdings, personal addresses. Published across multiple platforms simultaneously.

“These aren’t journalists,” her report said. “The profiles are being produced by consulting firms — three that we’ve identified so far. Each firm traces through a different shell organization to grant funding from community action committees.”

Dren looked at the feeds. Names he recognized — his supply chain director, three regional logistics managers, the head of the Tacoma fabrication facility. Each one profiled with the precision of an investigative feature: salary figures sourced from corporate filings, property records pulled from county databases, family photographs scraped from personal accounts.

Dren looked at one of the profiles — his Tacoma facility director. The man’s home address was listed. His children’s school was named. His wife’s workplace was identified. The profile was framed as accountability journalism. It read like a targeting package.

“Pull our exposed personnel into secure housing,” Dren answered. “Anyone who’s been doxed. Coordinate with the regional managers — they’ll know who’s most at risk.”

Dren sat with the report. The targeting wasn’t random — it was selective, aimed at the people whose removal would disrupt the logistics chain most effectively. Someone had mapped his organization the way O’Malley had mapped the firmware exploit — identifying the components whose failure would produce maximum systemic damage.

• • •

Jacksonville, Florida.

General Thomas read the federal directive on his tablet, set the tablet on the conference table, and looked at his chief of staff.

“Whitfield wants us to reroute the Savannah steel allocation to the Norfolk reconstruction zone,” he said. “Priority override. Presidential authority.”

His chief of staff waited.

"Norfolk is three months behind schedule because their zone commander couldn't manage a supply chain. We're on track because we can. And she wants me to give up steel that my contractors are waiting for — steel that's already in our yard — to bail out a zone that can't get its own house in order."

"The directive cites the emergency reconstruction authority," his chief of staff said. "Technically, the presidential override applies."

"Technically." Thomas picked up the tablet and looked at the directive again. "The same presidential authority that delegated command to regional zones eight months ago. The same authority that created this structure because Washington couldn't manage the reconstruction centrally. And now Washington wants to reach into my logistics chain and redirect materials because another zone failed."

He set the tablet down.

"Acknowledge receipt," he said. "File the directive. The steel stays in our yard."

"And if the Pentagon follows up?"

"The Pentagon can follow up all they want. My reconstruction authority comes from the delegation order. The same order that gives me operational control over resources allocated to my zone. Whitfield can't use the emergency authority to override the emergency authority."

His chief of staff made a note. The steel stayed. The Norfolk reconstruction waited. And the federal directive — a direct order from the President of the United States — was acknowledged, filed, and ignored.

It was the third directive Thomas had ignored that month. The first two had been logistical — personnel transfers, scheduling adjustments. This one was material. Steel. Tonnage. The physical infrastructure of reconstruction, treated as a regional asset rather than a federal resource.

Chen in Denver had been watching Thomas for months. When the Jacksonville directive was filed without action, Chen's office sent a quiet inquiry to Thomas's chief of staff: how had the pushback been received? The answer — no consequences, no enforcement, no follow-up — told Chen everything he needed to know. He began drafting his own list of federal directives to acknowledge and ignore.

General Park in the Great Lakes corridor didn't wait for the inquiry. She'd been operating with increasing autonomy since February, redirecting reconstruction resources to projects that served her zone's priorities rather than the federal schedule. When Thomas's non-compliance became known through the informal command network, Park stopped acknowledging the directives entirely.

Three zones. Three commanders. Three sets of reconstruction priorities that no longer aligned with Washington. The federal reconstruction authority sent instructions into a system that received them, processed them, and produced its own conclusions.

• • •

The Pentagon. Joint Chiefs' Conference Room.

The equipment request had been submitted twice.

General Aldridge, the acting chairman, looked at the two documents side by side on the conference display. Both requested the same mobile communications array — a satellite-linked unit capable of managing logistics coordination across a five-hundred-mile radius. Both cited reconstruction emergency authority. Both carried proper authorization signatures.

The first request was from the federal reconstruction coordination office, signed by the deputy director, routed through standard Pentagon procurement. Destination: Norfolk reconstruction zone.

The second request was from General Thomas's Jacksonville command, signed by Thomas himself, routed through the regional procurement authority that the delegation order had created. Destination: Jacksonville.

One communications array. Two valid requests. Two chains of authority that the system recognized as legitimate because the delegation order had made both of them legitimate.

"Which one takes priority?" Aldridge asked his logistics chief.

"Depends on which authority you recognize. Federal procurement says Norfolk. Regional authority says Jacksonville. The delegation order doesn't establish a hierarchy between them."

"That's because the delegation order was supposed to be temporary."

"Yes, sir."

Aldridge looked at the two requests. This was the third conflicting requisition this week. The first had been generators — Denver and the federal office both claiming the same units. The second had been transport vehicles — Park's Great Lakes command redirecting a shipment that the Pentagon had already allocated to the coastal corridor. Each conflict required adjudication. Each adjudication required choosing between federal and regional authority. Each choice alienated whichever side lost.

"Split it," Aldridge said. "Norfolk gets the array for thirty days, then it transfers to Jacksonville."

"Thomas won't accept a thirty-day loan."

"Thomas can file a complaint." Aldridge closed the display. "And tell the deputy director to stop submitting requests that compete with regional commands. We don't have the bandwidth for jurisdictional disputes."

The logistics chief left. Aldridge sat in the empty conference room and looked at the blank display where two legitimate, conflicting, irreconcilable requests had been.

The joint chiefs were issuing conflicting guidance because the system was designed to produce conflicting guidance. The delegation order had created parallel authority structures with no mechanism for resolving disputes between them. Every equipment request, every personnel transfer, every logistics decision was a potential jurisdiction conflict. The system wasn't breaking. It was functioning exactly as Haldane had designed it to function.

• • •

Congress. Beckett's Oversight Committee.

Beckett had expanded the scope again.

The original mandate — oversight of Dren Industries' reconstruction operations — had been broad enough. The expanded mandate — "presidential conduct during the Mars residency" — was effectively unlimited. Every decision Whitfield had made from Mars was now within the committee's purview. Every communication with Dren. Every directive issued through the reconstruction authority. Every expenditure, every appointment, every classified briefing conducted from Ares City.

The hearing room was full. Beckett sat at the center of the raised platform, flanked by committee members who had been carefully selected for their willingness to ask questions without knowing the answers.

The witness wasn't the deputy director Beckett had subpoenaed. The deputy director was seated behind the witness, looking uncomfortable. The man at the table was in uniform — pressed, decorated, the posture of someone who had spent thirty years being looked at by people who outranked him and had decided, at some point, that he outranked them back.

General Thomas had come himself.

He'd arrived without counsel, without prepared remarks, without the binder of documentation that subpoenaed witnesses typically brought. He'd walked into the hearing room the way he walked into his own operations center — as if the building belonged to him and everyone else was visiting.

"General Thomas," Beckett said. "Thank you for appearing before this committee."

"Senator, I want to be clear about something before we begin." Thomas's voice carried the room without effort. "I'm here as a courtesy. Under the current delegation order, my zone operates under regional command authority. This committee's oversight jurisdiction extends to federal reconstruction operations. My operations are regional. I am not obligated to appear, and I am not obligated to explain my operational decisions to this body."

Beckett's expression didn't change. The cameras recorded. The gallery shifted.

"That's an interesting interpretation, General."

"It's not an interpretation, Senator. It's the text of the order. I had my legal team review it before I flew up here. The delegation order grants regional commanders operational control over resources, personnel, and reconstruction priorities within their zones. It does not subordinate that authority to congressional oversight committees that were constituted under the federal framework the order superseded."

"The order was temporary, General."

"The order has no expiration clause, Senator. I've read it. Have you?"

Beckett paused. It was a shorter pause than the ones he usually deployed — the theatrical silences that let the room absorb his framing. This pause was genuine. Thomas had walked into his hearing and told him, on camera, that the committee had no authority over him.

"Let me rephrase," Beckett said. "The President issued a directive to reallocate reconstruction materials from your zone to the Norfolk reconstruction zone. You received the directive."

"I did."

"And you did not implement it."

"I assessed it and determined that the reallocation was not in the operational interest of my zone. The steel in question was already allocated to active projects. My contractors were waiting for it.

Redirecting it to bail out a zone that can't manage its own supply chain would have set my reconstruction back by weeks."

"So a regional commander can override the President."

Thomas looked at Beckett. "Under the current structure, a regional commander has operational control over resources within his zone. That's not overriding the President. That's executing the authority the President delegated to me. If she'd like to rescind the delegation order and take back operational control, she's welcome to try. But she'd need to explain to my reconstruction workforce why their projects are being paused so that Norfolk can have steel it should have secured through its own logistics."

"You're aware that two other zone commanders have followed your lead."

"I'm aware that two other zone commanders have read the same delegation order I have and reached the same conclusion. Independently."

"Independently," Beckett repeated.

"Yes, Senator. Independently." Thomas's voice didn't change. "Is there anything else? I have a reconstruction to manage."

Beckett looked at Thomas for a long moment. This was not how his hearings were supposed to go. The witnesses were supposed to be bureaucrats — careful, qualified, deferential to the committee's authority. Thomas was none of those things. Thomas was a general who had decided that congressional oversight was optional, and he was saying so on national television, and the worst part was that the delegation order's text supported him.

"Thank you for your courtesy, General," Beckett said.

"You're welcome, Senator."

Thomas stood, buttoned his jacket, and walked out of the hearing room without waiting to be dismissed. The deputy director remained in his seat, looking at the committee, looking at the door Thomas had walked through, and looking like a man who had just watched his organizational chart rewrite itself in real time.

Behind Beckett's hearing, the reconstruction caucus was splitting. The coalition that had held together through the first year — both parties, both chambers, unified by the shared understanding that rebuilding the country was more important than politics — was fracturing along lines that the astroturfed campaign had spent months widening. Regional members sided with their zone commanders. Coastal members fought for their reconstruction priorities. Interior members — Chen's allies — argued that the funding model was biased against communities that hadn't burned. The fault lines that Haldane's network had been feeding for months were now visible on the floor of the House, in committee votes, in the hallway negotiations that determined which bills moved and which died.

• • •

In transit. Eighteen days out from Mars.

Whitfield watched the feeds during the crossing.

She had eighteen days on the fast transport — Dren's ship, Dren's drive, Dren's crew. Eighteen days in a cabin with a display and a communications link that brought her everything happening on the planet she was returning to, delayed by the minutes that shrank as the distance closed.

She watched the Oregon blockade footage, the Portland incident, the Houston fire, the targeting of Dren's employee. And she watched Beckett's hearing.

She watched the talking points migrate from the street to the screen. Every network. Every feed. Every platform. The same language from outlets that had nothing in common — hard-right commentators and progressive reconstruction advocates arriving at identical conclusions through apparently independent reasoning.

They knew. They both knew the Fist was coming, and they didn't warn us.

Dren built weapons in secret. Whitfield let him. They worked together.

The deflection failed because they were incompetent, and two hundred million people paid for it.

Now she's on Mars, in his compound, using his ships, while we live in shelters.

The memorial is a distraction. The memorial is an insult. The people responsible for the disaster are asking us to mourn the disaster.

And underneath all of it, the election. The wound that wouldn't close because it had been designed not to close.

The legitimacy debate was entering its seventh month. The same committees that had amplified "stolen election" in November were still amplifying it in May — the language refined, the arguments sharpened, the audience expanded by six months of repetition. Governor Martinez in California had gone further than her initial statement. In March, she had formally declined to implement a federal reconstruction directive, citing "unresolved questions regarding the constitutional authority of the current administration." The directive had been routine — a reallocation of agricultural support funding between counties. The refusal was not routine. It was the first time a state government had explicitly tied non-compliance to the election's legitimacy.

Two other governors — both in zones that had voted for Turner — had issued similar statements within the week. Independent conclusions reached independently, in the same way Thomas and Chen and Park had reached independent conclusions about federal directives. The pattern was the same because the machinery that produced the pattern was the same — Haldane's committees, Haldane's funding, Haldane's dual-feeding strategy, producing identical fractures across different institutions through different channels.

Whitfield watched the feeds and saw the election debate running alongside the reconstruction debate running alongside the accountability debate — three separate arguments, three separate audiences, all of them funded by the same network, all of them serving the same purpose. The country wasn't having a political disagreement. The country was being operated on by a man who understood that democracy's vulnerability was its dependence on shared legitimacy, and who had spent twenty-five years learning how to corrode it.

The narrative was simple. It was emotional. And it was close enough to certain facts that correcting it required more time and complexity than the correction was worth. Dren had built weapons in secret — that was true. Whitfield had gone to Mars — that was true. The deflection had failed, partially, producing the tilt instead of a clean miss — that was true. Everything else was inference, framing, and the careful omission of context. But in a media environment where context was a luxury and attention was currency, the simple version won.

She turned off the display. She sat in the cabin and looked at her hands. The tremor was there — it was always there now. But it was quieter than it had been in Washington, quieter than it had been in the PEOC, quieter than it had been on the cot in the medical unit listening to a man say his daughter's name through the wall.

She was going back. She was going back with evidence that would break the narrative or confirm it, depending on how it was presented and who was listening. She was going back to a country that three men in different cities had spent months pulling apart — Thomas with his autonomy, Chen with his bitterness, Beckett with his hearings, and behind all of them, invisible, the man in Dallas who had been pulling strings since before the Fist was detected.

Eighteen days. Then the ground. Then the memorial. Then the truth.

• • •

Washington, D.C. May 2061.

Whitfield stepped off the transport at Andrews at 06:18 on a Wednesday.

The base was secure — perimeter checkpoints, restricted airspace, the full security apparatus that a presidential arrival demanded. Hunt was waiting on the tarmac with a motorcade and an expression that told her everything the feeds hadn't.

She walked to the car. The morning air was warm — late May, the humidity already building, the sky hazy with the dust that still hung over the capital eighteen months after the flyby.

The motorcade took the highway into the city. She could see the signs from the car along the route. Printed. Distributed. The same design she'd seen on the feeds. ACCOUNTABILITY. WHERE WERE THEY. THE DSA FAILED US. Taped to lampposts, stapled to plywood barriers around construction sites, held by people standing on overpasses who watched the motorcade pass with expressions she couldn't read at sixty miles an hour.

The White House was different. She felt it before she saw it — the weight of returning to a building she'd left under armed escort four months ago. The south portico had been repaired. The plywood was gone. The windows were new — reinforced glass, the same ballistic rating as before, installed during her absence. The wrought iron fence on the southeast perimeter had been replaced. New bars, new razor wire, the welds still bright against the old iron.

The divots in the stone where the bullets had hit had been patched. She knew where they were. She would always know where they were.

She walked through the south entrance and stood in the corridor where four men with automatic weapons had fought their way toward her. The marble was clean. The bullet scars had been filled and polished. The emergency lighting panels had been replaced. Nothing in the corridor showed what had happened there except her memory and the classified after-action report that she carried in her briefcase.

Hunt was beside her. He didn't say anything. He'd been in this corridor that night. He'd heard the gunfire through the PEOC door. He knew what the polished marble was covering.

"How bad is it?" she asked. Not about the building. About the country.

"Worse than the feeds," Hunt said. "Thomas isn't pretending anymore. Chen and Park are following his lead. Three zones operating independently. Two more wavering. Beckett has expanded the committee scope to cover everything you did on Mars. The military is splitting — three commanders report to the Pentagon, three report to their regional authorities. The joint chiefs are issuing conflicting guidance and losing credibility every time they do."

"Haldane?"

"Still in Dallas. Still operating. The audits have stripped some of his cover but he's dissolving entities faster than we can compel disclosure. Basin Range Holdings produced no response to the compliance order. The protective custody warrant is ready."

"Not yet," she said. "The memorial first. The evidence first. Then we take him."

She walked through the building. Past the Oval Office. Past the Situation Room — the PEOC access was down the corridor to the right, the reinforced door that had sealed between her and the rifles. She didn't look at it. She walked to the Residence, set her bag on the bed, and stood at the window.

The Ellipse was visible below. The protest camp was still there — smaller now, the portable heaters gone with the season, but the signs remained. The PA system was running. A voice she couldn't quite hear, reciting something she couldn't quite make out, in a rhythm that had become the background noise of the American presidency.

The country wasn't ungovernable. It was being ungoverned — deliberately, systematically, by a man in Dallas who understood that the fastest way to destroy a democracy was to make its institutions work against each other.

And Haldane was still free. Still operating. The protective custody order was signed and sealed and waiting in her briefcase next to the after-action report from the night four men tried to kill her in this building.

The memorial was in four weeks. The evidence was assembled. The timing was hers.

She looked at her hands. The tremor was there. She let it be there. It was part of the landscape now, like the protest signs and the patched bullet holes in the stone.

She went to work.

• • •

Washington, D.C.

Whitfield initiated the monitoring program on her second week back.

The recordings had confirmed what Dren's probe intercepts had suggested — Haldane had been communicating directly with the fleet. Not through intermediaries or institutional channels. A directional transmission from somewhere on Earth, aimed at a bearing past the heliopause, using a protocol that converted human language into something the alien intelligence could parse.

Someone on Earth was talking to the fleet. The probes had captured the traffic. Now Whitfield needed to find the transmitter.

She briefed it to a room of four people — her signals intelligence director, a communications specialist from the NSA's reconstruction-era remnant, and two military liaison officers from the joint chiefs' intelligence division. No staff. No aides. No paper trail beyond the classification header on the briefing folder.

"We're looking for a directional transmission originating from somewhere in the continental United States," she said. "High-power, narrow beam, aimed at a specific bearing in the sky. The bearing is classified and will be provided to your team under separate cover. The transmission may be intermittent — we believe the last confirmed transmission was approximately March of this year. It may resume."

"What are we looking for specifically?" the signals director asked.

"An antenna. Ground-based, probably fixed installation, probably isolated. The power requirements suggest a facility, not a portable rig. The beam characteristics suggest military or research-grade hardware repurposed for interstellar communication."

"Frequency range?"

"Unknown. The intercepted traffic was captured at the receiving end, not the transmitting end. Your team will need to scan across the plausible range for the target bearing. Start with frequencies that wouldn't be monitored by standard civilian or military systems — the transmitter was designed to be invisible to existing surveillance."

The signals director looked at his team. "That's a lot of sky and a lot of spectrum."

"Narrow it. The bearing gives you a direction. The power requirements give you a facility footprint. Cross-reference against known installations, power grid anomalies, and land use records in areas with clear sight lines to the target bearing. If someone built a high-power directional antenna in the desert, the power grid knows about it even if nobody else does."

"Timeline?"

"Before the memorial. June 24th. I want to know where the transmitter is before we go public with the evidence. If we can locate the facility, it becomes part of the disclosure. If we can't, we still go public — but the facility gives us the physical proof that someone on American soil was communicating with the intelligence that sent the Fist."

The team left with the bearing coordinates in sealed folders. Whitfield sat in the empty room and looked at her hands. The tremor was there, but it was quieter now. Steadier. She was acting, not reacting. The investigation was hers. The memorial was hers. The timing was hers.

The transmitter was somewhere in the desert. The monitoring program would find it, or it wouldn't. Either way, June 24th was coming.

• • •

And into this, Whitfield announced the memorial.

She did it on her third day back. Standing at a podium in the Rose Garden, the rebuilt south portico behind her. The protests were audible beyond the perimeter.

"One year ago, two hundred million people died," she said. "On June 24th, we will mark that anniversary. It will be more than a ceremony. It will be the truth about what happened, and why."

The announcement was broadcast on every network. Memorial ceremonies were planned for twelve locations — Washington, Los Angeles, Honolulu, London, Tokyo, Sydney, and six others along the flyby's damage corridor. Washington would be the centerpiece. The President would speak. The world would watch.

The reaction was immediate.

The first segment aired within the hour. A commentator on the reconstruction affairs feed — a man with a desk and a flag pin and the practiced outrage of someone who'd been waiting for this — leaned into his camera and said: "So the president who fled to Mars while two hundred million of her citizens died is now asking those citizens to gather and mourn. Let me say that again. She left. She went to another planet. And now she wants us to cry together. That's not a memorial. That's a campaign event."

The progressive channels hit the same note from a different angle. A woman on the DSA Today livestream, her voice measured, her framing surgical: "The memorial is scheduled for June 24th. That's the anniversary of the delegation order — the order that gave regional commanders the authority that Whitfield couldn't exercise herself. She's not commemorating the dead. She's commemorating the moment she admitted she couldn't lead. And she's asking us to thank her for it."

A retired general on a military affairs podcast, his tone clinical: "The security requirements alone for a memorial of this scale, in the current threat environment, will pull resources from three reconstruction zones. We're going to pause rebuilding hospitals so the president can stand at a podium and talk about the disaster she failed to prevent. That's not leadership. That's theater."

A panel discussion on the evening feed — four faces in boxes, the format that passed for debate in the reconstruction media landscape. The moderator asked: "Is this the right time for a memorial?" All four panelists said no. They used different words. They arrived at the same conclusion. The framing was consistent across outlets that should have had nothing in common.

By midnight, the hashtag #MemorialDistraction was trending in nine reconstruction zones. By morning, Novak's committee network had amplified it into thirty.

None of them knew what she was actually planning.

Ashford watched the announcement from the safe house.

She watched it twice.

• • •

Safe house. Location undisclosed.

"That's the platform," Ashford said.

Saunders looked up from the display where she'd been cataloguing the evidence package — organizing the recordings, the forensic documentation, the audit disclosures into a presentation structure that could be understood by a general audience, not just investigators and lawyers.

"The memorial," Ashford said. "June 24th. Washington. Every camera in the world pointed at one place. Whitfield speaking about what happened. And we have the answer to what happened."

"And you're going to use the memorial?" she asked.

"I want to present the evidence at the memorial. Whitfield is going to talk about the flyby. I'm going to explain why it happened."

Saunders was quiet for a moment. "If we transmit the recordings beforehand — release them through channels — Haldane's people will claim deep fakes. AI-generated audio. Fabricated evidence. The technology exists and the public knows it. A remote release gets dismissed within forty-eight hours."

"Which is why it has to be live," Ashford said. "In person. At the memorial. With the forensic chain presented alongside the recordings — the translation layer evidence, the Okoro testimony, the audit disclosures, the Meridian payments. Three independent investigations corroborating every recording. You can fake audio. You can't fake three forensic chains that were built by different people in different locations using different methodologies, all arriving at the same conclusion."

"And if they still say it's fabricated?"

"Then Whitfield confirms it from the podium. The President of the United States, standing on the National Mall, confirming that the evidence is real and that she authorized the investigation that produced it."

Saunders looked at her. "Does Whitfield know about this plan?"

"Not yet. But she announced the memorial for a reason. She said 'the truth about what happened and why.' She's not planning a moment of silence. She's planning a disclosure. I'm planning the mechanism."

"You're planning to walk into the most heavily secured public event on Earth and present evidence that a sitting philanthropist orchestrated the deaths of two hundred million people. In front of a crowd that's been told for months that Dren and Whitfield are the ones responsible."

"Yes."

"With what credentials? You're a journalist with a dead source, a dead protector, and a safe house that moves every seventy-two hours."

"I have nineteen recordings of Haldane's voice. I have the codes to decrypt them. I have three independent forensic chains. And I have Dren's testimony backing every technical element." She paused. "I also have you."

Saunders looked at the display. At the evidence package she'd been organizing for weeks. At the matrix of connections that had started with a logo change on the Wayback Machine and now encompassed a conspiracy that reached from Dallas to Mars to somewhere past the heliopause.

"June 24th," Saunders said.

"June 24th."

They started planning.

CHAPTER 22

Exposure

June 24th, 2061.

• • •

Washington, D.C. The National Mall. 09:00.

The morning was clear. A clear that felt deliberate — as though the sky had decided to cooperate with the gravity of what was happening beneath it.

The memorial stage stood at the west end of the reflecting pool, facing the Washington Monument. White risers, a podium, a wall of screens that would carry the ceremony to the crowds extending down the Mall and to twelve simultaneous memorial sites around the world. Los Angeles. Honolulu. London. Tokyo. Sydney. Six others along the damage corridor. Every surviving network was carrying the feed. Every camera was pointed at Washington.

The crowd was enormous. Hundreds of thousands — families of the dead, reconstruction workers, politicians, diplomats, military personnel in dress uniform, and the protesters. The protesters were there too. DREN AND WHITFIELD — WHERE WERE THEY WHEN WE BURNED. The signs were visible from the stage. The Secret Service had established a perimeter, but the perimeter contained the anger rather than excluding it. The chanting was audible between the speakers' remarks.

Haldane was in the third row. He'd been seated with the reconstruction philanthropists — the Foundation's contribution to the recovery had earned him a position of honor. He wore a dark suit and an expression of solemn gravity. The expression was practiced. Everything about Haldane was practiced.

He'd accepted the invitation because refusing it was impossible. The single largest private funder of reconstruction, absent from the one-year memorial of the disaster he'd helped fund the recovery from. The questions that absence would generate were worse than whatever Whitfield was planning. And Whitfield was planning something — he could feel it. The announcement had been too specific. "The truth about what happened, and why." Presidents didn't say that at memorial ceremonies. They said "never forget" and "we will rebuild." They didn't promise truth. Truth was dangerous.

But he was here. In the third row. On camera. Because twenty-five years of operation had taught him that the most dangerous thing a guilty man could do was act guilty.

Beckett was four seats to his left. They hadn't spoken. They wouldn't speak. The conspiracy required that their public relationship remain what it had always been: a senator and a philanthropist who moved in the same circles but had no particular connection. Beckett's face was composed, senatorial, appropriately somber. But Haldane could see the tension in his jaw. Beckett felt it too.

• • •

The White House. Two days earlier.

"Walk me through it again," Whitfield said.

They were in the Map Room — Whitfield, Dren, and Hunt, her Chief of Staff. The evidence package was spread across the table. Printed documents, signed attestations, chain-of-custody certificates. Evidence that couldn't be remotely deleted.

Dren laid it out the same way he'd laid it out on the Mars secure channel, but this time he was in the room. Three feet away instead of eleven minutes away.

"Four independent evidence chains. Technical — O'Malley's forensic trace from the position error through Okoro to Vickers. Organizational — Ashford's corporate mapping of the Haldane network, Meridian, Basin Range, the fellowship pipeline. Institutional — Saunders's ESA document, the killed reclassification, the nine outgassing advocates. And the recordings — nineteen conversations, twelve years, Haldane's voice giving direct orders. And most damning: Haldane in direct communication with the alien body that sent the Fist."

"Each chain was built by different people, in different locations, using different methodologies," Ashford said. She was standing at the end of the table — the first time she'd been in the White House, the first time she'd been in a room with the President. She didn't look intimidated. She looked like a journalist who'd spent eight months building a case and was ready to present it. "They converge on the same person independently. You can attack any single chain. You can't attack all four without arguing that four separate investigations, conducted by people who didn't know each other existed, all fabricated the same conclusion."

"That's the deepfake defense," Saunders said. She was seated at the far end, her tablet open, the presentation structure she'd been building for weeks displayed on the screen. "Any single piece — the recordings especially — can be dismissed as AI-generated. The four chains together cannot."

Hunt looked at the table. He'd been quiet through most of the briefing. He was a political operative, not an investigator, and the evidence was outside his domain. But the political implications were squarely inside it.

"This is enough to destroy him publicly," Hunt said. "I'm not sure it's enough to convict him in a court of law. And a court case could take years. His lawyers will challenge every chain. They'll attack the recordings as fabricated. They'll argue Okoro's testimony was coerced. They'll file motions that delay proceedings until the political environment changes."

Whitfield looked at him. "I know."

"If we go public and the legal case fails—"

"We're not going to court," Whitfield said. "Not first. Not as the primary strategy."

The room was quiet.

"Haldane spent twenty-five years building a system that used public narrative to override institutional process. He used fellowships to place people in positions of influence. He used funding to create dependency. He used Beckett to turn congressional oversight into a weapon. He used Novak to put anger in the streets. Every tool he used operated in public opinion, not in courtrooms."

She looked at the evidence on the table. "We're going to use his own tactics against him. We're going to convict him in the court of public opinion. Every screen on the planet. His voice. His orders. His network. Presented live, corroborated by four independent chains, confirmed by the President of the United States from the podium of the one-year memorial. By the time any court convenes, the verdict will already exist in the mind of every person who watched."

Hunt processed that. "You're bypassing the legal system."

"I'm using the memorial as the disclosure platform because the legal system has been compromised by twenty-five years of Haldane's placements. His people are in the judiciary. His money is in the legal infrastructure. His fragmentation campaign has paralyzed the institutions that would normally process this." She paused. "He destroyed the conventional path. I'm building a new one."

"And Haldane?"

"He'll be in the third row. Personally invited. He can't refuse without confirming every accusation we're about to make. He sits there, on camera, and hears his own voice on every screen in the world. His reaction is the confirmation."

"The protective custody order?"

"Executes the moment the broadcast ends. Brandt's team is coordinating with the Secret Service. Haldane doesn't leave the Mall."

Hunt looked at Dren. Dren looked back with the still, emotionless expression that was either the sign of a man who felt nothing or a man who felt everything and showed none of it.

"This is the right call," Dren said. "The evidence is unassailable. The platform is global. The timing is the one-year anniversary — the moment when the world is already focused on what happened and why. If we wait for courts, Haldane's lawyers buy him years. Years he'll use to continue the fragmentation. Years we don't have."

"And Ashford?" Hunt asked.

"I introduce her," Whitfield said. "From the podium. Not as a journalist — as the lead investigator in a presidential investigation. I give her the stage, the authority, and the platform. She presents the evidence. Dren presents the technical chain. I confirm it from the podium. Three voices, one truth."

"And Beckett?"

Whitfield almost smiled. It wasn't a pleasant expression. "Beckett will be in the audience. Four seats from Haldane. When the recordings play, every hearing he convened, every subpoena he drafted, every question he asked about Dren and me — all of it becomes evidence of obstruction, not oversight. He'll know it the moment the first recording plays. And every camera will be pointed at his face."

"One of the recordings names him directly," Dren said. "Haldane discussing the hearing strategy with Vickers. Beckett's name. His role. The coordination."

Whitfield's expression didn't change. "Then he won't just know. Everyone will know."

• • •

The National Mall. 10:15.

Whitfield took the podium.

The crowd noise dropped — not to silence, but to the dense, weighted quiet of a hundred thousand people deciding to listen. The protesters kept their signs up but stopped chanting. The cameras tightened on her face.

She spoke about the dead.

Not statistics. Names. Cities. The woman in Honolulu who called her daughter's school and got a recording because the school was already gone. The fire crew in Long Beach that drove into the tsunami corridor because the dispatch system said there were survivors. The bridge in San Francisco that held for eleven minutes after the pressure wave hit, long enough for a thousand people to cross before it fell. She spoke the way she always spoke — plain, direct, the twang surfacing under the weight of what she was saying.

She spoke for twelve minutes. Then she stopped.

"One year ago, I promised you the truth about what happened. I'm going to keep that promise now."

She turned slightly, looking toward the side of the stage.

"I'd like to introduce someone most of you don't know. Her name is Chloe Ashford. Eight months ago, she was a journalist investigating anomalies in the Haldane Foundation's corporate structure. What she found — what she and her team found — is the reason two hundred million people are dead. Not an accident. Not an act of God. A decision. Made by a man. Documented in his own voice."

She stepped back from the podium. "Ms. Ashford."

In the third row, Haldane's composure cracked. The name hit him the way the thermal imager readings had hit him in the Australian desert — a data point that restructured everything around it. Ashford. The journalist Oliver had failed to kill. Twice. The woman who had walked out of Arlington with Vickers's recordings while Okafor bled out on the study floor. She was supposed to be hiding. She was not supposed to be standing on the stage of the one-year memorial being introduced by the President of the United States.

He knew, in that moment, what was coming. Not necessarily the specifics of what Ashford had assembled. But the shape of it. The architecture. He recognized it the way he recognized all architecture — by its structure, by the logic of its construction. Whitfield had built something, and Ashford was the delivery mechanism, and the audience was the world.

The crowd noise shifted. Confusion. The talking heads on the networks were scrambling — this wasn't in the program, wasn't in the advance briefing, wasn't anticipated by anyone outside the Map Room.

Ashford walked to the podium.

She looked at the crowd. At the signs. At the cameras. At Haldane, in the third row, whose face had not yet changed because he was too disciplined to let it change before he understood what was happening.

"My name is Chloe Ashford," she said. "Eight months ago, I began investigating a connection between the Haldane Foundation and the events that led to the flyby. What I found, along with three independent investigative teams, is this."

The screens behind her lit up.

She started with a logo.

The screen behind her showed two images side by side. Fresh Start's original logo — the one she'd found on the Wayback Machine eight months ago. And the replacement — the bland, corporate version that had appeared between June 10th and June 22nd, the dates she'd given Novak in his office.

"Eight months ago, I found a logo change," she said. "A nonprofit foundation — one of the largest private funders of reconstruction — quietly replaced its logo during a twelve-day window. That's not unusual. Organizations rebrand. But the old logo contained an image that matched a symbol I'd seen in a document of data returned from the mission to explore The Fist. The old logo, the one that Fresh Start had been using for years, and this, an image returned from an alien object sent to destroy our planet."

On the screen the two images appeared, side by side. The resemblance was unmistakable. The implications, unfathomable.

She let the images sit on the screen. The crowd was thunderstruck. The dead quiet of people who couldn't comprehend what they were looking at.

"That," she said, "Is evidence of foreknowledge, of collusion. But how could this be? How could a simple non-profit know about an alien symbol? I pulled the thread. That thread led here."

The screen changed. The matrix appeared — the wallscreen version of what she'd been building in safe houses for eight months, the version Saunders had formatted for a general audience. A clean, readable map. Nodes and connections, color-coded, each one labeled.

She pointed to the first node. "The Haldane Foundation. Founded 2017. Assets in excess of four hundred billion dollars. Primary activities: reconstruction funding, institutional fellowships, policy research." She traced the line from the Foundation to the next node. "Meridian Technical Services. A private consulting firm. Board overlap with the Haldane Foundation advisory committee — three shared directors. Meridian was dissolved in 2044 and reconstituted in 2046 under the same board. During the gap, its contracts were serviced by Basin Range Holdings."

She moved to the next connection. "Basin Range Holdings. A shell company registered in Nevada. No employees. No public operations. Its sole documented activity was holding the lease on a facility outside Las Vegas — a facility that received industrial quantities of concrete, steel, and specialized equipment over a period of six years."

The crowd was listening. Not all of them understood corporate structure. But they understood the pattern Ashford was drawing — the shape of something hidden behind layers, the outline of a structure that existed specifically to be invisible.

"The Haldane Foundation funded a fellowship program. Over twenty years, that program placed individuals in governance positions, advisory committees, and institutional appointments across eleven reconstruction zones and multiple international bodies. Forty-three of those placements have been identified in positions of direct influence over reconstruction policy, resource allocation, and institutional oversight."

She paused. "That's not philanthropy. That's positioning."

She brought up a new display — four documents, side by side. Grant disbursements from the Fresh Start Foundation to four different civic organizations. Two from before the November 2060 election. Two from after.

"The same network that placed people in reconstruction positions also manipulated the 2060 presidential election," she said. "Not by rigging votes. By building the conditions that made the result contested before a single vote was cast."

She pointed to the first two documents. "Before the election: one committee funded to mobilize voters in interior reconstruction zones. A different committee funded to advocate for delaying the election in coastal zones. Opposite goals. Same funding source. Neither committee knew the other existed."

She pointed to the second pair. "After the election: the mobilization committee pivoted to 'stolen election.' The delay committee pivoted to 'decisive mandate.' Again — opposite messages, same source, same funding chain. The national debate about whether the election was legitimate was manufactured by a single network, arguing both sides simultaneously."

The crowd was quiet. This was different from the corporate structure and the fellowship pipeline — those were abstract, institutional, hard to feel. The election was personal. Everyone in the crowd had lived through November. Everyone had an opinion about the result. And now they were learning that the argument they'd been having — with their families, their neighbors, their coworkers

— had been scripted by the same man who had killed two hundred million people.

"The election wasn't stolen," Ashford said. "Every vote was real. Every count was accurate. But the conditions that produced the result — the suppressed turnout in California, the amplified anger in the interior zones, the legitimacy debate that followed — all of it was engineered. The same way the institutional delay was engineered. The same way the outgassing debate was engineered. Not by forging evidence. By shaping the environment in which evidence was evaluated."

She let that sit. Then she moved to the Vickers payments.

She brought up the payment records — the Meridian disbursement schedule that Saunders had found in the compliance filings. The screen showed a table: quarterly payments, fifteen years, to a personal account. A name.

"General Paul D. Vickers. Fifteen years of direct payments from Meridian Technical Services. One hundred and thirty thousand dollars a year. Personal account. No intermediary." She looked at the crowd. "General Vickers held an advisory position in the planetary defense oversight committee. He was the administrative signoff on the firmware update that caused the deflection error. The error that turned a clean miss into the flyby that killed two hundred million people."

The crowd shifted. The murmuring started.

"General Vickers was killed six weeks ago," Ashford said. "Before he could testify. But before he died, he gave me something."

She didn't say what. Not yet. The recordings would come later. She moved to the institutional chain.

She stopped. The presentation structure she'd rehearsed with Saunders had a clean transition here — from the organizational chain to the institutional chain. From money to documents. But she wasn't in the safe house rehearsing anymore. She was standing on the National Mall with every camera in the world pointed at her face, and the man who had ordered the murder of the person who should be standing beside her was sitting sixty feet away in the third row.

"I need to tell you about someone," she said. "Someone who should be standing here alongside me."

The screen behind her changed. A photograph — Greg, smiling, the one she'd looked at a hundred times on her phone in the months since. Relaxed. Alive.

"Most of you know this face," she said. "His name was Greg Harlan. He sold medical supplies. He was my —"

She stopped. The word sat there, unfinished, and the pause said more than any word she could have chosen. Whatever Greg had been to her — and it had never been simple, had never fit neatly into the categories that other people's relationships fit into — he had been hers, and now he wasn't.

"boyfriend." She cleared her throat and continued. "He was murdered in my apartment. Eight months ago. Greg wasn't the target. Greg wasn't part of any investigation. Greg sold medical supplies. He was a message to me to stop what I was doing. His murder served as an exclamation point."

Her voice was steady. She'd practiced this part. She'd practiced it alone in the safe house bathroom at two in the morning, saying the words to the mirror until she could say them without breaking, because she knew that if she broke here the cameras would show grief and the talking heads would call it performance and the evidence would be lost in the story of a crying woman on a stage.

"The man who killed Greg attempted to kill me twice after that. The same man killed General Vickers six weeks ago. The same man was killed himself during that operation, by a security professional named Daniel Okafor, who died shielding me from the explosive device the assassin was carrying."

She looked at the third row.

"The man who sent that assassin is sitting in this audience."

The crowd noise changed. The cameras moved — not to Haldane yet, not all of them, but the ones operated by directors who understood what was happening. The split screen was forming. Ashford on the left. The third row on the right.

She pointed into the third row. "Charles Haldane ordered the murder of Greg Harlan. Charles Haldane ordered the attempts on my life. Charles Haldane ordered the assassination of General Vickers. Charles Haldane sent a man named Oliver to do it — a professional killer, funded through the same foundation network I've just shown you, operating on direct instructions from the man sitting sixty feet from where I'm standing."

She was pointing, looking straight at Haldane. Not at the cameras. Not at the crowd. At him. The man in the dark suit with the practiced expression of solemn gravity, who was hearing his network described by the woman his assassin had failed to kill three times.

"Vickers gave me the proof before he died. Three men are dead because of what I'm about to show you. I owe them this."

Her voice cracked on the last word. Not a break, a crack, from holding something together for too long under too much pressure. Her eyes were wet. She didn't wipe them. She didn't apologize. She stood at the podium and let the tears sit on her face because they were real and because the man in the third row had caused them and because every camera in the world could see both of those things at the same time.

She took a breath. She looked away from Haldane and back at the screens.

"This is what they died for."

She moved to the institutional chain.

"This next section was assembled by Dr. Jessica Saunders, a scientific reporter, and my investigative partner."

The screen changed. Two documents appeared side by side. The draft ESA assessment on the left. The final version on the right. The differences highlighted in red.

"Three weeks after the initial detection of the object, the European Space Agency's internal analysis concluded that the spectral signatures were inconsistent with known cometary composition. The draft recommended immediate reclassification as a potentially artificial object."

She pointed to the right-hand document. "This is what the parliamentary committee received instead. The reclassification recommendation was removed. The language was rewritten to support continued observation under the natural framework. The revision was made at the Paranal Observatory by a senior official whose edits are visible in the document metadata."

She brought up the next screen — the fellowship connections. Nine names. Each one linked to the Haldane Foundation fellowship program. Each one connected to the institutional chain that had delayed reclassification by months.

"Nine scientists who publicly advocated for the natural interpretation — the interpretation that kept the world from responding to the threat — received Haldane Foundation fellowships. Nine. Recruited through the same pipeline, funded by the same source, placed in positions where their advocacy delayed the response by months. Months that cost cities. Months that cost lives."

• • •

In the audience, Saunders watched the screens.

The killed draft was on every screen in the world now. The edits were highlighted in red, the way she'd highlighted them on her tablet the night she'd found them.

She didn't cry. She watched the screens and breathed and let the evidence speak in the voice she'd given it. She hoped that at Paranal, Hamner would feel some level of vindication.

• • •

Dren.

Dren took the podium.

He didn't introduce himself. Everyone on the planet knew who he was. He stood at the microphone and let the crowd see him. Compact, still, his expression showing nothing that wasn't precise.

"Ms. Ashford has shown you the organizational structure," he said. "The money. The placements. The institutional manipulation. Ms. Saunders has shown you the institutional sabotage — the killed reclassification, the manufactured scientific consensus that delayed our response by years. I'm going to show you the technical evidence — how the sabotage was carried out, how we traced it, and where the trail leads."

The screen behind him changed. A single schematic — the parameter upload chain, stripped to its essentials.

"You all know that wave 3 fired early striking the Fist near the bow, and causing the tilt. One digit was changed in a targeting parameter. That digit caused the tilt. The engineer who entered it entered what his instructions told him to enter. The instruction file was altered afterward, to frame him. My forensics team traced the alteration to General Okoro, the military liaison assigned to oversee the deflection mission — a man sent to Mars to supervise the very operation he was ordered to sabotage. Okoro confirmed, under interrogation, that his instructions came from General Vickers."

He advanced the screen. The chain appeared — Okoro to Vickers, with the connection to Ashford's organizational matrix highlighted.

"General Vickers. Planetary defense. The man responsible for overseeing the very systems designed to protect us from the Fist. The same man whose financial records show fifteen years of payments from a Haldane-controlled company. Ms. Ashford's organizational trail and my forensic trail converge on the same network, built by the same architect."

He paused. Then he advanced to the next display.

"But the sabotage is only half of what we found. My team also discovered a covert communication relay hidden in the firmware of a decommissioned mining station in the asteroid belt. The relay was built into the station's code from deployment, a concealed transmission channel, all of it designed to be invisible to standard monitoring. The digital signatures on the firmware trace back through the same corporate infrastructure that connects to Meridian Technical Services — and from Meridian, to the Haldane Foundation. The same chain. The same architect.“

The screen showed the relay path — Earth to belt station to the Fist to the bearing at 130 AU.

"That relay was not communicating with anyone on Earth. It was not communicating with anyone in the belt. The transmission bearing points outward — past the outer planets, past the heliopause, to approximately 130 astronomical units from the Sun. And it was relayed by The Fist. The relay connected someone on Earth to an intelligence at the edge of our solar system. The same intelligence that manufactured and launched the object that killed two hundred million people – and was intended to kill everyone.“

The Mall was silent.

"Charles Haldane was in direct communication with the entity that sent the Fist. He sabotaged humanity's defense, possibly on their instructions. And when the Fist failed to destroy us, he leveraged the network Ms. Ashford described, to finish the job from the inside. The fragmentation of this country, the erosion of its institutions, the manufactured division you have experienced for the past year — all of it was designed to weaken us for what comes next.“

He looked at the crowd.

"The entity that sent the Fist is still out there. And thanks to the evidence we've presented today, we now know where they are, how they communicate. Charles Haldane gave us that — not willingly, but completely."

He stepped back from the podium.

And then Ashford played the recordings.

• • •

Haldane.

The first recording was from 2049. His voice — calm, precise, unmistakable — discussing the fellowship placement strategy with someone whose voice had been redacted. The language was operational. Clinical. The tone of a man managing a project, not conspiring to kill a species.

"The institutional delay needs to hold for at least a year. If we have that delay, the deflection window shrinks. And once the first wave of planetary defenses fail, as I have ensured they will, there won't be time to compensate."

Haldane sat in the third row and heard his own voice on every speaker on the National Mall.

His face didn't change. Twenty-five years of discipline held the expression in place — the solemn gravity, the philanthropist's concern, the public mask he'd worn so long it had become indistinguishable from his actual face.

Then he smiled.

It was deliberate. Calculated. The smile of a man who had decided, in the two seconds between the first recording ending and the second beginning, that the only play was dismissal. He shook his head slowly, the way a patient adult shakes his head at a child's invention. He waved his hand — a small gesture, loose-wristed, the universal signal for nonsense. A few people in the seated section looked at him. The cameras found him. He let them.

He waved his hand dismissively. "Cheap fakes," he said. Not into a microphone — to the people around him, loud enough to carry to the nearest cameras. "This is ridiculous. AI-generated audio. Anyone with a laptop can produce this."

He kept the smile through the second recording — 2053, the Ark, the Council's decision, his voice explaining the timeline to Vickers. He shook his head again. He leaned toward the dignitary beside him and said something with an expression of amused incredulity, as though they were watching a particularly unconvincing magic trick together. The dignitary leaned away.

He kept it through the third — 2060, the tilt, his voice instructing Vickers to sabotage Wave 3. "Whatever you can do to maximize the damage caused by the flyby." He was still smiling but the smile had hardened. The looseness was gone. The wave had stopped. His hand was on his knee now, and it was still.

The crowd was changing. The sound was changing. The signs that said DREN AND WHITFIELD were lowering — not all of them, not yet, but enough. The faces that had been angry at the podium were now angry at the third row. The cameras were finding Haldane the way cameras always found the center of a story — not because someone pointed them there, but because the geometry of attention had shifted. And what the cameras found was a man smiling while his own voice described the murder of two hundred million people.

The smile was the mistake. Dismissal works when the evidence is ambiguous. When the evidence is nineteen recordings corroborated by four forensic chains presented by the President of the United States on the one-year anniversary of the disaster — dismissal doesn't look like confidence. It looks like contempt. Contempt for the dead. Contempt for the audience. Contempt for the hundred thousand people on the Mall who had come to mourn and were now watching a man wave away their grief as though it were an inconvenience.

By the fifth recording, the smile was a rictus. By the seventh, it was gone. By the ninth, Haldane was sitting motionless, his hand still on his knee, his face showing nothing because the performance of dismissal had failed and the performance of composure was all that remained.

Beckett, four seats away, had been watching Haldane's performance with mounting horror — not performative horror this time, real horror. The horror of a man watching his co-conspirator try to bluff through a hand that had already been laid face-up on the table. Every smile, every wave, every "cheap fake" was making it worse — not just for Haldane but for everyone connected to him.

Five recordings. Seven. Nine. Each one another structural member failing.

Haldane could feel it. The weight of every camera, every eye, every feed and network and screen in every memorial site on the planet, settling on him like a physical force. His own voice, coming from the speakers, saying the words he'd said in rooms he'd thought were private, to people he'd thought were loyal, in conversations he'd thought were gone.

The twelfth recording changed everything.

Haldane's voice, discussing the hearing strategy with Vickers: "Beckett's committee is the lever. He'll frame the subpoenas around Dren's early detection data — the thirty-minute window. The hearings serve two purposes: they build the public case against Whitfield, and they keep the investigation pointed at Dren. As long as Beckett controls the questions, nobody asks the right ones."

Beckett was on his feet before the recording finished.

He turned to face Haldane — and pointed. His arm extended, his finger aimed at the man four seats away, and the gesture was so sudden and so raw that the Secret Service agents along the row shifted forward.

"Him," Beckett said. His voice cracked across the seated section, louder than it needed to be because it was aimed at the cameras as much as the man. "He did this. All of it. I had no knowledge of — this man came to me with — he manipulated the process. He manipulated everyone. Everything you just heard — that was him. Not me. Him."

He was still pointing. His hand was shaking. The senatorial composure, the practiced gravity, the careful calibration of every public gesture he'd made for thirty years — all of it gone. What remained was a man in a suit pointing at another man in a suit, on a stage built to honor two hundred million dead, shouting the oldest defense in the history of co-conspirators: it wasn't me, it was him.

Haldane looked at Beckett. The smile was long gone. What replaced it was something the cameras had never seen on Charles

Haldane's face: disgust. The disgust of an architect watching his materials fail. Beckett had always been the weakest structural member. Haldane had known that since Geneva. He'd used him anyway, because weak men were useful precisely because they were weak — they did what they were told, they performed when required, and when the structure collapsed, they broke first and pointed at someone else.

"Sit down, James," Haldane said. Quiet. The microphones didn't catch it. The lip readers would, later, when the footage was analyzed frame by frame. "You're embarrassing yourself."

Beckett didn't sit down. He kept pointing. He kept talking — faster now, louder, the words tumbling out in the disordered syntax of a man who had rehearsed a thousand senate speeches and was now improvising the most important statement of his life. "I was told it was policy research — the fellowship program — I had no idea about the scope — he came to me and said —"

The crowd nearest him saw it. They saw Haldane's stillness against Beckett's disintegration. They saw two men who had been sitting four seats apart in the reconstruction philanthropist section, one of them shouting accusations at the other while the recordings played.

That was the moment. The moment was Beckett, on his feet, pointing at Haldane, confirming by accusation what the recordings confirmed by content. One was sitting in silence. The other was screaming that it was all the silent one's fault.

The crowd didn't need a verdict. The third row had just delivered one.

By the fifteenth recording, the crowd had turned.

Not just the mourners. The protesters. And now Haldane's voice was coming through every speaker on the Mall, explaining how he had manufactured the anger they were carrying.

The signs came down. In clusters, in sections, a wave moving through a crowd. First near the screens, where the sound was clearest and the recordings were loudest. Then outward, spreading through the standing sections, through the protest zones, through the knots of union workers and community organizers who were hearing, for the first time, that the man who had funded their committees and printed their signs and organized their transportation was the same man who had killed the people they were mourning.

The chanting stopped. A different sound replaced it. A raw murmur that built into something louder. A sound that had no words because the words hadn't been written yet for what they were feeling. They had been angry at Whitfield. They had been angry at Dren. And now they understood that the anger itself had been manufactured by the man sitting in the third row, and the understanding made the anger change direction the way a river changes direction when the dam breaks.

The Secret Service perimeter held. But the geometry of the crowd was shifting — bodies moving toward the third row, phones raised, faces twisted with something that was no longer protest but something older and less organized. The agents along the seated section stepped forward. The barrier was psychological, not physical, and it was eroding.

Haldane could feel it. Not just the cameras now. The crowd. The heat of a hundred thousand people whose manufactured outrage had just become real outrage pointed at the man who manufactured it.

• • •

The podium.

Whitfield returned to the microphone after the nineteenth recording.

"The evidence you've just seen and heard was assembled by four independent investigations. And the recordings — kept as insurance by a man who understood that the network he served would eventually try to destroy him."

She paused. The Mall was not quiet. It was a different kind of loud than it had been an hour ago. The sound of a crowd that had been lied to and had just learned it.

"I authorized this investigation. I reviewed this evidence. I am confirming, as the President of the United States, that every element presented today is authentic, verified, and supported by a documented chain of custody. This is not fabricated. This is not a 'cheap fake.' This is not a political operation. This is the truth about why two hundred million people are dead."

She looked at the crowd. At the lowered signs. At the signs being torn apart. At the cameras.

"Charles Haldane is in the audience today. He was invited because this memorial belongs to everyone — including those who must answer for what happened. Mr. Haldane, a protective custody order has been signed. You will be taken into custody."

She paused.

"Senator Beckett. The same order applies to you."

The crowd noise surged. Something more primal than applause. The sound of a verdict delivered by a hundred thousand people simultaneously.

• • •

Beckett.

Beckett moved first.

He was on his feet before Whitfield finished speaking, looking for the nearest uniform. The Secret Service agents were already approaching. Beckett walked toward them — not away, toward. His hands were visible, open, unthreatening. His face had shed every pretense of composure. What remained was fear. Fear of the crowd. The crowd that was pressing against the perimeter. The crowd that knew his name now.

"I need to be taken into custody immediately," Beckett said. His voice was loud enough for the agents to hear over the noise. "I need protection. Now."

The agents flanked him. One on each side. They moved him toward the vehicle cordon behind the stage — fast, efficient, the practiced geometry of extracting a principal from a hostile environment. Beckett went willingly. Eagerly. The man who had spent months performing outrage was now performing compliance, because compliance meant a vehicle with locked doors and tinted glass between him and the people he'd been manipulating for a year.

The cameras caught all of it. The senator who had demanded accountability, demanding protection from the accountability that had found him.

• • •

Haldane.

Haldane watched Beckett leave. Watched the coward's exit.

He would not do that.

He stood. Slowly. Deliberately. The composure held because it was the only thing left to hold. Around him, the seated section was emptying — dignitaries and officials moving toward exits, the Secret Service creating corridors through the crowd. The crowd was pressing inward. The barrier between the standing sections and the seated rows was failing, bending, the agents stepping back to maintain distance rather than holding ground.

Haldane's private security materialized around him. Three men — his detail, positioned since the previous evening, loyal to the paycheck if not the man. The planned exit was east, toward the vehicle cordon where the protective custody detail was waiting. The planned exit was gone — the crowd surge after Whitfield named Beckett had buckled the perimeter, and the east corridor was a wall of bodies. The Secret Service was somewhere in that wall, fighting toward the third row, but the geometry of the planned interception had collapsed with the crowd control.

The detail lead made the call in two seconds. Not east. Lateral. South, through the seated section, away from the stage and the screens and the sound of Haldane's voice still echoing across the Mall. They moved in a tight formation — three men around one, shoulders clearing a path through panicked dignitaries and overturned chairs and memorial programs scattered on the ground like leaves.

A bottle struck the shoulder of the lead agent. Someone grabbed at Haldane's jacket — the agent to his right broke the grip with a practiced motion. The noise was deafening now. The organized chanting of the morning had become something formless and enormous, a sound that came from every direction and had no center.

They reached the south perimeter in ninety seconds. The fence was unmanned — the agents who had been posted there had been pulled toward the crowd surge at the east corridor. The detail lead cut the zip ties on a maintenance gate and they were through, onto the grass, moving fast toward Independence Avenue.

Haldane pulled out his phone and called the aircraft.

The pilot answered on the second ring.

"Ready the plane for immediate takeoff," Haldane said. "We're inbound. Ten minutes."

"Don't worry, sir," the pilot said. "We'll be ready for you."

Haldane ended the call. The detail was already at the street. Independence Avenue — four lanes, moderate traffic. The detail lead stepped into the road and stopped a grey sedan. He opened the driver's door, pulled the man out by his jacket, and put him on the pavement. Not violent — efficient. The driver started to protest. The detail lead showed him the weapon. The driver stopped protesting.

Haldane got in the back seat. Two of the detail got in front. The third stayed on the sidewalk — there wasn't room, and someone needed to not be in the car that was about to appear on every traffic camera between the Mall and Reagan National.

They drove. Fast, but not reckless — the detail lead knew that a speeding carjacked vehicle drew attention they couldn't afford. They took surface streets. The drive to Reagan National was six minutes in normal traffic. They made it in four.

The aircraft was on the tarmac at the general aviation terminal. Haldane could see it through the fence as they approached — his jet, stairs down, positioned for departure. The crew was standing at the foot of the stairs. Captain and first officer, in uniform, waiting.

Ready for him. Just as the pilot had said.

The detail dropped him at the terminal access gate and the sedan pulled away — fast now, no longer concerned with discretion. Haldane walked through the gate, across the tarmac, toward the aircraft. Three hundred meters of open concrete between him and the stairs.

He could hear sirens in the distance. Not close. Not yet.

"We need to move," Haldane said as he reached the crew. "Now. File for Zurich once we're airborne."

The captain looked at him. The first officer looked at him. Neither moved toward the aircraft.

"Now," Haldane repeated.

The captain looked at him for a long moment. He had the expression of a man who had spent the last forty minutes watching nineteen recordings of his employer's voice ordering the deaths of two hundred million people, and who had already made the only decision that mattered.

The captain turned and walked away. The first officer followed. They walked across the tarmac toward the terminal building without looking back, their footsteps quiet on the concrete, two people choosing to be unemployed rather than complicit.

Haldane stood at the foot of the stairs. His aircraft. His exit. His last escape route. Empty.

Behind him, the detail was gone — the sedan vanishing into traffic, the paycheck reaching its limit. Ahead of him, the stairs led to a plane that no one would fly.

He stood there for thirty seconds. The longest thirty seconds of his life. The sirens were louder now — approaching from the GW Parkway, the access road, converging on the general aviation terminal with the unhurried certainty of law enforcement that knew its target had nowhere left to go.

Three police vehicles. They pulled onto the tarmac and stopped in a semicircle around the aircraft stairs. Officers emerged. No urgency. No weapons drawn. Just the procedural machinery of an arrest that the broadcast had made inevitable.

"Charles Haldane," one of them said. "Please turn around and place your hands behind your back."

He turned. He placed his hands behind his back. The cuffs closed around his wrists — the first physical constraint he'd experienced in twenty-five years of operating above every system he'd built to constrain others.

The officer guided him to the nearest vehicle. Haldane looked back once — at the aircraft, at the empty stairs, at the tarmac where his crew had been standing. The distance between where he was and where he'd planned to be was three hundred meters and the rest of his life.

The door closed. The vehicle pulled away. Behind him, on the National Mall, the crowd was still making that sound — the formless, enormous sound of a nation learning who had broken it.

CHAPTER 23

The Aftermath

June 24th, 2061. Afternoon.

• • •

The National Mall. 14:00.

The broadcast had been over for an hour. The crowd hadn't left.

The screens on the Mall were dark now — the networks had cut away to analysis, commentary, the scramble of talking heads trying to process what they'd just witnessed. But the crowd stayed. Hundreds of thousands of people standing on the Mall in the June heat, holding phones that had recorded the evidence, looking at each other with the specific expression of people who had just learned that the shape of the world was different than they'd been told.

The signs were on the ground. DREN AND WHITFIELD — WHERE WERE THEY WHEN WE BURNED lay face-down on the grass, abandoned by hands that had been holding them an hour ago. Some had been torn apart. Some had been turned over and written on — new words, in marker, in pen, in whatever people had. HALDANE. 200 MILLION. WE WERE LIED TO. The handwriting was raw and uneven, the work of people who had never made a protest sign before because until an hour ago they'd thought someone else was making them for them.

Some of the protesters were crying. Some were angry, the anger redirected but not diminished, a heat with nowhere to go now that the man it belonged to was in the back of a police vehicle. Some were sitting on the grass, staring at nothing, the posture of people whose certainty had been removed and nothing had replaced it yet. They had come to the Mall knowing who the enemy was. They were leaving not knowing anything at all.

The chanting had stopped. In its place: the low murmur of a crowd processing something too large to process quickly. Two hundred million dead. Not an accident. Not an act of God. A man. A plan. A voice on a recording saying the words that turned grief into fury. And the fury they'd been carrying for months — the fury that had been organized for them, funded for them, printed on signs and bused to the Ellipse — had been part of the plan too.

That was the part that hurt the most. The signs. Their signs. Their anger. Manufactured by the man who had manufactured the disaster they were angry about. They had been tools in the hands of the man who had killed the people they were mourning. The anger and the grief had been real. The direction had been engineered.

Whitfield returned to thc podium at 14:15.

She hadn't planned to speak again. The evidence presentation was complete. The arrests were executed. The legal machinery was in motion. But the crowd was still there, and the crowd was lost, and a lost crowd in the capital of a wounded nation was something that couldn't be left alone.

She walked to the microphone. No notes. No prepared remarks. The Secret Service had argued against it — the security situation was still unstable, the perimeter had been breached during the arrests, there were too many people and too much emotion in too small a space. She overruled them the way she'd overruled every objection since the morning: by walking forward.

"I know what you're feeling," she said. "I know because I felt it too."

The murmur dropped. The Mall was too large and too full for silence — but to something that approximated listening.

"You came here angry. Most of you came here angry at me. At Dren. At the people you were told were responsible for what happened to your families, your cities, your lives. That anger was real. Your grief is real. The people you lost are real."

She paused. The twang was there — stronger than it had been during the morning's formal remarks, the accent that surfaced when the performance stopped and the person underneath started talking.

"What you learned today is that the anger was aimed in the wrong direction. Not by accident — by design. A man spent twenty-five years building a machine to point your anger where he needed it pointed, and it worked. It worked on you. It worked on Congress. It worked on me. We were all inside his machine, and none of us knew it."

She looked at the crowd. At the faces. At the torn signs and the abandoned megaphones and the people sitting on the grass with their certainty gone.

"That machine is broken now. The man who built it is in custody. The evidence is public. The truth is on every screen in the world. But the damage he did — the real damage, the damage that matters — isn't the buildings or the coastlines or the infrastructure. It's this." She gestured at the Mall. At the crowd. At the space between people who had been divided by design. "He broke our trust. In our government. In each other. In our ability to know what's true. That's what he was trying to destroy, and he nearly succeeded."

She leaned forward slightly.

"I'm asking you to do something harder than being angry. I'm asking you to come back. Not to me — I know I have to earn that. Not to the government — the government has to earn that too. Come back to each other. Because what's coming next — and there is something coming next, and I will tell you about it when the time is right — we can't face divided. We can't face it as regions, or factions, or parties, or zones. We face it as a country. As a species. Together, or not at all."

The Mall was quiet. A quiet that held its breath.

Then someone started it. Not from the stage or the VIP section. From the standing area, deep in the crowd, where the reconstruction workers and the union members and the people who had been bused in with printed signs were standing in the June heat with their certainty gone and nothing to replace it except the voice of a woman who was telling them the truth for the first time in a year.

"USA."

Quiet. Almost tentative. One voice.

Then another. Then ten. Then a hundred, and then the sound built the way sounds build in a crowd of hundreds of thousands, finding its rhythm, finding its beat, finding the cadence that turned a murmur into a chant and a chant into something that carried across the Mall and down the reflecting pool and off the face of the Washington Monument.

"USA. USA. USA."

It wasn't the chant of a rally or a protest. It was the chant of a crowd that had been broken and was choosing, in this moment, on this day, to start putting itself back together. The sound was rough and uneven and enormous, and Whitfield stood at the podium and listened to it and felt the tremor in her hands go quiet for the first time in months.

• • •

Federal Holding Facility, Alexandria. Two days after the broadcast.

Dren arrived at 06:00. Brandt was with him.

The facility was a converted government building — nondescript, secure, a place that existed for situations where the detainee was too important to put in a regular cell and too dangerous to leave unsecured. Haldane had been processed the evening of the memorial. He'd cooperated with the intake procedure the way he cooperated with everything — precisely, without emotion, as though he were checking into a hotel he found beneath his standards.

They met in a conference room. Reinforced door. No windows. A table, two chairs on each side. Haldane was seated when Dren entered. He looked as he always looked — composed, precise, the suit slightly wrinkled from two nights in custody but the expression unchanged. The philanthropist's mask was gone. What remained was the face underneath, which turned out to look the same.

Dren sat across from him. Brandt stood by the door.

They looked at each other for a long time.

"Mr. Haldane," Dren said.

"Mr. Dren."

"You know why I'm here."

"You want what I know." Haldane's voice was level. Clinical. "I have two things of value. The first is the communication system — the Nevada facility, the antenna, the translation protocol, the relay chain. The means to listen to what the fleet is saying and, if you choose, to respond."

He paused. Let the weight of that settle.

"The second is what they intend to do."

"And you're offering both."

"I'm offering the first as a show of good faith. The communication infrastructure. Location, access codes, operating procedures. You can verify it independently — send a team, confirm the equipment, intercept a transmission. Prove to yourself that what I'm giving you is real."

"And the second?"

"The second comes after we've reached an agreement on my future."

Dren was still. "What are your terms?"

"My life. Safe passage to Mars. House arrest under your direct authority — not Earth's courts, not Whitfield's political apparatus. Your custody. Your jurisdiction. Your guarantee."

"You're asking me to protect a man who killed two hundred million people."

“I’m asking you to weigh your options. You say I’m responsible for 200 million deaths. I accept that. Are you prepared for ten times that? Fifty times that? That is what you could face should my former associates decide that’s what they want.“

“When they arrive, if they arrive, they may find we are not precisely what they think,” Dren replied.

“Really?” Haldane asked. “And if they arrive tomorrow? Next week? You think you’re in any position to oppose them?”

“They aren’t that close,” Dren said.

“You’re quite sure of yourself, Mr. Dren. Are you willing to wager the planet that you are correct?” Haldane replied.

Dren looked at him for a long time.

“I can help you prepare, Mr. Dren. I have information you will find quite valuable, despite what it is you think you currently know,” Haldane said, flatly.

Dren paused, considering.

“Well played, Mr. Haldane. You are correct. I am not willing to gamble the species on the information I have at this moment,” Dren replied.

“I will verify the communication facility first. If it’s real, I will take your proposal to President Whitfield.“

“The facility is real. Nevada. Underground, north of Las Vegas. Ms. Ashford can give you the location. The directional antenna is on the surface, disguised as a decommissioned weather station. The console, the protocol software, the operating procedures — all inside. The access code is 10202021. Consider it earnest money.“

“Is that date significant?” Dren asked.

Haldane smiled. “It is the most significant date in human history, but only I know that. And now you do as well,” he replied.

Dren wrote nothing down. He didn’t need to.

“One more thing,” Dren said. He paused at the door. “The third reference in the Tolek communications. The anomalous string my team identified in the intercepts, alongside your designation. It’s me.”

Haldane looked at him. For the first time, something crossed his face that wasn't composure. Something that might have been surprise, or might have been the recognition that Dren had been reading his mail for months and he hadn't known.

"Yes," Haldane said. "They've been tracking you since the deflection. You're the variable they can't model. They wanted me to solve you. I couldn't."

Dren nodded. He left the room. Brandt followed.

• • •

The White House. That evening.

"Absolutely not."

Whitfield was standing behind her desk. Hunt was by the window. Dren was seated, which was unusual — he preferred to stand in meetings. He'd sat down deliberately, to signal that this was going to be a long conversation and she should settle in for it.

"He murdered two hundred million people. He tried to destroy this country. And you want me to let him go live under house arrest on Mars?"

"I understand the emotion," Dren said.

"The emotion!" Whitfield fired back. "200 million people are emotion!?"

Dren had never seen her lose her composure like this. When he responded it was with his calm, level voice.

"I am saying that we need to balance the future against vengeance for the past. 200 million are dead, yes. Executing Haldane will not bring them back. However, executing Haldane could very well lead to millions, or perhaps, billions more people dying. I don't believe that is a worthwhile exchange."

Whitfield took a moment to recover her composure.

"You're right. I hate it, but you're right. What he has, you really think it's worth the cost?" she asked.

"Potentially, yes. With verification. I want you to acquire the intelligence that determines whether the human species survives," Dren said. "Haldane is the price."

"The public watched me arrest him on live television. Every screen on the planet. The most-watched moment in the history of broadcasting. And I'm supposed to just let him fly off to Mars to live out his life? The public would never stand for it," she said. "The political exposure is —"

"Irrelevant," Dren said.

Whitfield and Hunt stared at him.

"If the Tolek arrive and we only know what we know now, the political exposure will be irrelevant because there won't be a political system left to be exposed in."

Whitfield sat down. She looked at her hands. The tremor was there.

"What exactly does he have?"

"Two things. First, the communication infrastructure — which he's already given me the location of. Nevada. I will verify. If the facility is what he says it is, we gain the ability to intercept fleet communications and potentially transmit. That alone changes our strategic position fundamentally."

"And the second?"

"The Tolek's intentions. Their timeline. Their plan for when they arrive."

Whitfield was quiet for a moment. "And he won't give up the second without the deal."

"He's a negotiator. He's playing the only cards he has. But they're strong cards, and he knows it. Additionally," he continued. "I believe I have a solution which will, to an extent, mitigate the political fallout."

Hunt jumped in, sharply, "How could you possibly mitigate the political fallout of the man who made Hitler look like a piker?"

"He dies," Dren said.

“What?” Whitfield asked. “You’re suggesting we lie to him and then execute him after he gives up what he knows?”

“No,” Dren said calmly. “We make it appear to the world like he died. Suicide. Goehring, to your Hitler analogy. Only without the actual death.”

“You want us to stage his suicide?” Whitfield asked.

“Yes,” Dren said. “His ‘death’ reduces your political cost significantly.”

Whitfield and Hunt looked at each other. Hunt said, “It could work. We’d get blamed for letting it happen, but that is a fraction of the cost of letting it be known that he walked on house arrest.”

Whitfield thought for a moment.

“I want something in return,” Whitfield said.

Dren waited.

“The weapon. The directed energy weapon your team reverse-engineered from the Fist. Full technology transfer. If I’m going to take the political risk of faking Charles Haldane’s death, Earth gets the means to defend itself independently.”

The room was quiet. Hunt looked between them.

“The full technology transfer isn’t possible,” Dren said. “The original Tolek cylinder — six tonnes of charged hafnium-178 isomer — stays on Mars. My team’s production capability stays on Mars. Those are strategic assets I can’t distribute.“

“Then we don’t have a deal,“ Whitfield said. She knew she had a weak hand, but she was going to play it as best she could.

Dren thought.

“What I can offer is this: a working prototype of the weapon my team has manufactured. The trigger mechanism specifications, the waveguide geometry, the emitter assembly — everything we have documented. And the crystal growth process — the seeding technique that allows new isomer to be grown from a section of the original lattice. A seed substrate from the Tolek cylinder, large enough to begin Earth-based production. You’ll have the weapon, the plans, and the means to manufacture your own ammunition. It will take time to scale, but the capability will be yours.“

“And you keep the original cylinder. And your existing production.”

“Yes.”

“So Mars retains military superiority.“

“One working weapon is hardly military superiority. Mars retains the ability to defend the species if Earth’s production isn’t ready when the Tolek arrive. That’s not superiority. That’s contingency.“

Whitfield looked at him. The look of a president calculating the distance between what she wanted and what she could get.

“I don’t like this deal,” she said.

“I don’t like it either,” Dren said. “Which is probably a sign that it’s fair.”

Whitfield almost smiled. “The logistics of the fake death. How?”

“Suicide in holding. There are precedents.“

“And the transfer to Mars?”

“Cargo transport. Sealed container, medical stasis, listed as classified material. He arrives on Mars under a new identity. My people hold him. He never sees freedom again, but he sees tomorrow.“

Whitfield looked at Hunt. Hunt looked at the ceiling. The expression of a man who had spent his career in politics and was now being asked to participate in the most consequential deception in human history.

“Do it,” Whitfield said. “Verify the facility. If it checks out, make the deal. Get me the Tolek timeline. And get me that weapon prototype before the ink is dry.”

• • •

Nevada. The next day.

Dren stood in the underground chamber — three hundred meters of reinforced concrete beneath the desert floor — and looked at the console. There was an incoming message in the queue. Dren followed the instructions Haldane had provided to decode the message. It was a demand for status. It seems Haldane's associates were not pleased.

He transmitted both forms to Chandra on Mars, and waited for the reply.

"The protocol structure matches," Chandra's response said. He had run the translation software against the intercept database his team had built. "The encoding framework is consistent with everything we've decoded. The translation seems legit."

Dren opened a secure channel to Whitfield.

"The facility is verified. The communication system is operational. Chandra has decoded a pending fleet transmission. His information checks out."

"Make the deal," Whitfield said. "Get the rest of what he knows. And start the arrangements."

"Understood."

Dren closed the channel and walked back to the communication room. He stood in front of the console — the system that Haldane had used to coordinate the near-extinction of the human species — and thought about what it would mean to use the same system to prevent it.

He flew back to Alexandria that evening.

• • •

Federal Holding Facility. The following morning.

"The facility checks out," Dren said. "Chandra verified the translation protocol against our intercept database. Your information is good."

Haldane nodded. The nod of a man who had expected this.

"The deal is approved. Fake death, Mars transfer, house arrest under my authority. Whitfield has signed the order. In exchange, I need two things from you now. The Tolek's operational plan — everything you know. And the names of every embed you placed in positions of influence. All of them."

Haldane studied him. Decades years of reading people across tables — donors, politicians, operatives, the Tolek themselves — and he could not find the seam. No satisfaction. No contempt. No performance of magnanimity. The man who had just offered to save his life looked the same as the man who had sat down.

"You must think I'm a monster," Haldane said.

He'd said it to provoke a reaction — any reaction. The word "monster" was a lever. It demanded denial or agreement, and either one would tell him something about the man across the table.

Dren didn't take the lever. "I think you identified a problem, as you saw it, and designed a solution. You then executed it with more discipline than anyone I've encountered," he said. "The fragmentation strategy — weakening the institutional response, distributing control through nodes you managed, ensuring that whatever survived would depend on your infrastructure. The engineering was sound. The premise was wrong, horribly wrong. But your actions were consistent with your beliefs."

Haldane stared at him. He had expected the word "monster" to produce anger, or denial, or the particular brand of moral revulsion that humans reached for when confronted with someone who had made calculations they couldn't stomach. Every person he'd ever sat across from would have given him one of those. Dren had given him a systems analysis.

"It appears the Tolek aren't the only ones who miscalculated with you," Haldane said quietly.

He gave Dren the Tolek plan. The approach timeline. Then he gave him the embed names. Most of them. The Earth placements. Enough names to fill a database. Enough connections to map the full network.

He held back the Mars names. Those may yet prove useful – either as assets or bargaining chips. Time and circumstance would tell. Even now, even in a concrete room with his freedom traded for his life, Charles Haldane was still playing.

• • •

The White House.

Whitfield made the calls.

Weber in Berlin first. Then Zhao in Beijing. Volkov in Moscow. Six others. Each call was brief. Each contained the same information: the fleet was real, the timeline was approximately eleven months, and the evidence was verified through a source she could not name.

The call lasted four minutes. When it ended, Weber activated the European Space Agency's planetary defense contingency — a program that had been on paper since 2059 and had never been funded. It was funded now.

The fake death was executed three days later. A staged incident at the holding facility. Suicide by poison capsule, the same kind which had been removed from Okoro. How it was missed would be the subject of inquiries – if the human race lasted that long. The government could withstand charges of incompetence, it had continuously throughout its history.

The arrangements for Nevada were put into motion. Dren would return to use Haldane's antenna. He had a message which needed delivering.

• • •

Secure channel. Nevada to Ares City.

Over the next two hours, Dren and Sato exchanged messages across the light-delay — each transmission carefully composed, each reply arriving minutes later, the slow rhythm of a conversation conducted between two planets.

"The timeline has compressed. Haldane's last communication with the fleet was March. They're adjusting their approach schedule based on the rate of fragmentation. Eleven months, not fourteen.

"The probes. They're past the halfway point. If the timeline is eleven months, the probes arrive in the fleet's operational space roughly when the fleet is preparing for final approach. Their current mission profile is reconnaissance. I want the option to change that. The probes are already at speed — we can't alter their trajectory significantly, but we can change their terminal behavior. I want targeting protocols uploaded to the swarm. Passive until final approach phase. If we get a clean fix on fleet positions from the intercepts, the probes retask for a terminal kinetic strike. Not automatic. Manual authorization required. Mine.

"I will attempt to use the Nevada facility to communicate. More comms means getting a better fix on them, particularly if they are in motion. They might be clever enough to delay their response so as not to give away their position. However, that won't matter, since the swarm will be able to get a fix using triangulation.

"Lastly, prepare one prototype DEW for transfer to Earth. A concession I needed to make to Whitfield. A full doc dump as well. Put it on a regular transport."

Sato's reply arrived sixteen minutes later.

"Understood on the timeline compression. Eleven months changes the production schedule for the DEW prototypes — I'm adjusting Yuen's fabrication priorities now.

"On the probes: upload package can be ready within forty-eight hours. Routing through the probe-to-probe relay is viable — the swarm's internal network can propagate the protocol update across all units. Targeting protocols will be passive until manually authorized. Confirming: authorization is yours alone, not automated.

"Understood on the DEW. I'll have it arranged. Of course, it might take a little time to package for transport.

"One question. If diplomacy is still on the table, what happens to the probes?"

Dren read her reply and composed his response. He thought about the transmissions the probe swarm had been intercepting for months. The fleet's directives to Haldane. The fragmentation mandate. The timeline. The assessment of Haldane's utility. "You are not indispensable. You are conditionally useful."

He sent: "Then the probes stay passive and we have reconnaissance data. The targeting protocols are a contingency. They don't fire unless I tell them to fire."

Fourteen minutes later, Sato's reply: "Understood."

A pause. Then a second message from Sato, sent one minute after the first: "That's poetic. Delivering a kinetic strike against those who sent the Fist."

Dren's reply was two words: "That's engineering."

He closed the channel and began the arrangements for Nevada.

• • •

The unraveling.

It happened faster than anyone expected.

Novak was arrested in Las Vegas four days after the broadcast.

He'd watched the memorial from the Foundation's headquarters — the nineteenth floor, corner office, the wallscreen that usually showed reconstruction logistics feeds. He'd watched all of it — the evidence chains, the recordings, Haldane's voice on every speaker. He'd watched the crowd turn. He'd watched Beckett taken into custody demanding protection. He'd watched Haldane's security detail carve through the chaos toward the south perimeter.

By the time Whitfield returned to the podium for the second time, Novak was already at his desk, executing the contingency he'd built for exactly this scenario. Transfer the crypto to cold wallets. Move the liquid funds offshore. Shred the paper.

He wasn't fast enough.

The FBI, operating under Whitfield's executive order, tracked him down in Las Vegas at 06:00 on the fourth day. He'd been renting a vehicle to take him to the Ark when an alert clerk recognized him. Size like his wasn't always an advantage.

On him, they found a collection of cash, gold, and crypto tokens. He'd hoped to ride out this storm in the Ark. Novak looked at the agents and raised his hands.

"I want a lawyer," he said. It was the most ordinary sentence he'd spoken in years.

The fellowship embeds began resigning within the week. Not all of them — some were legitimate scholars who had received Foundation funding without knowing the pipeline's purpose. But the forty-three individuals Sato had identified in governance positions recognized what the broadcast meant for anyone connected to the Haldane network. Seventeen resigned in the first five days. Eleven more were quietly removed by their respective organizations. The rest hired lawyers.

Beckett talked. Within forty-eight hours of his arrest he was naming names, mapping committee structures, detailing the funding channels he'd used to build the congressional pressure campaign against Whitfield. He gave up the hearing strategy, the coordinated media placements, the pre-written questions his staff had fed to sympathetic members. He gave up everything, quickly and completely, with the frantic energy of a man who understood that the first cooperator gets the best deal and the second gets nothing.

The regional commanders recalculated. Thomas in Jacksonville watched the broadcast from his operations center and spent three hours on the phone with the Joint Chiefs. By morning, he had formally resubmitted to federal reconstruction authority. Chen in Denver followed within the day. General Park in the Great Lakes corridor held out for a week before the political math became impossible — the public had turned, and independence from a federal government that had just exposed the greatest conspiracy in history looked less like autonomy and more like complicity.

The military zones began reintegrating. The Joint Chiefs issued unified guidance for the first time in four months. Equipment requests were processed through a single chain. The six semi-autonomous zones were still autonomous in practice — the infrastructure Haldane had built didn't dissolve overnight — but the trajectory had reversed. The country was no longer fragmenting. It was beginning, slowly and unevenly, to reconsolidate.

The international reaction was complex. Zhao in Beijing issued a formal statement condemning Haldane and the conspiracy, while privately ordering an acceleration of China's independent space defense program. Volkov in Moscow said nothing publicly, but the Foundation's Russian partnerships were frozen within forty-eight hours.

• • •

Ashford called Saunders from a hotel room in Georgetown. The first hotel room she'd slept in since the safe houses started. The first room she hadn't needed to leave in seventy-two hours.

"How does it feel?" Saunders asked.

"Strange. I am used to keeping my head down."

"What happens to us now?" Saunders asked. "Professionally, I mean. You're the journalist who exposed the biggest conspiracy in history. I'm the scientist who found the killed ESA document. Those aren't exactly résumé lines that lead to quiet careers."

"I've had three interview requests from networks since this morning. Two book offers. And a call from Whitfield's communications director asking if I'd consider a formal role in the ongoing investigation."

"And?"

"I told them I'd think about it. What I'm actually thinking about is the thing she said at the podium. 'There is something coming next.' She wasn't talking about the legal case. She wasn't talking about Haldane."

"The aliens."

"The aliens. The things Haldane was working with. The intelligence that sent the Fist. Whatever it is — whoever they are — they're still out there. And everything we just exposed, all of it, was one man's arrangement with them. The arrangement is broken. They're still coming."

"You think there's more to investigate."

"I think the investigation we just finished was chapter one. The other side — who they are, what they want, why they sent the Fist — nobody's told that story yet. Dren knows more than he's saying. Whitfield hinted at it from the podium. And the recordings mentioned coordination with an intelligence that nobody can name."

"You want to keep going."

"I want to understand what's coming. And I think the skills that found Haldane are the same skills that will be needed for what comes next." She paused. "What about you?"

"The ESA has been in contact. They want me to consult on the reclassification audit — a formal review of every decision in the detection chain, now that we know the delay was manufactured. It's institutional archaeology. It's what I do."

"That sounds like it could take years."

"It could. Or it could take a life time, if those aliens arrive and catch us as we are now." She paused. "Chloe. We did the thing. We actually did the thing. Greg and Okafor and Vickers — they're gone because of this, and what we did mattered. The recordings reached Dren. The evidence reached the world. The network has a voice and the voice is public."

"It mattered," Ashford said. "The cost was terrible. But they didn't die in vain.

"Take care of yourself, Jessica."

"You too. And Chloe — when the next story starts, call me first."

Ashford almost smiled. "You'll be the first call."

She ended the call and sat in the hotel room and looked out the window at a city that was still rebuilding from a disaster she now understood better than almost anyone alive. The investigation was over. The story wasn't. Somewhere past the heliopause, the authors of the Fist were still writing, and nobody had read the next chapter yet.

• • •

Ares City. Two days after the broadcast.

Raines asked to see Sato.

He'd been in the holding cell for three months. Three months of silence. Professional resistance. The blank, calculating face that had given them nothing.

The broadcast had played on the cell's monitoring feed. Raines had watched all of it.

When Sato entered the cell, Raines was sitting in the same position he'd occupied for three months — upright, composed, his injured hand resting on his knee with the careful stillness of a man who had learned to manage the pain without showing it.

"The network is gone," Raines said. "Haldane is in custody. The recordings are public. There's nothing left to protect."

Sato waited.

"I'll talk," Raines said. "Everything I know. The operational contacts, the communication protocols I used to report to Haldane. In exchange for consideration when this goes to trial."

"Haldane beat you to the punch, Raines," Sato said. "He's already given us all of that. Prisoner's dilemma, you lost."

"Are you sure he gave you everything?" Raines asked.

"What do you mean?" Sato asked.

"Sato." Raines looked at him. "Dren's control of Mars isn't as solid as he thinks it is. There are people in his operation — people he trusts — who were placed there the same way I was. I can give you names."

Sato's expression didn't change. But her posture did — the slight shift of someone who has just heard something that matters more than she expected.

"I'll pass this along to Dren," she said finally.

• • •

Ares City. Medical Center.

Jackson sat in the chair beside Inoue's bed at 14:37 and ate.

The numbers had been improving for weeks. Heart rate 52. Core temperature 36.4. Weight 39 kilograms — still skeletal, still fragile, but no longer the twenty-seven-kilogram figure that had floated unconscious in the pod bay. The refeeding protocol had stabilized her organs. The muscle recovery was slower — the medical team said months, possibly a year, possibly permanent deficits in the extremities where the tissue damage had been most severe. The cognitive assessments were encouraging but incomplete. Inoue had been conscious for short periods — minutes at a time, disoriented, unable to sustain conversation — and the medical team called these "windows" and said the windows would get longer.

Jackson had been present for three of the windows. Each time, Inoue's eyes had opened, tracked the room, found Jackson, and closed again. No words. No recognition that Jackson could confirm. Just the eyes — dark, sunken, aware for a moment and then gone.

Today was different.

Jackson was finishing the ration packet — the same time, the same ritual, the same chair — when the monitors shifted. Heart rate climbing. Neural activity spiking in a pattern the medical team had flagged as "pre-emergence." Jackson set the packet down and leaned forward.

Inoue's eyes opened.

They tracked the room. The ceiling. The monitors. The IV lines. Jackson's face.

They stayed.

“Jackson,” Inoue said. Her voice was thin. Dry. The voice of someone who had last spoken on Day 182 and was now finding the mechanism again after months of silence.

“I’m here,” Jackson said.

Inoue’s eyes moved around the room. Taking inventory. The medical center. The gravity — Mars gravity, not the micro-g of the Kludge. The warmth. The light. Things that hadn’t existed in her world for a very long time.

“Where,” she said. Not a complete sentence. The word was enough.

“Ares City. Mars. You’ve been in the medical center for—” Jackson checked herself. The number wasn’t important yet. “A while. You’re safe. Everyone’s safe.”

“Torres. Chandra.”

“Everyone’s fine. Torres, Chandra. They’re working. Dren’s got them on a project.”

Inoue’s eyes came back to Jackson. Something was moving behind them — the focused attention of a mind that was reassembling itself and had questions.

“How long,” she said.

“Don’t worry about that right now.”

“Jackson.” The voice was stronger. Stronger than a moment ago, the way a signal strengthens when the antenna finds the right bearing. “How long.”

Jackson looked at her. At the face that was still gaunt, still grey at the edges, still carrying the evidence of what she’d done to herself. At the eyes, which were clear for the first time since Day 175.

“You collapsed on Day 182. Alfred woke me. I got you into the pod. A rescue drone brought parts and fuel. I fixed the engines. We flew to Mars.” She paused. “It’s been about four months since we docked.”

Inoue processed that. Four months. Her eyes moved to the IV lines, to her arms, to the shape of her body under the thermal blanket. She was seeing herself for the first time since the collapse

— seeing what 27 kilograms looked like from the outside, seeing the cost of the calculation she'd made on Day 3.

"Did it work," she said.

Jackson understood the question. Not did the rescue work. Not did the transit work. Did the sacrifice work. Did the math hold. Were the crew ratios sufficient. Did everyone survive.

"It worked," Jackson said. "Everyone's alive. The ship made it. You did the math and the math held."

Something moved in Inoue's expression. Something older than a smile. The place where stubbornness and exhaustion met, except now the exhaustion was healing and the stubbornness was still there underneath it.

"Good," Inoue said. "That's good."

Her eyes started to drift. The window closing. The consciousness that had surfaced for two minutes was settling back down, the mind retreating to the deep recovery sleep that the medical team said was the best thing for her — the brain rebuilding itself the way the body was rebuilding itself, slowly, unevenly, with no guarantee of the final result.

"Inoue," Jackson said.

The eyes opened again. Barely.

"I eat at 14:37 every day," Jackson said. "Your time. I'll be here tomorrow."

Inoue looked at her. The eyes held for a moment — a moment of clarity, of recognition, of understanding what the time meant and why Jackson was keeping it.

Then the monitors changed.

The heart rate, which had been climbing steadily since Inoue woke, stuttered. A disruption. The rhythm that had been strengthening for weeks lost its pattern. The neural activity that had been spiking in organized waves collapsed into noise.

Jackson looked at the monitor. Heart rate fifty-three and falling, fragmenting. The waveform that had held its shape for weeks was breaking apart, each peak lower than the last, the intervals stretching into gaps that weren't intervals anymore. The neural activity readout had gone from structured spikes to static. She'd watched these numbers every day for four months. She didn't need the alarm to tell her what the static meant.

"No," she said. "No, no, no."

The medical team was already moving — the alarm had triggered in the corridor, and they were through the door in seconds. Jackson was pushed back from the bed. Hands on Inoue. Equipment. Voices calling codes and numbers and instructions that Jackson could hear but couldn't process because the monitor was showing the thing she'd been afraid of since Day 182.

Flatline.

Jackson stood at the wall, her hands at her sides, watching the medical team work. She didn't interfere. She didn't speak. She stood and watched and held the image of Inoue's eyes — clear, aware, recognizing her, understanding the time — and she held it because it might be the last thing Inoue had given her and she was not going to let it go.

The medical team worked.

The flatline sounded.

Epilogue

Nevada. The Ark.

• • •

Dren sat at Haldane's console and composed the first message humanity had ever sent to the Tolek with full knowledge of who was listening.

The translation protocol was running — Chandra's team had integrated it with the intercepted communications database within forty-eight hours of receiving it, and the structural patterns that had been opaque for months were now readable. Not fluently or completely. But enough to compose a message that the Tolek's systems would parse as intentional communication from a new source, not a continuation of Haldane's channel.

He wrote it the way he wrote everything. Edited before transmitted. Every concept weighed.

The protocol didn't work in words. It worked in structural relationships — concepts mapped to positions in a mathematical framework, meaning encoded through the arrangement of elements rather than the elements themselves. Chandra had explained it as "writing in architecture rather than language." Dren understood architecture.

He drafted in English on the primary display. The protocol rendered the structural output on the secondary — the alien encoding building beside his input like a circuit diagram, nested relationships and conditional operators and state markers that Chandra's team could read and Dren could verify by shape. Each time he revised a line, the structural output reconfigured. He watched the patterns shift, checked them against Chandra's reference library, revised again. Names didn't translate — the protocol had no mechanism for arbitrary labels. Identity was functional. You were what you did, what you affected, what role you occupied in the system.

He worked for an hour. Drafting, checking the structural rendering, stripping anything that didn't translate cleanly, rebuilding the sentences until the protocol produced output that matched the verified patterns from the Tolek's own directives. He was writing in their format. An assessment. The same structure their communications to Haldane had used. The same cold, mathematical precision — turned back at them.

When he was satisfied, the message read:

I am the individual who designed and executed the deflection of the primary instrument. I am the individual who identified and dismantled the network of your human agent. I am the third referent in your fleet communications — the variable your models could not predict.

Your models predicted that a wounded species would fragment beyond recovery. They did not. Your models predicted that a single human agent could engineer the collapse of a civilization. He could not. Your models identified me as an anomaly — a variable outside your predictive framework. I am not an anomaly. I am a characteristic. The species you assessed is a species that produces individuals like me as a matter of course. Your models failed because they treated an intrinsic property as an outlier.

You have two options. I present them as an engineering evaluation, in your format, using your criteria.

Option one: engagement. Communication with a species that has demonstrated the capacity to exceed your models. Discussion of coexistence, terms, and mutual constraints. This option carries uncertainty. You have acknowledged that uncertainty by designating me as a variable you cannot predict. Uncertainty is not weakness. It is information your framework cannot process. That limitation is yours.

Option two: conflict. Military action against a species that is now aware of the threat, aware of your fleet's position, aware of your timeline, and in possession of your weapons technology. A species that has the industrial capacity to prepare and eleven months in which to do so. A species whose primary characteristic — the one your models cannot account for — is that it adapts under pressure faster than your predictions allow.

I recommend option one. Not as a plea. As an assessment.

He read it once more. The protocol's structural rendering was clean, coherent. The Tolek would parse it as intentional communication from a new source, not a continuation of Haldane's channel.

He transmitted. The signal left the directional antenna and traveled outward at the speed of light, aimed at a bearing past the heliopause where a fleet was preparing for something it had been planning for decades.

Then he waited.

The response arrived thirty-six hours later.

It came through the same channel, in the same structural format, with the same cold mathematical precision that had characterized every directive Haldane had received for twenty-three years. The protocol parsed it cleanly. Chandra's team verified the translation.

No discussions. No conditions. No revised assessment. The Council's position is unchanged. The timeline is unchanged. The mandate is unchanged.

They were coming.

Dren read. He set it aside.

Eleven months. The timeline Haldane had confirmed. The fleet was not adjusting for diplomacy because diplomacy was a variable in their model they chose to discard. The message Dren had sent — the identification, the assessment, the offer — had been received, evaluated, and dismissed. The Tolek had heard from the variable they couldn't model, and their response was to proceed as planned.

So be it.

He opened the channel to Sato.

"The response is negative," he said. "They are coming. No conditions, no discussions.

"The probes. Using their projected speed, and that of the probes, compute the likely intercept point. That's our first engagement window — kinetic, not diplomatic. We will show them they still do not understand what they are dealing with. Perhaps that will get their attention."

He sent it and waited the fourteen minutes for the response.

"Understood. And if they adjust course after detecting the swarm?" Sato asked.

He replied. "Then we have their reaction profile and we adjust. But the probes are the opening move regardless.

"In the meantime, we advance everything. The DEW prototypes — accelerate production. I want a dozen operational units within six months, not two within three. The belt platforms — strip the deflection payloads, mount DEWs, add targeting systems. Every platform that fired at the Fist becomes a weapons platform. The nuclear shotgun arrays — redesign for anti-spacecraft engagement. Adjustable pellet spread, higher velocity, optimized for hull penetration. And I want a new class of platform — small, fast, maneuverable. A single DEW, a fusion drive, and enough delta-v to intercept and return. Space fighters. The concept has existed in fiction for a century. We're building them.

"The timeline is eleven months. Minus three for the probe intercept window. We need the first wave of converted platforms operational in eight months, and the fighter prototypes flying in six.

"The alternative is extinction. Or subjugation. Or whatever the Tolek have planned for a species they've decided isn't worth talking to."

The reply came, though he already knew the contents.

"I'll start the production orders tonight," Sato said.

He sat at the console in the underground facility that Haldane had built to survive the extinction of the human race, and he looked at the antenna readout showing the bearing of a fleet that had just told him it was coming regardless of what he said.

He had eleven months to build a defense against a species that had been traveling between stars while humanity was still learning to farm. Eleven months, two DEW prototypes scaling to twelve, a fleet of deflection platforms being converted to weapons platforms, a nuclear shotgun being redesigned for war, a fighter program that didn't exist yet, a translation protocol obtained from the architect of the worst crime in human history, and a fragmented civilization that was only beginning to understand what was coming.

It wasn't enough. You never go to war with what you want, you go with what you had.

He was reaching for the console to begin the platform conversion specifications when the transmission alert sounded.

Same channel. Same bearing. Same structural format.

Dren opened the message. The protocol parsed it. He read it.

He read it again.

He leaned back in the chair and looked at the antenna readout and the desert dark beyond the facility walls and the sky that contained, somewhere past the edge of what human eyes could see.

"Well," Dren said. "That was unexpected."

About the Author

Mark Kennedy got his start writing video games for the Intellivision at Mattel Electronics, and has spent the last thirty-five years as a cybersecurity engineer at Symantec/Broadcom, where he is a Distinguished Engineer. His career has taught him this lesson: every system has rules, every rule has a cost, and somebody is always looking for the exploit.

His research in Victorian-era criminal history has produced published work challenging established theories on the Jack the Ripper case, and his fiction draws on the same instinct — following evidence wherever it leads, even when the answer is uncomfortable.

He lives in Las Vegas with his wife Chloe and a household of cats and dogs.

Previous titles: The Devil's Own Luck (his debut novel) and Satan's Fist, Book 1 of Operation Clean Slate. Both available on Amazon.

He is currently at work on Satan's Consequence, the third book in Operation Clean Slate, a hard science fiction series.

www.ingramcontent.com/pod-product-compliance
Lightning Source LLC
LaVergne TN
LVHW010628110826
845149LV00014B/2809
* 9 7 9 8 9 9 4 9 7 3 1 7 2 *